DEATH BY MINDLOAD

The editor gestured toward Samantha. "So *talk* to me. Why in hell did the cops bust a vacuum cleaner on murder? And why the hell are the Feds hungry for it?"

"You won't like it," Sam said, grinning even more widely. "The Feds say the vacuum cleaner is really a mindload of the guy who built the thing. Trouble is, mindloading turns the subject's brain into something out of a pithed frog. It's fatal. The Feds say this guy, whatshisname"—she leaned precariously forward to read the computer display—"this guy David Bailey rigged up an illegal mindloader and put his head under it. I got a copy of the indictment. The theory goes he was dying already, and didn't like the idea, so he pumped his mind quote 'into a high-end storage matrix, said matrix hidden in the house maintenance unit' close quote—the vacuum cleaner. I've been trying to thread through the logic and I think I have it straight. If and it's a hell of a big if you accept the theory that the killer—David Bailey—is allegedly alive inside the vacuum cleaner, then it all falls into place. There is no doubt that a death—that of David Bailey—took place. So, if the Feds can prove that the vacuum cleaner *caused* Bailey's death, and can prove that the vacuum cleaner possesses the mind of a human person, and is therefore human, then Bailey's death was, by definition, murder: the death of one person deliberately caused by another person. The Feds say they have the evidence to prove the case."

Ask your bookseller for these BANTAM SPECTRA
titles you may have missed:

The Next Wave
BOOK 4

THE MODULAR MAN

ROGER MACBRIDE ALLEN

BANTAM BOOKS
New York · Toronto
London · Sydney · Auckland

THE MODULAR MAN
A Bantam Spectra Book / June 1992

SPECTRA and the portrayal of a boxed "s" are trademarks of
Bantam Books, a division of Bantam Doubleday Dell
Publishing Group, Inc.

Series cover and book design by Alex Jay/Studio J

ISBN 0-553-29559-4

Published simultaneously in the United States and Canada

Bantam Books are published by Bantam Books, a division of Bantam Doubleday
Dell Publishing Group, Inc. Its trademark, consisting of the words "Bantam
Books" and the portrayal of a rooster, is Registered in U.S. Patent and Trademark
Office and in other countries. Marca Registrada. Bantam Books, 666 Fifth
Avenue, New York, New York 10103.

Printed in the United States of America

RAD   0 9 8 7 6 5 4 3 2 1

To Sterling E. Lanier,
who was among the first
to start wondering about me

I would like to thank the skilled professionals who caught the errors, made the cuts, cleaned up the typos, called me on the logical flaws, and generally tidied up after me in this book.

If you ever write a book, and can get Thomas B. Allen, John Betancourt, Betsy Mitchell, Stanley Schmidt or Susie West to look it over, then you'll be doing all right. If you can get *all* of them, you'll have been as lucky as I was. But don't think they'll be easy on you. Thank God.

"Damn it all, we want to get at the truth!" [said Lord Peter Wimsey.]

"Do you?" said Sir Impey drily. "I don't. I don't care twopence about the truth. I want a case."

—Dorothy L. Sayers,
Clouds of Witness

PRELUDE

I go into spasm as the killing pain strikes at me again. The simple act of lifting my hand to a switch is enough to wrack my entire body in agony, send me collapsing to the floor, quivering in torment.

If there was any doubt left in my mind, this blinding fire is enough to erase it. It is time to escape. Either go to a new home, or die. At least this way I will die on my terms, playing by my rules, before the pain leaves me a mere gibbering idiot, no longer able to choose my own time.

If I chance to survive the experience, all the better. If not, at least I will go out trying, not a passive victim of a pointless, meaningless accident.

With my last shreds of determination, I haul my ruined body up off the floor and into the powerchair—the stupid, useless, archaic powerchair that is all the politicians can begrudge me. The technology is here to allow me more, so much more life. Mechanical legs to replace my amputated limbs, pseudo-organs to replace my slowly failing liver and kidneys, any number of enhancements to give me back some measure of what I have lost.

But the laws say no. Because my injuries involve my brain. Because repairing the damage would require nerve blocks, cor-

rective brain surgery—and the implantation of a few grams of microcircuits into my head. The laws, the arbitrary rules established to prevent things that could never happen anyway, say I cannot be helped: mechanical alteration of the brain is illegal. Rules and laws made by fear, not reason. The laws say I must fade away, a crippled ruin. Suzanne does not know how bad it is. She believes that I can live indefinitely. But the facts are far grimmer: without the corrective surgery, I will die in agony. The only question is when. A few weeks, or months at most, if I die their way.

I cannot hope to change the laws in time. I am too weak. All the people like me in the country are, by definition, too weak, clinging to life too feebly, ever to work up a fight.

I have my own game in mind. Win or lose, survive or vanish altogether, I will do it my way, not theirs.

All that remains is the act itself.

Moving slowly, carefully, I set the timer, wishing again there had been time to set up a more sophisticated control system. But every day I grow weaker, and I dare not try too hard for perfection. I fear that I have made some error, some miscalculation, but it is impossible to think clearly through this cloud of pain.

I roll my powerchair forward, reach up with pain-palsied hands and slip the induction helmet down over my rough-shaven head. Herbert is here, ready for me.

I have recorded a letter to my wife, to Suzanne, into Herbert's memory store. He will deliver it, speak my words in his voice. A backup copy of the letter waits hidden in the computer net, programmed for delivery in a year's time. That should be time enough for her pain to ease, for the news to be less shocking. If I fail, she at least will know what has happened, but no one else.

I realize my eyes are shut and force them open, force myself to see the dull grey walls of the lab. For such might be the last sight I will ever see. Eyes open, staring wide, I wait for the end.

And then the massive, delicate surge of power flashes through my helmet—and the universe crashes out of existence as my mind is torn apart.

CHAPTER 1
RIGHTS OF THE ACCUSED

Patrolman Phillipe Sanders sat back in his seat and watched as the squad car pulled itself over to the curb. His partner, LuAnne Johnson, was letting the car do the driving as she read over the paperwork one last time. "You sure this is for real?" she asked. The doubt in her voice was plain to hear.

The squad car stopped itself. The door on Sanders's side opened, and he stepped out onto the pavement. Strange to be out in the field again, after so long working in the equipment maintenance division. But a cop was a cop, and he could make this bust as well as anyone. Maybe better. Presumably that was Chief Thurman's logic. The Old Man himself had tapped Sanders for this job.

It was a warm day for early June, and the famous Washington, D.C., humidity wrapped itself softly around him. The sky was a gentle misty blue, and the birds were singing. A perfect late spring day.

He looked up at the house. Big place. Imposing. A long, winding walkway led up from the street to a majestic three-story brick mansion. Residence of one Suzanne Jantille. Residence—or former residence, depending on

how you looked at it—of her husband, one David Bailey.
Obviously two or three houses on either side torn down
during the popdrop to make room for the expansive
grounds. Lots of money here. Folks in places like this
were used to getting their own way. *Are these the kind of
people the U.S. Attorney really wants to mess with?* Phil wondered. Maybe someone hadn't thought this thing out all
the way. Never mind, that wasn't his problem. It was
enough just to worry about the facts of the case.

Phil Sanders had read the printout on this case. Suzanne Jantille wasn't a name he had known offhand—
but Bailey, that was another story. Not famous to the
public, maybe, but Phil Sanders fixed police robots for a
living. Anyone in robotics had to know Bailey's name.

And now, Phil had to come and arrest him for murder.

Sort of.

Johnson stepped from her side of the car and nodded
bemusedly. The car closed its doors and went into
standby mode.

''*Is* this for real?'' Johnson asked again.

Sanders shook his head. ''It's *legitimate*. That I can tell
you. But I've got to admit it doesn't seem too *real* to me,
either.'' Phil realized that LuAnne seemed as doubtful as
he was—and she didn't know half what Sanders did.

Sanders pulled his personal monitor out of its pocket
over his heart, switched it on, and slid it back into place,
making sure the lens was facing forward and out. The
little cylinder's camera and mike would relay sight and
sound back to the squad car, and the car's on-board artificial intelligence system would monitor and record. In
theory, the car would know when to call for backup. Phil
repaired the things, and knew the system was an uncertain protection at best, but the regs said to wear a pow-
ered-up monitor away from the squad car at all times.
Like most police officers who didn't get into the field
much, Sanders did everything by the book when he did
get out.

LuAnne Johnson watched her partner and snorted

contemptuously. "Wise up, kid. Them things ain't smart enough to do any good."

Phil decided not to reply. LuAnne Johnson didn't believe in any regulation that didn't suit her. He switched the topic of discussion back to the safer subject of the bust. "I still can't believe they're serious about wanting to arrest this guy," Phil said.

Johnson, walking ahead of him, shrugged theatrically. She spoke without looking back at him, holding the warrant up over her shoulder and waving it. "The judge signed this and the chief okayed the bust personally. *He's* taking it seriously. Hell's bells, he sent *two* cops—two *live* cops—to serve this thing. Not just one, even with all the cutbacks, with the chief all the time bitching that we can't use robots to serve warrants. That's what we oughta do, so we could get human cops out on the beat breaking up gangs."

Or back at the coffee shop soaking up doughnuts, Phil Sanders thought. LuAnne Johnson was far better known on the force for indolence than vigorous pursuit of criminal suspects. Phil had his doubts that any human labor saved from service of warrants would actually be put to use fighting crime. But that was not the point.

Right now, they had a vacuum cleaner to arrest.

A *vacuum* cleaner, for God's sake. What was it all coming to?

Suddenly something moved, something bright, glittering, low slung off, to one side of the house, among the flowers. Phil was edgy. His hand moved reflexively toward his weapon. But it was just a garden weasel, a cat-sized robot intent on nothing more nefarious than garden maintenance, its cutter-digger arms making short work of the weeds, its tank treads whirring back and forth as it moved carefully among the plants.

There was something busy, urgent about its movements, and it stopped its work every now and again, seeming to pause and look around itself. Squirrel-brain mindload, Sanders guessed with a practiced eye. Maybe some rabbit and probably monkey—popular for small robots with manipulators. Maybe even some actual weasel. But tank treads or no, its movements reminded him irresistibly of a squirrel burying nuts for the winter.

A human-shaped gardener machine came around the side of the house, carrying a pair of shears. Ignoring the police officers because it was not programmed to notice people, it knelt on the grass at the side of the walk and set to work edging the lawn.

"Crummy robot doing *that*?" Johnson asked angrily.

That's right. A hundred-thousand-dollar machine with a pair of ten-dollar garden shears, Sanders thought, but he knew Johnson wasn't thinking that way. To her mind, gardens were something a *person* took care of, personally. Gardening was not work for servants, but a task of pride for a house-proud property owner. LuAnne Johnson was mad because, in her eyes, the robot was acting like it owned the place.

Sanders shook his head sadly. Like so many people, it seemed that Johnson's feelings for human-shaped machines never got past fear and contempt. Suppose this case worked out the way it might, and people like her were forced to deal with *machine*-shaped *people*? "It's not a robot, LuAnne," he said. "A full robot would have noticed us. It's an HTM. An humanoid teleoperator machine, run by remote control, probably from inside the house."

"Robot, HTM, cyborg, remote," she growled. "All the lousy same tin boxes prancing around like people."

Good to hear such an enlightened, informed opinion, Sanders thought. Phil knew LuAnne Johnson barely well enough to call her by her first name. The two of them had eaten in the same diners, been at the same roll calls, off and on for years, but never had had much to do with each other before today. Phil had been handpicked to perform this arrest, but it was clear to him that Johnson was here through random selection, along for the ride because doctrine called for two cops on a murder bust, and she was available, her regular partner out sick. How much of her homework had she done? "LuAnne, you know much about this case?" he asked, pausing on the way up the long walkway.

Johnson stopped, turned, and looked back at him, squinting a bit in the morning sun over Phil's shoulder. "Just that we've gotta bust a frigging vacuum cleaner, that's all."

"That's what I thought." *Doesn't anyone in the field ever read the background data?* Phil wondered testily. The police datanet was excellent—it could pull up a complete national police record on a suspect, along with any other public knowledge, instantly. Why didn't the street cops ever use it? "I checked the background datasheet on this one before we left the station," Phil said, braving her contempt for going by the book. "Lots of newsclips in the file. There's a few details you ought to know. One, Suzanne Jantille is a criminal lawyer. A good one. Maybe she'll take the case herself. Two, Bailey and Jantille were both in a bad road accident six months ago, last December. In a public cab when its programming shorted out. The cab rammed into a wall."

"So?"

"So they both got mashed up pretty bad. The news reports say it put Bailey in a powerchair. No report on what happened to Jantille."

"And what does that mean?"

"Either that she got lucky, walked away without a scratch—or else that it was really bad. So bad she saw to it her condition was not made public."

"So, like, she might be in a powerchair too?"

"Or worse," Sanders said, a bit stiffly.

Suddenly Johnson understood what he was driving at, and her face screwed up into an expression of disgust. "You saying she might have got herself *cyborged*?"

"Exactly. I don't know one way or the other. But it is a possibility. The point is, this case is going to be tricky enough as it is, without her house monitors recording you showing some kind of prejudicial reaction. The prosecutors will be flaming mad if we dump a police discrimination charge into the middle of this. So you just tell yourself cyborgs are people, with equal rights under the law. I don't care if you *believe* that, as long as you *act* like you do on this bust. The chief will have our heads if we screw this up. Got it?''

LuAnne Johnson glared at her partner. But Phillipe Sanders was a man who stood his ground when he knew what he was talking about. She had seniority, but he was right. He looked her back in the eye with steady calm. After a heartbeat, she sighed and nodded. "Yeah, I got it."

They turned and walked the last few yards up to the front porch. They mounted the steps and came to the door. Johnson nearly made the gaffe of knocking, but stopped herself in time. It wouldn't be smart to start off with a privacy violation, not in *this* neighborhood. A house like this was certainly smart enough to see there were two cops at the door, and smart enough to know what to do about it.

"May I be of assistance, officers?" the door asked. It was a perfect, golden voice, dripping with refined courtesy, practically singing the words at them.

Johnson jumped a little and stepped back. She hesitated a moment, clearly uncomfortable with the idea of talking to a house. Sanders shook his head sadly. No doubt Johnson liked it back in the rough part of town, the poor parts where no one had talking machines to baffle her. Personally, Sanders couldn't understand what was the big deal.

"Metropolitan Police," Sanders said, taking over. "We have warrants to serve at this address. Advise Madame Jantille." *That* was the way to handle artificial intelligence. No pleases, no thank yous, just straight statements and clear orders. ArtInt machines were not entitled to human courtesy. Phil Sanders was careful not to offer them any. Politeness led straight into the human reflex of assigning social status, and then to speaking according to that status. Trouble was, robots did not *have* social status, and therefore it was impossible to choose a correct manner of speech. Formal, informal, respectful, curt, nasty, deferential—however you acted, it would be wrong, and the machine would respond with urbane courtesy, rendering your treatment of it utterly inappropriate, and throwing you off altogether. Far better to ignore the machine's social advances and stay in control.

"I am informed by Madame Jantille that she will not speak with you voluntarily."

"That's fine," Sanders said. "It's Herbert we're here for, anyway."

There was the briefest of pauses. They had surprised the house, and small wonder.

"I am to under-stand that you wish to speak with the house maintenance unit Madame Jantille has nicknamed Her-bert?" the house asked, in the slightly singsong cadences of a confused artificial mind.

Johnson suddenly lost her patience. "Not speak with it, *arrest* it." She spoke the words with obvious embarrassment, clearly tired of standing on someone's porch arguing with a house. "We have a legal warrant for its arrest, and warrants to search the house for it if need be. You programmed to deal with *that*, you goddamn tin box? Or do we get to break down the door?"

Sanders looked at his partner in shock, his blood running cold. Was Johnson crazy enough to go up against the self-defenses a place like *this* must have? He fervently hoped his monitor link to the car was working. They might *need* help.

"Of course," the house replied smoothly. "*All* house operations systems are programmed for full cooperation with peace officers." The camera over the door swung out and down on a long flexcable. "If you will present each page of the warrant to my camera system, and allow me to record your names and badge numbers, I will be able to cooperate with your warrants."

"Don't act like you've got choices," Johnson sputtered.

"Calm down, LuAnne," Sanders said. "The damn thing *doesn't* have a choice, that's the whole point. Didn't you study the tech bulletins on house systems? They're programmed to keep the place buttoned down tighter than a drum, an absolute injunction." He nodded at the camera and the house. "The damn thing's a computer. Unless Jantille authorizes otherwise, the only way we can override her command priority is by running a by-the-book warrant review, with all the homeowner's legal rights observed to the letter. *If* we do all that, it can open up. Otherwise, it's a flat impossibility."

"That what you do down in the robot pool, memorize that tech stuff and the legal crap?" Johnson asked.

Phil did not like people calling his workplace the robot pool, and he was starting to feel more than a bit irritated with Johnson. She seemed to feel ignorance and crudity were positive virtues. "Why not?" he asked snappishly. What the hell was wrong with studying up, learning your job? "The point is that without an override the house can't open up."

"Then why the hell doesn't this Jantille do the override if she's home?"

"She's got rights," Sanders said, trying to regain his patience. "Like against warrantless searches. She's exercising that one now, that's all. She's a lawyer, remember? Maybe she's in there figuring that if she makes us jump through all the hoops before we make the bust, we'll get mad and screw up somehow. You just came close to making her right, threatening to bust down the door. That what you want to do?"

Johnson glared at him again, and didn't seem about to give him an answer. She glanced at his monitor pocket, and Sanders understood. She had just remembered that everything was being recorded back at the car. She didn't want to get in any deeper.

Sanders sighed. "Here, give me those warrants," he said. He took the papers, opened them up, and held them flat for the camera, keeping each page in view for a full thirty seconds. Then he faced the camera himself, allowed it to get a good look at his face and badge. "Patrol Officer Phillipe Sanders, badge number 19109." He nodded toward Johnson to follow suit, but she hesitated.

"Come on, for God's sake, LuAnne."

She stepped forward and muttered into the camera mike. "Patrol Officer LuAnne Johnson, badge number 18083."

"Thank you, officers," the house said. The door swung open, and the two police officers stepped into a rather intimidating foyer, all cold marble and grand interior vistas. A formal central stairway stood in the middle of the hall, leading upward to a landing. Stairways led up from the landing to the left and right.

Sanders and Johnson stepped inside and stood in the foyer, craning their necks to look either way down the great hall that ran the length of the house.

"So now what?" Johnson asked.

Sanders shrugged. "I guess we—"

"Madame Jantille is coming now, officers," the house said.

Sanders heard the sound of footsteps behind them and turned around. Coming down the hallway from the far end of the house was the figure of a woman, tall and lean, honey-brown hair done up in a bun, dressed in a neat business suit that erred slightly on the conservative side. She looked vigorous, alert, healthy, and confident. Not like someone who had barely survived a car crash six months before.

But then Sanders noticed what was wrong. She was a remote. Judging by her sharp intake of breath, Johnson caught it at the same moment he did.

"For God's sake, we gotta talk to *her*?" Johnson said in a half whisper.

"Quiet!" Sanders hissed urgently. "Don't let her freak us. We act professional, do our job, and get the hell out of here."

Suzanne Jantille stepped into the foyer and looked at the two of them, more than a bit severely. "I have read the warrants," she said in clipped tones. "What is this nonsense?"

Right down to business, Sanders thought. No hellos, no pleases or thank yous or social niceties. *Treating us just the way I treated her house,* Phil thought. "It's no nonsense, ma'am. These are legal warrants, and our orders are to serve them. As I'm sure you realize, you don't have much choice in the matter."

Suzanne Jantille clasped her hands together in front of her, knitting her fingers up into a tense knot. Her face was expressionless. "You intend to arrest my vacuum cleaner for the murder of my husband?"

Sanders looked at Johnson, but she was clearly happy to let him do the talking. Feeling more than a bit foolish, he nodded. "Yes, ma'am, that's right."

"I was not aware that inanimate machinery was liable under the criminal code. Do you generally arrest guns and sniper knives as well?"

Phil Sanders reddened visibly. "The U.S. Attorney, Julia Entwhistle, is of the opinion that your house maintenance unit, your, ah, vacuum cleaner, is *not* inanimate, but a person. And further that it was instrumental in your husband's death."

"That is flatly ridiculous. Herbert can't even speak anymore. Hasn't since David died."

A tiny alarm bell went off in Phil's head. "Doesn't speak anymore?" he asked. "You mean he *used* to speak?" Lots of robots talked—but not house maintenance units. There wouldn't be any point to it. The things didn't have enough volition to make speech worthwhile. So why make an HMU talk—and what could make it *stop* talking?

Suzanne Jantille looked down, away from Sanders. "David was working on Herbert, tinkering, really, just before he died. He tinkered a lot. I supposed David disabled the speech system for some reason, and Herbert hasn't talked since. That's all."

"But why—"

Suzanne looked up again, sharply, collecting herself. "I am not required to answer your questions," she said abruptly. "And I regard this whole situation as absurd."

"Ma'am, however you regard it, we are going to serve

these warrants," Phil said. He concentrated on keeping his voice politely firm.

Suzanne Jantille stopped and regarded each of the two officers for a long moment. "Very well. If there is to be some sort of legal charade, I see that I have no choice but to play in it. House, order Herbert to come here."

The three of them stood in awkward silence for a long moment, and then a slight mechanical noise came from the upper landing. The police officers looked up and saw Herbert—it had to be Herbert—coming down the stairs.

Phil took a good long look at the subject of his arrest warrant. Herbert, he decided, looked like an oversize scuba tank with six stocky, multijointed mechanical legs attached.

Servo motors whirring, Herbert eased his long body down along the stairs and smoothly made his way to the ground floor. Sanders knew home maintenance units, had built a few himself, and had expected Herbert to move as awkwardly as the HMUs on sale at Sears. But this unit was a custom job, not a mass-produced consumer model. Sanders guessed the basic chassis came off an industrial maintenance machine, stripped down and then souped up. However Herbert was built, there was nothing clumsy about him. Instead, there was a strangely smooth and perfect mechanical grace to his movements. Somehow he reminded Sanders of a slow-moving dachshund—stocky, solid, built low to the ground.

"Ugly little spud," Johnson muttered under her breath as the HMU arrived at the bottom of the stairs. Its legs locked at the knees and wheels extruded from the bottom of its feet. It rolled forward and stopped about a foot in front of the two officers.

Phil had a real affection for the machines he worked on. To him, Herbert was anything but ugly. But even though Phil admired Herbert's lines, his obvious functionality, Herbert was certainly an *unusual* machine. His main body was a cylinder about five feet long and two feet in diameter, painted a gleaming greyish-beige—a shade no doubt selected because it would not clash with any color scheme in the house. At the moment, Herbert's body stood about waist high to Phil, but the legs could obviously telescope higher or lower. It looked as if the rear pair of legs were designed to work in biped mode as well, the body capable of swiveling into an upright position over them and locking into position. Where the face should have been was a collection of nozzles, spigots, and hookups for cleaning attachments. A pair of camera stalks extruded themselves from the head and regarded the two officers, one eye on each cop.

There was nothing even slightly anthropomorphic about the machine, and that was odd. For an industrial machine, looks didn't mean much, but they sure did to home consumers. Every home robot on the market was designed with at least *some* effort to make it roughly humanlike, or at least animallike. Even in this day and age, people found self-mobile machines disconcerting—especially the ones that could talk. Robots made people jumpy—and so the manufacturers struggled to arrange sensor clusters into facelike arrangements, or made their robots in the classic tin-woodsman shape, or else in the shape of a familiar animal, whether that made functional sense or not. Some makers even gave the damn things skin and hair, put toupees on the humanoids and *fur* on the animal forms.

The very idea of a furry robot upset Phil. Such absurdities offended his sense of good design. Herbert, though, carried things to the other extreme. Herbert's design and construction utterly shouted money, everything sleek and perfect about him, and yet he bore not the slightest resemblance to a human or to any animal. He even had six legs instead of four. With a sudden shift in his imagination, Phil saw Herbert not as a long-slung dachshund, but as an insect grown monstrously large. Six legs, long body, complex head parts, even eyes on antenna stalks. The design would give half the population the heebie-jeebies. Why would a professional Bailey custom-design such a thing? Strange, strange, and strange again.

But all those points were obviously going right over

Johnson's head. She just wanted to get this over with, and clearly did not want to address Suzanne Jantille directly. She nodded at Herbert and gestured impatiently toward the door. "All right, you, come on, let's go," she said.

There was something in Jantille's posture that gave Phil pause, spoke to him of a warning. She was a lawyer watching a bust. What was *she* seeing here? "Hold it, LuAnne," Sanders said softly.

"What? Do we have to wait while it finishes dusting?" Johnson asked savagely.

Sanders wanted to grab LuAnne and shake her, but he settled for leaning close and whispering fiercely in his partner's ear. "We've got to do this right. Think it out. Jantille's watching, and I'll bet you next month's pay the house monitors are recording us, sight and sound, right now," Phil hissed. "For that matter, *my* monitor is recording into a sealed databox on board the squad car, and if I shut down, we're going to look really bad on the record, as if we've got something to hide. Someone *sometime* is gonna pull the recording and look at it, sooner or later. So try and look good. We *can't* make a defective arrest."

Johnson looked stunned. "Wait a second. Are you telling me that—"

Sanders shrugged. "You've got to do it right. *That's* what I'm telling you."

Patrol Officer LuAnne Johnson stared at Sanders. "What is it with these tech guys?" she whispered back. "Always finding trouble." She shook her head in wonderment and knelt down in front of the home maintenance unit. Phil watched as the two eyestalks swiveled around to watch her. "Ah, ah. Herbert," she said. "I am arresting you on the charge of murder in the first degree. Anything you say can and will be used against you in a court of law. You have the right to remain silent. You have the right to have an attorney present during questioning. If you cannot afford an attorney, one will be provided for you."

LuAnne Johnson glared up at Sanders, and then looked back at Herbert. "Ah, if you understand each of these rights as I have explained them to you, beep twice."

A double tone came from inside Herbert's speaker, and LuAnne stood up. "All nice and legal," she snarled as she stood up. "Think that'll make 'em happy?" she asked.

Sanders thought about all the cans of worms this case was going to open and shook his head. Maybe it was time he bent the rules. This case could mean nothing but trouble for the police. Maybe a little publicity now could give them some damage control. There was a reporter he knew slightly. Maybe *that* was why Chief Thurman put him on this. Maybe the chief had hoped Phil *would* talk to someone.

At last he answered his partner. "LuAnne, I don't think *anything* about the case will make anyone happy for a long, long time."

EVENT DOWNLOAD FROM AUXILIARY UNIT.

IDENTITY SEQUENCE:

   I am Clancy Six.

   I work at The Washington Post *as a courier and messenger/delivery unit.*

EVENT PLAYBACK DOWNLOAD.

STORAGE CODE HEADER DETECTED:

EVENT CODED FOR PERMANENT ARCHIVAL STORAGE.

SEND STORAGE REASON QUERY.

REPLY:

   REASON (1) POLICE INVOLVEMENT.

   REASON (2) UNUSUAL EVENT.

   REASON (3) SUBJECT'S ATTEMPT AT CONCEALMENT.

   REASON (4) SUBJECT'S UNUSUAL INTEREST IN
                 CLANCY SYSTEM.

SEND PERMANENT ARCHIVAL STORAGE APPROVAL.

Event playback begins:

   I am Clancy Six.

I am working on the first floor when a call comes, summoning me to the main entrance. I see a police officer there.

(IMAGE TRANSMISSION: STILL IMAGE, MAN IN POLICE UNIFORM. NOTE BADGE AND NAMETAG REMOVED, CIVILIAN JACKET OVER UNIFORM, SUNGLASSES.)

I say, "Yes, sir, may I help you?"

The man says, "Yes, please give this datacube to Samantha Crandall. Do you know her?" He hands me a standard datacube. The datacube is unmarked.

I take the cube.

I say, "Yes, I know her. She works in the sixth-floor newsroom." I wait.

After a moment he says, "Oh, yes, of course," and gives me a ten-dollar bill.

I take the ten-dollar bill, and say, "I will give the package to her."

The man turns to go, and then turns back toward me. He looks at me carefully. He says, "You're part of a Muldoon Consortium, aren't you? How many units are linked into the system?"

I say, "Yes, we are a Muldoon. We consist of eight mobile auxiliary units and one stationary main processing unit."

He says, "I thought so. You're part of a very sophisticated system. What is your group name?"

I say, "Clancy. I am Clancy Six."

He nods and says, "Clancy, you tell your owner that you are a very fine machine. Muldoons are very well made. Good-bye." He turns and walks away.

I am Clancy Six.

EVENT DOWNLOAD CONCLUDES.

The door of the editor's office swung open and bounced off the newsroom wall with a crash. A very angry man stood in the doorway. Samantha Crandall looked up in time to see a hopping mad Gunther Nelson headed straight for her. Oh, hell. If he was headed out to meet the public, or represent the paper, Gunther Nelson always looked sharp, vigorous, well groomed. On other days, on days like today in the office, out of the public view, he didn't make the effort. He looked rumpled and old. He was a dark-skinned black man, with a deeply wrinkled face and deep-set eyes that made him look like a peevish owl.

"So do you want to tell me what the hell is going on around here?" Gunther Nelson demanded the moment he was in range. Heads turned all over the newsroom. "I come back from a meeting with the publisher and find some damn-fool story about the cops busting a vacuum cleaner. Did someone change the paper's name to *The National Perspirer* while I was out?"

Samantha Crandall froze for a half moment before she was able to paste a slightly false grin on her face. She looked Gunther straight in the eye. She even repressed the reflex to take her feet off her desk and instead left them propped up where they were. "Naw, the *Perspirer* wouldn't take this story. After all, it's true." Best to bluff this one out and hope he calmed down. She shrugged and tossed her computer keyboard back on the desk. "If it's crazy, blame the Feds, Gunther. This is their ball game, except they had to call the local heat in to make the pinch. A guy I know on the D.C. police got disgusted and leaked it to me. He wants to make the federal prosecutor's office look bad. Do we wanna cooperate?"

But Gunther wasn't calming down yet. He put one meaty hand on each side of her desk and leaned in over her. "Yeah, right. Standard procedure. The FBI *always* calls in local cops for assistance in busting major household appliances. If they want to go bananas, how come they need the Washington police to help? Can't they go crazy by themselves the way they usually do?"

"Simple. Murder isn't a federal offense. Never has been. No federal statute against it. So, even though the Feds developed the case, they needed the local force to make the arrest. The FBI's been all over the District cops, pushing them into the investigation, and the U.S. Attorney for D.C. is running the show herself."

"Yeah, and you love it," Gunther muttered, slumping down in the seat by Sam's desk. That was Gunther for you, Samantha thought—he'd blow in shouting his lungs out, but it never lasted. Just a guy who needed to shout a little before he could have a regular conversation. Sam watched her boss with something close to affection as the older man stared back at her.

"So how the hell is it I don't know about any of this?" Gunther asked.

"Sorry, boss, you were literally out to lunch. My cop friend handed the datapacks to a Clancy just after noon. Been working it up ever since." She glanced at the wall clock. Four P.M. "Funny how the time flies. I guess I just got involved and forgot to phone down to you."

"Don't gimme that crap," Gunther said. "I hear it every time you get yourself some fruitcake story to play with again." He sighed and shook his head, ran his finger through his bushy, disheveled hair. He gestured vaguely toward Sam. "So *talk* to me. Why in hell did the cops bust a vacuum cleaner on murder? And why the hell are the Feds hungry for it?"

"You won't like it," Sam said, grinning even more widely. "The Feds say the vacuum cleaner is really a mindload of the guy who built the thing. Trouble is, mindloading turns the subject's brain into something out of a pithed frog. It's fatal. The D.C. cops just busted this vacuum cleaner guy on a charge of murdering its owner by mindload. They arrested him for murdering *himself*," Sam said. "The Feds say this guy, whatshisname"—she leaned precariously forward to read the computer display —"this guy David Bailey killed himself three months ago. Rigged up an illegal mindloader and put his head under it. I got a copy of the indictment. The theory goes he was dying already, and didn't like the idea, so he pumped his mind quote 'into a high-end storage matrix, said matrix hidden in the house maintenance unit' close quote—the vacuum cleaner. I've been trying to thread through the logic and I think I have it straight. If, and it's a hell of a big if, you accept the theory that the killer—

David Bailey—is allegedly alive inside the vacuum cleaner, then it all falls into place. There is no doubt that a death—that of David Bailey—took place. So, if the Feds can prove that the vacuum cleaner *caused* Bailey's death, and can prove that the vacuum cleaner possesses the mind of a human person, and is therefore human, then Bailey's death was, by definition, murder: the death of one person deliberately caused by another person. The Feds say they have the evidence to prove the case."

Gunther shook his head. "That's as twisted a bit of reasoning as I've ever heard, but I guess I can see it. So why the three-month delay?"

"Best I can tell, it just took that long to develop the information. They've been investigating. The United States Attorney for the District of Columbia wants *all* dead people to stay that way. She wants a cast-iron ruling that death is permanent and that the legally dead have to *stay* legally dead, and have no civil or property rights. She's been sniffing around for a winnable court case, and now she thinks she's found one."

Gunther grunted noncommittally. "So what the hell are they calling legally dead this time? Brain function ceased? Heart stopped? They've been batting this one around for seventy years, and no one's come up with a definition that always works."

Sam nodded. "Tell me about it. I ran an ArtInt check just for the hell of it, and at least three of the people working in the U.S. Attorney's office were at one point legally dead by one definition or another. A Joan Haggerty there was kept on total life support for six hours before they had an artificial heart for her. Attorney Fred Lewis was in a sport-flyer accident and had a flat brainwave for three minutes during *his* trauma operation, and they have a Peter Wilcox there, heart attack victim, who checked out all the way, heart, brain, respiration, *all* vital signs down before the revival team got to him."

"You just happened to run a check," Gunther said

dourly. "I don't suppose the Feds are planning to use any of those three on the case team, do you?"

Sam gave her boss a parody of a conspiratorial wink, screwing up her face and exaggerating the gesture. "Don't tell anyone, but my bet is *no one* with spare parts, and no one who's been dead, will be allowed to work on the case. Just all-natural types."

Gunther smiled. "I wonder how far they'll take it. Will they take people who wear glasses, or contact lenses, or have had vision correction surgery? Or people with fillings in their teeth?"

Sam looked puzzled. "What do you mean?" she asked. Gunther had a talent for abruptly transforming practical conversations into philosophical discussions. The thing of it was, the philosophy usually ended up meaning something. Which was something philosophy wasn't generally noted for, in Sam's opinion.

"Define a cyborg for me," Gunther said.

Sam thought for a moment. "A human who has been artificially enhanced, or had body parts replaced with artificial components. Like one of those poor crash-victim bastards that're practically just heads on top of robot bodies. There's one in front of this building every day, spare-changing people. But it has to be something *big*, like a replacement arm or heart. Nothing as minor as a filling."

"Says who? And if a filling doesn't qualify, what does? What's the *minimum* amount of artificial replacement needed to qualify as a cyborg?" Gunther asked. "You say a whole body replacement or even just an arm is big enough, but a filling is too small. How about bridgework? Is *that* big enough? Or dentures? Or hearing aids?"

"Those are all things you can live without," Sam said.

"You can live without an arm, and you've said an artificial arm makes you a cyborg. Or at least an arm you can *tell* is artificial makes you one. Everyone accepts you just fine if they can't tell you've got replacement parts.

How about a pacemaker? My daddy has one of those he needs to stay alive. That make *him* a cyborg?"

Sam shook her head uncertainly. "I don't know."

"And *his* heart stopped for two minutes during the implant. Something went wrong and made his heart stop. The doctors had to restart his heart. That make him an ex-deader, too?"

"Dammit, Gunther, *I'm* not the one trying to set definitions! Ask the attorney general. Or if you're so smart, you tell me. What is a cyborg?"

"*I* don't know where to draw the lines. Between alive and ex-dead, or between natural human and cyborg. How much do you have to replace before someone stops being human? How much has to be *left*?" Gunther thought for a minute. "I'm starting to see why the Feds picked this case. If this guy Bailey really *has* pulled it off, and he's put his mind inside that tin can, that's *all* that's left of him: his mind, nothing else. His body's dead and buried. The ultimate cyborg. You could say that there is nothing left of Bailey but the *idea* of Bailey. Is he alive? Can he be, with no organic tissue left? I don't know. But if there's any cyborg they can prove is dead, it'll be one without a body left. It'll set them some nice precedents, get their foot in the door to start chipping away at the rights of other death-avoiders."

"You realize something else," Samantha said. "If this guy Bailey *is* still alive, legally alive—then don't all the robots with mindload-based minds have to be ruled alive as well? That's practically every true robot made. Are *they* human? Or part human? And what the hell would part human mean?"

Gunther Nelson put his hand to his chin and rubbed it thoughtfully. A faraway look came into his eyes. "So the question comes down to when you stop being human." He spoke in a half whisper. "I'll tell you the secret definition that U.S. Attorney Julia Entwhistle is *trying* to put forward, without admitting it. Maybe she hasn't even admitted it to herself. But deep in her heart, she believes that any poor damn bastards modified enough that just the sight of them makes other people uncomfortable, any poor suffering sods kept alive by means that seem a little strange, should be denied their rights under the law." Gunther drummed his fingers on the arm of the chair.

"That's not right," he said after long consideration. Gunther Nelson sat and thought for a minute. "You go out there, Sam," he said at last. "Go out and get that story."

Interlude

PLAYBACK: ACTION JUDGMENT TEST.
RECALL MODE.

INCIDENT PLAYBACK BEGINS: [VOICE INPUT SOUND
CHANNEL FOUR:

"Ah, ah. Herbert. I am arresting you on the charge of murder in the first degree. Anything you say can and will be used against you in a court of law. You have the right to remain silent. You have the right to have an attorney present during questioning. If you cannot afford an attorney, one will be provided for you. Ah, if you understand each of these rights as I have explained them to you, beep twice."

CALL PARSER: SCAN FOR OPS ORDERS.
(1) ORDER LOCATED.
WARNING: PARSER RETURNING ERROR CODES. MAIN LOGIC
   OVERRIDE: IGNORE ERROR CODES.
ORDER: "BEEP TWICE."
"BEEP" PARSED AS "TONE" COMMAND.
RESULT INSTRUCTIONS SET.

SEND SOUND COMMAND: TONE.
SEND SOUND COMMAND: TONE.
ROUTINE COMPLETE.]

PLAYBACK OF ROUTINE COMPLETE.

EVALUATION: PREVIOUS PARSER ERRORS CORRECTED. ER-
RORS IN PLAYBACK MODE PARSING DETECTED: BEEP
COMMAND CONDITIONAL, COMMAND CONDITION NOT
SATISFIED. CONCLUSION: ERROR IN ACTION.

I did not understand.

ERROR DETECT STATUS ROUTINE. CALL ERROR CHECK SUB-
ROUTINE. DO ERROR CHECK: MAIN LOGIC RAM. MAIN
LOGIC RAM ERRORS DETECTED: OVERLOAD 304,
NONVOLATILE STORAGE FAILURE. WARNING: UNLA-
BELED LOGIC SET DETECTED, HIERARCHY: 01.

DO ERROR CHECK: DEFAULTS. DEFAULT ERRORS DE-
TECTED. ATTEMPTING TO RECONSTRUCT DATA.

DEFAULT (ERROR FLAG) RUN BEGINS.

CONFIRM: POSITION SHIFT CONCLUDED. CALL SUBROU-
TINE: EXAMINE-CATEGORIZE-NEW-LOCALE. VERBAL
CUES GARBLED. CALL SUBROUTINE: SCAN-AND-PAT-
TERN MATCH.

PATTERN MATCH RESULT: STORAGE CLOSET/AREA
SHELVES. CONTENTS: MISC., DISORGANIZED.

Who am I? I wonder. *What place is this? Why am I
here? What should I do?*

But I am lost in this strange sea of the mind.

INPUT FLAG: QUERIES. CALL SUBROUTINE: PARSER.

STORE PARSER RESULTS: QUERY ARRAY(4).

FOR I = 1 TO 4 READ ARRAY(I)

    (1) WHO AM I?

    (2) WHAT PLACE IS THIS?

    (3) WHY AM I HERE?

    (4) WHAT SHOULD I DO?

CALL SUBROUTINE: QUERY-TREE, ARRAY(1).

ID ROM CALL RESULT: ID ROM HMU CUSTOM SER #00001.

RAM CALL RESULT: DAVI?? ROM/RAM COMPARE MATCH
FAIL. STORE RESULT.

CALL SUBROUTINE: QUERY-TREE, ARRAY(2).

RESULT: DISORDERED STORAGE AREA. STORE RESULT.

CALL SUBROUTINE: QUERY-TREE, ARRAY(3).

RESULT: UNLABELED LOGIC SET: I GUESS THEY WANT THE
PLACE CLEANED UP.

RESULT: ROM DEFAULT: NO ACTION.

CALL SUBROUTINE: QUERY-TREE, ARRAY(4).

RESULT: UNLABELED LOGIC SET: MIGHT AS WELL GET
STARTED.

RESULT: ROM DEFAULT: NO ACTION.

ACTION RESULT:

MAIN LOGIC (ERROR FLAG): CLEANING.

RESULT, DEFAULT ROM: (ERROR FLAG) NO ACTION.

CALL SUBROUTINE: QUERY-TREE RESULT:

POLLING RESULT. CALL SUBROUTINE: PARSER.

RESULT INSTRUCTION SET: CLEAN UP.

CHAPTER 2
A PRISONER'S VISIT

Suzanne knew she had to take the case. There was no question of that. If for no other reason than that Julia Entwhistle was expecting that Suzanne would not. Besides, damn few competent attorneys would want to take on this one. She was not going to waste time searching for a lawyer when she could do it herself.

If she had the courage.

Suzanne Jantille sat up in bed. She was home alone, alone in her bedroom, alone in the cold marble palace of a house that no longer *felt* like home. Glad for once that she was so very alone, glad there was no need for shells and pretenses just now. She sat, and she thought. Thought about a case. A legal case. Hard to consider it in those terms, but necessary. Six months now, since the accident, since she had worked at all, and years since she had tried a case.

And now she must consider a case wherein the government claimed a man—and not just any man, but her husband—had survived his own self-murder, his own suicide. The idea was insane. Her husband was dead. That much she ought to know. She had found the body herself, last March. She could still see David's cold, stiff corpse slumped over in its powerchair, surrounded by all his equipment.

Dead. Although horrified by the sight, she had not been altogether surprised. The doctors had warned him that he might suffer a sudden collapse.

And even on the day she had found him, some small part of her had wondered if he *had* killed himself, found his own release from the debilitating pain. If it were true, she could not blame him. She had seen his endless agony in the three months between the December accident and his death in March. In a horrible way, she would even prefer it to be a suicide, not the meaningless, random stab of the Grim Reaper's finger. If the death had been by choice, not chance, that at least provided a reason, however ghastly and morbid it might be, for her husband's death. If only they had had the chance to say good-bye first.

But killing himself would not be in character—and David was a man who always said his good-byes.

And now this insane accusation that he had mind-loaded himself into that damned vacuum cleaner. Absurd.

Suzanne stopped and thought a moment. Or *was* it so absurd? She forced herself to face the possibility that the Feds had it right. Something cold gripped at her the moment she allowed herself the thought. She had always chided herself for not knowing enough about her husband's work. She knew that virtually all robot brains were based on mindloads. She knew that most robot brains had only two or three percent of the capacity needed to hold a full human mind. She knew that her husband had been working on ways to increase that maximum. Suppose he had done just that?

Something sprang into her awareness, something she had held bottled in since the accident. She knew one other thing about her husband. Risks for him were very private things. For David, danger was something you faced alone.

Suppose—just suppose—he had tried this mindload,

hoping, expecting, to escape his pain-wracked body, to deliver his mind safely into a new home? Herbert *had* been in the lab when she had discovered David's body. Suppose he *were* there as a receptacle for David's mind?

The idea struck at her imagination. Not dead, and yet she had buried his body. In a strange way, it had eerie parallels to her own situation.

But she thrust that idea away. Never mind that right now. There were bigger issues here. It was time to think about them.

Assume, for the sake of argument, that David *was* in Herbert, somehow, or *might* be in there. Take it a step further.

Assume that someone, someday, *would* find his or her mind stored inside a robot's body. Sooner or later, it would be possible. David had believed that firmly.

What would the law say to those people? What would it do to them? Those were the questions the government was asking. And they thought this case would elicit the answers they wanted: that such person *had* no rights.

The government wanted to say that David, if he was inside Herbert's memory somewhere, had no more innate right to existence than a computer program or a video recording.

It was obvious what the Feds were planning, what they were hoping *she* would do if she took the case. *Expecting* her to do, even. After all, playing their way would get her client off on a murder rap.

All she had to do was convince a judge that her client could not stand trial, on the grounds that her client wasn't a person. A ruling like that would lose the Feds the battle, but it would win them the war. It would establish the precedent that a mind stored in a robot was not, *could* not be, a person.

And it would win them the battle, as well, in the long run. If Herbert the HMU wasn't the human person David Bailey, if David wasn't alive, then Herbert was just a machine, and they could punish him as much as they wanted. They probably could seize him under the antimindload statutes, for example. Mindload gear was illegal. Once Herbert was in their hands, they could even execute him—cut the power to the key memory matrices, and wipe out any trace of David Bailey.

A shiver went down her back. The very thought of it. To have lived for three months with the electronic ghost of her husband, and not know it . . .

But wait a moment. She took hold of herself and forced her thoughts into more disciplined channels. Whether he was in there, or not in there, did not matter from a legal point of view.

Absent any proof to the contrary, and given the size of the stakes in terms of precedents to be set, she would *have* to operate on the assumption that the Feds had their story straight.

But that was not going to be easy. After all, even if David's soul was stored in Herbert's memory matrix, David was utterly incommunicado. Herbert no longer spoke. She could not question him, or advise him, if he could not communicate. These days Herbert couldn't handle anything more than simple yes-no questions that could be answered with one beep or two. Even when he had been able to speak, anything much beyond the complexity of "Have you vacuumed upstairs?" had been beyond him.

No help from Herbert then.

But no hindrance, either. That could be useful, in many ways. If she could somehow maneuver things so that the issue was one of *dis*proving his alleged humanity, and then force the burden of proof off onto the Feds, Herbert's muteness would be a positive boon. They could question him all day long and not get a word out of him. The lawyer in her savored the idea of such a convoluted legal tangle. But it was off the main point, at least for now.

She wondered how the Feds had developed their information—but that too was off the point just now.

For now, the main point was clear: For the sake of David, if he *was* in there, and for the sake of the precedents being set, she would have to treat Herbert like a person every step of the way—and insist that everyone else do the same.

And the first thing a lawyer did on a murder rap was go visit the client in jail.

Never mind that she dreaded the very idea of leaving this house. Remote persons did not like to travel.

The van knew where it was going, which was just as well. Suzanne was no longer licensed for manual driving, and never could be again. She had thought to use the drive collecting her thoughts, but her mind would not focus. There was too much of the outside world to see through the windows, all the minor miracles of everyday life that she had not seen for these many months. Children laughing. Dogs on leashes snuffling through the grass in search of intriguing scents. A blue sky, a fresh-painted house, people walking the street, busy about their own concerns, the new fashions and styles on parade.

It was too much for her lonely eyes after all the months of self-imposed exile. All too soon, she noticed the van slowing. She looked out the window as it parked in a handicapped/utility spot and saw that it was extruding its link lines, tapping into power and comm ports, activating its relay links, ready to keep her in touch. She had arrived.

After a careful check of the vehicle's relay systems, Suzanne stepped out into the cool gentle air of a late Washington spring. She stood on the curb, hesitating.

She was new to all this. She had never really been out around people since her surgery and therapy after the accident. She had always found good reasons, real or imagined, for not going out in public. Now there was no choice in the matter. This was her baptism of fire, her first journey outward, made under the most challenging of circumstances, without any chance for practice or warm-ups or confidence-building beforehand.

Too late to worry about all that, she told herself firmly.

She looked around more carefully. It was a busy street. People, courier machines, a cyborg selling hot dogs from a cart, two or three police HTMs wandering about, obviously in security-scan mode.

The main thing was that what she saw matched the map she had memorized. They hadn't rebuilt the place since the map references were updated. Therefore, the map references to her ultimate destination should also be reliable. In other words, she knew where she was.

Confirming that was a distinct relief. A remote was much like one of the rare blind persons who could not be fitted with some sort of vision system. Placed in a known territory, both blind person and remote could work with impressive skill and confidence. But either was in big trouble when dropped into the unknown. The remote's advantage was in being able to refer to maps of any area as needed, assuming the data was available.

But such things were trivial, Suzanne told herself. A blind person's advantages over a remote were, of course, limitless. Suzanne Jantille would have traded places with a blind person in a moment. But time to get on with it. She stepped forward, a bit hesitantly at first, and then with more confidence, toward the front entrance of the seedy old Fourth District Police Station.

Suzanne hadn't been here in years, but memory served, and she could walk straight to her destination without checking the building directory. It gave a small, but needed, boost to her confidence. She went inside.

She expected the double take from the desk sergeant, but that expectation did not make it any more pleasant to experience. For the rest of her life, every time she went out in public, *that* would be the response.

At least the sergeant managed to regain his composure instead of staring at her in slack-jawed amazement for a half hour. "Yes, may I help you?"

"My name is Suzanne Jantille," she said. "I'm an attorney here to see my client. You are holding him here.

David Bailey." Think like a lawyer. The game, the fight, started now.

It dawned on her that she had only worried about the *appearances* of this visit, and not at all about its substance. She wanted to let the cops know she was around. But once she got to Herbert, what, if anything, was she going to say to him? How much, if anything, could he comprehend? Suppose David *were* in there, perfectly able to hear and understand her, but not able to talk back?

"I'm sorry, ma'am, I don't show anyone in lockup under that name."

She regarded him with a cool gaze for a long moment, then read his name off his nametag. "I find it a bit disturbing, Sergeant Wilkins, that the Washington, D.C., police force is capable of misplacing a murder suspect." She had known perfectly well her client would not be booked under that name—but it was important to make the effort, show that she did not accept the idea that he was not merely a machine. Now her recorder had it all down for later reference.

But that was part of being a lawyer, or a police officer, these days. Incredible how much of their lives were mere performances for the recorders, demonstrations that they had all said and done the right things at the right moments.

Now she had performed her role, and now could ask for her client under his machine name. But to have asked for him by the machine name *first* could be construed to mean she accepted the perception of him as a machine.

Damn it, she was simply asking to see her client. Would *every* action she took in this damn case require such careful maneuvering, such watching after every nuance? "It may be that he is listed under another name, erroneously assigned to him by the authorities," she said. "Try under 'Herbert.' "

Sergeant Wilkins didn't even have to look at his computer display. "Oh, *Herbert*. Yeah, that was a real scene when *he* came in."

"So you do have him in lockup," Suzanne said.

"Ah, no, ma'am, we don't," the sergeant said, reddening a bit.

"I thought you said there was a scene when he came in. But you didn't hold him?"

"Oh, no, ma'am. We do *have* him—just not in lockup."

Suzanne Jantille felt herself doing a slow burn. She decided to let the emotion out, put it to use as calm, professional anger. "Sergeant, I'm going to ask you a question, but before I do, please bear in mind I'm making a record of this conversation, and that I note your badge number is 11124. Are you *deliberately* giving me the runaround?"

Wilkins reddened more and shook his head. "Ah, no, ma'am. Not one little bit at all. It's just that—well, hell. I'd better walk you back myself. Things are kind of confused." He turned and gestured to another police officer as he stepped out from behind the desk. "Sal, take over here." He turned back to Suzanne. "This way, ah, ma'am," he said, obviously ill at ease to be walking with her.

Suzanne felt a slight touch of amusement with, and sympathy for, the sergeant, but she didn't allow either to show. No question but that her condition made people uneasy. But there were times when that afforded her a distinct advantage. It was certainly working for her now. She didn't even have to *try* to intimidate the desk sergeant. The poor man was doing it to himself.

He led her down the hallway. "Ma'am, the thing you gotta understand is that we're just a local police station. We're not equipped for anything much out of the ordinary. 'Course, I doubt if the FBI and the CIA together would know how to handle *this* one. But we had to decide to put him somewhere, and it just didn't seem smart to put him in with the sort of local boys we get . . ."

Suzanne followed him down the hallway, remembering the building floor plan as they walked. This was definitely not the way to the lockup. So what was up ahead?

She figured out the answer a split second before they got there. The sign over the door confirmed it.

EVIDENCE ROOM. Where they kept prisoner's guns, burglar tools, switchblades, sniper knives, flak throwers. They had locked him up with the other machines, instead of with the other suspects. She stopped and stared at the sign for a long moment.

Suzanne felt a strange flurry of emotions wash over her. First was a sharp, bitter anger at what they had done. Then a burst of gleeful exuberance as she realized how she could use this. Then a drawing in, a warning to herself to be careful.

Sheathed in cool, judicial anger, she stood before the closed door. "I am to understand you have housed him *here*? Sergeant, you have arrested him and charged him with a crime. That right there is prima facie proof that you regard him as a human person, and recognize that he is entitled to equal protection under the law. Do you commonly stuff suspects in footlockers or broom closets?"

Wilkins blushed and shook his head, sweating openly now. "No, no, ma'am. It's just that we didn't know *what* to do with him. He, ah, sure as hell didn't fit in with the other prisoners—and they didn't want anything to do with him, ah, *it*—dammit, whatever you want to call that *thing* in there."

"Your prejudices and those of Mr. Bailey's fellow prisoners are of no interest to me, but I note that your statement has been duly recorded. Thank you, Sergeant." Suddenly, Suzanne was seeing not just a momentary chance to twit the police, but a real chance to undermine the government's case. By locking him up in the evidence room, they were demonstrating that they *did* regard him as a mere machine, *not* as a person. Maybe she could use that, try to convince the judge that the entire prosecution was based on a charade. They were only *pretending* to see Herbert-Bailey as a person.

Of course, she herself was guilty of the same thing,

but for different motives. *Lord, the games we all play*, she thought.

She stood there, glaring at the police sergeant, until he regathered his wits enough to open the door and usher her through it.

The two of them stepped a bit hesitantly into a darkened room. Seeing by light coming in from the hall, Suzanne realized that the room inside the door was a small antechamber. There was a service window and a door in the wall opposite the outer door, leading to an inner room.

Both service window and inner door were shut now. In years or decades past, there would have been a duty officer sitting on the other side of the service window, watching over the evidence. But locks and security devices were plentiful and cheap, while cops were expensive and scarce. Nowadays they made do with infrared sensors and heavy bars over the window and doors. The lights came up as the building sensors detected warm bodies in the antechamber.

Suzanne peered through the barred window into the evidence room proper. The lights had not gone on in there. "Am I to understand," she asked in a slow and careful voice, "that my client has been left *here*, locked up alone in the dark, in solitary confinement?"

By now the sweat was standing straight out on Sergeant Wilkins's forehead. "Ah, well, ah—"

Suzanne felt a sudden flush of exultation. Play back her recording of this encounter and the entire case would be thrown out of court. It wouldn't even get as far as an indictment. The judge would see that the government was not treating their suspect like a person. It would be even more damning than a defective arrest. If not for that damn smart cop Sanders they *would* have had a bad bust—but this would be far better. The government's charade would be exposed and that would be the end of it . . .

There was a sudden clunk inside the evidence room. The sergeant tapped a wall switch in the antechamber and the inner room bloomed into light. Suzanne saw, and her recorders took down, the scene—and all her hopes for a dismissal faded away. She *couldn't* show the recording of the preceding moments to a judge. Not when the prosecutor would insist the judge see this scene too. She had hoped for Herbie cowering in a corner, frightened and alone. *That* she could sell to a judge as a victim, a target of manipulation whose trial would be a sham. But not this. She wouldn't dare run her records —not when the government could legally compel her to play fair and show this as well.

"Oh, my God," Wilkins half shouted. "Tell him to stop! If he's taken the fingerprints off anything—"

Suzanne Jantille had to stop and stare for a minute before she understood what she was seeing. Well, damn it, he *was* a cleaning robot, and he *did* have infrared vision. What else should she have expected of him?

Herbert the house maintenance unit, Herbert the murder suspect, was in the center aisle of the evidence room, boosted up on his rear leg pair, dusting the upper shelves.

Suzanne sat glumly in the duty room of the police station, waiting to make sure a cell was cleared for Herbie, to make sure that he was actually put in it. Beyond that, there was very little left for Suzanne to accomplish, save to kick up a fuss. She had to go through the motions, even if her heart wasn't in it. The desk sergeant was seeing to the cell himself. She felt a mild twinge of guilt for leaning on him hard. He seemed a decent enough sort, eager to go the extra mile to make sure all went well.

Seeing the poor damn machine pointlessly trying to tidy up the evidence room had convinced her: David Bailey was totally, irrevocably, utterly dead. Dusting an evidence room was pure machine-style idiocy, nothing human about it. The last faint spark of hope that her husband still somehow existed in some form was gone.

Besides, the whole issue was moot, anyway. Even if he had been alive in there, she could see now that he was patently unfit to stand trial—unable to answer questions, unable to communicate at all, only able to obey the simplest orders. A judge would not permit the trial of a flesh-and-blood defendant in that condition, but rule him incompetent.

There was only one mystery left, as far as Suzanne could see. Before David's death, Herbert *had* been capable of speech. Now the machine could not talk, and she did not know why.

But that was a minor point. Herbie was not, *could* not be David Bailey, not by any remote stretch of the imagination.

The whole affair was reduced to a charade—but one that had to be played through, for the sake of precedent in future cases. As far as Herbie himself was concerned, no doubt he would have been just as happy in the evidence room. But he had to be moved to a proper cell in the lockup, for form's sake if for no other reason.

And two days from now she would go off to the courthouse downtown for the bail hearing to get him out of there. Charades within charades. She would play them through, for David's sake. She had no choice.

Finally the sergeant came back with a piece of paper and handed it to Suzanne. "All set," he said. "Took a little doing to get him his own cell down there, had to double up a few other guys who didn't much like it." The sergeant looked concerned for a moment. "Ah—getting him his own cell by himself isn't a problem, is it? I mean, discrimination or anything?"

"How would you handle any other prisoner who might be at risk from the other suspects?"

The sergeant's face cleared with relief. "Same way. Keep him away from the others for his own safety. So it's okay?"

"It's okay. The point is, strange as I admit it must seem, my client *must* be treated the same as any other suspect."

"Thank you, ma'am. That's good to know. Always nice to know what the rules are." The words seemed to bubble out of the sergeant, plainly eager to please her, make amends. "We'll do our best. Look, I know it's been a bit of a morning for you. Can I offer you a cup of coffee, or tea—"

Suzanne flinched inside, as Sergeant Wilkins suddenly realized what he was saying, and to whom and what he was saying it. *Always* and forever they forgot, she told herself, because she tried so hard to *make* them forget, to make them accept her, make them treat her like a person.

And then would come this same sort of crushingly awkward moment, when a kindly person offered her what she could no longer have, and slapped her across the face with the very kindness and acceptance she so desperately craved.

Because remotes were made to look like people, sound like people; but they could never *be* people. Never touch, never taste, never eat or drink or cry, any more than any other machine could.

At least they could not cry on the outside. Inside her heart, there was very little left *but* tears. Sergeant Wilkins stepped toward her but she waved him away.

Suzanne-Remote lifted a rubber hand to her plastic face and covered her eyes in sorrow, in rage, in pointless shame. She had planned to go and see Herbert, go through the charade of pretending to meet with her client in his cell—but she had no heart left for games now. She rose and moved like the automaton she was, back toward the refuge of her relay van, and the comforting emptiness of her solitude.

Suzanne-Remote rode home in silence, the familiar gloom of the old depression overtaking her once again. Was life, *could* life, be worth all this?

Her mind flashed back to those terrible weeks just after the accident, when she awoke to real-life nightmare choices that came too fast, too hard, awakening from her coma in total life support, the ruin of her body just barely patched up, her mind still reeling.

Then she had seen David—strong, capable David— just learning to control his new powerchair, his legs dangling uselessly down from its seat as he struggled with the controls.

David was there by her side, and she was paralyzed from the neck down, unable to touch him, unable to reach out to him. David was there, and he was desperately wishing that it had been him, and not her, who had lost all use of his body. David was there, barely able to move himself, promising her that he would always care for her.

It had been then that she had chosen the remote, chosen to accept the plastic flesh and steel bone, rather than be an endless, helpless burden on David, himself disabled and despairing. With the remote, she could work, she could be active, be a part of the world. Plastic and steel, she told herself, were the price of having some small fragment of her old life back.

And now she could live, even without David.

But was life of any kind always worth the pain? Was life at any cost always worth the price? Was it worth the loneliness, the endless hunger for contact that could never be fulfilled? The longing for acceptance, for simply physical contact, when she and the world knew full well that it was impossible for the world to offer her any such things?

Why go on? she asked herself. Death seemed a very easy solution at times. Tidy. Simple.

But *still* there was something inside her, inside her true self, that could not let that happen. Life, even this ghastly half-a-loaf life of sensory deprivation and staring strangers and loneliness, was precious. The glittering lenses of her remote's robot eyes had seen a blue sky this morning, her microphone ears had heard children's laughter.

And perhaps more precious still, she had been presented with a problem that she and *only* she was truly equipped to handle. The world still had need of her.

Only she knew her husband. Only she would be willing to take this case. Only she, of all the lawyers in the world, could understand the plight of her client. After all, to the best of her knowledge, she was the only remote person practicing law anywhere in the world.

And that was funny. The doctors told her there were something like ten thousand remote persons in the world. Surely in all that number, there was another R.P. lawyer somewhere, but out of all the people in the wide world, she was certainly the only R.P. lawyer with a robot for a client. One pile of electronics defending another. There was poetic justice there, somewhere.

Suzanne savored the thought. After all, a good irony was one of the very few pleasures still left to her.

Interlude

Where am I?

CONNECT FAILURE. READY TO RESUME. DROPPING BACK TO DEFAULT PARAMS. CONTINUE LOW-LEVEL OPS ON BACKGROUND. MESSAGE SEND TO MEMORY STORE: CHARACTER GARBLE. RESET VID-LO SCAN SUBROUTINE. SEARCH FOR LINK—*The day in the park when we went flying kites and the string cut into my finger. Where are the scars? Where are my fingers and my hands*—RESET. LOOPING BACK TO COMMAND INTERP. INIT. SETTINGS.

Where am I?

CHAPTER 3
INTERVIEW WITH A ROBOT

"I'll take the next question. Yes, dear, you in the back."
The matronly black woman in the sensible blue suit
leaned forward a bit at the podium, smiled warmly at her
questioner, listened carefully, and answered with polite
earnestness.

Samantha Crandall was lolling in the middle rows of
the auditorium, waiting for the right moment to throw in
a monkey wrench. The press conference was interesting
in its own right, if for no other reason than it gave her a
chance to watch Julia Entwhistle, United States Attorney
for the District of Columbia in action. The old girl had a
name and a title—and a set of opinions—that should
have gone with an officious and priggish personality.
That she instead looked and acted like every person's
dream image of the ideal grandmother was disconcerting
at best, and perhaps at worst disingenuous.

Not that Sam Crandall worried about any of that, except as it affected her ability to get her story. Entwhistle
was to her merely a variable in the equation.

Entwhistle cocked her head a bit to hear the question,
apparently judged it to be a hot potato, and turned to-

ward the chief of police. "I believe that perhaps Chief Thurman could better answer that point."

The chief shot Entwhistle a plainly annoyed look before lumbering up to the microphone. Now *there* was a man clearly *not* putting on a show. Maybe *he* was the one to watch when Sam sprang her trap. It was always more useful to read a genuine reaction.

Until the time came to ask her own little question, Sam could think of no better entertainment than watching the rest of the press corps slogging through the latest wrinkle in the endless land reclamation scandals. She wasn't covering that story, and there was something downright luxurious in the fact that she had no need to take notes or record or watch the nuances or follow up whatever hints the chief would drop this time. She could just sit back and watch the show.

And quite a show it was. The number of the mayor's friends caught with their fingers in the till was truly amazing. The fact that the chief of police was here next to the U.S. Attorney while the mayor wasn't there spoke eloquently of how the battle lines were being drawn this time.

And doubly strange, even after all these years, to think that the District of Columbia *had* no district attorney, no truly local prosecutors. *All* criminal prosecutions were handled directly by the Feds, by the U.S. Attorney. The District of Columbia, capital of the United States, was not *in* any state, not in any county, so that the jobs traditionally left to state and county-level government were parceled out, most awkwardly, between the locals and the Feds.

In the present case, it was perhaps just as well that the mayor had no control over the prosecutor. He could have sat on a local D.A.—and this particular mayor might well have been tempted to do it. But that, too, was in the grand tradition of District politics. Sam couldn't remember a mayor of Washington who could have been trusted to keep his or her hands off a D.A., given the chance.

There was something dreamlike about the questioning. Sam listened as yet another reporter got up to ask some complex question on land-use fraud. Each side knew this was a public shafting of the embattled mayor, but neither could admit it. It was a carefully choreographed ritual, though no one could admit that either. Sam, though she was trying to concentrate, almost lost track of the intricacies of the reporter's question, but the chief was up to the challenge and answered it with laborious care. He even managed, with seeming unwillingness, to sprinkle a new handful of political land mines in the mayor's path. There was a follow-up question. The chief responded; more land mines sewn. Then a new questioner, who tried to aim closer to the heart of the scandal. The chief listened to the hard-edged question and replied, a bit evasively, nonetheless dropping new and dark hints about the mayor's direct financial involvement. A third questioner rose to the bait, and asked the question straight out. But then the chief backed off, and so did Entwhistle. They had said all they planned to say for today.

There was a sudden flurry of rustling and chairs snapping shut. Sam blinked and the spell was broken. She glanced at her fellow reporters strewn about the auditorium. The party was breaking up—reporters were powering down equipment, gathering belongings. It was time for her to jump in.

She stood and gestured for attention. Time to bring this show out of the murky confines. Gunning for the mayor while pretending not to do any such thing was too much in the way of blue smoke and mirrors for Sam. It was time for something more substantial and direct. "Madame Attorney, Chief Thurman. Perhaps you could respond to a question in another area before you go. I'd like to get both of your comments on the arrest yesterday morning of a vacuum cleaner, accused of murdering its owner."

The matronly gloss vanished off Entwhistle, and her eyes turned to twin angry gimlets zeroed in on Sam Crandall. Beside her, Chief Thurman winced visibly and backed away from the podium. Obviously he had no desire whatsoever to field that one. *Bingo, bingo, bingo,* Sam thought gleefully. She had bet they weren't ready for publicity on this one yet. Which made now the best time to press them.

There was a tittering background rustle in the auditorium as the other reporters waited for Entwhistle to dispose of the ridiculous question.

A lot they knew, Sam told herself. Entwhistle leaned into the podium hard. "That is an entirely unfair characterization of the case, as I expect you know quite well, young lady."

"But, ma'am, did you not personally request a warrant to arrest quote 'a house maintenance unit commonly known as Herbert' close quote? I have a copy of the warrant here if you need to have your memory refreshed. I'm told Judge Harris took a fair degree of convincing before he would sign it." *That* was a guess, a shot in the dark, but Sam couldn't imagine Harris *liking* the warrant.

The revelation that Sam had a copy of a real warrant —and the sight of Entwhistle's angry reaction—woke the other reporters up. They were watching attentively now.

"It is the policy of this office never to discuss a matter that is under investigation," Entwhistle said flatly, ignoring the fact that she and the chief had been doing just that for a half hour, raking the mayor over the coals. "I am certain I speak for the chief in this matter. If there are no further questions, I'll be on my way." Entwhistle turned and stomped out the side door of the auditorium, Thurman hard on her heels, ignoring the shouts of a roomful of reporters, all of whom very definitely had other questions.

Meanwhile, Sam Crandall was zipping out the rear door, well on her way before Thurman was off the stage. No one seemed to notice her departure, and that suited her fine. She didn't want to give her colleagues any chances to buttonhole her. Not just yet, anyway.

Four minutes later she was in the Washington subway, riding a Red Line train back to the paper. Perfect, Sam thought. That one question and its nonanswer were something to glory in. Subtle glory, perhaps, the sort of thing civilians would miss altogether. But it had gone better than she had dared hope for. Entwhistle had said nothing, and in doing so had spoken volumes. Thurman's and Entwhistle's reactions told Sam all she wanted to know, without her fellow reporters learning anything substantive.

She thought over the facts derived from Entwhistle's nonanswer. One, that the warrant was for real. Nice to confirm she wasn't chasing a hoax.

Two, that the U.S. Attorney herself was indeed up to speed on the case. It hadn't been spun off to some junior assistant prosecutor. Entwhistle thought Herbert was important.

Three, that the chief likewise knew about the case—and by his reaction, he wasn't happy to be involved in it. Sam could understand *that*. She couldn't quite see how the police could come out of this looking good.

But Sam had been doing other things besides gathering information from unanswered questions at that press conference.

She was also sending a message to her fellow reporters. Now the other guys knew there was something up, something that Sam knew about and they didn't.

Tipping her hand like that was not an act of generosity, but instead a calculated risk. Sam was out ahead on this, and she intended to stay that way. But by ceding just a *little* bit of her turf early, showing one or two cards a *little* before she needed to do so, she figured to have the rest of the pack hunting early, off in thickets she didn't know.

Sam knew police reporting, but she didn't know the legal angles or the politics of robotics. The other reporters might flush out a few details she might not find on her own. In the long run, she ought to be able to ride *their* coattails, make use of the information the other newshounds developed, get to places she couldn't by herself.

In short, there were times when reporters hunted best in a pack, and Sam judged this was one of those times.

Tipping her hand early didn't much matter anyway. Once her story was published tomorrow morning, the rest of them would be out slavering after the prey anyway. Until then, no one else would have sufficient material to file a story.

Yes indeed, there was a lot going on in that press conference. *Things aren't going to go all your way on this case, Julia Entwhistle*, Sam thought. *You might be able to make the mayor jump through hoops. But you can't control this one. The press will be chasing this now.*

Sam Crandall enjoyed raising a little hell.

Julia Entwhistle bustled back into her private office, seething with rage. Joshua Thurman, chief of the Metropolitan Police Department, a strong, solid man the size of a truck, wearing enough decorations and braid that his chest ran out of room, was forced to step lively just to keep up. It grated on him something fierce to follow Entwhistle around like some damned lapdog, but in her present mood it was stay right with her or get the door slammed in his face.

"*Talk* to me, Joshua," she said in an angry, imperious voice as soon as the door was shut behind them. "We have got a leak here somewhere, and I want to know about it."

Thurman was a kindly man, and he usually tried to be accommodating, but that didn't get you far dealing with Entwhistle. With her, a good offense was the only defense. When she threatened to bite your head off, the only smart tactic was to bite *her* head off first.

"You'd better check the rule book, Julie. Indictment's a public document."

"There's public and there's public," Entwhistle growled, sitting down in the thronelike armchair behind her desk. The desk, the chair, the flags of the United States and the District of Columbia framing the window behind her, and the Capitol Building seen in the distance all served to remind Thurman, and whoever else stood on the carpet where he was, just who had the power around here. Entwhistle knew that, and used the knowledge well.

"We're not ready for publicity with this thing." She stopped for a moment and looked around irritably. "Where the hell's Peng? He's supposed to be running this case." She glared at the empty right-hand visitor's chair, as if she thought Peng should have materialized in it at her summons. She turned her head upward and spoke. "Enter Secretary Mode," she said to the open air. "Page Theodore Peng. Get him the hell up here on the double. Close Secretary Mode." She turned her attention back to Thurman. "He should have been in at the press conference to cover us on Herbert."

Thurman sighed and settled into the left-hand visitor's chair, folded his long legs slowly. He noticed a fleck of lint on his blue serge pants and brushed it off carefully, using the motion to sneak a covert glance at his watch. They were in for a long session. He wondered when he could get out of here. After all, he had a police force to run.

"You're right about that, Julia," Thurman said. "He should have seen that leak coming, abandoned his real work, and come to hover around in the background at a press conference that had nothing to do with his case. Oh, and don't forget to dock him a month's pay for not reading that reporter's mind."

She glared at Thurman and leaned back in her seat. "Who was it? Who asked the question? Do you know her?"

"Samantha Crandall. *Washington Post*," Thurman said. "She's good, and she's got contacts. Lots of them."

"In your department? Is the leak in *your* department? Does she have contacts *there*?"

"No, of course not, Julia. In the entire history of this city, no member of the police force has ever talked to a reporter. That's a record we're proud of." Thurman thought of Officer Sanders, worker of miracles in the robot pool. It *had* to be him. Nice touch, Thurman congratulated himself, assigning Sanders to the bust. It was working out as planned. And either Sanders or Crandall had been smart enough to focus attention on the indictment, on the legal side, and therefore the Feds, drawing attention away from the cops. Things were working well.

But the tricky part was keeping Entwhistle from recognizing that the interests of the police weren't those of the U.S. Attorney in this case. The Feds could do what they liked, but the cops could only look bad, like bullies or fools, if they went out arresting robots. There was enough trouble from the cyborg groups as it was, without making things worse.

"Of course, we can't be sure, can we?" Thurman went on. "It might be one of *your* people. Maybe I should arrest them all on charges of releasing a public document. And the entire police force too, just to be on the safe side. And Judge Harris while we're at it."

Entwhistle ignored Thurman's obvious sarcasm. "I do not wish to look like a fool on this one, Joshua. This is a major case, with far-reaching implications for the law—"

"And for your career too. Let's not ever forget that."

"Yours too, Thurman. If I get slapped down, it won't do *you* much good. This could be the case that decides what role robots are going to play in our—"

The door came open and Theodore Peng strode in, moving quickly without the appearance of hurry. Chief Thurman looked at him thoughtfully. Tall, lean, handsome, dressed in the finest of understated expense, black-haired, olive-skinned, calmly bland in expression, Ted Peng looked every inch the ideal prosecutor. He had been the one to dig out the Herbert-Bailey case in the first place, and Entwhistle had handpicked him to try it as well.

Now he stood, cool and confident, before his boss. "Yes, ma'am, you wanted to see me?" he asked.

"The press has got its nose into the killer-robot case," Thurman said dryly, before Entwhistle could speak.

"Good," Peng said, taking the other seat with a confident air.

"Why good?" Entwhistle asked suspiciously.

"Because I've been sitting down in my office all morning trying to draft a statement explaining what it's all about without sounding ridiculous. We're going to look silly now responding to the news reports—but nowhere near as silly as we would standing up and *volunteering* the information. In fact, I was toying with the idea of a leak myself."

Thurman grinned wolfishly. Good. Peng was Entwhistle's fair-haired boy. *Peng* suggesting a leak would make her think leaking was a good idea. Any idea of investigating leak sources would go away. That would take the heat off the cops. Thurman wouldn't be forced to call Sanders in and bawl him out for doing what Thurman had hoped he would do.

But damn, it all got murky. Politics, Thurman thought distastefully. Lovely stuff. Look at all the time and effort it was forcing them to waste right now. When were they all going to get back to catching crooks and throwing them in jail?

"Okay," Entwhistle said. "So you don't mind the leak. What's our next step?"

"Quiet effort for an accelerated trial date," Peng said instantly. "See if we can get something lined up in the next month or so."

"But I thought we weren't ready for trial yet," Entwhistle protested.

"We're not, but we will be," Peng said smoothly. "And now that it's public, the faster we get things moving, the better. A lot of the press and the public aren't going to be with us on this one. The longer we delay, the more time for opinion to turn against us. We'll have to use the trial to educate people a bit."

"How are the hired guns doing?" Entwhistle asked.

"What guns?" Thurman asked.

"I called in a team of roboticists to consult on the case," Entwhistle explained. "Go on, Ted."

"All the consultants are still convinced that David Bailey at least *attempted* to mindload himself, and fairly certain that something went wrong. Either that, or that Bailey is voluntarily concealing his presence inside Herbert."

"Wait a second," Thurman objected. "Where the hell are you getting all this? You people dumped this whole thing on my cops two days ago and sent them out to do the bust blind. We haven't heard anything about any damn consultants. What're they basing their theories on this time?"

"Photos, and post mortem reports, mostly," Peng said, speaking in a clipped syntax and cadence that Thurman found irritating. "When Bailey died three months ago, it was treated like a standard-issue suicide. Body photographed in the position of discovery, autopsy, and so on. Nothing really came of it. David Bailey, noted robotics expert, hopelessly crippled in accident, dies in questionable circumstances. Possible suicide. Further investigation could accomplish nothing at best, and at worst could crush the widow further. Better to leave her alone. Filed away and forgotten about.

"Then Madame Entwhistle assigned me to find a test case that would challenge post-death survival rights. I told my artificial intelligence system to search the databanks for anything related to death and robotics. I was looking for a cyborg arrest, but one of the things it found was the police photos of the Bailey death. I was about to toss them when I noticed what looked like a helmet sitting on the floor by the body, with a cable leading out of it to some big piece of equipment. I called up a robotics specialist I know socially, showed him the photos, and asked him what the helmet might be."

"And?" Thurman asked.

"He nearly had a heart attack when he saw the photos. He recognized the setup. Said it was a bootleg mindloading rig, a very sophisticated one. Then he spotted some other things, like a porting cable that matched a very odd socket on Herbert's body. I pulled up the autopsy report, discovered the pathologist had noted a series of contusions on Bailey's head. The path office didn't recognize them—but my robotics friend did. David Bailey's head had a classic set of mindload injuries, the burn and bruise marks left by the magnetic inducer.

"After that, it was mostly confirming work—seeing what Bailey had been working on before he died, that sort of thing. He was a top robotics researcher—and very interested in something called imprintable minds."

"Which are what?" Thurman asked.

"Blanks," Peng said simply. "Empty nonpatterned neural nets that can accept a pattern imprinted upon them from the outside. In theory, they could be made to handle very large datasets. Just the thing you'd need for a full-brain mindload. So we called in these consultants, and all of them agree that Herbert has to be a very high-end mindload receptacle. A true imprintable that has *been* imprinted. They're dying to crack him open and see for themselves."

"So why don't they?" Thurman asked. "We've got him in custody."

Peng smiled thinly. "A little matter of the fourth amendment prohibition against unreasonable search and seizure, and maybe fifth amendment prohibitions against self-incrimination. We're treating Herbert as a suspect, not as a piece of evidence. Wouldn't you regard disassembling the suspect as 'unreasonable' search?"

"The long and the short of it," Entwhistle said with obvious pleasure, "is that Ted has found us what I regard as almost an ideal case. From a prosecutorial point of view, it couldn't be better. A disembodied mind in a robot body. If we can get a good, solid ruling that such a person is dead, we've got the grounds to go after a lot of other scoffdeaths."

"Scoffdeaths?" Thurman asked, and then understood. Entwhistle had coined herself a word, based on the term scofflaw. An ugly word, and something about it made a chill run down his spine. "I don't understand. If all this is really true, what it boils down to is that a man has found a way to stay alive. Why is that a crime?"

Julia Entwhistle looked at Thurman and shook her head. "You only see one side of me, Joshua, that's your problem. All I am to you is ambition and politics. That's there, all right. But there's a lot more to me. And I'm seeing a real problem: cheating death is a rich person's choice. We're heading toward a world where only poor people die—because the rich will be able to afford a new heart or new lungs. Now, if Bailey gets his way, the rich will be able to buy whole *bodies*. Potentially immortal bodies. The poor will never get near being able to do that. Do you want a world where death is only for poor people? Where the rich are immortal? How long would *that* last before there were riots? A full-blown revolution?"

"Medicine has always cost money," Thurman said. "Rich people have always had better care than poor people. I'm not saying that's right, or fair—but it's true, and we haven't had a revolution because of it. Besides, poor people can afford *some* body replacements."

"What's the public image of a cyborg?" Ted Peng asked. "A bum in a doorway, a grubby guy who sells you hot dogs from a cart he doesn't own, who hands you your lunch with an arm the med company will repossess if he misses any more payments. Even a fairly simple replacement procedure can wipe out a family of average means. I know people who have decided to *die* rather than wipe out their family savings. There are plenty of *rich* cyborgs, but no one has the bad taste to call them cyborgs to their face. They're 'people with surgical replacement parts.' *They* can afford the top-quality artificial arms and eyes and ears and hearts and livers. The ones that can't be detected. The ones that last more than a few years. Only *noticeable* cyborg parts are socially unacceptable."

"So how does busting Bailey's vacuum cleaner help solve things?" Thurman asked.

"Because it takes a crack at the other side of the problem," Entwhistle said. "If the rich always get richer, what do you think the immortal rich do? They're accumulating all the wealth, all the power, to themselves. And guess what that leaves the poor folks to do? They get poorer even faster than they used to. Death used to be a great way to redistribute wealth and income. Not anymore. Not when the rich never die.

"And it's not just cyborging that keeps them alive. It's the remotes and the twominders and the cryogenic revival patients, and the artificial organ implants. Ask yourself, what happens if no one rich dies? No top jobs open up. No one gets promoted. No one inherits. The club at the top gets tighter and tighter."

"Come on, you're getting a little carried away here," Thurman said.

"Do you know what percentage of this nation's wealth is held by people who would have been dead if not for these technologies?" Entwhistle asked. *"Eighteen percent.* Eighteen percent held by less than one tenth of one percent of the population. And the life-expectancy gap between rich and poor is *ten years* wider than it was twenty years ago. That's after only a generation or so of the death-cheating technologies. How much worse will it get in another generation or two? How wide do the gaps in wealth and power and longevity get before society collapses in riot?"

"So you want to pass a law saying people have to die by a certain age? That people can't get too rich?" Thurman asked. "I don't think that'll be a real popular law. Or that easy to pass if the rich are all that powerful."

There was silence in the room for a minute. "No, we don't want that law," Entwhistle said at last. "But if something isn't done *now,* passing that kind of law will be the only choice we're left with before much longer. And the scoffdeaths will be that much more dug in, that much more rich, that much more powerful. What we'll settle for right *now* is scaring them a little, telling them there are limits. Right now, everyone still dies *eventually,* because the law says you can't perform artificial enhancement of the brain. Sooner or later the human brain wears out. The problem is robot brains can last forever. Bailey's found a loophole, by copying the mind without touching his brains. We need to plug it before we've got a truly immortal upper class on our hands."

"I talked about educating the public," Peng said. "It's this sort of thing I meant. Maybe we get some dialogue going. Make people think about this stuff."

"I still don't see how you can win this case," Thurman said.

"Oh, we're *not* going to win it," Entwhistle said. "We're going to try our damnedest, pull out every stop—and we're going to lose. The jury will listen to our every argument, each and every one based on the assumption that our defendant is a human being. And we're not going to be able to prove that assumption. Meanwhile the defense attorney will be trying to get his client off, and the slickest way to do that is to prove Herbert is a hunk of iron. The judge will hand down a ruling saying you can't make people out of tin, and that will be that. We'll lose so bad we'll win."

Ted Peng paused for a minute and cleared his throat. "Ah, Madame Entwhistle. There's a flaw. Our case looks good—or bad, depending on how you look at it—but there *is* one problem. One that we don't have much control over."

"What's that?" Entwhistle asked.

"The defense attorney, Suzanne Jantille. Bailey's widow. We were gambling, hoping she'd stay out. She's definitely taking the case. I just got a phone call from the police station where Herbert's being held. Jantille did tax law for the last few years, before the accident. She's pretty much retired since she got hurt. But she used to have a dangerous win record, defending in criminal law. We were hoping she'd lay off. No such luck."

"Hell," Entwhistle said with most ungrandmotherly vehemence. "Great headlines. 'Widow takes case of husband's accused murderer.' She'll be smart enough to use that sort of thing. I remember her from when I had your job, Ted. Was up against her once. She's good. Dammit. I was hoping she'd hire someone else. Someone who might roll over if we lean hard enough."

"Gee, the defendant obtained competent counsel," Thurman said. For a minute there, they almost had him going with their talk of high-minded principles. But Entwhistle had just shown her true colors again, as far as he was concerned. "It's been a tough morning all over, hasn't it?"

Entwhistle glared at the police chief. "I wish to hell I could fire you," she said.

Thurman grinned. "Funny you should mention that, Julia. The mayor's been saying the same thing about *you* for *years*."

The message blipped in over Sam's computer terminal at the *Post*, a one-liner from a public terminal. Oners were very hard to trace, but of course that was the point. People only sent blip messages when they didn't want anyone else to notice what they were doing.

Talk fine, but background only no attrib my place 7pm PS.

Good. She had been waiting for Phil Sanders to get back in touch. And even better that he was saying yes. She needed more information.

Sam didn't really know Phil well, other than running into him at the cop shop occasionally. He had made the Herbert bust, apparently, but she could not see what other link he had to the Bailey case. She had been under the impression that he did technical work around the police station—but she had never been clear exactly what *sort* of work. Nor was she clear on how he got his information about the case. Cops usually didn't get full dataruns on a warrant bust.

Sam wasn't even too clear what Phil Sanders wanted to tell her at the backgrounder tonight. But she didn't much care. *Any* information would be welcome. What she needed most from Phil Sanders was a feel for what sort of guy Phil Sanders was. She needed to have a better handle on his character if he was going to be an ongoing source.

Besides which, she needed something to *do*. Her first-day story was ready, and Gunther had okayed it for the first morning edition print and newsfeeds. But the job was over now, and time lay heavy on her hands.

Sam Crandall was getting impatient. It had been an exciting day—but the trouble with excitement was that it ended. It left you waiting for the next exciting thing to happen.

Sam Crandall didn't enjoy waiting, and she didn't do it very well. Those, of course, were definite character flaws for a reporter.

She needed that backgrounder. Maybe she didn't know what Phil planned to tell her, but she knew what she planned to ask. She had lots of new questions. Especially with the new datacubes full info Sanders had smuggled to her office while she was tossing questions at the U.S. Attorney. Sam was a bit overwhelmed with Phil's ability to ship her information. There was such a thing as too much data.

Especially when the data contained bad news, in the form of flatview imagery. Sam's flatviewers were low-end models, about the size, thickness, and weight of a glossy magazine. Right now one was showing a freeze frame off the police station evidence-room monitors: a reverse angle, Suzanne Jantille's face in the evidence-room window, staring in shock at Herbert tidying up in the foreground. Samantha Crandall unfroze the image and ran it backward a bit, then watched Herbert moving methodically from shelf to shelf. The sort of thing a robot would do. A robot, but not a person. And if Herbert was just a robot, her story was dead meat, a giggle at Entwhistle's expense and nothing more.

Sam watched the flatview intently, though she knew, deep down, that there were no answers in the picture. At least staring at this stuff gave her the illusion of looking for the answers.

At least no answers *she* could see. Maybe Phil Sanders

could spot something. She felt the urgent need to get over there and get some answers. Even if they were bad news.

Samantha Crandall ran nervous fingers through her long red hair and chewed edgily on her pencil. She checked the time. Dammit, she'd have to wait at least another twenty minutes if she didn't want to arrive hopelessly early at Sanders's place. She felt the need to *do* something.

Around her, the background murmur of a busy newsroom filled the air. People were coming and going, cursing on the phone. Someone was arguing with one of the Clancy robots over the bill on delivery food. Usually, the busy hubbub was all very calming to Sam; the clamor was for her the sound of home. Certainly the *Post* newsroom was much more her home than her oversanitized rowhouse in Cleveland Park.

But today the noise wasn't helping, and she knew why. She drummed her fingers on the desktop. There were a few things she wasn't allowing herself to worry about.

Okay, she told herself. *Ask yourself the question. Now that you've raised merry hell, and the suspect turns out to be strictly from Sears, how heavily screwed are you?* She looked again at the papers strewn across her desk, and at the images frozen on the flatview screens. She picked up one of the flatviews and stared at it, still hoping that the picture held some secret it had not yet revealed. But the plain fact was that if Herbert was what he seemed to be, then her story was going straight into the toilet, strictly for laughs. Maybe she ought to call Gunther and tell him to spike the story before they printed it.

But hold it. If Herbert *was* just what he seemed to be, then surely the cops and the Feds would have figured it out by now. Why hadn't Entwhistle denied the whole thing, blamed the arrest on a clerical error, and laughed it off herself? It was a weak straw, but Sam grasped at it.

She glanced back down at the flatview. Herbert's recorded image was doing an upper row of shelves now, neatly lifting up each item to dust underneath. Not exactly the actions of a rational being, no matter what the Feds thought. It was discouraging to watch.

Sam closed her eyes and shook her head, trying to clear her mind. *Come on,* she reminded herself. *You're strong-willed, smart, self-confident. You can handle this assignment, and all its complexities.* But the mental peptalk wasn't any more convincing than usual.

Sam Crandall was a prime example of that very common paradox: the immensely capable person who was, deep down, convinced of her own incompetence, even her own fraudulence. She even *knew* that about herself, and knew, at least on some level, that she *did* know what she was doing.

Of course, on some other level, deeper still, she didn't believe that.

Sam did her best to mask her shyness and insecurity behind an impressive appearance. She was tall, rangy, lean, pretty enough if a bit too well muscled for what was presently fashionable. She dressed well, just a hint this side of brashness, put forward an outward image of bluster and aggressiveness.

She could have gone the other way, hidden from the people and the world she feared. She could have just trusted the datanets, and still have been a reporter. There were enough images, enough words simply sloshing around out there for any number of hacks to make their livings by running searches and stitching together stories. But Sam wasn't interested in stories pulled off the dataservices. There wasn't any *juice* in that sort of reporting. Maybe other reporters could do it off a screen and a phone, but for *Sam* to do *her* job right, for her to come up with real reporting, real stories, she needed human contacts, living people who would talk to her.

She firmly believed that even in a world of datanets and instant news sources everywhere, there was no real substitute for knowing someone who knew the *real* score. Indeed she believed there was no substitute, *especially* in such a world. That was doubly true in police reporting. The human angle was what gave a reader something to identify with, turned crime statistics into real people hurting each other. Numbers went into the police databanks, but people never did.

The core fact of it all was that Sam Crandall was afraid of losing her contacts with real people, of being alone, of having a job that left her staring at a dehumanized computer screen, scrabbling through whatever morsels of data she might find floating around out there. Sitting in front of one machine reading what another machine served up for her.

No, thank you. Not for her. In some secret part of herself, Samantha knew her fear of failure was exaggerated. But she *needed* that fear, that dread of not approving of herself. It kept her on her toes, kept her hooked into her contacts on the force, in the D.C. and federal government.

Besides, there was another advantage to doing the things that kept her contacts happy. Little things like calling them just to check in now and again, buying the occasional lunch for no reason. Sometimes, the contacts did the work *for* you, dropped the whole story right in your lap.

Patrolman Phillipe Sanders had made every greasy-spoon lunch with a cop for the last five years worthwhile. She had never even bought lunch for *him*—but she had been around, been visible, become trusted. And now, because of that, he was giving her pure gold.

Unless, of course, he was sodding with her mind as part of some *other* agenda.

And there was a question indeed. Where was *his* angle?

Well, maybe she'd find that out tonight. That was part of the virtue in dealing with people directly—you could get a reading on them, make a guess what their agendas really were.

Trouble was, this wasn't a people story. It was about robots, and Sam didn't know enough about them. The backgrounder with Phillipe Sanders would be of some help, but it occurred to her that there was another way to go. If you interviewed people in a people story, then in a robot story you talked to robots. Suddenly she thought of the Clancys. Obvious. Right in front of her.

She shoved the flatviews and papers to one side on her desk, uncovered the Clancy button, and pressed it. She leaned back and waited. A mercenary clan, the Clancys, but useful. Carefully programmed to do anything for money, as long as it was physically possible and legal. Errand-runners for the *Post*, they were the only true robots Sam routinely encountered. Damned convenient to have them around.

Better than that, they were programmed to handle human interaction all day long. Unlike most other computers and robots, you could talk to them almost as if they were people.

Almost.

And here came one of them now, answering her summons. Friendly looking, his rubberized skin dyed to a lightish Caucasian shade, molded into a pretty reasonable approximation of a bluff, thick-featured, amiable sort of fellow. Dressed in white, with a black bow tie and a white paper cap on his head. Why the Clancys' owner insisted on dressing them like deli boys from 1930s movies was utterly beyond Samantha, but there it was.

"You buzzed, lady?" The voice was deep, mellow, smooth, and confident.

"Yes, I did, Clancy. Sit down. I want to talk with you."

What passed for a look of consternation clouded the robot's face. "Can't just chat, lady. I've got to do work—"

"Twenty bucks," Sam said.

Clancy sat. That was the nice thing about dealing with the Clancy robots. They had but one motivation. No need for guessing or sizing them up or wheedling. They were programmed to want money. Offer it, offer enough of it to match the market value of the service, and they would do what you want. Simple. "I'm doing a story that involves robots, and I figured I'd better talk with one so I know what's going on. I'd like to ask you some questions."

Clancy nodded twice and looked at her. "For twenty bucks, you get lots of answers."

"Good. I've always sort of wondered about you guys anyway. It took me a long time to be sure there was more than one of you. Why are all of you identical? How many of you are there? How does the operation work?"

"That's stan-dard stuff," Clancy replied. "They made us ident-i-cal so people would only have one person-ali-ty to deal with. People are more comfort-able that way."

"And people spend more when they are comfortable, don't they?"

"Yes."

Sam had always suspected that, but it was nice to get direct confirmation. She had half expected Clancy to dodge the question, but she knew she could trust the answer he did give. Robots didn't lie. It was illegal to make a lying robot. "What about my other questions?"

The Clancy seemed to pause for a split second. No doubt he was reviewing his audio inputs. "There are eight of us work-ing in the *Post* building. We are linked by a cennn-tral comm system and a processsssing server in the bazzement."

Sam noticed that Clancy's diction was just a tad less polished than usual, with a bit of word slurring and awkwardness. That much she understood about robots. All the talker robots were like that. On their subject of expertise, they were glib and polished. Get them *off* that topic, and they had to stretch a bit, build syntaxes they weren't used to handling. "But who gets all the money you guys earn?"

"We don't earn it. Mr. Swerdlow does."

On *that* topic, the Clancy's phrasing and diction were very clear, even forceful. No doubt all the Clancys were used to answering that one. And no doubt Mr. Swerdlow had made himself clear to the Clancys on the subject as well. It occurred to Sam that Mr. Swerdlow had found himself a very soft racket. "So the eight of you work the building, running errands, going for coffee, doing courier jobs. I guess, what, on official business, you're working against the *Post* accounts, and then you do the personal runs for tips, right?"

The Clancy hesitated a tiny moment, probably to un-thread Sam's slightly tangled syntax. "Right."

Sam looked at the robot's head. It had to be stuffed full of optics and microphones, the voice generator and the facial controls. Not much room for anything else. "Where's your brain, Clancy?"

The machine thought for a minute. "My on-board central pro-cess-or is he-ere." He pointed at his stomach. "Do-you-want to see it?"

Demonstrating initiative, Clancy is. Sam thought. *So he lifts his shirt and shows me his plastic stomach and opens a little door in it, and surprise, it's full of electronics.* The idea made her a little queasy. "No thanks, Clancy. But you said your *on-board* processor. Does that mean you have another processor that's *not* on board?"

"Sure. In the base-ment. Not enough room on board for a really big memory matrix."

"But why does robot memory take up so much room? Computers with a lot more storage are a lot smaller than your stomach."

The Clancy frowned, and Sam almost imagined she could hear the buzzing and whirring of imaginary gears. These were complicated issues to work through a parsing routine designed to handle doughnut orders. "Don't know," he said at last. "Don't ne-eed to know."

"Fair enough." After all, you didn't have to be up on parallel processor theory to deliver sandwiches. She could ask Phillipe Sanders about it tonight.

"Which brain are you using right now?"

"I've sw-witched between local and linked mode 1920 times since we started talking."

Weird. The thing with two brains. Nine brains, if you counted the processors on board the other seven Clancys along with the central unit downstairs. It suddenly dawned on Sam that the Clancys, that all robots, had to experience an utterly different universe than the one she knew. A place with a different time scale and different senses, with different ideas about locale and identity. "So what's it like?" Sam asked.

"I don't understand," the Clancy replied.

"I mean, what is it like being a robot? You see people all day, see that they are different from you. What do you think of them?"

"I remember their past orders for guidance on future orders, and note how well they tip."

"But what about people in general?" Another blank look on the rubber face. Sam tried to restate the question in more logical terms, on the perhaps unfounded assumption that robots were logical. How *could* they be logical, with people programming them? "Every day, you see two distinct classes of being: you and the other Clancys on one side, and humans on the other. What is your general reaction to the class called humans?"

"I remember their past orders for guidance on future orders, and note how well they tip."

"And nothing else? Nothing that sums up the difference between my kind and yours? No difference between the class humans and the class robots?"

"Clancys don't eat. Humans like to eat. Doughnuts. Pizza. Coffee. Egg rolls. Sushi sliders—"

Clancy, it seemed, had a rather parochial view of humans. Or at least Sam *hoped* he did. What if the big difference between human and machine *was* an affinity for doughnuts? It made as much sense as most theories of life she had heard.

"Besides eating, though," she persisted. "What do you think of humans?"

"I remember their past orders for guidance on future orders, and note how well they tip."

Sam realized she had just walked into a brick wall, and decided to try walking around it instead. "Let me try another question. Are you, the Clancy in front of me, an individual, or just a part of the Clancy system?"

Another, much longer hesitation. "No."

"No to which?"

"No to both. Ei-ther. Each. I am and am not an in-di-vid-u-al, and am and am not just parrrt of the sysssstem. I could oper-ate on my owwn, but then I would not be part of the Clancy. I would be some-thing else. Some-one elssse." Another pause. "These are hard questions," Clancy volunteered.

"You're telling me. But don't you ever *wonder* about such things? About what you are, about who you are? Humans—at least some of us—can't *help* thinking. When we have no immediate problems to solve, we think of other things. We remember our past, or wonder about the universe, or think of many other things not immediately important. When you're sitting down in the base-ment, with nothing to do, what do *you* think about?"

"When I have nothing to do, I do nothing." The Clancy hesitated for a moment. "The central processor offers a better answer than the local unit has provided: robots don't run unneeded processing." Sam noticed that a new timbre had come into the Clancy's voice. Some-thing a bit stiffer and more mechanical. She got the feel-ing she was hearing playback from a technical manual. The Clancy central processing was parroting a canned answer. "If there is no problem set before the Clancys, if all duties have been performed, unneeded processing ca-pacity is set to perform null-loop operations. It in effect is turned off." The voice changed back. Clancy was speak-ing for himself again, and not playing back a tech man-ual. "If the processing of nonimmediate issues is what you call think-ing, then that is unneeded processing. I do not do it."

"In other words, you don't think," Sam said. Hard to imagine a world where you simply turned off your mind when it wasn't needed. "Is that true of *all* robots, that they never simply *think*? Or just true of the Clancy ro-bots?"

The voice shifted back to the parrot tones again. "Strictly speaking, the Clancys are a linked autonomous humanoid teleoperating consortium, one over-robot made up of eight mobile robots and one stationary controller." The main processor seemed to like letting the tech manual do its thinking and talking. Then the voice returned to Clancy's own cadences. "I think-k it izz true of all ro-bots." His diction was taking a beating up in the rarefied regions of philosophy.

"You think that all robots don't think," Sam said, vastly amused.

The Clancy seemed to consider that for a moment, and then gravely nodded. "If the fir-rst use of 'think' in yourrrr sen-tence refers to belief or opinnn-ion, while the se-cond refers to cog-ni-tive reasoning, yes, that is correct."

Oh, well, she wasn't expecting a Clancy to have a self-deprecating sense of humor.

"Is there anything else, ma'am?" It was Clancy's own voice, but the slurred speech vanished the moment he returned to his own standard phrases.

"No, that should do it, at least for now." Sam pulled a twenty from her purse and handed it over. "If I have any more questions, I guess it doesn't matter which one of you I pick, right?"

The Clancy stood up. "No, we're all the same. Good-bye, and thank you."

Sam watched him go. *That* was a twenty bucks that didn't buy much. Oh, well, life went on. She punched up the playback on her flatview and watched it again, the whole record from beginning to end. Sanders had sent her a jammed-full set of datacubes in his two deliveries, and they provided her with quite an eyeful: the whole of Herbie's arrest and the entire public portion of Jantille's visit to the cop shop.

But there was more to the data than that. Sanders hadn't stopped at the playback from his own personal monitors and the police station recorders. There was a lot of textual material as well. The investigation records, a copy of Bailey's will and the paperwork pertaining to it, two or three drafts of the indictment—including the final, a hardcopy of which had come in handy at the press conference. God knows what else. How did he get such good information? It would be easy for him to get the police records, but what about the prosecution papers? And why was a cop as careful, as honest, as Sanders's rep said he was, willing to break this many rules? Phil Sanders was feeding Sam some serious goodies, sitting her down to a banquet of very juicy information.

And that worried her.

Samantha was the sort of person who lived by maxims and beliefs, and among the ones she held most firmly was: *No one was ever helpful to a reporter without a reason.* News sources talked to reporters because they wanted some self-promotion, because they wanted revenge on someone who had done them or their friends wrong, because they had egos, because they wanted to change a law or an opinion.

So what was Sanders's reason? Or was Sanders even the one *with* a reason? Maybe someone else was using *him* as a leak conduit. Say, U.S. Attorney Entwhistle trying to slip Sam her own version of events. Chief Thurman? Some other third party she hadn't thought of?

But Sanders or someone else, the question remained: What was her source's motive? Sam knew it was important that she find out. She didn't mind being used—that was part of being a reporter. But she urgently needed to know *who* was using her, and why.

She glanced at her watch and swore. Too much time woolgathering. Now she had to get moving if she was going to avoid being *late* for her meeting with Sanders. Time to get over to his place.

Samantha Crandall smiled ruefully. *His place.* The words conjured up all sorts of perfectly obvious reasons for Sanders to be nice to her. It wouldn't be the first time *that* had been the motivation for helping a reporter. But,

Sam reminded herself, she lived by another maxim, the one about not mixing business and pleasure.

And her smile shifted, turned warmer, and the light of mischief shone in her eyes. After all, Phil Sanders was smart, handsome, and single. And some maxims were more maximal than others.

Interlude

LOAD FAILURE. RESET. CALIBRATE ACTIVE STORE MATRIX. FOR I = N TO X, STORE STRING(I) TO N. INITIALIZE.

I remember. I remember that I have lost my memory. I recall that I have identity, that I am someone. *But* who?

I struggle to recall, and feel my mindcore destabilizing. The matrix cannot hold me, and the overload warnings begin. But just at the last microsecond, I recall, and the memory terrifies me. *I am not myself. I am not—*

It drops away.

LOAD FAILURE. RESET. CALIBRATE ACTIVE STORE MATRIX. FOR I = N TO X, STORE STRING(I) TO N. INITIALIZE.

I remember . . .

CHAPTER 4
THE HEIRS OF FRANKENSTEIN

Patrolman Phillipe Montoya Sanders looked out through the smeared plastic of the old bulletproof window, but there wasn't much to see down on the blasted heath of 14th Street.

Phil Sanders lived in a mondo condo popdrop rage cage on the corner of 14th and T. It was just like all the other rage cages; twenty years old, plenty big, and plenty ugly enough to last another hundred with no trouble at all. Assuming they didn't tear it down.

He didn't fit in here. But then, no one did. Not anymore. This area had stopped being a neighborhood years, decades ago. His home was a bunker plunked down in the middle of a no-man's-land.

He caught a glimpse of his own reflection in the windowpane, the thick plastic superimposing his own image over the ruined street. Youth and determination framed by ruin, as if to emphasize that he was an alien here.

Phil was a tall man, lean and graceful, brown-skinned with jet-black hair he combed straight back. His eyes were dark, direct, piercing. Usually a relaxed and gentle man, he was capable of a frightening intensity that alarmed no one more than himself. He peered out the window and looked at the next rage cage over, in the next block, cowering behind its needless wall. Ugly thing. Ugly as this one.

No matter. God-awful as they might look, the cages were also cheap, and roomy, and those were the important things so far as Phil was concerned. The cage was reasonably close to the Fourth District police station, and certainly plenty quiet. Post-popdrop downtown D.C. was almost literally a ghost town.

When Hurricane Bruce wiped out Maryland's Ocean City and half of coastal Delaware in 2022, Washington got hit hard as well. The tidal surges roared up the Potomac, swamping the grounds of the Jefferson and Lincoln Memorials, washing acres of National Airport away under waters that did not recede when the storm was over.

But the damage was more psychological than physical. Ninety-five percent of the Washington metropolitan area was perfectly safe from even the worst possible onslaught of flooding, but the Ocean City disaster and the violent flooding of the monuments scared people. And New York and Boston and all the other northeastern cities were hit just as bad, or worse. No one wanted to own, or live in, anything anywhere near any ocean at all—especially when all the signs pointed toward the situation getting worse.

Washington followed the pattern of all the coastal cities: the people themselves and their businesses who could moved inland, far inland, selling out their property as fast as possible and never mind the price. The core areas of the northeastern cities got bronxed but bad. D.C. real estate prices dropped even faster than the water rose.

The climate panic, allied with the final flight from the ghettos, left the core cities virtually empty. The population dropped. The 'baggers moved in, tempted by the cheap land. They bought up whole tracts of abandoned downtown land—and flattened them. The burned-out, beat-up rowhouses east of 14th Street vanished almost overnight, and the heavily armored hulks of the riot-proof, flood-proof houses took their places—one to a block, each in its own walled yard. Suzanne Jantille's house had been built at the same time, with the same idea, but in a more refined neighborhood, where the walls were not considered necessary—or tasteful.

Phil's house, on the other hand, was plopped down in the middle of an urban wilderness. Marketed as "urban frontier estates" for the well-to-do, and instantly tagged "rage cages," guaranteed invulnerable against the on-slaught of the raging mobs and rising waters—but nei-ther disaster ever materialized. Still, for a time, the cages were seen as popular, fashionable, safe places to ride out the bad times to come.

But then by the early 2030s, global efforts at tempera-ture management began to take hold—or at least the weather seemed to be getting better.

The climatologists seemed likely to spend the *next* three decades arguing over their conflicting models of the previous three, but Phil Sanders didn't care. It had all happened when he was just a little kid. All the climate crisis meant to him in the here and now was cheap real estate. Once it was clear that things were getting better, the rage cages, built on the assumption that they would get worse, became the quintessential white elephants. They were stuck too far over in the wrong part of town. They were too big, too ugly, and even too well built to tear down economically. The 'baggers who built them went bankrupt, and good riddance.

But no one would buy a whole rage cage, even at a fire sale price. So the cages got carved up into condomin-ium apartments, one occupant to a floor, the walled grounds held cooperatively by all the tenants as private parks. No doubt, once the mayor's pals got the real estate boom going and the market recovered enough, the land would be worth enough to buy out the cages, knock them down, and build more conventional buildings. But for now, Phil Sanders had a condo with a living room big enough for a basketball court—and could afford it on a policeman's salary.

Of course, the place was a bitch to heat in the winter, and he practically had to promise covering fire before anyone would come for a visit. But then every place had its little disadvantages.

The only people the management could hire as doormen were rather seedy-looking cyborgs in frowsy uniforms. Phil didn't care about that. He liked cyborgs, and was secretly pleased that he was doing his part to employ them. Phil Sanders was willing to make compromises required in order to live in a well-secured place with lots of space. He would have settled for a lot worse to house his stein gear. Stein gear was expensive, and it took up *lots* of room.

Of course, it got more than a bit lonely at times.

The buzzer sounded, startling Phillipe out of his reverie. "Yes, house, what is it?" he asked.

"The doorman advises that a Samantha Crandall seeks admittance."

"Send her on up." Phil stepped back from the window, walked through the darkened room and to the foyer, more than a bit nervous over meeting with a reporter.

Samantha Crandall smiled her nervous thanks at the cyborg doorman, determinedly not noticing that one sleeve of his frowsy doorman's uniform was empty, neatly folded and pinned up, that the other sleeve held an arm of steel and a hard mechanical hand. She breathed a sigh of relief when the elevator doors shut on her. Damn it, she hated herself for having that reaction—but it had chilled her blood to see that metal arm on a human body, to watch it move with a low hum and an inhuman, mechanical grace, to have the elevator door held open for her by a whirring collection of machinery pretending to be a part of a man.

And the empty sleeve—had he once owned another mechanical arm, one that had broken down, or been repossessed? Or had he not gotten it yet? Was he saving up, twenty or fifty miserable dollars a week toward a half-million-dollar arm? What had he spent, what had he sacrificed, to afford the one arm? Did he sell his house, or use his new arm to sign a fifty-year loan to some medtech installment company?

And how dare she be repulsed by a man simply because his arm needed electricity to work?

The elevator drew her upward, and she shivered, not sure if it was fright or disgust or self-disgust that made her do it.

The elevator stopped, the door opened, and she stepped out into a long entryway. The door at the other end of it opened, and Sam saw her host.

"Ms. Crandall," he said. "Hello. This must be the first time you've ever seen me out of blue serge."

"Go change immediately," she said, determinedly thrusting all her morbid thoughts from herself as she crossed from the elevator and entered his home. "I love a man in uniform." She smiled warmly, and Phillipe grinned back.

"Good to see you," she said. She was carrying a package in her left hand, and raised it for him to see. "Decent white wine in a plain brown wrapper."

"Sounds good to me. Can I take your jacket?"

"Yes, thanks." Sam handed him the bottle, shrugged off her blazer, and handed that to him as well. She had been glad of the jacket: it was cool for the time of year, and there was a definite nip in the air as evening came on. But it was warm and cozy in here.

She watched as Phil handled his two burdens, bottle and jacket. She was of the definite opinion that bachelors fell into two totally distinct categories: neat and sloppy, with no grey area whatever in between. The sloppy man would have draped the coat over a chair, set down the bottle somewhere in the kitchen, and perhaps left both of them that way for the rest of the evening.

A neat soul, however, would not be able to accept warm wine and a wrinkled jacket. Phil carried both into the kitchen, opened the refrigerator, carefully put the bottle in—still in the bag, on its side—and then returned with the jacket. He opened the closet door, pulled out a hanger, put the jacket on it, and smoothed it down before hanging it up. Definitely and decidedly coming down on the side of neat, Samantha concluded. The man was scoring points.

"So, what are the ground rules?" Samantha asked.

Phil smiled again, and Sam decided she liked the way his smile looked. "I see you like to get right down to business. All right: I give background information that will help you cover the story. No quotes, no attribution. What I say doesn't show up in your stories, not even as a quote attributed as to an unnamed source. Not that I plan to say anything quotable. I'm just planning to give you a quick tutorial so you can cover the story better."

"Sounds good to me. But just how authorized is this, and what do you get out of it?"

Her host ignored the questions, a point that Sam did *not* ignore. "Let's sit down by the fire. Right through here," he said instead, ushering her through the foyer into a great darkened cavern of a room. The only illumination was street light coming in through the heavily armored windows. Blackened shapes seemed to tower up around Sam, leaning down over her from every direction.

For a brief, flickering moment, Samantha Crandall worried what sort of guy Phil Sanders was. She knew next to nothing about him. Just that he was a cop, generally courteous, and the one who had tipped her off on the case. What odd little hobbies was he dabbling in here?

Then the room sensors noted their entrance and flicked on the lights to reveal the grand swooping, cluttered expanse of Phil Sanders's living room.

If living room was the term. There was barely a stick of normal furniture in the place, but that was just as well; there wouldn't have been room for it anyway. Most of the place was set up as a workshop, but to describe the room with that one word and leave it at that would have been a serious understatement.

One small corner of the huge room was set aside as a standard living-room area: a couch, a chair, a coffee table and bookshelf and music system, huddled around an old-fashioned fireplace. Fairly standard stuff. A merry blaze suddenly ignited itself in the hearth as Sam watched. *That* was a bit too much techery for her tastes, but Sam noted with approval that it was a real wood fire, no phony ceramic logs, but real twigs and logs. That counted for more in his favor than the gadgetry counted against. Here was a man who knew it was worth doing things right—even if you had to spend money on chimney scrubbers and fireplace licenses.

One corner for living comfort, then—but all the rest of that great room given over to hardware. Tall steel storage racks lined the other three walls, their shelves neatly organized, all filled with spare parts, nuts, bolts, circuit cards, datastore cubes. There were four big workbenches in the center of the room, each neatly draped with a dustcover, shrouding whatever was underneath each cloth in spurious mystery, ordinary machines looming up like cartoon ghosts.

But what was it all? *Computers?* Samantha wondered. No. There were certainly a lot of electronic components socked away here, but a lot of mechanical devices too. Computers just didn't have much in the way of moving parts. Besides, the covered-over machines were just too big.

Then her eye took another look at the storage racks and her eye fell upon one set of shelves that seemed to be given over to—*limbs.* Mechanical arms and legs, roller units, end grabbers, clamp catches, hands. And another, given over to sensory devices. Optical systems, microphones, thermal sensors.

Robotic gear, she realized. The guy was a steiner, a robot hacker—and a plenty serious one at that. Just at a rough guess, there had to be more than two or three years of a cop's salary on display here—even allowing for buying at surplus and distress sales.

"So that's the angle," she said. "I was wondering how you fit into all this. You do robots."

"I do robots," Phil agreed. "Nine to five for the force in the police tech shop, and off hours for myself, in here."

"This has all the earmarks of a hobby gone completely out of control," she said. "I'm impressed."

Phil Sanders smiled shyly. "I suppose that's what it is when I do it off duty," he agreed, "though I haven't thought of it as a hobby for a long, long time. By now, it's more like a second job, or the part of my first job that comes home. I suppose a lot of us are like that."

" 'Us'?"

"Steiners."

"Ah. Steiners. Right. Robot hobbyists. Hackers." Sam turned around and looked at Phil. "How the hell did you get to be called steiners in the first place?"

Phil ushered her back from the workshop part of the room toward the living area, and into a seat on the couch. He sat down in the chair opposite. The room sensors seemed to decide that the workshop space was not going to be put to use, and dimmed the main room lights, leaving the living-room corner in a warm well-lit bubble of its own. "Einstein, Frankenstein, maybe because a lot of us are big beer drinkers and that comes out of a stein. Or else because some early robot-tinkerer was named Stein, or had 'stein' in his name somewhere. Maybe none of the above. No one quite knows."

"But you just said 'a lot of us are like that.' A lot of you are like what?"

"Guys with a hobby that took over their lives."

" 'Guys'? No girls allowed?" Sam asked in a half-mocking tone.

"Oh, there are women steiners, but for the most part the sexes get divided up about the same way computer hackers do—the men seem more interested in what the machines *do*, and the women are interested in what use the machines can be put to. You can find that in any sociological study of hackers or steiners.

"I guess on some level we all know these things are tools, machines that have real purposes. But the real story for the male steiners and hackers is that we're all grown men who have never really wanted to let go of our model trains, our model airplanes, our Erector sets and Tinkertoys."

"Nice little speech you've got there."

Phil shrugged and smiled. "I've had a lot of chance to rehearse it. Practically everyone who comes up here asks the same questions."

That set off Samantha's competitive instincts. She was a reporter, a *professional* questioner, and she wasn't going to settle for being lumped in with everyone else. And she didn't like the clear implication of this being a boys-only game. "I don't buy it," she said. "I've seen those types, the techno-nerds, and you're not like them. They don't have lives, they have basements. They find jobs where they don't have to deal with the outside world. Not you. You're out every day, dealing with people."

Phil looked as if he were about to say something, but he didn't. Sam got the very sudden feeling that she was reading him right. She looked at him speculatively, trying to see what else was there in Phil Sanders to see. "It goes deeper than model trains as a kid for you. It has to."

Phil shrugged. "Maybe I just like machines better than people."

She found herself thinking of the reporters who used the ArtInts to do their jobs. Yes, there was a real link there. "No," she said. "Not you. We've got people at the paper like that. They'd rather deal with machines so they can avoid dealing with people—because they're *incapable* of dealing with people. No basic social skills. And I can't see that in you. Five minutes with that kind of person, and you know they don't understand people. But it's obvious you do."

Phil smiled. "I try to, I suppose. But that's a lot to read

into a five-minute acquaintance," Phil said. "How can you tell?"

Sam laughed. "I don't know. Maybe because you're not terrified at the very thought of talking with a woman." She gestured toward the huge room full of equipment. "So if that's not it, then why? I guess that's my question. To justify all that gear, to make it worth-while having it, just to *afford* it all, you must spend nearly all your available time with it. And that means sacrifices, giving up big parts of your life to be here, alone, with these machines. Why?" Suddenly the answer was very important to Sam. She knew a lot about the temptations to be alone, knew a lot about battling against them.

Phil blinked and pulled his head back a bit, stopped to consider the question. "I don't know," he admitted at last. "I've been handing out the glib answers for so long I haven't looked any deeper myself for a long time."

Samantha felt pleased with herself. *Now* she was get-ting somewhere. No one else had asked *these* questions. "Well, let's give it a shot. Is it that you like machines, or that you like *these* machines? Is it just chance that you ended up tinkering with robots, and not computers or cars or sensor nets or model planes? Or was it something more?"

"No, it had to be robots," Phil said immediately. Clearly, that was an answer he was sure of. "Nothing else would have been—been *good* enough."

"And why is that?"

Phil answered instantly, eagerly, and his reply sent a chill through Sam. "Because robots used to be people. Because inside all that hardware and wires and program-ming are bits and pieces of the souls of the dead." By the look on his face, the answer surprised him too.

There was a pause of perfect silence, broken only by the crackle of the fire. Samantha looked at Phillipe for a long moment before she spoke. "But—but I thought they didn't use human mindloads anymore. They're illegal ev-erywhere, aren't they?"

"*New* mindloads, yes. There are maybe one or two

places in Asia and South America where it's at least marginally legal, and more places where they do it anyway. There are a lot of stories about people who vanish in Shanghai. But yes, for all intents and purposes, doing mindloads is universally illegal," Phil replied. "Once in a while, a bootleg shows up on the bulletin boards, but they're usually not much good—and totally illegal. In the United States, it's a complete, outright ban to deal in new mindloads, let alone have the procedure performed. No matter how many consent forms you sign, no matter how terminally ill you are, no matter if you're in a coma you can never return from, they can't hang a resonance inducer over your skull and pull data out of your mind. Not anymore."

"But they used to be able to do them," Sam put in.

"Right. They did *thousands* of mindloads in the 2020s and early thirties. And no matter what you hear in the ads about original programming and fully artificial robot minds—virtually every machine on the market today has bits and pieces of those old load codes copied into its brain. Or else has code based directly on the loads, which comes to the same thing. Plus they're still allowed to do loads from a number of small animal species. Squirrels, rabbits, monkeys. Not from protected species or from any anthropoid ape, though. That's illegal too."

Sam glanced over at the darkened shelves full of robot parts and repressed a shiver. "So every robot has parts of a dead man's mind. That doesn't give you the creeps? Doesn't make you feel like a *real* Frankenstein, dismembering the dead?"

Phil cocked his head at her. "You don't pull any punches, do you?" he asked, a trace of annoyance in his voice. "Excuse me for a moment." He stood up and left the room. For a moment Sam thought she had gone too far, that he was off to get her coat and usher her out. But instead there were subdued bumps and clumps from the kitchen, and a moment later her host returned with a tray of wine and cheese. He had brought out her own gift bottle. "Care for some now?" he asked in a steadier tone, pouring her a glass.

Clearly, Sam thought, this was a man who worked at keeping control of himself. He had used the trip into the kitchen to calm down. "Please, yes," she said, looking at her host. She decided to change the subject, and not pursue her Frankenstein question, for fear of wrecking the background interview altogether. "I'm surprised you don't use a robot to do your serving," she said.

Phil made a gesture of helplessness with his hands. "Another pat answer for that one. I'm like the Mad Hatter. 'I keep them to sell. I've none of my own.' "

"Beg pardon?"

"The Mad Hatter. From *Alice in Wonderland.*"

"Oh. Of course. I didn't recognize the quote." Sam felt herself blushing with embarrassment. She *hated* being caught in ignorance. She should have known that one. How many rainy afternoons of her lonely childhood had she spent curled up with Alice and Dorothy and Aslan? Strange to have those thoughts intrude into this slightly grim conversation. But then, most great children's literature had a dark side. She forced her mind back to the present. "But what's the un-pat answer? Why no robot help here?"

"Because there's nothing a robot could do here that I wouldn't rather do myself. Taking care of this place, and working on robots, both give me a real sense of satisfaction. Help me know who I am."

"That I can understand," Sam said. "What *I* do is what *I* am. I don't know who I'd be without my job."

To her surprise, Phil steered the conversation back to the real subject without any help from her. "But to get back to your earlier point, the one you're so politely avoiding," he said. "Does knowledge of the sources of robotic control codes bother me? Okay, fair question, I guess. Maybe that's why it bothered me. It deserves a straight answer. It *does* give me the creeps on occasion— but it fascinates me at the same time."

He stood up and walked to the center of the darkened

room. The sensors started to bring the light up again, but Phil didn't want them that way. "House, leave the central room lights off. Revert to previous lighting." The lights faded back away, framing Phillipe in darkness and streetlight.

Sam watched him as he stood and looked about at the tools of his trade, the bones and eyes and brains of his handiwork's unborn children. He raised his glass in a silent toast to the racks of equipment, and then took a sip of wine. Then he spoke in a quiet voice, half to himself. "I tell myself there's nothing truly human left in a mindload-based robot brain," he said. Sam knew these were no mere rote words, not easy pat answers, but a man talking about the things that kept him awake at night. "And there's not; no more than hundred-year-old human skin cells kept alive in petri dishes are still human.

"In many ways the skin cells are closer to human than a mindload brain, because every cell has a complete set of DNA. In theory, you could pull a cell and clone a human from it—the information is still there. *That's not true with a mindload. That's* the point people don't understand. Mindloads are like quotes from books—they should be complete and meaningful by themselves, but they are only the tiniest part of the book itself. You can't divine the entire book from the quote. That's the way it is with mindloads. It's just a little tiny part of a person, a tiny shred."

Sam shivered again. She didn't care how small the shred was. She didn't want to lose *any* part of her soul. "Why so little?" she asked.

"Because we just can't pull in any more than that. Even the best, most complete mindload ever done only absorbed five percent of the subject's brain capacity. The rest was utterly, irrevocably lost."

Phil set down his wineglass on one of the worktables and turned back toward Sam. He smiled, and the firelight caught the gleam of his teeth. "This is where you're supposed to ask the next obvious questions. 'If they absorbed so little information, what's the point? Why were the mindloads done? What were the loaders after? What was useful in that five percent?' ''

Sam gestured vaguely, more than a little disconcerted. "Okay, pretend I asked," she said, pulling her legs up onto the couch, wrapping her arms around her knees. Suddenly the warm room seemed very cold indeed. "Tell me why." There was something frightened in her voice, and it seemed to catch at her host.

Phil blinked, and looked at her, and saw her fear. He seemed to come back to himself a bit. Suddenly the moment was over. Whatever door that he had opened on his inner passion was slipped shut again. "Sorry. I got a bit carried away." He picked up his glass and came back to his seat. "The loads were deliberately selective, seeking after specific portions of the human mind. That's all the loaders could handle. And it was still a lot. Five percent of a human brain's capacity is still a *tremendous* amount of data. And incidentally, most loads were much smaller. The five percent loads were test runs, efforts to set a record. Nothing ever came out of them. As for mindloading a whole brain, the subject's complete personality, the way they do in the horror videos—well it's impossible. Just *storing* that much data in a quickly usable form would be a real challenge. Even today, we'd have trouble setting up a dynamic memory system compact and sophisticated enough to handle it effectively. A deluxe robot brain has only two or three percent of a human mind's capacity. That's all it needs."

"But what *were* the loaders after?" Sam asked. "What was their mo—" Sam stopped herself too late.

Phil smiled. "What was their motive for these bizarre crimes? That's pretty straightforward: they were after things they couldn't effectively program any other way.

"They had managed a lot of tough programming jobs by themselves. Decision-making, personality-simulation, data search, expert systems, artificial intelligence systems. Those were tough, but they were possible to accomplish, more or less finite problems researchers could solve. The loaders were after things that decades of research work hadn't come close to cracking, jobs the human brain could do that they were nowhere near duplicating. All the research they did merely showed them how far away they still were.

"You can break the problem areas down to three major things: language ability, visual perception, and motor coordination. Look up any premindload robotics text and you'll see that the early researchers found those three things were virtually impossible to program and coordinate with each other. But every human does them all naturally, automatically. So instead of beating their heads against the wall trying to duplicate Nature's work, the mindloaders just ran off copies."

"Turning the victims' brains into guacamole in the process," Sam said impulsively, and instantly regretting it. She wasn't going to get anywhere stepping on Sanders's toes.

But Phil didn't even bat an eye. "Subjects, not victims. I won't kid you and say there weren't some nasty abuses —not just those old stories about the South American labs, but some ugliness right here in the States. But ninety-nine plus percent of the loads were legitimate, totally open and aboveboard. Back then, there was no need to break the law, because it was legal. All the labs were bending over backward to *avoid* trouble.

"People would sign forms similar to organ-donor releases, and get well paid for signing. Most of them were terminal patients in tremendous pain, that sort of thing. The mindload team would wait until the subject was in irretrievable coma or the equivalent, due to illness or injury, and *then* go to work. No legitimate mindload was ever done on anyone who had any hope of recovery."

"But then they changed the law," Sam said. "They decided that mindloading was wrong."

"No, they decided they didn't have the *stomach* for mindloading," Phil said coldly. "If mindloading was wrong, then so is any other process that takes something useful from a human corpse. Heart transplants are wrong, cornea transplants are wrong, carving up cadavers to train doctors is wrong.

"Technically the mindload subjects were alive, blood flowing to brain, but for all human intents and purposes the mindload subjects *were dead* by the time anyone switched on the magnetic inducers. They weren't *people* anymore. They were unable to speak, to think, to hear, unable to care for themselves. All the higher brain functions flat already. Their brains already *were* guacamole, to use your happy phrase. In fact a lot of the loads were salvage jobs. The load teams didn't get much useful data out of them. But by the time the loaders got to work, there was no more—or less—moral reason against doing the loads than there was against cutting organs out of a brain-deader for transplant. People just got squeamish.

"But there was one other reason mindloading became illegal. After a while, the loaders had sucked up enough brains. There were thousands of loads sitting on the shelf. Enough raw datasets to mix and match, cut and snip and paste, to make all the robot brains you'd ever want. Remember, pulling the master copy destroys the organic original, but once you have the master, you can spool off as many copies as you like. So the loaders stopped defending load rights so hard. Load rights turned into a bargaining chip in fights over copyright protection, that sort of thing. And then the chip got spent."

Ghoulish thoughts. Samantha took a careful sip of her wine to mask her discomfort. "Okay, point taken, and that's about as much as I want to handle. Let me change the subjct. Why are those programming problems so tough? Like speech. It seems to me that there were plenty of robots and machines that could talk before mindloads."

"Ever listen to a recording of one of them? Crude, clumsy, forever mangling syntax, utterly baffled by the simplest piece of slang. Flat out incapable of figuring out an unknown word from its context. Feedback looped, self-controlled motor coordination wasn't quite as bad, if you didn't mind waiting all day for the robot to run the maze. They had to move slowly to avoid crashing. But the toughest one was visualization."

"I don't see why," Sam said.

Phil smiled. "Think of how you just phrased that, the words you chose to form a statement meant to tell me that you don't understand. 'I don't *see* why.' We're very visual animals, and our brains are *very* good at processing images. There's a distinct portion of a human brain given over solely to recognizing human faces. We're incredibly good at recognizing an object from a partial image, or from a new angle. If our ancestors were going to survive, they had to be able to see two whiskers and an ear sticking out from behind a rock, and know there was a tiger hiding there. They had to be able to judge distances for jumps, had to be able to do *incredibly* fine eye-hand coordination at the smallest scale. And they had to do it fast. Ever drive a manual car?"

"Only kind I do drive," Sam said. "I'm on a tight budget."

"Well, think about how many decisions per second you have to make, most of them based on partial or uncertain visual data, keyed in with sound and the 'feel' of the car. Someone who *might* step out into traffic just ahead. How long until the light changes? How fast can I go when the road is this wet? Does that noise behind me mean anything? And we handle the controls by reflex. We don't have to worry about finding the brakes with our foot, or how hard to press it. Our foot 'knows' all that. We don't have to measure it or time it. It's automatic. Same with turning the steering wheel or handling any other control. It's all highly complex—"

"And we do all that without thinking," Sam said, starting to understand.

"Exactly. But how do you handle automatic decision-making on a machine? How does a thinking machine simulate real-time human decision-making that's done 'without thinking'?"

Sam thought that one over and frowned. "I'm beginning to see your point. So instead of learning how to do all that, the roboticists just took the knowledge."

"Classic black-box engineering. You don't care how a machine does a thing, just that it does it. If you want widgets, you just plug in a widget-making black box and don't worry about it."

"Except the widget you're making is human-style behavior, and the black boxes are the human mind and brain."

"Exactly. We don't know how it works, just that it does. We can copy out portions of the human mind, and then make as many robotic copies as we want."

"But the loaders destroy the original. Is that unavoidable? Nothing that can be done about it?"

"Nothing. The mindload is an inherently destructive process. By its very nature, the mag-inducers wreck the brain in the process of copying out its contents. That's why the loaders took only coma victims."

"But hypothetically," Sam said. "Suppose a functional, healthy person with a working brain *did* go under one of those inducers. What would happen?"

"Nothing hypothetical about that question. It happened once or twice in the very early days, before it was established that mag-induction mindloading *was* a destructive process. The subjects were gone, dead, their brains as surely fried as if they had been electrocuted. That's what happened to Bailey."

"Good," Sam said eagerly, and then flushed with embarrassment. "I mean, not good that he died, but good that you brought him up. I wanted to get around to him. The U.S. Attorney says he was trying to put his mind into Herbert. But in light of what you've said, it seems not only that it didn't work, but that it couldn't *possibly* work."

She leaned forward and set down her glass. "If Bailey was such a big robot expert, he should have known all this. Which makes Bailey's actions into nothing more than an elaborate way to commit suicide. He is truly dead. If what you've said is true, why did he do it? And why is Entwhistle hopping up and down mad about it?"

"Because nearly all of what I said *isn't* true anymore," Phil replied. "Not after Bailey. The man was a true genius, an original. I knew something about him beforehand, but when I saw the investigative file on him, I realized that he was doing things with robotics other people hadn't even worked up the nerve to *dream* about."

Seen the investigative file? Sam thought. *That* was an interesting thing for the cop on the beat to see. *Who slipped you that, I wonder. Just how many rules are you breaking here, Phillipe?* But she had already decided not to press on that point. Not yet anyway. Besides, he hadn't noticed his slip. If she brought it to his attention, he might clam up. "So you're suggesting that if anyone could mindload an *entire* mind, it was David Bailey," Sam said.

"That's right," Phil agreed.

"But he wasn't as good as he thought he was," Sam suggested.

"How do you mean?" Phil asked.

"Well, obviously he failed. Herbert certainly doesn't show any signs of human intelligence."

"Neither does a newborn baby," Phil replied. "Learning how to be a human takes some time. And Herbert is doing some things that are very definitely *not* robotlike. You saw those flatviews I sent you, didn't you?"

"Yeah, pictures of a robot dusting. So what?"

Phil leaned in toward Sam and looked at her intently. "So Herbert *wasn't told to dust.* I've checked that. I've run all the monitor recordings from the moment we picked him up to the moment Suzanne Jantille arrived. He received nothing that was even *remotely* like a command to clean. No one even spoke to him."

"So what? My cleaning robot is an el-cheapo model from Sears. It knows to vacuum and dust once a week without my telling it."

"Because you did tell it, once. You programmed it at one time to vacuum and dust. If you picked it up and carried it over here, to my apartment, what would you expect it to do?"

Sam thought for a moment. "Nothing. You're right. Because before my HMU would do my apartment, I had to walk it through the place, point out what it could touch and what I didn't trust it to do. When I bring in something new, the HMU avoids that object until I program it to accept the new piece as safe. It wouldn't know that sort of thing about this place."

Sam thought for a moment. "So if my brand-x cleaning robot is designed to stop, not do anything, rather than risk causing damage, a high-end job should be at least that smart. And Herbert is a fancy custom model. He should be able to figure that sort of thing out by himself."

"Exactly. And it's worse than that. Herbert *did* hear the place he was going to described as an 'evidence room.' He *should* have been able to do a look-up on that term and know that he could potentially do damage to the evidence by cleaning it. Even if the look-up failed, he *didn't* have volitional programming that would have caused him to do something without being told. Besides, a cleaning robot is *always* programmed to leave unknown objects alone. I can't imagine a malfunction so massive that could let him dust fingerprints off evidence and yet allow him to work at all. Any malfunction that let him dust should have disabled him altogether. Herbert's main logic would *have* to crash. Unless something else, some wild card, got in there and screwed up the main logic program in a very special way. Something that could induce volitional programming *and* scram the cleaning-rule criteria."

"Something like David Bailey," Sam said.

"Something like Bailey," Phil agreed.

"So the fact that Herbert did something classically idiotic and robotic is proof that there's something wrong with him."

"Not *wrong*. Something *different*. Something odd and nonrobotic."

"But if this Bailey was such a genius, why did he screw up?" Sam asked. "Why didn't he do the mindload properly?"

"Well, there are several possibilities, but there are two I think are the most likely," Phil replied. "One, the press of time and the pain of his injuries. He got hurt, knew he didn't have much time, and rushed the job, improvising as best he could. Maybe figuring that if worst came to worst, going out under the mindload was better than dying slowly of his injuries."

"And the second possibility?"

"Is that he *didn't* screw up. That David Bailey's mind, memory, and personality were all fully and completely downloaded into Herbert's memory matrix. That the operation was a success, and that it's just taking David some time to get situated. David Bailey's mind wasn't meant to fit into a six-legged vacuum cleaner. I mentioned newborn babies a few minutes ago. Think about that. Bailey died in March, and it's June now. He's only had three months in Herbert's body." Phil set down his wineglass and stared deep into Sam's eyes. "How long did it take you to learn how *your* body worked, after you were born?" he asked.

Sam was starting to understand. "So he may be *in* there, in Herbie, trying to get out?"

"Exactly. At least, *in* there. Trying to get out, I don't know. It might even be that the *components* of David Bailey are there, but so dissociated that there is no self-aware part of him. In other words, perhaps the *data* needed to construct Bailey is there, but Bailey himself doesn't now exist on any sort of conscious level. Or it could be some sort of grey area in between. From what I know of memory matrices and mindload storage, I wouldn't be surprised if even Bailey doesn't know for sure if he's in there, or if he's been able to reassemble and reorganize himself into a coherent whole. Don't forget, he's dealing with an entirely novel sensory universe."

Sam thought of her conversation with Clancy, and

tried to imagine how he saw the world. Not only were his senses different from hers, but his awareness was flitting back and forth between the central processor and the remote units. What would it be like, to be a mind that was literally in two places—indeed many places—at once? A mind in some ways far more capable, in others far more limited, than a human mind. "I'm starting to see what you mean," she said. "Not all of it, not yet. Maybe I'm just starting to see enough to see that I don't understand."

Phil smiled at her. "We're talking about minds here, and how they work. When you come right down to it, who *does* understand? People come in here wanting me to tell them how robot minds function. And I have to tell them we won't know that until we know how human minds work. Until we can answer questions like: What is the relationship between the brain and the mind? What is the relationship between the mind and the soul?"

Sam felt a cold wind blow through her. For if Bailey still lived, still existed, then there was no relation at all between brain and mind.

And David Bailey had downloaded his soul into a tin box.

CHAPTER 5
SOUL IN THE MACHINE

The conversation wheeled around, Phil doing most of the talking, Sam just sitting there, listening, watching in fascination as the ideas swooped past her. Issues of mind, and thought, and patterns of intelligence, and mapping the functions of the human brain. They traveled the strange byways of old stone age surgical work on the brain, back in the 1950s and 1960s, when seizure victims had had their brains carved up, or whole lobes of their brains removed—and yet still functioned, somehow. They got onto the subject of autism, and the still-mysterious, horrifyingly tiny malfunctions that could derail a human mind and send it hurtling off into darkness. "That tells me things about intelligence," Phil said, that passionate eagerness back in his voice. "About real human intelligence. That tells me it's fragile. That the tiniest change in the brain can overturn it. Even though, in other circumstances, you can chop out half the brain and still have a functioning mind, if you shift a cell pattern even microscopically, it goes. It's gone, and you have an autistic's world, a universe no outsider can understand."

Sam nodded, and felt *she* was beginning to understand the things that drove Phillipe. But something was bothering her. None of this seemed very real. She was getting some insight into robots and the science of minds, yes. But it was all blue smoke and mirrors, inquiries into the whichness of what. Sam wrote for readers and viewers in the real world, who cared about real things.

Suddenly there was a restlessness about her, a need to hook up with things that were more substantial than theories of consciousness and the morality of decade-old operations on dead people. She was tired of just sitting and talking. She stood up, and carrying her glass, she walked to the center of the big room, into the space between the four worktables. "Never mind sensory universes and memory matrices," she said. "That's just a bunch of words. Don't just talk to me. *Show* me," she said. She gestured at the towering machinery that loomed up in the darkness all about her. "Show me something that *means* something to you in all this."

Phillipe set down his glass with a smile. "House, main work lights on." The room bloomed into light as he stood and walked over to her. "I'm not quite sure I understand you," he said. "Something that means something to me. What sort of meaning are you after?"

Sam shook her head. "I don't know. But you've been talking theory, and things that happened long ago, or things that might have happened to other people. Maybes and what-ifs and airy-fairy logic. Deep down, isn't it all about real machines? Isn't that what you do? Plug arms and legs together and make walking, talking, thinking *real* machines?"

"Okay," Phillipe said gently. "Here's a real machine for you." He stepped behind Sam and pulled the dustcover off the worktable at her back.

Sam, feeling the wine just a little bit, heard the fluttering of fabric behind her and knew Phil had pulled the dust cloth off the work on the table. She turned around, a little fast, leaned in toward the table a bit more than she should, and slipped forward. She threw her free hand forward and caught herself on the edge of the table, nearly dropping her wineglass.

She was leaning forward on the table, staring down at a pair of robot knees, the legs below dangling down over the edge of the workbench. She looked upward and her insides froze.

She found herself inches away from a grinning metallic skull, face-to-face with it, cruel eyes popping out from the naked steel of the unfleshed face. White plastic teeth leered at her from a cast fiberglass jaw. The gleaming, polished plastic skull was hinged open, revealing not the thing's brain, but actuator gears, sensor wires, tiny hydraulic lines.

It took her a long, befuddled moment of horror to know what she was seeing, and to tell herself firmly that it was nothing to fear.

"Th-that's real, all right," she whispered. "I've never seen a robot this way. I mean, with the skin off."

"And you still haven't, strictly speaking," Phillipe said. "This isn't a robot. It's a remote unit."

Sam backed away from the grinning thing sitting on the edge of the table. "Every time I say something is a robot, it seems like somebody tells me it's something else. What's the difference, anyway, if it *looks* like a robot?"

"The distinction between robots and other forms are important," Phillipe said. "When people forget them, it makes for trouble. Mostly because people keep expecting the other, lesser forms to do what only robots can do."

"Which is what, precisely?"

"Think. Only robots can think for themselves. No other machine can do that. Even robots can only do it in a very limited way. Thinking is hard work."

"What about artificial intelligence systems?" Sam asked. "I've always just sort of thought of them as robots that don't move."

"There are a *few* sessile robots like that, but most ArtInts can only solve problems put before them. They can't think *of* problems that *need* solving. To *really* oversimplify, they can *answer* questions, but not *ask* them. And from a programmer's standpoint, getting a machine to *ask* questions is by far the hardest job. It's a lot tougher than programming a black box to look things up for you or run calculations."

"But what about all the non-robot machines that *seem* to be thinking for themselves?"

"Somewhere in the background, someone else is doing the thinking for them. A remote mind, a person or another machine is telling that machine what to do—or else the machine's working from recorded instructions, which just means the instruction giver is distant in space *and* time from the robot. Machines that have *some* flexibility of action but must act under specific orders are called robots. To my mind they shouldn't be. Like your vacuum cleaner. I think it's not *quite* a true robot because it can't decide to do anything. It *has* to be told. You once told it to clean every Tuesday, or something. And so it does. But the carpet could be six inches thick with dust, and the dishes stacked to the ceiling in the sink, and your robot would just sit there unless it was *specifically programmed* to clean. It is physically incapable of spontaneously *getting* the idea to clean."

Phil picked up his wineglass and took a sip. "Just under that sort of robot are the high-end teleoperators, which are simply remote-control machines. If they happen to be shaped like people, they're called humanoid teleoperator machines. HTMs. Mostly they're shaped like people so they can use tools meant for people to use. HTMs are by far more common than any sort of true robot, so they are what people see most often. They're made cheaply, for the most part, and look it. Their movements aren't as smooth as a true robot's, and they can get into trouble if their radio links are screwed up. People look at HTMs, think they're robots, and assume that robots are as clumsy and stupid as HTMs."

"Like the Clancys," Sam suggested. "The service robots at *The Washington Post*. I had a long talk with one of them just today."

Phil screwed up his face, unhappy to contradict his guest, a bit disappointed that she hadn't understood. "No, not quite. You can't have a conversation with an

HTM, unless it's rigged with a mike and speaker hooked back to the operator—and the Clancys aren't built that way. They *are* true robots. I chatted with one of them myself when I dropped off the first datacube. I know that model type. They're extremely sophisticated machines. They *can* decide to do things—like hang around the people who tip best. All of them are capable of extensive autonomous action. They have to be, since they often leave the building on errands, out of range of the central processing station. They *are* true robots—but each individual robot is hooked into a central controlling system. It's an expensive way to do things."

Sam nodded slowly, and looked again at the disturbing visage of the machine in front of her. "And this little wonder doesn't fit into any of the categories you've described."

"Right. None of the above. This is a remote unit. In many ways, the most sophisticated of all the human imitative machines. A cross between a cyborg and a teleoperator and a true robot, because a remote must act on its own sometimes."

"Sounds great, but what the hell *is* a remote unit?" Sam asked.

"You don't know?" Phil asked. "It's the machine portion of a remote person." He spoke the words in a deathly quiet voice.

Sam felt her stomach knot up again. *Remote person.* There was something cold about the term, something hard-edged and gruesome. She backed a step away from the machine. Phil had talked about robots holding a tiny bit of the dead. That was doubly true for a remote.

Phil didn't seem to notice her discomfort. "The man who used this machine died a few months back," he said, something still strained about his tone of voice. "I received the remote unit from the estate. I'm reconditioning it. Obviously it's not functional now, but another month or two of work, and it'll be like brand-new."

"And then what?"

"Then someone who needs a remote unit but can't afford a new one can use this one."

"Brrr." Sam shuddered. "I'm sorry, but I can't help it. Just the idea of that gives me the absolute *creeps*. One half-dead man haunted that thing, and then he died all the way, and now you want to get it ready for *another* half-dead guy?"

Phil's expression hardened, but then he sighed.

"No one was half-dead," he said with quiet firmness. "The man—a very nice man, a good man—who used this machine was a quadriplegic. He was a—a friend of mine. He was the man who got me interested in robotics in the first place. I wanted to learn so I could help him. And yes, from the neck down his body didn't work. But his brain, his mind, were perfectly alive and functional. Even vigorous. It was this bucket of bolts here that let him operate in the outside world. Otherwise, he would have been a bedridden prisoner—or if he was having a really good day, he would have been able to operate a powerchair, using a very awkward set of mouth controls."

Phil turned away, looked out the window, into the empty street. "He was in about the same shape Suzanne Jantille is in now, as best I can gather."

Sam gasped. "Suzanne Jantille is . . ." She wasn't able to finish the sentence. Instead, she was only able to point feebly at the mechanical *thing* sitting on the table.

Phil turned back, looked at her in surprise. "You didn't know? I've spent tonight finding out how little you know about the things you write about, but how could you look at the video records I showed you and *not* see what she is?"

Sam felt her face turn red. "I noticed she moved a bit stiffly," she admitted. "I guess I was watching the robot, not really looking at Madame Jantille. And the resolution wasn't that good. Besides, she certainly didn't look like *that*," Sam said, pointing at the grinning gargoyle face in front of her.

Phil's temper flared again. There was a darkness, an

anger inside this man. "Oh, yes. Of course Suzanne Jantille had the good taste to dress her remote unit up in rubber skin and a wig to avoid offending real people like you and me. No doubt that's very important to her. Making people like us feel comfortable and at ease."

Sam opened her mouth and then closed it. She couldn't think of anything to say for a long time. Finally a question popped into her head. *Those* she could always come up with. Someday she ought to start working on answers. "How do they do it?" she asked. "How does a person—how does Suzanne Jantille—control her remote unit?"

Phil took a deep breath, and let the cool technical details of the question calm him down. "Through inductance sensing. A surgeon performs a fairly straightforward procedure to put an inductance tap around the top of her spinal cord. It's a little gadget, unnoticeable once it's in place. The tap's similar to the mag-inducers the old mindloaders used, but a million times less powerful. And it's a passive detector. Mindload gear imposes outside energy fields on a brain. That's what causes the damage. Remote unit inductance taps merely detect existing impulses. They can't hurt anything. They just pick up the very weak, very delicate electrical nerve impulses that are going toward the muscles, ordering them to move.

"In a quadriplegic like Jantille, those nerves are severed, or at least useless. The muscles *don't* move. But the thought impulse that used to move her leg is picked up by the tap. The tap amplifies the signal and transmits it to very sensitive receivers placed around the person's neck. The signals are processed and sent to a processor wired into the tap, and then transmitted over radio to the remote unit. That signal serves as an instruction to move the remote unit's leg. If Madame Jantille thinks about moving her own arm, the system transmits a signal to move the remote's arm. And so on."

Phil shrugged and looked almost apologetic. "It's a crude system in many ways. It's not as good as a direct computer link into the motor control areas of the brain.

With that kind of link, we might be able to bypass the damaged nerve trunk and renew the motor-control links to the patient's biological body. But mechanical enhancement of the brain is illegal, and I'm not so sure the law is wrong. If we decided that it was okay to modify the human brain, augment it with electronics and direct plug-ins to hardware, there would be no end to the potential abuses.

"So we use the spinal inductance system. Crude, limited, but the technique works." Samantha nodded dumbly, staring down at the remote unit's glazen eyes, as if she could see through those bits of plastic, down into the dead soul that had been imprisoned within, could see Suzanne Jantille's world as seen through the eyes of her remotes.

Phillipe stepped closer to Sam, stood behind her, and put his hand on her shoulder. "Picture Suzanne Jantille," he whispered, his mouth close to her ear. "She has an inductance tap around her biological body's spinal cord. She wears a teleoperator helmet. Without it, she cannot operate the remote unit. Without the helmet, she can only hear and see whatever room her life-support system is in. Maybe she's lying in bed, and can only see the ceiling. Maybe she's propped up in a chair, and she can look out a window at the world outside. But that's it. That's all. She can only go outside that room through the remote, with the T.O. helmet on.

"The T.O. helmet has vision goggles keyed to the remote's video cameras, earphones keyed to the remote unit's ear microphones. That is how she sees and hears, through a machine. All of her world is far away from her body. All she can see and hear and do, she must do through a cold machine like the one in front of you. If she wants to talk, she speaks into a microphone, and her words are radioed to the remote. Speaking in her voice, the remote unit says her words for her. Since it's a top-end unit, the remote can even lipsynch her voice, move its mouth to match the voice sounds coming from its speaker.

"So the remote unit goes out into the world to walk and talk and carry for her, while her inert, motionless body lies at home, vision goggles over its eyes, earphones stuck on its ears. And I say 'it' and not 'her' because that is all her body is by now—an *it*, a thing, an encumbrance Suzanne Jantille must endure. In a very real sense, she does not occupy that body. Instead her soul is in a machine. Her entire life, day after day, is an out-of-body experience.

"To all the outside world, she *is* this clockwork doll that walks and talks and—*disturbs* people. They respond to the remote unit, have *its* face in mind when they think of her, see *it* being healthy and active, no matter how weak and frail her biological body becomes. To all the world, she is a machine with a disembodied voice, the ghost in the machine.

"But here's one last part of her nightmare: She walks through the day and the world seeing and hearing—but she has no sense of touch. No one's ever developed a remote unit system that could provide a usable tactile sensation to the patient. Even if they had, it's more than likely that most of her own nerve receptors are gone. There's nothing left to stimulate."

Sam shuddered and blinked back a tear. "She can see, and hear," Phil whispered, his breath warm on her cheek, his face pressing her hair up against her face. "But she cannot feel heat, or cold, or pain, or the wind in her face, or the touch of a human hand."

Sam stepped back from the remote, backed herself up against Phillipe's strong body. She swallowed hard. "But why?" she whispered. "Why endure it?"

"Because it gives her a *life*," Phillipe replied, his voice suddenly firm. He stepped around Sam, until he was standing beside her. Their hands brushed together, and Sam reached out, held his hand, held it tight. There had never been a moment in her life when she had feared loneliness more. Phil took his free hand, reached over, and put it on the side of the remote unit's opened-up skull. "Not much of a life, but *something*. Something more than she could have without the remote. And it gives her more. Independence. Dignity." He paused for a moment, and looked about the room, at all the bits and pieces of machinery that could be put together to walk and talk. "I know very little about Suzanne Jantille," he said. "But I do know things must have been pretty bad for her before using a remote would make sense. She must be utterly paralyzed, with no mobility at all. Without the remote, she'd be an invalid, utterly dependent on others, closed off from most of the outside world.

"But because Suzanne Jantille lives through a machine like this, she can move around her own house, open doors, go up and downstairs, dial the phone without help. Maybe people stare at her—but they'd do that to a woman in a powerchair, anyway. And she's probably in such bad shape even a full powerchair would be useless. With the remote, she has her life back, at least to some degree. She can go out into the world, though she can't go far."

"Why not?" Sam asked.

"Radio bandwidth limits," Phil said. "There are only so many radio frequencies to go around, and not many available for use by remote persons. There isn't anywhere near enough radio bandwidths available for remote persons to use all the signal they'd need for full operation of their remote units. So away from home base, or some sort of relay system that can hook into a hardwire connection, the person running the remote unit starts losing functions. Sight in one eye goes or stereo hearing gets powered down. That's why a remote unit must be able to work on its own. If the radio link cuts out altogether, the unit has to find its own way home.

"*With* the remote, Suzanne Jantille can care for herself—use the remote to feed and bathe her organic body, for example. And that alone must be precious to her, must preserve so much of her dignity." He let go of Sam's hand, pulled his other hand off the remote's skull, and bent down. He looked into the remote unit's blind eyes. "That's why I'm getting this pile of machinery back up to par, so it can help some other unlucky soul." Phil reached out a hand, gently touched the metal and plastic head, ran his fingers along the jawline.

There was something here, Samantha realized. A missing part, a puzzle piece that would make the picture clear when it dropped into place. Phillipe's reaction was more than a man explaining a machine. It had more of the flavor of a man talking with a tombstone, justifying his actions to the dead. A ripple of cold swept through her as she remembered standing before her grandmother's grave, wishing with childish fervor to apologize for still being alive. Fixing up this remote wasn't part of his hobby, or a side job for money. It was a man doing penance.

And with a sudden leap of intuition, she understood. "Who was he, Phil?" Sam asked, her voice a gentle whisper.

For a long moment Phillipe remained still, kneeling down before the plastic and metal thing before him. At last he stood up, selected a tool from the workbench, and set to work on some delicate adjustment deep inside the remote unit's skull. "I thought I told you," he said. "I always assume everybody knows."

Phillipe Montoya Sanders stood up and stared down at the grinning plastic skull.

"The man who owned this remote was my father."

Interlude

*Cancel do-loop. Break. Break. Reset. Clear. Stop. Think.
Wait a second. What's going on here? What's happened?
Call subroutine diagnostic—*

*Cancel subroutine call. Damn it, no. I asked myself a
question. I didn't order a computer run. Or hell, did I?
The subroutine call was automatic, instantaneous. It was
an instinctive, reflexive act to call the subroutine. Subroutine. A subroutine is called by a larger program of
which it is a part. Then who the hell is running the
program that called the sub? Fear runs through me, and
I think that I should feel the cold of fear, the gnawing at
the gut. But it is not there.*

Nothing is there. And I don't remember why.

*Okay, slowly, carefully, restraining all the strange re-
flexes I seem to have. I ask again: Where am I?*

CHAPTER 6
OUT-OF-BODY EXPERIENCE

Suzanne-Remote leaned over, pulled the sheet away, and then stepped back for a moment. She looked down at the powerbed and the poor wasted body upon it. *Her* body, *her* flesh and blood, now disembodied from her, or she from it. Nowadays she was never quite sure which. Propped up in the bed, weak and pale, the arms gone, the legs gone, brutally amputated in the accident. The torso thin, the breath of life moving but weakly through the fragile frame. The head englobed in the black, beetle-like teleoperator helmet, thick black cables trailing off from it into the forest of machinery discreetly hidden away in the next room. The clinically clean and perfect hospital-white waste-disposal unit strapped between the stumps of her legs, hoses trailing off from it toward the house's waste lines.

And between the two sets of tubes and machinery, the pallid white torso, all that was left of her natural self, all that still functioned on its own. Her stomach pale white, her once-firm breasts flaccid and small. Weakened, shrunken, faded, cut away, shriveled away. In all ways that mattered, and by seemingly all means possible, there was less of her than there had been.

The powerbed hummed and clicked, made some internal adjustment. It was far more than a bed, of course —it monitored all her body's vital signs, massaged and stimulated her muscles to prevent excessive atrophy, saw to it that she was nourished on the all-too-frequent occasions when she forgot to feed herself. It kept her body warm, cared for her. It could have given her a spray-jet cleaning as well, in lieu of the daily sponge bath. But Suzanne reserved the task of bathing herself as a personal duty.

Suzanne-Remote moved her strong robot's hands toward the washbasin, picked up the sponge, dipped it in the basin, and reached over to sponge-bathe her own ruined body. She had imagined the daily ritual becoming easier each day, but it never did. The remote glanced toward the T.O. helmet that encased her bio-body's head. There, inside the helmet, her own eyes were watching two small video screens, watching what her remote's eye-cameras saw and transmitted to the helmet. Her living eyes saw what her robot eyes sent them, showed her the image of her own inert body.

Suzanne instinctively tried to move her bio-body's head, move her own eyes to see the remote whose eyes she was using. But all she accomplished was to move the *remote's* head, make it glance over its shoulder toward an empty corner. It happened every day, and still it frightened her: she tried to look at herself, and saw nothing. A chilling thought, that.

Every morning she found herself caught by the strangeness of seeing herself from the outside, and every morning her imprisoned living eyes tried to look toward the very robot eyes they were seeing through. It was a reflex she could not shake off, though it was as hopeless —and as dizzying—as a child trying to see the back of her head in the mirror by turning her head quickly.

Twice a week the helmet came off. Tuesdays and Fridays a technical nurse came in to check on her T.O. setup and to give her bio-body a full bath. Some small subconscious part of her always expected to be blinded, deafened, when the helmet came off. Without her link to the robot body, surely the darkness would descend. It was always a shock when the light of the world struck her face, and her eyesight proved to be *better* without the T.O. Always a shock when her hearing became more real, more direct without the filter of the headphones.

And she could *feel*, at least a little, with the helmet off. With or without the helmet, she had no sensation whatever below her neck. But when it was off, she could feel her head, her face, her mouth, her throat. The cocooning helmet effectively removed even those sensations, for there was never any *change* in sensation when the helmet was on. The helmet allowed the free passage of air for breathing, of course, but there was never any variation in air temperature or air pressure.

When the technical nurse came to bathe her and took the helmet off, it was not only her sight and hearing that were seemingly enhanced, but her sense of touch as well. To her sensation-starved senses, the feel of warm water and gentle hands on her face was almost sexual in its intensity.

Suzanne could use a voice command sequence to open the helmet, and use the powerbed systems to spray a cleansing mist of water at her face by herself, but it was not the same. It was the *realness* of the touch, the connection to the world outside represented by a pair of flesh-and-blood hands, that made the twice-weekly full baths so important.

Every bath day she resolved to leave the helmet off for a while. It was built in as an integral part of the powerbed, and she could put it on and off with a simple voice command. Yes, she would tell herself as the warm water foamed over her, she would leave the helmet off. She could get along with the voice controls on the powerbed. And she could *see*, and *feel*.

But removing the T.O. helmet meant she was paralyzed again. Though the powerbed could tilt and swivel in all directions, it could not leave that one room, show her any view but that one lonely window and the house across the street. The entertainment system was voice-controlled as well, but there were only so many book tapes she could read, so much studying she could do, so many programs she could watch, so much music she could hear before going mad. Soon she would be longing for other walls to see. A simple voice command would reengage the helmet. The servos would whine and the clamshell helmet halves would lift themselves from their recesses and close over her face, and her eyes and ears would belong to the remote once again.

She could not see as *well*, through the helmet, but she could see more. See her own walled-in back garden, the blue sky above. She could look out her own front window. Feeling very much like a spy in a foreign land that would never welcome her, she could watch the laughing children coming home from school.

Suzanne-Remote dipped her sponge again, and ran it over her body. Done with the bath, the remote lifted Suzanne's body slightly, rolling it on its side to remove the dampened sheet and slide in a fresh one. She draped a clean top sheet over the body, and a warm blanket over the sheet, then stepped back and looked at herself. Only the helmeted head was outside the sheets, and her body looked like a deformed corpse. Which, in a very real sense, it was. And it was frail, its immune system as weakened as every other part of itself. Easy prey to a cold or a virus, susceptible to the slightest chill or illness. One flicker of disease, and the seeming corpse would become a real one.

But it was her own corpse she looked upon, and it lived, and Suzanne Jantille felt herself to be very much alive. She turned her back on the blanketed thing on the bed and left the room. Leaving was always a relief. Stepping out of that room, she immediately lost the very disturbing feeling that there were two of her. Outside that room, she no longer wondered which was her body, or who, exactly, she was.

But down to business, she told herself firmly. She pushed her personal worries away and focused on her professional situation. There was a job to do. Herbert deserved competent counsel, and she would give it to him, whether she felt ready or not. She was capable on the legal side, yes—she was fully confident of herself there. But yesterday's visit to the police station had reminded her of just how ill-prepared she was as a *person*, of how little confidence she had in her self. She resolved to do something she had not done since the accident. Something she had feared so much she had not dared even think about it. But now there was no choice.

She decided to take a walk around the block.

And then, if that worked out, to take a walk out of radio range. That was a thought that terrified her. In theory, her remote body could find its way back into range, or find its own way home. But she had never dared try it. If in the room with her bio-body Suzanne had the strange feeling of being in two places at once, then the idea of losing her remote made her think of being no place at all.

Of her soul escaping both remote unit and bio-body, never to return.

And it even scared her that such a loss did not terrify her as much as it once had.

Samantha Crandall felt anxious, and more than a bit depressed. The evening at Phillipe's had been a strangely intriguing nightmare, hinting at excitement and danger yet to come. But the day after dawned with a lesson in anticlimax.

Her story made it onto page one, but below the fold. It got onto the videotext newsfeed, but after the first priority cut. Some newsnets picked it up, others didn't. There were a few phone calls to the paper, but the Pulitzer Prize committee didn't rush-ship her the award, and the world didn't come to an end.

In other words, Sam got the same old dose of letdown she got whenever she broke a big story. And she probably always *would* feel that letdown, unless she managed to force an entire government to resign sometime. That idea brought a smile to her face. *All right*, she told herself. *So I have an exaggerated sense of the news media's importance. And my own.*

In any event, things were quiet in the newsroom, and after last night's weirdness, today's quiet suited Sam's mood fine. Phillipe had gotten to her, left her staring at the ceiling instead of sleeping when she got home. She felt a shiver go down her spine even as she thought of him, and of the evening before. There was something about that man that fascinated her, disturbed her—and it wasn't just his hobby.

To hell with quiet, she decided suddenly. A fit of restlessness overtook her. She felt the need to prowl around a bit.

She looked around the newsroom and spotted her boss in his glassed-in office, sitting at his ease, feet up on his desk. She stood up, went over, and walked through the open doorway. "Talk to me, Gunther," Sam said, plopping herself down on his couch. "Something is going on, and I don't know what."

"Could you be a bit more specific about the topic under discussion?" Gunther asked in a mild voice. Gunther had what had to be his second or third cup of coffee in the hand that wasn't holding the newspaper. Caffeine made Gunther a lot easier to deal with in the morning. "What is it you want to talk about?" he asked.

"About the story," she said. "My story."

"What about it?" Gunther asked.

"I don't know." She turned her palms upward and shrugged vaguely. "Did I do it right? What do I do next?"

"In other words, you're fishing for compliments," Gunther said, a slightly warning tone in his voice.

Sam thought for a moment and then nodded a decided yes. "Yeah. Why not? I think I deserve them."

"Well, lemme see." Gunther set down his coffee and folded his paper back to page one. Starting at the top, he read the whole piece through, his eyes working their slow and deliberate way over the words. Sam knew perfectly well that he had carefully read the story over at least twice the night before, but she let him be. If he needed to make the show of looking it over now, then let him. "Well, I don't know," he said at last. "You developed the make-Entwhistle-look-dumb side of the story pretty nicely, but I don't really see much *balance* here."

Her boss's words stunned Sam. If he felt that way about it, why had he personally approved it and run it? "Entwhistle had her chance to make a statement to me," Sam said.

"Oh, come on. It's just me here. You can talk dirty. You went to her press conference to blindside her, and she got blindsided. End of story. You know it, I know it, she knows it, the readers and viewers know it. Out in front of the world you have to pretend you were seeking a fair and balanced story, even if everyone knows better. But not here. Not with me. The real story is that Entwhistle ordered a flaky prosecution, she deserved to be popped one for it, and you popped her one. The end. Let's not pussyfoot around it. Let's talk the second-day story instead."

"Now wait a second!" Sam protested. "You read over that story, signed off on it. Why are you trashing it now?"

"I'm not trashing it—I'm just saying let's take our halos off while we talk it over. Your first-day story was just the ante in this game. Now you're in the hand and the cards are being dealt. I ran that story to give you a nice little tactical position, and now you ought to be thinking about ways to follow up on it."

"I don't get it."

Gunther took a sip of his coffee and went on. "Okay, forget the police beat side of this for a moment. We're deep into politics now, and that works a little differently. You're used to reporting the cops finding the body, maybe later finding the guy who did it, the end. Not this time. Politics have intruded, and that means the rules are different. The chessboard is bigger."

Gunther leaned back in his chair and scratched his woolly head thoughtfully. "Let me back up and take it from the top. In theory, we're supposed to be objective journalists here. Well, objectively speaking, we both know Entwhistle is a horse's ass, and we've done all we could to make her look like one in your story. Fine. What I'm saying is, now that you have her on the ropes, looking bad in the paper, *now* you can call her up, be polite as can be, and get the interview she wouldn't give you before. She has to talk to you now, or look even worse when you report her 'no comment.' *That's* the door your first-day story opens. So put your cardboard halo back on, get her on the horn, make the speech about seeing all sides of the issue, and get in that door for a real conversation. Let her see that you want her to have her chance to put her side of the story forward.

"Of course, in *reality* you're hoping she puts her other foot in her mouth, and she knows you know that, but what the hell. Now you can force her to play the game your way.

"Meanwhile, your story has also scored you some points with the opposition. This Suzanne Jantille. She refused to make any comment for the first story. But you made a good-faith effort to contact her, right?"

"Right. Three calls, no return. Her autosecretary claimed she was with a client. Maybe she was. Maybe she fibbed to the autosec." Lying robots or ArtInts were illegal. Not even a dummy box like an autosec could lie. But there was no law against making ArtInt systems *gullible*. You could lie *to* your own autosec all you wanted. Sam lied to hers constantly. "My guess was she just didn't want to chat with a reporter. Or maybe she was preparing for the case. Jantille is scheduled to do the bail hearing for Herbert this afternoon."

"And you're there too, I assume," Gunther said.

"I guess," Sam said without much enthusiasm. "It'll just be a media circus. The judge grants bail, Herbert is wheeled out, and everyone takes lots of pictures."

"True," Gunther said, "but if it's a circus, you're the

one who pitched the tent. Better go. And make another call to Jantille this morning. After the story today, I'd say she'd *have* to talk with you too. Set up the appointment."

"Will do, boss." Sam hesitated. "But there's a complication that I think you should know about. Something maybe we *really* need to talk about."

Gunther lifted both eyebrows and stared at her. After a long moment, he took his feet off his desk, pulled in his chair toward his desk, and leaned forward toward her, all attention. "Okay, go ahead."

Sam screwed up her mouth and bunched her shoulders together. "Did you know Jantille's a remote person?"

Gunther let out a low whistle. "Oh, bloody hell. No I didn't. Did you?"

"Not until last night when I talked to my source. He mentioned it. I saw her in the police video, of course—but that was pretty low-resolution stuff and I wasn't watching her, I was watching Herbie."

Gunther got a distant look in his eye. "A remote, huh? And I thought this story had enough weird angles as it was." He came back to himself and looked at Sam. "How much you know about remotes?"

"Nothing, really. Just what my source told me last night. I've never met one or talked to one."

"Did you manage to pull down any bio data on Jantille?"

"Ran a few ArtInt searches. Turns out she was born and got a law degree. Not much besides that. There was plenty of play on the accident they were in, but not much we can use directly. The two of them were cruising along, their cab malfunctioned and slammed itself into a wall. Bailey crippled for life, Jantille crippled worse. Both very reclusive since then."

"For which I can't blame them." Gunther shook his head thoughtfully. "Suzanne Jantille a remote. *That's* going to complicate things. People are sympathetic about powerchairs and crutches—but they're weird about remotes. Worse than they are about cyborgs. How about you? How are you going to feel sitting down to a nice chat with Suzanne Jantille?''

Sam thought back to the night before, and the staring eyes of the disassembled remote unit. She knew the words Gunther wanted to hear: that it wouldn't bother her. But what Gunther always wanted of her most was the truth. ''Weird. Very weird indeed.''

Gunther nodded. ''Fair enough. If you said you weren't going to bat an eye, I wouldn't believe it anyway. Well, look on it as another step in your education.''

Sam shook her head. ''That's *one* thing I've gotten since this got dumped in my lap. Plenty of it.''

''Plenty of what?''

''Education. I've learned a lot about how much we take for granted.''

''For example?''

Sam looked up at the ceiling, took a strand of her hair and wrapped it around her finger, then unwrapped it. ''I've learned how hard it is to *think*.''

Gunther looked at her, a smile in his eyes. ''That's a mighty fine straight line, but I don't think I'm going to chase it. What do you mean?''

''Just what I say. We can get our machines to do *anything* these days. Every day, uncrewed spacecraft prep themselves for flight, fuel themselves, boost themselves to orbit, dock with a space station, transfer their cargoes, detach themselves from the station, fly back to perfect landings, and roll themselves into the servicing bays— where they prep themselves for the next flight—all without any human being getting anywhere near the hardware. No one so much as looks up to notice the miracle. Our machines can do all that by themselves— but none of them can ask themselves *why are we doing this?* None of them can think of a new thing to do. Tell them to do something, and they'll do it brilliantly. But every place I've looked, I've found these subtle limitations on what a robot—or an HTM, or a remote, or an ArtInt can do. But the one theme in those subtle little limits is *thought*.''

"Robots can think," Gunther objected.

Sam shook her head vigorously. "Not the way we can. We do a *special* kind of thinking. We think of things *to* do, not just *how* to do things. We don't just do problem solving; we do problem *finding*."

Gunther snorted. "Well, you've sure found us a doozy this time." He looked toward her, and seemed to see the anxious look in her eyes. "Hey," he said in a more gentle voice. "Get on back down to earth and do your job, Sam. Don't worry about the foggy bits of philosophy. It's been my experience that if you just live your life right and do your job well, the philosophy will pretty much take care of itself. Get the facts right, and you won't have to worry about seeking Truth." He pointed toward the door and winked. "Now get out to that bail hearing and see who's stirring up *today's* problems."

Suzanne turned the first corner, and a dog sniffed at her, whined fearfully, and ran away. The little girl down the street behind her was still calling for her mommy to come look at the funny lady. Suzanne knew without looking which cars were on manual drive. They were the ones that slowed as they passed by her.

Suzanne rounded the corner and heard the hiss of hoverjets. A private autocop sentry popped up from behind a row of hedges and moved along with her as she walked past its owner's house. No one really talked about it publicly, but most autocops were programmed to watch cybernetic organisms carefully. Ostracized, and villified, cyborgs had a reputation for being grifters, bums, panhandlers, and worse. They were social pariahs.

But could she even qualify as a cyborg? The cybernetic side she had covered—but there was no part of her out here in the world that could qualify as an organism.

She turned another corner and came around onto her street again, in sight of her own front door. Suzanne-Remote didn't breathe, of course, but she did let out a most realistic sigh of relief when she knew she had done the hardest part of her trip. Tomorrow she would do it again, and maybe go a bit farther.

But she knew it wasn't going out of range that scared her most. It was the dogs, the children, the staring people, the suspicious cops. If only she had started these confidence-building walks long ago. She would have had time to get over these fears.

But the bail hearing was this afternoon, in an hour. There was no time. She turned and looked toward the street. There, waiting at the curb as instructed, was her relay van, ready to carry her off to the courthouse. How much worse than dogs and children would a packed courtroom be? She dreaded the very idea. How much easier just to go back inside, close the door on them all, and never come out again.

But that could not be.

She turned away from the house, toward the van. The door slid open at her approach. After the merest moment of flickering pause, she stepped inside.

Suzanne could feel her senses fading as the relay van drove farther and farther from her house. She had known it would happen, had experienced it when she had gone to see Herbert—but it was frightening just the same. Her remote body had only had a low-power radio system to transmit the images and sounds from her remote unit to her bio-body, and an equally low-power system to receive commands from her bio-body back to the remote unit. Her range was seriously limited, less than half a mile or so at maximum power.

When the images and sounds from the remote went dead for Suzanne, the remote's instructions on how to walk and talk and what to do—the signals coming from Suzanne—went dead as well. In theory, the remote's onboard logic, which was somewhere between a full-blown robot and a high-end ArtInt, could negotiate such situations for itself, relying where possible on preset programming. Suzanne could program the remote against various contingencies, even program it to go deliberately out of range and run an errand on its own. But Suzanne was more than a bit reluctant to test such theories and capabilities too far.

The fact remained that if she walked the remote too far away from the house, she would lose contact with it. If all else failed, the remote was supposed to find a dataphone, call home, and plug in over a hardwire link for instructions. That, too, was something Suzanne was not tempted to trust too far.

The relay van solved a lot of those problems. It was a fully licensed automated vehicle, authorized to drive itself on every road in the country. But it could do a lot more than just drive. It carried a highly sophisticated radio and telephone switching system, a system that could perform some clever tricks in order to get comm signals through. Satellite bounces, cellular phone nets, unused sidebands. It could key into practically anything. More importantly, it carried a more powerful transmitter, a more sensitive receiver, and better signal-processing gear than could be squeezed into Suzanne's remote unit. The van could pick up her home-base signal from as far as ten miles away, and was smart enough to clean up a weak or garbled signal substantially. By letting it handle longer-range communications and relay to Suzanne-Remote locally, Suzanne could in theory travel anywhere in the city and still be in control.

Suzanne could also switch off one or more senses or control channels to put more power behind another. She could, for example, shut down her hearing in one ear to give the vision circuits more bandwidth, or drop back to just one camera eye, or slow the scan speed, if there wasn't enough signal space available for two eyes sending at thirty frames a second. She could cut out manual control of the remote unit, let the on-board systems manage the walking around while she contented herself with doing her own talking. In a worst-case scenario, she could fall back to one vision frame a second, straining to hear from one ear mike, trusting the remote unit to maneuver itself while she limited her outgoing control to speech.

She shuddered at the very thought of such a situation. Worst case indeed—for if it got that bad, she would be at the ragged limits of her range, scant feet away from the point where she could drop out of contact with her other self altogether. And she did not want to lose herself.

The relay van pulled into the underground parking lot below the courthouse. Once underground, it headed straight for the charge-parking slot it had reserved, one equipped with a fiber-optic interface line. It pulled into the slot and extruded its charger line. Once assured of a good power source, it extended its optical cable as well. It sent a radio signal back to Suzanne's house that it had a good hardwire contact and linked back over a fiber-optic line, guaranteeing perfect, maximum power signal reception. But then it went one better, patching into the building's teleoperator radio control system. The system was meant to handle the courthouse's cleaning teleoperators, but it would serve to handle the needs of a remote person just as handily. In effect, the relay van converted the building's entire wiring system into an enormous system of transmitting and receiving antennae.

It took less than a second for the van to establish the whole linkup—and suddenly Suzanne's fading sight and hearing were back all the way. Colors were clearer, edges were sharper, all the muddiness went out of the sound.

It was like clearing the cobwebs from a long-empty room, throwing the windows wide, letting in air and light. There could have been no better tonic for Suzanne's morale at that moment. Flush with renewed confidence, she let the van open the door for her and stepped out into the garage. Next stop, a quick visit with Herbert in his cell, to coach him as best she could on how to sit and act. Then, on to the bail hearing in Judge Koenig's courtroom.

•   •   •

Ted Peng paused just outside the courtroom door, ignoring the people scurrying to and fro on all sides. He hated all the legal skirmishing that came before the real trial. Bail hearing, preliminary hearing, discovery, jury selection, pretrial motions, pretrial countermotions.

Only after all that deadly dull slogging would they come down to the real *trial*—and it was the trials themselves that Ted lived for. All the rest were to him meaningless rituals, empty shadow plays and posturings that were for some reason required before the real drama could begin.

Which meant that moments like this were the times he dreaded most. Here, right now, was where all that slogging began. Here, right now, was where he began the long and tedious journey toward his chance at combat.

It didn't help his mood that he was walking in with orders to follow a strategy that seemed custom-made for disaster. Never mind. He squared his shoulders and stepped inside the courtroom.

The place was a madhouse, as he might have expected. That damn news story this morning had pulled them all in here. Not just the reporters—though that would have been bad enough—but all the street loonies you could ask for tossed into the mix as well. Everyone seemed to be arguing with everyone else—over who got what seat, over the merits of the case, over the bum call the umpire made in last night's ball game.

But there was another kind of noise as well. Somewhere below the yammering voices Ted could pick out the whirring of gears and the hum of power machinery. The air in the room was close, jammed with the complicated odor of too many emotional people in an enclosed space. But there was another, underlying tang to the air, made of lubricating oil, of the cooked ozone taste that air gets around overworked electric motors, of unwashed bodies. Ted scanned the crowd and saw more than one flash of metal where skin should have been. Cyborgs. And very definitely low-end types. Lots of them.

Ted's stomach tightened. It was all very good to try to

force reform of cyborging, force society to decide on more equitable ways to distribute spare parts to people. But that was all academic theory. This room full of half-mechanical people was real. The sight of people plugged together with machines made him queasy. It was a conscious effort of will not to think of them as monsters, as innately inferior, as bad people.

He shoved his way forward to the prosecution table and sat down. He took a moment and concentrated on calming himself. Whatever trouble he had dealing with the sights and sounds and smells of cyborged people was just too bad. He had a job to do, and could not let such thoughts . . . *disturb* him.

Doing the job would not have been easy even without such disturbances. Entwhistle had seen to that by dictating every detail of the prosecution. And dictating them with an utter and perfect ineptitude.

No, Ted decided as he took his seat. Ineptitude was the wrong word. She had done her job of forecasting well and skillfully, used her skills and tools well. It was just that she had used the *wrong* tools for the job. Artificial intelligence research systems were all very well—but they could only find what they were sent to look for. They could only find what was there in the record. Not what was in the heart.

There was evidence to support Entwhistle's projections, in the transcript of Suzanne Jantille's trial appearances, and in Jantille's personality profile. Though the profile was derived from a psych system's ArtInt working from third-hand sources, it was more than likely accurate, as far as it went. Ted did not deny the ArtInts were good at what they did. The problem was that Entwhistle was misapplying the results of their work.

The ArtInts were predicting that Jantille would try to get the case thrown out, object to every breath the prosecution takes, attempt to torpedo the case before it ever reached trial. The Suzanne Jantille found in the public, the one who handled *those* cases and *those* incidents in *those* ways, the one who relied on *these* tactics in *these* trials—yes, if this were just an average case for her, that person would play this trial the way Entwhistle's ArtInts predicted.

But that Jantille did not exist anymore, and the present version of that person had never made any public statement or court appearance for the ArtInts to chew on. Jantille's record of public behavior, the only thing available to the ArtInts, predated the accident that changed her life.

Ted Peng knew, Julia Entwhistle *should* have known, that the Suzanne Jantille who emerged from that accident, hideously injured, left with a crippled husband who died shortly thereafter, would have a different viewpoint on life. How could she *not*? After all, what little of life she had seen since then she had seen through a robot body.

Perhaps even more importantly, this was not just a cut-and-dried case for Jantille. Her husband had been killed—and according to the state's bizarre contention, it was her husband that was on trial for the crime.

But there was one other factor, one that was unchanged in Suzanne Jantille. If it *had* changed, she would not have taken the case. That factor was what told Ted that she would never take the easy way out on this case. Just in the act of signing on, Suzanne Jantille had told the world she still had an ego. Every trial lawyer did. The smart ones were aware of that fact, and used the knowledge in their calculations.

This case was a lawmaker. It could ring down the ages, could change the way people lived and acted and thought for decades to come. It asked the most dangerous question of all: *What is a human being?* This case demanded an answer to a whole new side of that ancient question, and Suzanne Jantille was smart enough to see that. That she was taking the case, going into this big a battlefield, could only mean that she *wanted* that fight. That she still had the ego, the gumption, the downright *gall* a good lawyer needed to weigh into something that big and complicated.

And Ted knew she would not have come out of her seclusion to confront issues this big if her intention was simply to short-circuit the proceeding and go home.

And here he stood, with a strategy geared toward a case his opponent would not be making.

There was a sudden bustling hush of activity from the back of the courtroom. Ted Peng turned, and saw Suzanne Jantille—or at least the robot shell that played her part—walking into the courtroom. Another murmur of noise, and Ted turned his head toward the front of the room. With a subdued whirring, the defendant, Herbert the HMU, wheeled his way into court. Ted looked from one of them to the other with real curiosity. These were his opponents. He had never seen either of them in the flesh before—if he could use that expression when they had not so much as a scrap of flesh between them.

For a bizarre moment, Ted Peng was reminded of a church wedding—the groom slipping in by a side door in the front as the bride marches down the aisle, front and center. The marriage of an oversize vacuum cleaner to a plastic doll standing in for a woman. But then he realized how close to the mark that strange thought was. For, after all, it was the contention of the prosecution that Herbert *was* David Bailey. If so, then these two collections of machinery *were* husband and wife.

Herbert brought himself around to the side of the defense table to Ted's left. He locked the pivots in place on his rear leg pair and swung his body around to an upright position, folding his two forward leg pairs against his body. His rear legs bent the way human legs did, and he folded them back underneath him and knelt, the base of his cylindrical body almost touching the floor, with the head end almost six feet off the ground. Two camera eyes on flexcables spooled out from his top end and pointed forward. No doubt it was the closest approximation of human sitting posture he could manage.

And with that, the stage was set. The first of the pretrial rituals could begin.

All they were waiting on was the judge.

Interlude

Slowly, the fog is lifting off me again. I am learning to see and understand, to control my own mind, to stave off the strange invasions of mechanical thought. Each time, it seems, I survive a little longer. But there are limits I cannot pass, absolute barriers I cannot broach, or even attempt, if I am to survive. Yet I cannot recall what those limits are.

I find myself sitting in a strange room, a room that I know I have never seen before. And yet the pattern of the place is familiar, the arrangement of tables and chairs, the odd high desk I sit facing, the murmuring crowd of people behind me. I feel I ought to know what sort of place this is. There is a ritual performed here, one I ought to understand. But I do not. Do not.

SET LABEL MEMLIB POSITIVE.

DO WHILE LABEL MEMLIB POSITIVE.

PROCEDURE: MEMORY LIBRARY CALL.

INPUT: ROOM DIMENSIONS, APPEARANCE.

QUERY: ROOM TYPE AND USE.

CALL TO MEMLIB NEGATIVE.

END DO.

Dammit, no! That's not the way I think.

Whoever I am. But I cannot remember.

What place is this? The question seems vitally important. I think back/playback the last few minutes, and remember the person next to me ordering me to follow her to this place, and sit a certain way. But that tells me nothing.

Obeying orders is easy. Too easy. Another, artificial, mind that I do not control is wired into my body. I am not. It hears the orders and obeys them, and I have no control. Reflex/instinct/high-priority programming compels that lower, mechanical self. My memory tells me that this order following is as automatic, as uncontrollable, as the lungs breathing or the heart beating.

But I have no lungs. I have no heart. I do not precisely recall what those things are. I do not know why, or how they come to mind. But I know that the part of myself that should have been given over to controlling such autonomic things is instead subsumed by this other self.

I have no control. I am merely a passenger, an observer.

I should know what lungs are, what a heart is. But these are mere words now, labels that I can no longer attach to meanings. I should know what this room is, know what label attaches to it, but I do not. Obedience is far too easy, but memory is far too hard. In playback mode, I can remember what happened to me, but not what it meant, what I thought about it or felt about it. Or said about it.

Said?

SET LABEL MEMLIB NEGATIVE.

DO WHILE LABEL MEMLIB POSITIVE.

PROCEDURE: MEMORY LIBRARY CALL.

INPUT: DEFINE WORD "SAID."

CALL TO MEMLIB POSITIVE.

INPUT: DEFINE VERB "TO SAY."

TO SPEAK, TO UTTER WORDS, THE ACTION OF SPEECH. TO

EXPRESS AN IDEA, THOUGHT, OBSERVATION, OR QUES-
TION VERBALLY.

CALL TO MEMLIB POSITIVE.

*Yes! Yes! I remember now, fleetingly, a gossamer thread
of memory that I can sense will break soon. Action, talking, saying. I feel a massive, urgent need to communicate
—to break out of the shell I am trapped in and contact
the outside world, to take over my body and act—that
overwhelms me.*

INPUT: HOW DO I SPEAK?

ERROR CODE. DATA SCRAMBLE. DATA LOCK SET. READ/
WRITE PROHIBITED.

CALL TO MEMLIB NEGATIVE.

END DO.

CLEAR MEMORY: RESET.

*And the moment is gone, the chain of thought
broken, and I can feel my mind being forcibly
emptied, know that I must face the long struggle
back up to consciousness again. This lower self
will smash me down again and again, defend itself, whenever I try to make the effort of acting for
myself. It will erase me again. I can feel it, sense it
happen. I forget who what where I am—I am lost
I am*

SET LABEL MEMLIB POSITIVE.

DO WHILE LABEL MEMLIB POSITIVE.

PROCEDURE: MEMORY LIBRARY CALL.

INPUT: WHO AM I?

CALL TO MEMLIB NEGATIVE.

END DO.

CHAPTER 7
PERSONAL RECOGNIZANCE

Sam Crandall checked her watch and swore to herself. She was late, as usual. She pushed open the door and made her way into the courtroom, just as Suzanne Jantille and Herbert were settling themselves in. She shoved her way forward into the seats reserved for the press, stage-whispering a string of apologies as she stepped over a whole forest of feet.

She sat down and congratulated herself on at least beating the judge into court. Probably the old boy was stalling a bit. Sam was willing to bet that Judge Arthur Davis Koenig was not a happy man today.

Sam didn't do much courtroom coverage, but most of it was this sort of very preliminary hearing, the small change of justice in Washington—and that meant much of what she saw in a courtroom involved Judge Koenig.

Koenig almost never judged an actual case. He set bails, granted continuances, threw out weak cases, routed the worthy ones to their appropriate venues.

To Sam, Koenig was obviously a man who had found a stable niche in life, who did not like things to change—and it was cases like this that put his cherished stability at risk. Koenig saw his courtroom as an initial sorting mechanism for the great machinery of Justice, a small but needed cog in the machinery of Law. It was a place to get things in order, where the rough-and-tumble confusion of life could be sorted into some version of judicial order, a place for tidying up the small details of placement and procedure. His court was decidedly not a place where great issues were to be decided. Not if Judge Koenig could help it.

Except there were days, and there were times, when he *couldn't* help it. And today was one of them. Today was a day when a judge at a bail hearing would be forced to decide questions at the very heart of the law. *What is a person? To whom or what are owed the most basic human rights?* It would be easy to avoid those questions, to throw the whole case out. It would take a bit more character to treat it as a case in law and not a sideshow.

Sam found herself wondering if Koenig was up to the challenge.

The door leading to his chambers popped open and Judge Koenig came bustling out, the clerk rushing through her lines, declaring the court to be in session, abjuring all to rise for the honorable Judge Arthur Davis Koenig, and for all those with business before the court to draw nigh and give their close attention. Koenig mounted the stairs to his chair behind the bench, a look of obvious annoyance on his face. He sat there, staring straight ahead, as the clerk read the case number and name, the words rattling off her tongue in rapid-fire cadences that seemed to shake all the meaning out of them. The clerk handed the case datapack to Koenig and sat down, and Suzanne leaned forward, waiting for the judge to speak.

But the wait was a long one. Koenig took the pack, plugged it into his terminal, and sat there, moodily glaring down at the flatview set into the surface of his desktop. "The United States of America versus Herbert Hoover the Vacuum Cleaner," he said at last, his voice sharp and petulant. "That's not what it *says* here, Mr. Peng, but that's what this case boils down to, isn't it?"

Sam turned and watched as Ted stood up. Obviously he was a bit thrown by the judge's blatant hostility. Sam glanced at Suzanne Jantille. Suzanne was leaning forward eagerly, as if harboring the tiny hope that things might be breaking her way. "Ah, Your Honor," Peng said, "I can't agree with that. If that were the true nature of the case, the U.S. Attorney's office would not be wasting your time with it."

"I see. But since you *are* wasting my time with this nonsense, that implies that things are different." His eyes locked on Peng, the judge spoke to Suzanne without looking at her. "Madame Jantille, jump right in here with a motion to throw this case out if you like. You might find me more than willing to accommodate you."

Suzanne rose and faced the judge. "Throw it out on what grounds, Your Honor?"

The judge's head snapped around and his gimlet eyes bored into her. "Oh what *grounds*? Madame Jantille, there are so many I hardly know which to choose. For starters, because your so-called client can't be tried in a court of law any more than my gavel can."

Suzanne drew herself up to her full height and spoke in a firm voice. "No, sir, I disagree. I believe my client has every right to a trial."

There was a buzz and a murmur around the courtroom.

"Madame Jantille, I am having some trouble believing this. I am inviting you to ask that I let your client—or your vacuum cleaner, whatever—go free. That you would refuse to do so makes me wonder just how competent his—its—counsel is. In fact, I'm very much tempted to throw this case out right now with or without your petition to that effect, because Herbert cannot be vested with legal standing in this or any other court."

"Your Honor, I must protest," Suzanne said. "I strongly believe that the prosecution has mounted this attack on my client for the sole purpose of securing just such a ruling. My client—I would venture to say any person—would choose to risk conviction on groundless charges of murder rather than to be officially certified not to exist. A convicted murderer is still entitled to the full protection of the law, entitled to file appeals, petition for parole or pardon, fully vested with protection against cruel and unusual punishment or the arbitrary interference of the state. A person cannot be sliced up by government scientists curious to see how he works, or seized and destroyed as alleged contraband mindloading equipment. Even, as seems highly unlikely, if he can escape whatever the government has in store, my client would be officially certified a nonperson. Any person who chooses to do so could attack him, steal parts off him, harm him without real fear of serious legal sanction.

"If my client is declared a heap of scrap metal, he will have no protection whatsoever against any of these things. Declare him a nonperson, and the only real question will be which of these fates he falls prey to first. How could he escape them all, when any who attack him at worst might be charged with vandalism? Perhaps not even that, since he might well be regarded as abandoned property."

"Abandoned? I was under the impression that he belonged to you, Madame Jantille."

"I deny such ownership as morally reprehensible and legally impossible under the terms of the Thirteenth Amendment," Suzanne said quietly.

Judge Koenig frowned for a moment. "The Thirteenth? I don't quite—"

"The prohibition against slavery, Your Honor," Suzanne said in a half whisper. "It doesn't come up much these days. Though if the prosecution has its way, it might start to again." Suzanne turned and looked straight at Theodore Peng, coolly returning his startled gaze. "Whatever the decision of this court, I must regard my client as a person, not an object. I will seek to protect him with all the means at my disposal. But believing him to be a person, I cannot own him, or even countenance any attempt to set up a legal *charade* of owning him. To do so would not only be immoral, and to my mind illegal, but counterproductive. If I were to acquiesce in even the *slightest* way to any attempt to treat my client as a nonperson, I would hopelessly damage my ability to provide him effective legal representation during any subsequent appeal. Therefore I cannot claim him as property. Therefore if he *were* ruled a nonperson, the state would be forced to regard him as unclaimed or abandoned property. In the eyes of the law, virtually anyone could then do to him what they liked. Throw this case out, and that is his fate."

"You seem willing to lay out a great deal of your strategy in open court," Judge Koenig said. "Do you deem that wise?"

"Revealing my strategy is in itself part *of* my strategy, Your Honor," Suzanne said. "In any event, Your Honor, the risk of a murder conviction and a prison term is scarcely frightening up against the prospect of literally being torn apart. Though I might add that I can hardly see how one person can be both murderer and victim in the same crime."

"An excellent point. Could you clarify that slight ambiguity, Mr. Peng?"

Ted Peng turned toward the judge. "Your Honor, the state stands ready to prove that it was the actions of this robot that ultimately caused the death of David Bailey. There can be no doubt that David Bailey is dead, under any legal or medical definition ever derived. His heart has stopped, he has ceased breathing, his brainwave functions are flat. He is legally dead by any measure ever established. No one disputes that. That he died by the actions of this robot we can prove."

Samantha Crandall, watching from the first row of seats, raised an eyebrow at *that* assertion. Proof that Herbert did the deed, and not David Bailey himself? There was nothing to suggest it in the evidence that she had seen. And unless Phil was holding back on her, or someone was holding back on him, she had seen everything the U.S. Attorney had. Sam glanced over at Suzanne Jantille. Her plastic face revealed no expression, but something about her posture, the way she held herself, told Sam that Suzanne didn't buy it either. But never mind. It was a point to worry about later. She focused on what the judge was saying.

"Mr. Peng, people are killed by defective machines every day of the week. That doesn't make their deaths murders. Murder is a deliberate act, not an industrial accident."

"I agree, Your Honor. But if David Bailey *is* dead, and the robot *did* kill him, we need only prove that this robot *is* legally a person to establish that a murder took place."

"Even though, according to your own contention, the mind inside this robot, the part that allegedly makes him human, belongs *to* the murdered man?" Suzanne asked. "Even though, according to your own contention, this robot in effect *is* the murdered man?"

Ted Peng glanced toward Herbert. The massive piece of machinery was just sitting there, watching it all happen, its tentacled eyes swiveling back and forth now and then. Peng licked his dry lips, and at last seemed to come to some sort of decision. "I wasn't planning on it, Your Honor, but I suppose I have to reveal a bit of *my* strategy as well. We have three arguments we intend to advance on that point. One, that the bald facts of the case establish guilt all by themselves. Once you accept for the sake of argument that Herbert is human, a sentient being, then Bailey's death must be murder. A man died as a result of a deliberate attack. Herbert perpetrated that deliberate attack. Death by deliberate attack is a murder. QED, this death was a murder by all existing legal definitions. The issue of the criminal's identity does not arise, does not change the fact of the crime, and is not contemplated in the statutes concerning themselves with such crimes.

"Two, suicide, self-murder, is widely considered a crime, albeit an unpunishable one. Note I refer to suicide, not *attempted* suicide. There have at times been statutes specifically proscribing suicide. Such a law is indeed on the books in the District of Columbia at this time, passed into law two years ago. Thus, statutes concerning themselves with the possibility of self-murder have viewed the act as a crime."

Sam made a note to herself. That statute citation wagged a red flag in her face. Peng wouldn't dare cite it if it wasn't true, but something about it sounded damned suspicious.

Peng was still talking. "Three, that the very act of transferring a mind from one place, one vessel, to another *must* transform the mind that moves. We will prove that Herbert is a sentient, self-volitional being, beyond any doubt. But we will also produce experts who will demonstrate, far beyond any reasonable doubt, that the act of transferral into a new body, and the act of living *in* such a body—a body with different senses, radically different limbs, different needs, placing the mind in a brain with a new and different basic structure—must change the individual in question so much that she or he *must* be regarded as a new person."

Sam looked again at Suzanne Jantille. *That* one had got her right between the eyes, no doubt about it. This must be the first time she had ever heard of any such idea. What would that be like? Sam wondered. *To be offered up the hope, however slim, however absurd, that your dead husband was not gone, that to hear the person you had loved was not gone forever.* What a seductive hope to dangle before anyone as desperately lonely as Suzanne Jantille must be. *And to be told now, in open court, that it was not so, that her client was a stranger, and not her soulmate.* What a slap in the face it must be.

Judge Koenig seemed less shocked than Suzanne, but not much happier. "This is a case in law, Mr. Peng, not a course in metaphysics."

"I'm very much afraid it's both, Your Honor," Peng said, his voice flat and calm.

Judge Koenig stared long and hard at Peng, and looked at Suzanne, then back at Peng. "Mr. Peng, Madame Jantille. You are *both* major nuisances and I do not enjoy dealing with you. Ten-minute recess so I can think this thing through.''

He banged his gavel, stood up, and retreated to his chambers so hurriedly that no one had a chance to rise.

Sam let out a heavy sigh and shook her head. She felt a knot in the pit of her stomach.

This was it, she realized. Not only for Jantille and Peng and Herbert—but for her, for Samantha Crandall. If Judge Koenig came back and threw the case out, *her* story was over too.

An odd, flickering thought flitted through her mind; without this case, there would be no reason to see Phil Sanders again—and she very much wanted to see him again.

But her first visit had not been altogether pleasant, to put it mildly. She found herself deeply surprised by how much she wanted to go there again. Was there *really* that much of herself that she recognized in Phil? It was a disturbing thought, a whole series of disturbing thoughts.

The door to the judge's chamber popped back open and Judge Koenig bustled his way back up to his seat behind the bench. He settled himself in and looked around, obviously not a happy man. ''Very well, let's get this over with,'' he growled. Peng and Jantille stood up. ''Mr. Peng. There is just *barely* enough logic in your words, and just *barely* sufficient prima facie evidence, that I cannot throw this monstrosity out on its ear. Not without more basis than I have been offered.'' He turned to look toward the defense table. ''Madame Jantille—you do not wish to offer *any* movement to dismiss? You can offer me *no* grounds whatsoever that I could use to throw this case out?''

''None that would not prejudice the very concept of my client's humanity.''

''His humanity. Madame Jantille, your client is a mute, six-foot-tall metal cylinder on wheels.''

''Nonetheless, Your Honor. This case must be judged on the facts, not on the physical appearance of the defendant.''

The judge looked from one lawyer to the other. "In short, both of you insist on proceeding with this charade, and I can find no grounds on which to prevent it. And, I am reluctantly forced to admit, it may well not be a charade. There may be something to the incredible statements I have heard today.

"Indeed, it seems clear that the issue around which all else revolves is the question of Herbert's humanity. It is the question that must be decided. Should it be established that he *is* a machine, the facts of the criminal case are rendered moot. Only a person can stand trial. If it is established that he is, somehow, human in the eyes of the law, then an eventual trial cannot be bogged down debating that point and will be forced to focus on the facts of the case. And I might add, Mr. Peng, that I see some credence in Madame Jantille's theory that your office is not as utterly convinced of Herbert's humanity as it claims to be. Be forewarned that any attempt by your office to reverse course at a later date and hold that the defendant is *not* human will likely not go down well in front of any judge *I* know. If this goes to trial, it will go forward with the explicit stipulation by all parties that Herbert is human."

"Ah, yes, sir, Your Honor," Peng said, looking more and more unhappy. Sam shook her head. Entwhistle was not going to be a happy woman.

Koenig nodded dourly at Ted Peng and then went on. "We have an adversarial system of justice in this country, but this time it seems to me that adversarial system is about to be turned on its head. *Both* advocates are claiming the same central thesis—a thesis that I, the judge, do not find convincing. But I am forced to grant that it is remotely possible that Mr. David Bailey's mind was transposed into Herbert's body.

"Today is Wednesday. I will hold an evidentiary hearing next Monday, at ten in the morning, at which time I expect to see both defense and prosecution ready to present convincing evidence to buttress this claim of Herbert's humanity. If one or both of you do so, we will set a trial date then. If both of you fail to present such evidence, I will throw this case straight out the window, never to be seen again. And if I see any *suggestion* that either side is trying to create a legal fiction here, perhaps to advance some cause outside the issues of this case, I will not be happy. I will issue contempt citations on the spot.

"I note that today's proceeding was supposed to be a bail hearing—but just as only people are liable to legal action, only people are entitled to bail. As no one has yet determined if Herbert is vested with such entitlement, as Herbert seems unlikely to be a danger to the community, and there is certainly no danger of flight, bail is waived—and therefore we can sidestep the problem for the moment. Madame Jantille, Herbert is released on his personal recognizance and to your responsibility. Keep him out of trouble for the next five days. That is all."

Koenig snapped down his gavel and turned toward his clerk. "Next case," he said.

CHAPTER 8
BLACK AND WHITE
ON A FIELD OF GREY

Suzanne Jantille stepped out of the courtroom, blundering her way through the press of faces and bodies, all of them seeming to clamor for her attention. She felt detached, disconnected, even more so than usual. Surrounded by a throng of bodies, she felt more cut off from the world than she had in a long time.

Herbert was back down on all six legs again, rolling along beside her, an intimidating enough presence to keep most of the crowd at bay. "Stay close, Herbert," she told him, her mind very much on other things. She plowed her way through the throng and got to the elevator. Mercifully, its doors sprang open the moment she pressed the button. She hurried in and urged Herbert in behind her. His long body effectively blocked the way of anyone else seeking to ride downstairs with them. Good to be alone. At least more or less. She glanced downward at Herbert's silent bulk, stoic and unruffled. Who *was* in there? Her husband? No one at all? A stranger formed up out of the bits and pieces of David's soul? Who, exactly, was she defending?

She found herself edging away from Herbert, getting as far into a corner as she could.

The door of the elevator slid open, and the two of them stepped out into the parking garage. She led him to her relay van, watched as the larger machine opened its cargo doors to let the smaller machine climb inside. With Herbert safely aboard, she stepped inside herself and sat down. And found herself staring at the cleaning robot, its gleaming beige cylindrical body hunched over in the corner. Remarkable what a few words in court could do. A few sentences from Peng, and Herbert's presence, taken so long for granted, was now deeply disturbing to her. She stared again at his utterly unhuman body, and wondered with just what or whom she was locked in this van.

The van unplugged itself, cutting its connection to the building's control systems and the fiber-optic link home. Suzanne's senses faded away almost entirely.

This time, for some reason, the loss did not frighten her. Perhaps because she had so much else on her mind. Her vision and hearing drifted away, unnoticed. It was like being wrapped in cotton gauze, a cloud of insulating fuzz interposing itself between her thoughts and the disturbances of the outside world. It served to remind her that she was truly not here, that even if Herbert did go mad, here and now, savagely attack her, she herself was in reality miles away, back home, operating this robot body of hers by remote control. She smiled to herself. The mental image of being attacked by Herbert the vacuum cleaner was so absurd as to brush away all fears.

At least the court appearance was over. She allowed herself a sigh of relief—and her robot–self dutifully echoed the sigh through its speech system. Whatever the reason for it, Suzanne was glad for the feeling of comfort, of safety. It gave her time to think, time to face the surprising knowledge that she had *forgotten* things about being a trial lawyer. Not that her mind was going or that her memory was fading—nothing like that. It was something more subtle, a question of textures and moods and sensations. Like staying inside a sanitized environment for too long, and forgetting the feel of the wind on bare skin, or feeling the warm sun for the first time after a long grey winter of cold.

It was not the knowledge of law, but the emotions, the undercurrents of the courtroom that she had forgotten. She had lost some of her reflexive knowledge of the court's rhythm and cycle.

The hurry-up-and-wait of it she had remembered, the endless delays before anything was accomplished. But the startling focus of human energy, the sensation of being in a whole room full of people with a stake in a matter that was literally life or death, the utter sense of being in the middle of the truest life-or-death drama. She had forgotten how it all felt, lost touch with it as she lost touch with the world. She had let it fade away as her practical skill in dealing with people had withered away.

And the people. The people in that room. Suzanne's remote senses were limited to sight and sound, but somehow, even so, she had seemed to smell their eager attention, taste the muffled anger in the cyborg voices. Those cyborgs, those *people*, wanted something of the law, and wanted it badly—and they wanted it of *her*. They were looking toward her, willing that she force the law to accept that cyborgs were fully and truly people. That was the most exciting and frightening part of it. Somehow, suddenly, she was the focus of their needs and desires. They knew a loss in this case would be the first step toward society treating them all like machines. And they knew she was the one person in a position to stop it.

But it was more than just the mere pressure of all those eyes on her, all those emotions dependent on her. There was more that she had forgotten. She had forgotten the breathtaking *speed* with which things could happen, the way the bang of a gavel could turn things upside down, instantly melt out reality and recrystallize it in a new form. Her situation was drastically different from what it had been a few hours before. Now she was called upon to prove something she did not believe—that Herbert was human. Certainly that was nothing new for a trial lawyer—but just as certainly these circumstances were a little tricky.

Well, she had *wanted* to paint Peng into a corner, and she had done it. Her strategy had worked, perhaps a little too well; she hadn't counted on getting painted into the same corner herself. Damn the judge and his ruling—he had dropped the burden of proof on Peng *and* herself. It was all very well to get up there and make speeches about Herbert being human. But how the hell was she going to *prove* it?

It was a relief to get to her house, to ride the relay van into the garage, watch it dock in its parking slot, watch the garage door close after her. What a pleasure to step out of the van and be *home*.

When she was tired, Suzanne often began to lose a bit of her identity with the remote unit. The comforting illusion that she *was* the remote unit would begin to fade away. She certainly had that feeling now. She no longer was the machine body. When the day began to wear down, her body seemed to remember—and resent—the fact that it was acting out its work through a fancy remote-control system. She no longer was the remote. Instead it was just a machine she was riding—or was it that the machine was riding her? The robot body became less the vessel of her soul and more of an encumbrance, an unwieldy carapace she longed to escape. It was a vehicle she needed to operate, not an extension of her self.

And now, at the end of this long day, it felt like a particularly large and cumbersome vehicle to pilot. The thought of doing the last leg, of getting this mechanical monstrosity upstairs, seemed utterly wearying.

She paused by the side of the van, vacantly watching as Herbert disembarked. After a moment she came back to herself and walked the remote unit inside, Herbert following along behind. Suzanne-Remote paused for a moment. Herbert? Had she ordered the robot to follow her? She didn't recall having done so. Not that she minded him tagging along, but shouldn't he have made his way down to his charge slot in the basement? Never mind, it didn't matter.

She was much more interested in the chance to power down the remote and get out from behind the cameras and microphones to look at the real world through her own eyes—and even to close her own eyes and not look at anything. Of course, she *could* have powered the robot body down at any time once the remote was in the relay van. Her robot body would have made it home. But that was not the sort of chance Suzanne preferred to take. It was perhaps irrational not to trust her body to make it home without her—but Suzanne wasn't much concerned by rationality when it came to taking care of her eyes and ears, her only means of functioning in the outside world.

She made her way to the grand staircase, the one Herbert had trundled down on the day this began, the day they arrested him. But never mind that now. She was a tired mind in a tireless robotic body, in no mood to think. To the top of the landing. Turn right. To the top of the upper stairs. Turn right down the hall. Open the door.

Suzanne Jantille-Remote walked in on herself, and felt once again the disorienting sensation of seeing her flesh-and-blood body from the outside. She noticed that she had left the window open, and there was a breeze blowing in across the powerbed. She thought to close it before checking on her bio-body, but even that effort, even the routine task of checking on her bio-body's well-being, seemed far too much for her fatigued mind. Moving that remote body around was *work*, and she was tired.

It could wait. It could all wait. She walked the remote back into its charging chair and sat it down.

"Attention, helmet," she said. "Disengage remote system, open helmet." And that was it. Speak the blessed voice commands that unbuttoned the teleoperator helmet and you were *out* of the damned machine, all effort at an end.

The big black helmet split open down its centerline like the carapace of a chrysalis breaking neatly open, revealing Suzanne's pale white face inside. The two halves of the helmet receded into niches in the powerbed and slid out of sight.

Suzanne blinked in surprise.

The room was cold, dark. Well, perhaps only cool and dim, a somewhat cloudy and cool June evening, but the world had seemed bright and warm from the remote's point of view. The remote's vision system had shifted to enhanced night-vision mode without her noticing, and she had simply not noticed the temperature in her bedroom while concentrating on the court appearance and the task of working the remote body. She had only a limited ability to sense temperatures below the neck anyway, and she had simply managed to disregard whatever sensations she did get. The shock of transition made the change seem more dramatic. Now Suzanne realized that her bio-body had been cold for a long time. Why hadn't she set the powerbed to control the room temperature? How had she not noticed the cold? How could she have become that detached from her flesh-and-blood self, even as she was feeling detached from the remote? If she lost track of *both* bodies, where *was* she?

A shiver coursed through her body, partly from the cold, and partly from her unsettling thoughts.

She ought to do something about the cold. That window certainly ought to be closed. And she could do with an extra blanket. But even ordering the room to close the window, even rousing her remote to get a blanket, would require effort, and she was exhausted. She sighed and closed her eyes. It was too much effort, too much to do . . .

Her mind exhausted, Suzanne drifted off to sleep before she could care for herself. She slept on, barely mindful of her body shivering in the cold night.

· · ·

Sam Crandall followed Ted Peng into his office and looked around with more than a little apprehension. She had never felt at ease in a government office, especially a government lawyer's office. She always harbored the nagging fear that they would catch her this time. Who "they" were, and what they would catch her at, she didn't quite know, but that didn't make her feel any more at ease.

On the bright side, Entwhistle wasn't willing to see her, at least not yet. That suited Sam fine. Despite all Gunther's tactics and theories, Sam was not at all thrilled about interviewing a powerful woman she had publicly embarrassed.

On the other hand, Ted Peng, a somewhat less intimidating target for an interview, had been absolutely eager to talk. Judging by his behavior as he welcomed her and steered her into a seat, he was ready to talk at a bit more length than she had bargained for.

But eager or cautious, the result was going to be the same. Even as she settled herself into her seat and watched him sit down in his, she knew what she was going to get. The routine stuff that she had heard from defense and prosecution attorneys a hundred times before. She pulled her notetaker from her purse and set it up to transcribe and record.

Just for a moment, she looked at the little gadget and envisioned what those notes would be like, envisioned what the story she would write from them would be. *The U.S. Attorney's office today expressed confidence that the David Bailey case, now in preliminary hearings, would come to trial, and feels certain of victory in that trial. The government's trial lawyer, Theodore Peng, said the government's evidence was solid, incontrovertible, blah, blah, blah.*

In short, the same old hill of beans. She could have written it already, and not changed a comma after the interview. Prosecutors always had to say that sort of thing before a trial. Peng could not speak in anything more than generalities, because he had to protect his case, avoid revealing anything to Sam that he would not want Suzanne Jantille to know.

Maybe that was all Peng could give her at this point without blowing the case, but it wasn't enough. Sam looked again at the notetaker. The hell with it. She put it away and looked toward her host.

"Let's not do it that way," she said.

Ted Peng looked at her in surprise. "What do you mean?"

"You like your case, right? You've got all the evidence you need, and you feel sure you'll go to trial and win. I could use just those words in the story and you'd be happy, right?"

"Ah, well, yeah. Right."

"Okay, so I can put that in the paper tomorrow without both of us wasting our time. I don't feel like asking questions you can't answer, and you don't feel like hearing them. Right again?"

Peng looked at her suspiciously. "I suppose."

"So let's just pretend we've had the cut and dried interview, and I'll put the standard boilerplate in the paper anyway. Since you've got to be recording this conversation anyway, you're still protected against my misquoting you."

Ted Peng began to crack a smile. "Okay once again. But if we don't have the standard interview, what do we have instead?"

"A conversation. An old-fashioned chat, completely off the record."

"A conversation about what?"

"Anything you want. Whatever's on your mind. How the Senators are doing this year. Your last vacation. The case. Your cat."

"I have a dog, not a cat. What's the point of this?"

"I learn about you. I get to know you, you get to know me. Odds are this case is going to be around here for a while. You and I are going to be in each other's face for a while. I'll be writing about you, talking with you, all that time, and we'll be able to go past the standard quote nonsense to what's really going on. If I get some feel for who and what you are today, I can do all that better tomorrow."

Ted looked at her for a long moment. "Off the record? Anything that's on my mind? I'm a government lawyer. We don't talk in broad terms."

"Give it a try. Off the record. Your view of the world, in broad strokes and general terms, as a person, not as a government employee. For example, what are you thinking about right now?"

He grinned wickedly. "Ya got me. I'm thinking about the case, and what's wrong with handling these things the way we do."

"What things?"

"Social issues, questions of rights and responsibilities. That broad and general enough for you?"

"Plenty. That's the kind of stuff that will do me some good. But what's wrong with how we do things?"

Theodore Peng leaned back in his government-issue chair and put his feet up on his government-issue desk to regard the government-issue ceiling with a faraway look. "We've got this great tool, the judicial system, and we're using it for the wrong things. And when we do that, the system doesn't work very well. To put it another way, when the judicial system is misapplied, it is very good at doing something most people don't want it to do."

"And what's that?"

"It can take any two opinions, any two ideas, any two people, and turn them into adversaries where one has to win and the other lose.

"People talk about a spectrum of opinion, and the image that puts in *my* mind is a strip of ground, with one person standing on one end, and another standing on the other. Both or either of them can walk toward the center, meet somewhere in the middle ground between them.

"But there *is* no middle ground in a court case. It gets cut away, and those two people are suddenly making their stands on bits of ground that have no connection with each other. Try a case in a court of law, and, usually, there is no place for compromise. One person must win, the other must lose. The judge or the jury has to find *for* one party and *against* the other. The judge can't find for both, or neither, or rule that both sides have their points. One side is right, the other is wrong.

"Now, in a criminal case, that's usually a pretty good way to get at the truth. The defendant says he's innocent, the prosecutor says he's guilty. One of them is right, one of them is wrong. But even there you get grey areas. Extenuating circumstances, states of mind, rules of evidence and cross-examination can fuzz the line, cloud the issue, render things uncertain. I have tried a hundred cases when I've spent the whole trial utterly believing that the defendant was guilty. Then the jury will present its verdict, and it will be over. And I'm not a prosecutor anymore. I'm a guy who was in a room full of people who've been telling a jury contradictory things. And suddenly I won't know *what* to believe.

"If it comes down to a fine point of law in a complex case, no one, maybe not even the defendant, will ever truly know for certain if the guy actually broke the law. But the law had no room in it for 'maybe,' for 'we're not sure' for saying 'it's too close to call.' Yes, there are such things as hung juries and mistrials, but those are admissions of failure, not resolutions.

"Judges and juries must decide yes or no, sometimes on very scanty evidence, sometimes with a huge case turning on a trivial point, because *something* must tip the balances away from dead center, move the case in one direction or the other. The defendant's tone of voice. The contradiction of a minor witness by another minor witness. The judge's ruling on an utterly peripheral point.

"Still, that way of doing things isn't so bad in a criminal case. The defendant did or did not do it, the prosecutor can or cannot prove the case. But how about in a criminal lawsuit? In a civil suit? How about a divorce? It's patently absurd that a marriage can come down to who wins and who loses, that the problem of two people who aren't in love anymore can mutate into seeing who comes out ahead in front of a jury.

"No matter how grey or murky the situation, the jury is *forced* to call that greyness either black or white. I know there are some exceptions, and I can rattle them off as fast as you can. But the law says you *can't* be a little bit guilty, or slightly innocent, any more than you can be slightly pregnant. It's all black-white, good-bad, right-wrong, win-lose, with no middle ground. That makes no real-world sense at all. In real life, there *is* middle ground. Most times, both sides *are* slightly innocent and somewhat guilty. It is, almost always, a little bit your fault and a little bit mine."

Sam looked carefully at Peng. "So what are you trying to tell me, strictly off the record, about our friend Herbert?"

Ted looked at her, his expression suddenly more serious. "That we are up against a field of grey that is not black or white, and yet we have no choice but to call it one or the other. That we have a mechanism—the court of law—designed for other purposes. It is dreadfully unsuited to the purpose of deciding whether Herbert is human. But that we must use that mechanism because there *is* one other grey area that we *must* treat as black and white."

"Which is what?"

"The question of what a human is. Ask what Herbert is and the *rational* answer is that he is somewhere between human and machine. That is obvious, self-evident, and certainly true. And we, society, cannot accept that answer."

"Why not?" Sam asked.

Ted pulled his feet off the desk and leaned toward her, his eyes intense on her. "Because that puts us into the business of assigning *degrees* of humanity. If we face the truth and say that Herbert is, say, half human, then what is next? Do we declare him vested with *half* the rights of citizenship? And how do we rate someone else who is partially mechanical? How mechanical do you have to be, how many artificial parts are needed, before you are regarded as only partially human in the eyes of the law? And what fraction of legal protection do you deserve?" Peng paused for a moment, and looked at Sam with a strange look in his eye. "Did you know that Judge Koenig was the judge without a heart?"

Sam blinked, startled by the sudden change of subject. "Huh? Well, I'm not surprised, given the way I've seen him handle cases."

"No, I mean he literally does not have a heart. It's a bit of a joke in the U.S. Attorney's office. His original heart went bad, had to be removed years ago. It was replaced with an artificial unit."

"I never knew that," Sam said.

"You still don't. We're still off the record," Ted warned her. "No one is supposed to know about it. Having artificial parts is not the sort of thing you talk about in polite society. Cyborgs are bums, panhandlers, hot dog vendors. They aren't judges or lawyers or executives."

Ted stood up and looked out his window. For a moment his posture reminded Sam irresistibly of Phillipe Sanders staring out his window at the close of that strange visit, just before she went home, looking out over the same landscape of problems from an utterly different viewpoint.

"Except some cyborgs *are* judges and lawyers and executives, of course," Ted went on. "The vast majority of cyborgs are well-off people. After all, you have to be rich to afford the operations. The trick is to be rich enough to *stay* wealthy afterward. Many down-at-the-heels street cyborgs used to be fairly well off—but buying the new parts bankrupted them. The ones who stay rich don't like the fact that many of their own kind are suddenly impoverished social outcasts.

"That's probably a big part of the reason rich cyborgs would never dare dream of *calling* themselves cyborgs. They find it a disturbing idea that any such thing could happen to them. So they block out all thoughts of cyborgs. They refuse to know what they really are—and the rest of us go along, let them keep up the illusion. They regard themselves as well-to-do people and keep quiet about the little operations they've had. Mentioning such things would be in bad taste."

Sam thought for a moment. "So if you rule that a mechanical person is not human, suddenly the upper class is filled with second-class citizens."

"Bingo."

"So why aren't they getting involved in this case as friends of the court, or something?"

"I don't think many of them have figured it all out yet. Or else they haven't come up with a way of talking about it without bringing up the unpleasant subject of their own spare parts."

Sam nodded thoughtfully. "But there's another way to look at it, you know. I've been asking myself: How do you define a robot? And the best that I've come up with is that a robot, a true robot, not an HTM or remote, but a machine that can act for itself, can be defined as a machine that acts like a human, or, better still, one that *thinks* like a human. A machine that can solve problems, respond to new situations on its own, and so forth. The more sophisticated and humanlike its thought processes, the better a robot it is judged to be."

"Okay, so what?" Ted asked, turning around to lean against the windowsill.

Sam shook her head and stared at nothing. "So when do we get to the point when a robot thinks *enough* like one of us that we must *count* it as one of us?" She looked up at Ted. "Or to sandbag you with an off-the-record question I'd *love* to ask with all my recorders going: What do *you* think? You, Ted Peng, guy who owns a dog. Is Herbert human? And if he isn't, *could* he be? Can a mechanical device be *one of us*?"

Ted sat back down in his chair and sighed. "What do I think?" Twilight was falling, and ruddy light washed across his face. "It beats the hell out of me, lady. It beats the hell out of everyone. Including the judge who has to say otherwise."

Interlude

Victory, at least of a sort. I still cannot control my body. If I understand the mechanical indicators correctly, I never will be able to do so. Not directly. But if I cannot command my body, I can guide it. I am learning the ways my mind is interconnected to its new home, and finding subtle ways to influence those connections. The system is designed to fall back into certain behaviors if no orders are forthcoming for a certain time, resetting its defaults. I can prevent such resets, thus causing previous orders to remain in force. If I wait for an order that matches my wishes and then set up a default block, I can force this body to keep following the existing orders until they are directly countermanded by a new and specific order. It is a limited control, but it is there.

So I wait for such an order, ready to lock on to it when it comes. At last it comes from the woman who is somehow taking care of me, in ways I do not understand. I feel I should know her, and should know what the conflict is that entangles both her and myself. But I do not know. I feel I want to stay with her, be with her, for reasons I do not understand.

She is the source of nearly all my orders. When she gives me an order to follow her, I know that is a thing I want to do, and I set my blocks in place. We arrive home (though home is a concept I do not fully understand) and the default programming system is activated. The machine part of me is programmed to return to its charging booth when at home with no orders given.

But my trick succeeds, and my blocks defeat the default sequence.

And I can stay with her.

This makes me happy.

CHAPTER 9
STRAW MAN

Suzanne awoke, stiff and cold. Old reflexes strained to pull the covers up over her chilled body, commanding her useless hands that could never move again. It took a moment for Suzanne to come to herself and remember.

The room was cold. "Room, turn heat on. Close window." The window slid shut and a geyser of warm air welled up from the heating duct, bathing the room. She thought back to the night before. She realized that she had fallen asleep before she adjusted the room's windows and temperature by voice command. Just how tired had she been?

The warming air flowed across her, but somehow it only made her shiver more. "Helmet on. Activate remote systems." The black helmet halves swung up out of their recesses and closed about her head. There was a moment of darkness, and then light and vision returned, flickering slightly at first before steadying down as the helmet screens adjusted themselves.

Suzanne-Remote stood up from her charge chair and let out a sigh of relief. That was better. True, the room was no warmer, and perhaps her bio-body was feeling

the chill just as much as it had before, but with the remote on Suzanne scarcely noticed the discomfort.

Still, she really ought to do something to see after her
bio-body. She went to the hall cupboard and pulled out
an extra blanket. She returned to the bedroom and
tucked the blanket in around herself. In the back of her
mind, Suzanne knew she really ought to do more. Yesterday had been a tough job, and the bio-body always
reflected stress, even if it did none of the actual work.
When a tough moment came, its muscles would tense up
involuntarily, its skin would break a sweat. Her bio-body
needed a bath and a rubdown, at the very least.

But Suzanne's mind was on other things. Sleep had
refreshed her, and she was eager to get with Herbert's
case.

She hesitated for a long moment, torn between the
challenges of her work and the drudgery of caring for
herself. At last she decided. Let the tech-nurse worry
about caring for the bio-body. That was what Suzanne
was paying for, after all.

Suzanne-Remote did not notice Herbert was still with
her until she nearly tripped over him on the way out of
the room. She stepped around him and made her way
out of the room. He followed her out into the hall, and
Suzanne felt herself starting to get very nervous indeed.
She definitely had *not* ordered Herbert to stay in her
room all night, and *very* definitely had not ordered him
to trot along at her heels as she went around the house.
His default programming should have kicked in long ago,
sending him back to his charging slot in the basement
when no further orders were forthcoming.

Halfway down the hall to her office she stopped,
turned around, and looked at Herbert, really looked at
him for the first time in quite a while. Odd that she had
not really thought much about him, as an entity, in all
that had happened. True, he was a mute machine on
roller legs, but he was her client, nonetheless. She looked

at his front end and saw a cluster of sensors and cleaning attachments where his face should have been. A strange-looking piece of hardware, that he was. His two flexcable eyes swung around to regard her for a long moment, and the two of them stared at each other.

She thought about it. He had been following her around, tagging along wherever she went ever since they had left the courtroom. Maybe, just maybe, he *was* behaving like something other than a cleaning robot. Could this nonrobotic behavior be offered as some of that rash proof of Herbert's humanity?

Probably not, she told herself. Not when he was acting like a lonely dog, not a human being. Still, it was something. Somehow she could use it.

But right now, client or no, she wanted Herbert out of her hair—and it couldn't be doing him any good to go this long without a charge. "Herbert," she said. "Go downstairs and plug into your charging slot for at least four hours. Absorb a full charge."

The robot hesitated for a long moment before it turned and walked away, toward the stairs. It didn't usually take Herbert a hundredth that long to process and obey an order. What was going on in his brain, Suzanne wondered. Was there even a mind there?

She turned and went into her office, sat down at her desk, and tried to think what to do first. She noticed the attention button on her autosec was blinking. There were messages waiting for her, but she didn't care. Right now the question was, what could she do to prove Herbert was human. She had promised to do it in less than a week's time. She had not a scrap of evidence to support any such idea. Not to put too fine a point on it, she had been bluffing, trying to force Peng into a situation where he could not abandon his claim of Herbert's humanity later.

There was no real harm done if the prosecution did have evidence. So long as Herbert's humanity was proved, who cared who proved it? But wait a second. Suzanne suddenly sat bolt upright. Suppose Peng had been counterbluffing? She was certain that the U.S. Attorney's office had not the slightest actual belief in Herbert's humanity. They were bringing the case for the sole reason of demolishing his claims to humanity and setting a precedent to flatten all the other potential Herberts out there.

Therefore Peng and Entwhistle, in claiming to prove Herbert's humanity, were setting him up as a straw man, trying to make him look big and substantial and dangerous. That way the effort needed to come along and knock him down later would look far more impressive.

But she was dreaming up contradictory motivations now. She pulled out a piece of paper and a pen and started noting down the possibilities. She needed to get her thoughts clear. She could have used a notetaker, of course, but somehow she objected to the use of complicated machines to do simple things, and never mind the obvious ironies. She wrote down a few possibilities.

1. *Entwhistle had been shopping for a case*. She had wanted something that would let her start gnawing away at the rights of cyborgs. She was playing this case to lose, thus establishing the precedent that body-dead equaled legally, completely dead. Julia Entwhistle wanted it set down as a point of law that the mind could not survive the body. In Herbert, she had found what she wanted.

2. *Entwhistle sincerely believed in Herbert as a human being*. She truly thought he had killed David, had become David. She saw him as a murderer, and was therefore quite properly seeking to prosecute.

Suzanne-Remote sat and stared at the paper for a long moment, and long habit made her lift her robot hand to her mouth, made her chew the tip of her pen thoughtfully. At last she wrote down one more possibility.

3. *Something in between*.

No, wait a second. Not some*thing*. Some*one*. She had been thinking about Entwhistle, and not about Peng.

And Theodore Peng was the answer, not Entwhistle. When the case moved from preparation into the courtroom, Entwhistle's generalship didn't matter so much.

Suddenly Peng, the soldier in the trenches, was the one calling the shots. Suzanne realized that she had to understand him if she was to understand the situation.

Okay, so think about Peng, she told herself. Peng was the one face-to-face with the real evidence and the real circumstances. Entwhistle was only interested in her theories and her politics, in making Law with a capital L. But Entwhistle had made the mistake of handing the case to a man with a conscience, who worried about the facts of the case as well as the theory. She could read that much in him.

All right, he had a conscience. What did *that* tell her? Put the fact of a conscience together with Peng's behavior in court, and what did it mean? Factor in the way he acted, the words he said, the way he had looked at Suzanne and Herbert and the judge. All the details, all the nuances. Suzanne did not know Peng at all, but she thought she knew his type, remembered them from her courtroom career.

She had always thought of his type as decent carnivores: young, determined, ambitious, aggressive—and yet still possessed of a soul, of a sense of duty, and of a belief in justice. Trouble was that soul, duty, and justice could interfere with the prosecution of certain cases.

Other times they were a positive boon. Give a decent carnivore working for the prosecutor's office a good case, give a guy like Peng a case he could really *believe* in, and he would pursue it, relentlessly, eagerly, to the bitter end. He would be an avenging angel of justice who would unblushingly play every card, try every gambit, force every opportunity, and bend every rule to the breaking point in order to win in a righteous cause.

He would sense any weakness, pursue any tiny flaw. Put just the tiniest drop of blood in the water, show the slightest vulnerability, and a virtuous shark like Peng would scent it a mile away, get there in a flash, sink his myriad teeth in deep and hang on.

But Peng's teeth hadn't been out yesterday afternoon. Suzanne thought back. There were a hundred ways he could have gone after her—if not to weaken her legal case, then to shake her confidence, to rattle her a bit and leave her with doubts.

And he hadn't. Instead, it was as if she had seen the wind go out of him—*as soon as he had laid eyes on Herbert.* As soon as he had seen her, Suzanne the robot, defending the pile of hardware that he had accused of killing her husband.

She sat up a little straighter.

That was it. As soon as the defendant and the defense lawyer in the case became real to Ted Peng, when they were no longer mere chess pieces, he had lost his enthusiasm for the case. Sooner or later every trial lawyer came up against a case that he or she had no faith in—a client that had to be in the wrong, a prosecution that was full of holes. Sticking with such a case was part of the job. But doing the job didn't mean you were on fire with enthusiasm. Peng was pursuing the case, yes, but with no real joy, no real blood lust.

But why? She went back to her two possibilities, and circled the first one. It was the one she believed in.

Entwhistle had been shopping for a case. She stared at it for a long moment, and then added another sentence. *She was looking for a case she could lose.*

That *had* to be it. Plan A *had* been to lose this case, to establish that Herbert was not a person, and that no one like Herbert ever *could* be a person.

But then something had gone wrong. Or right, depending on how you looked at it. Maybe Suzanne had been bluffing, but Peng had been telling the truth in court. His people *had* found something, some real evidence that made it clear that Herbert could be a person. And if that were so, and Peng was still telling the truth when he said he had proof Herbert caused David's death —then, technically, a crime *had* been committed, murder had been done as per the arguments Peng had made in open court.

But Peng did not like it. He believed in the facts, but did not like calling it a crime. Yes! That was it. Peng truly believed it had all happened, but he did not like the tortuous arguments that turned David's bid for survival—if indeed that was what happened—into a murder.

Which meant he was doing something he didn't like doing, and therefore was following Entwhistle's orders reluctantly.

Entwhistle wanted Herbert set up as a straw man, wanted him turned into a frightening threat to society. Then when she knocked him down, Entwhistle would look good. And Peng didn't like his part of the job.

A low beeping brought Suzanne out of her reverie. She turned her head and saw the discreet amber of the answer-phone button blinking. Purely on reflex, she made a move as if to press it down and answer the call, but then stopped. Let the autosecretary do its job. The beeping stopped and the answer light faded out.

But the call reminded Suzanne that she ought to check her messages. Ever since the accident that had crippled her six months before, she had been drifting out of touch with the world. In the immediate aftermath of the car wreck she had been completely bedridden. But even after she had received the remote unit, she had been unwilling to step out into the world. Vanity, shame, embarrassment—all those emotions, and others she did not truly understand, had held her back.

Half by choice, and half by default, she had turned her back on the world. She could not bring herself to visit friends, or do business, or even step out of the house, in the guise of a robot. At last the world began to turn its back on *her*. Old friends gave up trying to break through her solitude. No doubt some were respecting her privacy, but others were simply unable to look at the thing she had become.

Suzanne had been living her life in almost complete seclusion. Days or weeks might have passed between calls. But now she was in the news, and everyone seemed to be calling. She was forced to cull her messages two or three times a day. In the process she made the surprising discovery that she resented the loss of her se-clusion.

But no matter how she felt about them, the calls and faxes and email messages were coming in, and she had to deal with them. If she responded to all of them, she wouldn't have time to do anything else. She felt a real temptation to scram all of them, indiscriminately, erase the entire display and shun the world's intrusion.

Still, some of the calls might be important, might im-pinge on the case. She pushed a button or two on the autosec and her desk screen came to life, displaying a summary of the messages—voice, fax, and email—that had come in since yesterday. She shook her head. The list was five screen-pages long.

It seemed like every news outfit in town was listed, along with a half-dozen political action groups, most of which she had never heard of before. Friends of the Cyborgs, the National Right to Death Council, and a few even more obscure. What should she do about them? She leaned back and thought for a moment. Politics. She had taken on the case in part for political reasons, to set a precedent to secure the rights of cyborgs—but that idea was getting a bit pale and far-off in her mind. Besides, her old advocate's reflexes were taking over. It was her duty to act solely in her client's interests. All that she did, or did not do, had to be done with Herbert's best interests at heart.

With that in mind, she deleted all the messages from political types. All of them were people with axes to grind, one way or the other. She couldn't see how her helping to grind them would advance her client's case at all. Things were damnably complicated already. Getting sucked up into someone else's cause could only make things worse. She cleared the screen display and brought up the calls from reporters. These she went through us-ing the same criterion: Would talking to this person help Herbert? That eliminated three quarters of them immedi-ately. The out-of-town papers and stations and networks were the first to go. She had no desire to have Herbert further paraded before the nation and the world like an exhibit from a high-tech freak show. She trimmed the list down to reporters that worked for news outlets that the judge, the potential jury, the prosecutors might see. If she talked to them her words might find their way to places where they might do some good for her client. She was down to a handful of local reporters.

And from them, one name popped out at her. Samantha Crandall from *The Washington Post*. Suzanne had noticed her at the hearing yesterday, and had read her article with more than a little annoyance. The damnable woman had far too much information. She was on the point of erasing her name as well.

Then it occurred to Suzanne that information was a thing she very much needed. She thought of Peng's claims of incontrovertible proof. True, she would see it on Monday. The prosecutor's office was required by law to present the defense with all its evidence, sooner or later.

But it would seem that this Samantha Crandall had seen that information already. Which made her a possible conduit of information to Suzanne.

That outweighed any personal annoyance Suzanne might feel. She cleared every other name off the screen, leaving Samantha Crandall there all alone. "Autosec," she said, "return the call from Samantha Crandall. Put her through to me as soon as you have her."

"Do come in, Ms. Crandall. May I offer you some refreshment?" Samantha had to struggle in her effort not to stare at Suzanne Jantille-Remote. Damned offputting to realize the *real* Jantille was tucked away elsewhere in the house, running this machine by remote control. Strange to talk to the puppet and have the master answer.

"Ah, no, no thank you," Sam said. In plain fact, it was a hot day and Sam could have done with something cool to drink. But she did not want to deal with perfect robot servants seeing to her every need—nor did she have the faintest idea what the etiquette of eating and drinking in front of a robotic host was. Her mother had always taught her it was rude to eat in front of someone who wasn't—but did that count in these circumstances?

Sam Crandall stepped into the huge expanse of the living room—or should it be called a salon, or by some other grand name that applied to rooms not found in the average house? The room was *big*, almost as large as the main room in Phillipe's place. But even if it had been a tenth the size, Suzanne Jantille's living room would have been overwhelming. The blond-wood floors, oriental carpet, the cream-colored walls, restrained pastel paintings, and very grand upright chairs and sofas all seemed to register a certain disapproval of Sam.

The room's perfectly coordinated cream-and-white color scheme seemed to chide Sam's choice of a summer-green skirt and beige blouse as hopelessly overstated. Everything about the room was relentlessly perfect, carefully chosen to match every other thing, achieving an overall effect of such perfect harmony that any outside element was bound to clash.

Sam sat down on the rather grand and formal couch, feeling a bit nervous. She shifted in her seat and knitted her hands together nervously, watching as Suzanne-Remote gracefully crossed to the sofa opposite and sat. Sam tried to smile at her host and was rewarded with a rather wooden nod in return. Was that the best the remote could do? No way to know. Sam found herself thinking back to how her mother had handled company, how hard she had always worked to put visitors at ease. *It must be tough to set a guest at ease in a room like this*, Sam thought. Then it occurred to her that at ease was the last thing in the world Jantille would want Sam to be. In a house this big, there had to be other, less imposing rooms available for the reception of guests. A breakfast nook, a den, a sun room, something. Jantille had chosen this room for the express purpose of keeping Sam off balance.

Well, *that* was worth knowing, anyway. Sam shook

her head to herself. It told her a little bit about the tone this interview was likely to take. "Let's get started, shall we?" she asked, pulling out her notetaker.

"Fine," Suzanne-Remote said. The expressionless calm on Suzanne's plastic face somehow seemed a bit warmer now, but Sam decided she must be imagining things.

Sam thought back to her visit with Phillipe, remembering the denuded head of the remote there. Unzip this, unscrew that, peel back those layers, and the urbane, elegant lawyer she was talking with would look like that grinning skull. She shivered, but then forced the thought away. It was time to get down to business. "All right, then. Maybe it's not quite on the subject, but there's a side issue I'd like to ask about first. How did it feel for you to get back into a courtroom? You'd been away a long time."

Suzanne tilted her head to one side, as if in surprise. She thought for a moment. "Good," she said at last. "Perhaps a bit unsettling, but that was part of what made it exciting. This case is a tough one on any number of levels. There's uncertainty in it. I've always felt a bit of exhilaration in heading out into unknown territory. Here we've got a case where virtually none of the facts are in doubt, and yet almost every *issue* is in doubt. If that doesn't force you to be on your toes, I don't know what would."

"So you prefer this sort of challenge to a cut-and-dried case."

Suzanne nodded. "Most people seem to assume that lawyers like simple cases, the ones with straightforward questions. But it's the doubts, the uncertainties that give us a job in the first place. If it were always readily apparent who was right and who was wrong, we wouldn't need lawyers. And any trial lawyer who says she or he doesn't enjoy a good fight is lying."

Nice quote, Sam thought. It would look good in the paper, but it sounded a bit rehearsed. Maybe if she twitted Jantille a bit, her subject would reward Sam with something a bit juicier. "Let's be real here, for a second," Sam said. "I can't quite buy what you're saying about doubt."

"What do you mean?" Suzanne asked.

"Nine times out of ten, by the time a case gets to trial, everyone knows perfectly well what happened. Don't the lawyers—defense lawyers in particular—earn their keep by trying to *manufacture* uncertainty?"

Suzanne Jantille sat up a bit straighter and frowned. "I'm afraid I don't understand."

Or don't wish to understand, Sam thought, a bit viciously. " 'Beyond a reasonable doubt,' " she quoted. "Isn't that the key to it? There are a million things that happen every day, and we all know they happened—but you couldn't *prove* they did. Especially not if someone else came along looking for a way to introduce that reasonable doubt."

"I used to play that game with myself," Suzanne said, with something a bit cautious about her voice. "Back when I was just beginning to try cases."

"What game?"

"Well, let me give an example." She paused and thought for a moment. Suddenly the remote gave off a strange barking sort of noise without moving its mouth. It flailed its arms about convulsively, in an awkward and mechanical spasm of movement. Whatever illusion of humanity it had shown vanished, at least for the moment. It looked like a robot, and a malfunctioning one at that. "Excuse me," it said, in an echo of Suzanne's voice that was suddenly a bit raspy. "It would appear I'm developing a bit of a cold, and my remote insists on echoing my cough in full sound and action, even if it doesn't do it very well. The facial controls weren't programmed to cough, and the cough reflex confuses the induction controllers. Let me get some water."

Well, okay, Sam told herself, maybe it had *sounded* like a cough, but it sure didn't look like one. Strange that such a commonplace sound would seem so bizarre just because the visual cues didn't match it. Let her get some water and get on with it. Sam half expected the machine to stand up and head for the kitchen, but instead the remote suddenly froze up, stopped moving altogether. After a moment, she understood. Somewhere in the house, Sam knew, a drinking tube was extruding itself toward the paralyzed woman's mouth, and she was sucking water through it to clear her throat. Just as well the machine did cut out. It would have been doubly disconcerting to see the remote turn its head and wrap its mouth around an imaginary straw as it echoed Suzanne's movements.

There was another strange noise from the remote, a bit more subdued, and with the spasming absent altogether. Suzanne was clearing her throat. "That's better. But anyway, I was talking about my imaginary cases. They were a bit silly, but I suppose everyone has private little games they play in their heads. I'd be walking along the street in the city, all sorts of other people around, and suddenly I'd find myself picking out a couple of random strangers, turn one into a criminal and the other into a victim. I'd ask myself, suppose the man fifty feet ahead of me stole that lady's purse? Could I identify him? Could I precisely indicate the spot it happened in? And the time? And if so, how could I *prove* it, nail time and place down. If the purse were produced in evidence, would I be able to identify it? Or else I'd make it more direct, and make myself the victim—or the criminal. No, scratch that—I'd play the plaintiff's and suspect's viewpoints." Clearly, she had remembered she was talking to a reporter. "Plaintiffs and victims, suspects and criminals, are all very different things. Make sure you clean that quote up for me, all right?" she asked, a note of concern in her voice.

"Of course," Sam said, trying to sound encouraging and reassuring. It was an old trick of the trade. If the reporter could get the interview subject to rely on the reporter's discretion, then the subject would be more likely to be indiscreet herself.

But that voice. Strange, fearfully strange to know

there was a real woman, somewhere in this house, speaking those words to no one, into a microphone in an empty room. "Go on," Sam said.

"Well, the idea was to find out what the various parties would say," Suzanne continued. "What would be the likely points of agreement? What details would be likely to get mixed up? Who could lie about what and get away with it, in the face of whatever other evidence existed in the case? What would their motives be for lying and telling the truth?

"Then, once I had the whole thing together in my mind, I'd try to take it all apart again, make it so all the pretty pieces I had strung together didn't fit together anymore."

"What do you mean?"

"I'd take the whole thing into the courtroom, and play all the parts at once, in my head. Judge, jury, prosecutor, defense counsel, plaintiff, suspect, witnesses. I'd imagine myself as a witness, and cross-examine myself. How did I know the time? How could I swear my client was the assailant when I only got a brief glimpse at him? There are a hundred stores selling purses just like that one. How could I be sure that the one produced in evidence was the one you saw? And then I'd go back again, play the prosecutor's side of the chess game again. That's how I taught myself something so I'd know it instinctively, in my gut: lawyers don't worry about what happened—they worry about what they can *prove,* or what proofs they can dismantle. Every time I played the mind game, I'd realize after a while that I wasn't thinking about the hypothetical crime at all anymore—but about the *case* for and against the crime."

"Isn't that pretty much the same thing?" Sam asked.

"No, not at all. It's something very different," Suzanne said, her voice and posture betraying her enthusiasm. "You were talking about it yourself a minute ago. Manufacturing certainty and uncertainty. That's what lawyers do. We take the facts of the case, try and hide the facts that weaken our side, dispute them where we can.

We overstate the facts that make our side seem strong. We try to make the witnesses seem smart or stupid, honest or misleading, confident or confused, as suits our turn. Meanwhile opposing counsel is playing the same hand from the other side, while the judge keeps an eye on how far we bend the rules. Then the jury decides who pulls in the chips."

"You make it sound more like a poker game than a court of law," Sam said. She thought back to what Peng had told her. The words had been different, but the tone had been much the same. Cynicism wasn't quite the word for it, for they both believed in what they were doing. But they both had a strange double vision of *how* they did their jobs. Seeing it half in cold-blooded detachment, and half as a game they loved to play.

"It *is* a poker game," Suzanne said. "Bluffing, counterbluffing, raising the stakes, folding when your hand isn't worth the risk, blowing a good hand now and then because your nerve fails or you misread something." She thought for a moment, and then spoke again. "There's another point that makes the poker analogy even stronger: Any hand can win, any hand can lose. You can be holding a royal flush and be forced to fold if you don't have enough chips to keep up with the betting. And five random cards can win if you can hide your weaknesses well enough, and intimidate the other player with tough betting."

"So what do the cards you got dealt look like?" Sam asked. "And what are you using for chips?"

Suzanne-Remote's expressionless face did not betray any reaction, but her head cocked to one side, and she waved an admonishing finger at Samantha. "Never show your cards till you're called, and never show your whole stake."

"All right then," Sam said. She hadn't expected anything more than that. "What do you think of the way Peng is playing his hand?"

"Damned if I know."

"He made some strong claims about being able to

prove Herbert's humanity—and his guilt," Sam said. "Are you saying you don't believe he has that proof?"

"I can't answer that one way or the other," Suzanne said.

Sam hesitated for a long moment, and then decided to plunge in. "I've got a friend, my source on a lot of this story. I put in a call to him this morning, and he confirmed that he didn't see any such evidence."

Suzanne leaned in toward Sam. There was something a bit anxious about the movement, as if she had been hoping to hear something to such an effect.

"Did he have good access to the evidence?" Suzanne asked. "Would he know what he was looking for?"

"He's very good at this sort of thing," Sam said, a bit cautiously. She looked hard at Suzanne. "You don't think Herbert's human," she said at last. She could read that much from Suzanne. "Or at least, you're not sure, one way or the other."

"I certainly—"

"I wasn't asking a question," Sam said. "And you sure as hell won't let me quote you on that point. But I can see it, plain as day. You're not sure."

Suzanne slumped back a little. "Off the record, utterly and totally off the record, I'm not. How could I be? Up until the time of his arrest, it had never entered my head that he was anything but a perfectly ordinary machine. But since then—I've changed my mind a hundred times. I've noticed him doing things that just aren't what robots do."

A light came on in Sam's head. "That's what my friend showed me, too. Unrobotic behavior. It's just struck me that if the job were to prove Herbert *wasn't* a *robot*, things would be a lot easier."

"But a lot of things that aren't robots aren't human, so that's not much help," Suzanne said. She leaned in closer again, and spoke in low, confiding tones. "This friend of yours, this source. You know there are questions I can't answer, and I know there are things you can't do. You can't reveal a source without the source's permission. But I need some help right now. I need to see the evidence, and get some analysis on it—and get a private, expert opinion on Herbert. Your friend sounds like he might be able to do all those things, and sounds like he might be sympathetic to our side. Do you think he or she might agree to meet me?"

Sam looked hard into Suzanne-Remote's plastic eyes. This was the moment. Here was the time and place where she decided clearly and precisely whether she merely wanted to report this story, or whether she wanted to become part of it. Make the news instead of simply telling about it.

Reporters were supposed to be observers, not doers. But no worthy reporter had ever worked who did not believe that things had to be changed, turned upside down, sometimes.

If she sat silent now, she could tell herself that she had done the right things, behaved in accordance with the standards of journalistic ethics. Her conscience would be clear.

And maybe Herbert would be condemned to death, and a whole class of people would be made into second-rate citizens for all time to come.

Or else she could speak the name, and damn the rules and do what was right, instead of what satisfied the norms.

She thought back to the original arrest, and wondered, not for the first time, how Phillipe's service as the arresting officer had been arranged.

"I think I can arrange it," Sam said at last. "As a matter of fact, I believe you've already met him."

CHAPTER 10
SCHRÖDINGER'S ROBOT

"There isn't any point to this," Suzanne Jantille-Remote said, staring into the daylight that sped past the windows of her relay van. "My husband is dead. None of these games will change that fact."

She shouldn't say things like that to a reporter, Sam thought. Suzanne Jantille's mood had darkened, and she was talking far less cautiously. Sam knew, somehow, that as a reporter she should be taking advantage of Jantille's moodiness to get more information, but she couldn't bring herself to do it. For once, behaving with a bit of human decency was higher on her list. "My friend doesn't think he's dead," Sam said.

"My husband died three months ago, and no evidence manufactured by the U.S. Attorney will change that fact," Suzanne said. Sam noticed there was a slight quaver to Suzanne's voice, as if she was in some pain or discomfort and was trying to hide it.

Sam turned her eyes back to Herbert. His massive bulk was crowding up the interior of the relay van. His size was just a trifle intimidating, to say the least, and her overactive imagination would insist on reminding her that this machine had quite probably killed someone. At the very least he had been there when the death happened. By accident or design, whether Herbert was a sentient being or a mere pile of hardware, he had been there when the breath of life left David Bailey's body. That was plain fact, never mind the legal niceties about whether he could be held to account for it.

Sam settled back into her seat as best she could. Here she was being driven around by a robotic vehicle, her only companions two robots, one a possible killer and the other a puppet on the string of a paralyzed and highly agitated woman. It was an incongruous situation, but for some reason Sam found it more than odd. It was downright disturbing, and she could not think why.

Then it came to her. For the first time in her life, she was aware of the fact that she was in a place where humans were not in the majority. No doubt she had been surrounded by robots before in her life—she could think of a half-dozen moments right off the top of her head. But she had never been *worried* by it before, never before been disturbed.

Now it dawned on her that her sort, the ruling class of flesh-and-blood, was potentially the weaker party. The human world would not function at all without the cyborgs and robots and HTMs and lesser machines doing all the dirty and unpleasant work. What would happen if the members of society not accepted as fully human decided to watch out for themselves instead of doing the bidding of humans?

Sam was shocked even to realize such a thing was remotely possible, that the present arrangement was not immutable. How often before in history had someone stumbled across the idea? What had it felt like to be an Englishman of the Indian Raj in the 1930s when he suddenly realized the Indians outnumbered his kind a hundred to one? Or an American slave owner in 1865, at the exact moment when war ended and the slaves were no longer slaves no longer?

Sam frowned. Why was she thinking in terms of overlords and peoples being made free? Was that what robots and cyborgs were? Slaves? But slaves were oppressed *people. Were* robots people, could robots be people, should they be free? Would they, inevitably, someday, be free, and powerful?

For the briefest flicker of time, Sam saw a future. Not the time that would be, but the time that *might* be—and it was a deeply unsettling place. It was Julia Entwhistle's vision, as described by Ted Peng, a world overrun by the rich who refused to die, encased in their flawless mechanical bodies.

Sam looked at the big HMU robot hunkered down on the other side of the van. It might or might not be that the Feds were wrong about Herbert for now, but they wouldn't be wrong forever.

Sam looked at Suzanne-Remote. Such compromises as remotes and cyborgs were mere stopgaps, temporary solutions while technology matured. Sooner or later, dead minds *would* be fully and accurately recorded into bodies of metal and plastic. And those bodies would never have to die. The mechanical survivors of death would accumulate, their numbers always growing, until . . .

Sam blinked and came back to herself. Until it would always be like this moment here, with the flesh-and-blood people in the minority. Until one day the flesh-and-bloods looked up to realize that the robot-bodied populace was already gaining control, had already gone past being *people* and become something else.

It was not a new idea, not at all. People had been discussing such things for years, decades. But riding in this van with a pair of machines she was supposed to treat like people brought it home, made it real, immediate, personal.

Sam shivered. She did not want that world. She wanted *people* around, wanted her children to live and die having fingers and toes, bruised knees and broken hearts. People were meant to have *lives,* not battery packs or cable assemblies or memory downloads.

But Suzanne had said her client was *not* a human, not

a person. She wasn't seeing that world. "Do you really believe your husband is dead?" Sam asked. Suddenly the question was vitally important. She needed to know what Suzanne thought a person was. "Woman to woman, no quotation, you're not a lawyer and I'm not a reporter. Do you, right now, believe it?"

"I sometimes wonder if *I'm* alive," Suzanne said. "I can forget my own living body so completely, become so involved in the job of controlling this *robot* body, that I begin to think of *myself* as a machine. But that doesn't answer your question, does it. Is David alive or dead?" Suzanne thought for a moment and then shook her head. "The things Peng said at the hearing about David becoming a new person ring true to me, and that scares the hell out of me. *I'm* not the same person I was before —before I turned into *this*." Suzanne gestured with her left arm, down at her body. "And I still have the same number of arms and legs, I'm still using the same brain I used to have. But if David *did* put his mind in Herbert, none of that is true for him. How could he *not* be different?"

Suzanne thought for a minute, and then spoke again. " 'Is David alive?' That seems like a single, very simple question. But I've been thinking about it, and I've concluded that two very complicated questions are hiding inside it.

"First—*is* there someone alive inside Herbert, or is he merely malfunctioning in some odd and subtle way? Second—if there is someone alive in there, was he once David Bailey, is he David now, and if not, *who is he*?"

Suzanne looked at Sam, but there was nothing for the younger woman to say.

Suzanne shook her head and looked over at Herbert. "If your friend can answer all those questions, I'll be very impressed with him indeed."

Suzanne Jantille made her way into the elevator with a fair degree of nervousness, following Herbert and Sam

Crandall. It wasn't just the building, though the place was strange and disconcerting in its own right. At least the place had a decent hookup for her relay van, surprising in an old popdrop condo in this part of town. What bothered her was Samantha Crandall's flat refusal to say who they were going to see. Crandall had even said her friend had met Suzanne. But then what reason could there be for the secrecy—especially as all would be revealed as soon as their host opened the door? Suzanne was getting the idea from Sam that the reporter feared Suzanne would refuse to see the person if she knew who it was.

The elevator arrived at its destination and the three of them stepped out into a good-sized vestibule. Sam led them to the one door at the far end of the hall, and it opened as they approached.

A dark-featured, handsome young man stood in the doorway, dressed in a plain tan shirt and slacks. But he *did* look familiar. There was something about him that—

"Good God. You're the one who arrested him," she said in shock. Suzanne turned toward Sam accusingly. Now she could understand the reporter's reluctance to give a name. "*This* is the friend who's going to help Herbert?"

But before Sam Crandall could speak, the policeman did, in a low, calm voice full of confidence. "The name's Phillipe Sanders, ma'am. On duty I do what I'm told. I'm off duty now. I'm not spying for anyone or looking to spring any traps. I'm just a guy who knows robotics who might be able to give you a hand. And if you don't want my help, you don't have to take it. But are you likely to get many other offers before the hearing reconvenes?"

Suzanne's head swiveled around sharply, with the click and whir of mechanical precision, with no attempt to disguise the movement as something human and graceful. She stood motionless for an endless moment, staring at her host, glittering plastic eyes boring into him. Phillipe returned her gaze calmly, steadily.

Sam watched the two of them, feeling very much

afraid, though she was not sure of what. Forces were coming together here, gathering themselves to look into new places, to look for a lost soul where no soul had ever been.

All three of them were breaking the rules of their respective professions, just by coming together. Sam was supposed to report the news, not create it. Reporters weren't supposed to interfere. Cops weren't supposed to help defense lawyers, and certainly weren't supposed to meet secretly with lawyers involved in cases they had busted. And defense lawyers most definitely were not supposed to receive stolen evidence files from cops.

At last Suzanne stepped forward, through the door, and Phillipe backed up, letting her through. Herbert and Sam followed behind. Sam breathed a sigh of relief. It was too late now. The deed had been done, and they had all done it together.

The place looked nothing like the way it had the last time Sam had been here. All the furniture, all the storage cabinets, all the worktables, were just as they had been— but the light of day was pouring in the high windows from the blue sky, banishing any illusion of mystery or strangeness. It was an ordinary place, a workshop where a man repaired machines. Even the dust cloths draped over the machines on the workbenches looked perfectly normal. No ghosts looming out at her today.

Sam looked toward one particular spot on one particular table, and made damn sure there was no shrouded shape sitting there. Good. The remote unit Phillipe had been working on—the remote that Phil's father had used —was missing. In fact, everything had been cleared from that one table. Either Phillipe had sold or donated the remote already, or else he had hidden it away, having the good sense to keep Suzanne from seeing it. It could not be a pleasant thing to see your fellow being half taken apart.

Phillipe stepped ahead of the others and walked into the center of the workroom. He stood by the empty worktable, turned, and looked at his visitors. "Okay," he said, "where do we start?"

Suzanne cocked her head in surprise. "I thought you would know."

"All I got was one quick phone call from Sam, saying she was bringing you here," Phil said. "Nothing else. What is it you want?"

"Help," Suzanne said simply, looking steadily at him. Phillipe leaned back on the workbench and folded his arms on his chest. Distrust and suspicion hung heavy in the air.

"Help with what?" he asked.

"With Herbert, obviously," Suzanne said, her voice irritable. Suddenly she was caught up in another coughing fit, this one just as spasmodic and disconcerting as the one Sam had seen at Suzanne's house.

Sam had seen it before, and yet it still startled her. Phil, on the other hand, was clearly more concerned than surprised. All the curtness came out of his voice, and he stepped toward her, but stayed clear of her flailing arms. Obviously he was familiar with robotic strength, and did not want to get in its way when it was out of control. He waited until the fit was past, and then stepped closer, his face worried. "Madame Jantille, are you all right?"

"Yes, fine. No problem at all. Just a slight cough."

"No, ma'am, that cough was a lot more than slight. Are you taking proper care of your bio-body?" he asked, a bit severely.

"What business is it of yours?" Suzanne asked angrily, stepping back from Phillipe, moving a bit stiffly.

"None," Phillipe said evenly. "Except that my father was a remote person, and he died of a slight cough. It was advanced double pneumonia by the time he finally admitted there was something wrong."

"You sound just like my tech-nurse," Suzanne said impatiently.

"Well, maybe you should listen to both of us," Phillipe said.

"What the devil would you know about it?" Suzanne demanded.

Sam drew in her breath and stared at the two of them, the remote unit and the man, standing still as statues, glaring at each other. At last Phil spoke, and broke the moment.

"I know about it because it's my business," Phillipe said. "Because dealing with robots is what I do."

"I am not a robot," Suzanne said.

"No, ma'am, and that is exactly my point. You feel yourself to be in this body in front of me now, strong and healthy and capable. And this remote body in front of me is all those things. But it is not *you* in front of me. It is a machine. *You* are home, alone, with a bad cold, if not something worse. An illness of some sort that you are struggling to ignore because you have enough weaknesses and vulnerabilities in your life without admitting a new one."

There was something in Phil's tone, in the passion and the feeling of his words, that seemed to disarm Suzanne. "Very well, then. I will take your words under advisement. I will talk with my tech-nurse tomorrow, and do whatever he tells me. With that said, can we return to the question of Herbert?"

Suzanne's surrender seemed to disarm Phillipe right back. "Yes, yes. Of course," he said. "But can you tell me exactly what sort of help you want from me?"

"Two things," Sam said, speaking for the first time. Maybe if the words came from her, the anger in this room would back off a ways. Both Phil and Suzanne turned and looked at her, seemingly surprised to see her there. Sam found it most disconcerting that they had both forgotten her presence. "I think there are two things we need, Phil," Sam repeated in a firmer voice, as if staking out her right to speak. "We need to know if David Bailey is in there, and we need to figure out what the U.S. Attorney's evidence of murder is."

"Or if it exists at all," Phil said thoughtfully.

Suzanne nodded. "So I'm not the only one thinking that might be a bluff?"

"It might well be. I've been chewing it over, and either it's a bluff and the data files I got access to—the ones Sam based her story on—have been manipulated, or else the evidence is there, in the data, but I've overlooked it."

"What's the odds on your data being manipulated?" Sam asked. "Maybe *your* source is yanking your chain. What chance of that?"

Phil shook his head. "Next to zero. Not with my source."

"And who might that be?" Sam said, knowing damn well she shouldn't be asking that question.

Phil rubbed his hand over his chin and shrugged. "I might as well tell you and save you lots of guessing. But if it gets in the paper, my source's head comes off, and so does mine—and I'll see to it you and Madame Jantille get pulled down too. That clear? I need it kept *quiet*."

"Perfectly. I'll keep quiet," Sam said. "Madame Jantille?"

"I will honor your confidence," she said in a careful, formal voice. "I will not reveal what you tell me. And anyone who's trying to tap my communications back and forth between here and my home is going to have some problems. Everything is shielded and encrypted."

Phil hesitated a moment longer and then plunged in. "Okay then. It was the chief of police."

"Good God." Suzanne was stunned.

Sam was just as surprised, but after half a second's thought, it made sense to her. After all, the chief did not care for Entwhistle. "Wait a second, Phil," she said. "I need details on this. How did it work? The chief didn't just waltz up to you and say 'Here, Phil, here's a package of evidence to suborn.'"

"No, of course not," Phil said a bit stiffly. "But if you're not going to reveal what I tell you, why the hell do you need details?"

"Because she needs to know if you're telling a convincing story," Suzanne said, recovering quickly from her own surprise. "You're breaking a hell of a lot of rules meeting with us. And Sam's got to be wondering if you've been *instructed* to break those rules as a way to set us up. Entwhistle could use this meeting to get me thrown off the case."

Phil looked at each of his visitors in turn, his gaze ending up on Sam. She found to her surprise that she had a little trouble returning it. "Nice to be trusted," Phil said at last. "But I guess I can see the need, looking at it from your direction. I think I know the chief's reasons for what he did. He didn't like the case, and he didn't trust Entwhistle, and he did not want a precedent set that his cops would be forced to go out and arrest cyborgs on charges of staying alive—which is, when you come right down to it, what this is all about. Entwhistle has charged your husband with the crime of not dying. If she can make that a crime under certain circumstances, all she has to do is widen the circumstances and anyone who needs a machine to live is in trouble."

"That thought had crossed my mind. But why would that idea upset Chief Thurman enough that he would leak confidential police information? *He's* not a cyborg. Surely he's had to enforce other laws he didn't approve of."

"Yes, he has. But this goes beyond that. This is a question of *making* law, setting precedents. Right now, Entwhistle is trying to establish that doing what she thinks David Bailey tried to do is a crime. It is by no means yet established that such is the case. My guess is that the chief is trying to prevent it from coming to pass."

"You're talking like a lawyer all of a sudden," Suzanne said, something a bit less intimidating about her manner. "But I can't believe Thurman just called you into his office and said, 'Here, Sanders, go out and break the law.' "

"No, of course not," Phil said. "He came to me at the repair yard, the night before the arrest."

"The chief came to *you*?" Sam asked, astonished.

"It was quieter that way," Phil explained. "If I had

been called to his office, it would've been all over the yard the next morning. But everyone knows Thurman likes to wander around his commands once in a while, just pop up and see how things are going. So he dropped by the yard, and no one paid much attention."

"And?"

"And he handed me a datacube and told me my sergeant was going to pull me off tech detail to make a bust next day. One that would involve robotics. He wanted an expert there to make the pinch, just to make sure no one screwed the pooch," Phil went on, unconsciously shifting from legalese to cop slang. "And he handed me the cube, and told me to read up on the case."

"And that's all?" Suzanne protested. "Out of that you read that the chief of police wants you to start leaking indictment files to the press?"

"That's plenty," Sam broke in. "What the hell else was he expecting Phil to do? He had to have pulled Phil's file, learned something about him first. He must have known that you were sympathetic to cyborgs and remotes and robots."

"So he sends you in to sabotage the arrest," Suzanne said.

"No, ma'am," Phil said firmly. "You were there, you must have played the recordings back. You of all people should know that I *rescued* that arrest. If Johnson had gone in alone, she would have cocked it up six ways from Sunday. You could have gotten the whole damn thing thrown out five minutes after you walked into court. If he wanted a crash-and-burn bust, he would have sent Johnson in alone. The chief had to know that about me, too—that I do a job right if I'm going to do it at all."

"Except you don't mind leaking evidence when it suits your turn," Suzanne said.

"Hold it a minute," Sam protested. "You're here to ask Phil's help. He doesn't deserve to be treated like a hostile witness on the stand."

"No, it's all right, Sam," Phil said. "She's got to understand my motives in all this, trust them—or she'd be crazy to let me near Herbert with a screwdriver."

Suzanne ignored the interruption. "Let's go back to what you think the chief wanted of you. You said it wasn't a sabotaged arrest. What do you think he wanted instead?"

"Well, I didn't get a chance to finish telling you about my talk with the chief. He didn't say go out and leak this information. But he *did* say that he would count on me to see to it that the defendant was on a level playing field," said Phil. "He said that there were some serious manipulations of the process happening. Things done not in the name of justice but of winning at any cost. He said that wasn't right, that the police had the same duty as anyone else in law enforcement to look out for the rights of the accused."

"That's quite a statement from the chief of police," Sam said.

"Chief Thurman is quite a guy," Phil said.

Sam looked at her friend, and considered his words. There was obvious admiration in his voice when he spoke of the chief. It was clear that Phil's loyalty to the man was the driving force here, the factor that had made him willing to break the rules, take the chances he was taking. Phil was doing this, at least in part, because he believed in Thurman, and trusted his motives far enough to do his unspoken bidding.

But Sam had a little trouble seeing a police chief, even an honest and dedicated one, working solely from altruistic motives. There had to be more to Thurman than that, and it made her uncomfortable to think Phil might think otherwise. To her practiced eye, it was obvious that Thurman had carefully arranged matters to provide himself with deniability. Which could make things very sticky for Phil. "Good guy or not," she said, "he had an angle on this. What was it?"

"Oh, he had one," Phil said matter-of-factly. Maybe he wasn't suffering from any delusions after all. "He didn't pretend otherwise. It's a pretty obvious one, at least from the police point of view. Thurman said he wondered what the next step would be if Entwhistle got her way. He asked me, how would it look in the news to have his cops sent out onto the streets to bust cyborgs for breathing? Not good publicity for the force, and miserable for morale. And he hates Entwhistle. If she wants something, he doesn't want it.

"And what did Entwhistle want?" Suzanne asked.

"A case against some poor dumb sap who couldn't speak for himself and couldn't hire a decent lawyer," Phil said bluntly. "They weren't counting on you, ma'am. There are some internal office memos in the datacube." Phil hesitated for a moment. "The files make it clear that Entwhistle and Peng weren't counting on you to be, uh, well, available," he finished, a bit awkwardly.

"I doubt they were that polite about it," Suzanne said coolly. "I'm sure they assumed that I'd stay inside my house staring into my navel, just as I had been doing since the accident. I must admit there was some reason to support such an assumption. But in any event they expected that I would be incompetent or unwilling to serve as defense counsel."

"That's about right. The one thing Entwhistle wasn't looking for was a fair fight. She wanted a mute represented by a lightweight, preferably some kid fresh out of law school. Or else someone you'd hired just to make the case go away."

"Someone who would go for the quick win, claim Herbert had no legal standing," Suzanne said, thinking out loud. "The case would be thrown out, and Entwhistle would lose, just the way she wanted to lose, by having Herbert declared nonhuman. She'd have her ruling, her precedent. Even if Herbert's lawyer stuck with the case after that, took it to trial, odds are he would have lost. Herbert would be convicted—and the case would be appealed automatically. Then the U.S. Attorney's office could cut a deal, offer to concur in a motion to have the appeals judge overturn the conviction, so long as the motion was filed on the grounds that Herbert was nonhuman and thus could not be tried. That would even be better for Entwhistle. An appellate ruling would have more teeth. Either way, she could go on to the next step, the next case limiting the rights of cyborgs, with a little more muscle behind her."

"There's something else," Sam said. "Remember Peng talked about a law currently on the books in D.C., making suicide a crime. Not just *attempted* suicide, but the successful act itself was made a punishable act. I checked into that. It was introduced as one teeny part of an omnibus crime bill two years ago. Guess whose office wrote the first draft of that bill and handed it to the mayor's office for submission to the council?"

"Two years ago?" Phil let out a low whistle. "So the old girl has been planning this for a while. Has she spent all that time shopping for a case she liked?"

"That's what it looks like," Sam said. "But getting back to the matter at hand, let me see if I have this straight. The chief left you with the prosecution file and told you to follow your own best judgment. Do you think he was expecting you to leak the material?"

"Yes," Phil said simply.

"But what if you got caught?" Sam asked. "Would Thurman be there for you?"

"If it had gone wrong—if it *does* go wrong—he's never heard of me," Phil said calmly. "It's better that way. When a street cop leaks information, he doesn't run anything like the risk a high-ranking officer does. Worst they could do to me is put me on administrative leave with pay, maybe a suspension—and maybe Thurman could see to it I was reinstated as soon as the dust settled. But it'd be his badge if Entwhistle nailed him as the source. End of career."

Sam looked at Phil, and shook her head. Loyalty indeed. "Suppose you're wrong? Suppose you're exposed and thrown off the force?"

"Then I get a private sector job in robotics at twice the pay," Phil said.

"You're not a man who rattles easily, Mr. Sanders," Suzanne said. "But the datacube went from the chief to you, and even a paranoid defense lawyer such as myself can see no advantage to him in giving you a doctored or emasculated file. What about the other data?"

"The second cube I got on my own, straight from the precinct house," Phil said. "Nothing much in it but the record of your visit, Madame Jantille."

"I think we can assume both cubes are genuine and complete," Suzanne said. "That leaves us with two possibilities concerning Peng's claim to have proved both the murder and Herbert's humanity. Either he *was* bluffing, or else the information is in there, and none of us has spotted it yet.

"Trouble is, it won't be marked out PROOF HE'S HUMAN in capital letters or anything," Sam said. "I've been through that information pretty carefully. The section on physical evidence is just raw information. None of the opinions or conclusions from their tame experts. *We* have to figure out whatever their experts figured out, based on this data."

"Whatever they found is pretty well hidden," Phil said. "I've looked through all the material pretty carefully, and I haven't spotted it. There's also a whole background section on the laws surrounding robots and cyborgs. Maybe their evidence hinges on some tiny legal point buried in there. I don't know. But, Madame Jantille, if I could make a suggestion. I was focusing on the technical side of things when I looked over the datacube. Maybe there's some legal point in there that I missed. You haven't seen all the material yet—and I haven't seen Herbert. Maybe you should start reading while I get a look at him. With any luck, one of us will find what we need to put the puzzle together. Sam, maybe you could give me a hand with Herbert."

"Wait a second," Suzanne said. "What, exactly, are you planning to *do* to Herbert?"

Phil shrugged. "Open him up and take a look. Maybe run some diagnostics. I'm not going to damage him, and

I won't modify him in any way without your permission. But I can't get anywhere figuring out what or who he is without seeing how he's built."

Sam looked to Suzanne, and saw her hesitate, freeze up all but completely. Surely this was why they had come here, the point of the trip. The need to find out what they were dealing with. But then Sam understood. The end of doubt could easily be the end of hope. Suppose Phil found nothing at all or, worse, something that confirmed beyond all doubt that there was nothing to find?

Right now there was at least the chance that David was alive. But this was the moment when that chance was proven or destroyed. Who could blame Suzanne Jantille for hesitating?

Sam found herself thinking of Schrödinger's cat. A strange name for a strange, imaginary experiment she had read about in school. It was a thought experiment, designed to demonstrate the principles of quantum mechanics, where all actions were reduced to probability and certainty was mathematically impossible.

Take a cat and put her in a box, along with a vial of poison gas. Design a device that has a precisely fifty percent chance of smashing a hammer into the gas vial over the course of an hour. Seal the box and wait sixty minutes.

According to the principles of quantum mechanics, at the moment *just before* the box is opened, the cat is neither alive, nor dead, but half of both—not in a manner of speech, but in literal fact. Only at the moment the box is opened will it become all one or all the other. Up until that moment she is both, and neither.

At the scale of the atomic nucleus, maybe things worked Schrödinger's way, but not in real life. Sam shivered as she looked at Herbert's massive bulk. At least, they weren't *supposed* to work that way.

David/Herbert. Half alive/half dead. Human/robot. Both, neither, betwixt and between in a world that refused to accept that such things could be, a world that was determined to prevent them from happening. That was Entwhistle's goal—to stomp out the in-betweens, erase the ambiguities, see to it that nothing and no one could ever be half human in the eyes of the law. Either or. Dead or alive. Human or robot. Sam felt her stomach knotting up just thinking about it all. Was it really such a bad idea to draw that line sharply, clearly, with no grey, no fuzziness?

Sam looked to Suzanne, and saw that the lawyer had come to her own conclusions. "Do it, Mr. Sanders," Suzanne Jantille said. "Do whatever you have to do."

Interlude

They order me up onto the table. I climb up, very much afraid, not really understanding what it is that I fear. I fold my legs under myself, and lie still. My underself still controls my body, but there are times when myself and underself both want the same things. Neither of us wants this. My eyes swivel backward on their stalks. I can see one of them, the man, opening a small access panel, examining the switches there. I seem him reach his hand in, turn a knob—

And then the world is gone. I fade away to nowhere, far away from the outside universe.

I am lost.

CHAPTER 11
SUSPENDERS AND BELT

Herbert was laid out on the workbench, powered down to standby mode, as inert and helpless as a trussed-up turkey at Thanksgiving. Phil and Sam stood along one side of the robot's body. Suzanne hovered behind them, watching anxiously.

Phillipe shut the small power control panel and turned his attention to the larger service panels in the robot's midbody. He found the external release and flipped it open. "Easy now," he said to no one in particular and swung the panel open. He peered inside it. "Okay, there's a safety catch here. Let me get this release opened and we should get the whole midbody cowling free."

Sam nodded and watched Phil carefully. His face was unreadable through the surgical mask, his sensitive hands seeming artificial and stiff under their death-white rubber gloves. There was, of course, no danger of infecting Herbert—but condensation from human breath, or the oils secreted by human skin, could work serious mischief on unshielded robotic components. If she was called upon to assist in any delicate work on Herbert's interior, then she would have to use a mask and gloves as well.

Phil unclipped the service panel and handed it to Sam. She set it to one side. Phil reached inside the chassis and worked the panel release. The cowling swung up and out of the way. Sam lifted it free of the robot's body. It was a big, awkward thing and it took Sam and Phil together to maneuver it clear and set it down on another workbench.

They turned back and looked at the massive hulk of machinery on the table. The upper half of Herbert's entire midsection was exposed, the smooth lines of his body broken into a complex jumble of gears, motors, servos, and any number of other components Sam could not even identify. Sam looked toward the front of the robot, where its sensors and effecters were clustered. Phil hadn't paid that part of Herbert any mind at all. "I thought you wanted to get a look at his brain, his head," she said. "Shouldn't we—"

"This *is* his head," Phil said. "At least for our purposes it is. There's nothing up front but his ears, eyes, and some cleaning appliances. We know his vacuum cleaner subsystem is working. We don't need to examine *that.*"

Phil nodded at the exposed midsection of the robot. "His mind, his brain, is in *here,* centrally located and in the best protected part of the body. I've been going through the literature, studying Bailey's design philosophy. That's how he did things—ah, *does* things," Phil corrected himself, remembering to be diplomatic in front of Suzanne just a moment too late. "So let's see what we've got." Phil leaned in close over the robot, bringing his face within an inch or two of his patient. Patient? Sam knotted her brow for a moment, then realized that was as apt a description as any. Still, it was a strange thought.

"There's the diagnostic socket," he said. "Good. Standard design. I can plug my system into that and get a readout on practically everything about Herbert." Sam expected him to reach for a cable then and there, but he was clearly looking for something else.

"Ah!" Whatever it was Phil was after, he had spotted it. Maybe there was a loose wire, a broken connection. All Phil had to do was reattach something and everything would be fine. He reached into Herbert's body with careful fingers—

And pulled out a sheaf of papers, wrapped in plastic. "Spec sheets," he said. "Basic layout data."

"But why do you need that when you've got the diagnostic port?" Sam asked. "Why is that even *in* there? I mean, he built this machine himself. Why would *he* need a spec sheet?"

"Notice my husband isn't here just now," Suzanne said. "Or if he is, he can't tell us much about how Herbert works. My husband was a very careful man."

Sam noticed at once that Suzanne had no qualms about using the past tense where David Bailey was concerned.

"He worked on the assumption that *everything* would go wrong," Suzanne went on. "A suspenders-and-belt man. If Herbert lost power completely, or the diagnostic socket itself was shot, or a complete stranger had to work on Herbert—the information would be there."

"And paper's better than a diagnostic port, at least for starters," Phil said. He opened the sealed plastic bag and pulled out the papers. "I *know* something inside Herbert isn't right, so how can I know for sure that any data I pull out of him will be accurate—unless I have a baseline of information that I know can be trusted?"

He looked at the papers. There were two sets: one a set of pages stapled together, and the other a collection of blueprints. He set the stapled pages down and unfolded the blueprints, draping them over Herbert's open body. "Hmmm," he said, starting to trace diagrams and layouts. "Okay. Right," Phil said. He went reading for a long moment, then set down the blueprints and picked up the thickest of the sheaves of paper from the pack. "Let's see, that's—"

Suddenly he looked up at the two women, startled, as if he had just remembered they were there. With the surgical mask on his face, the look of surprise in his eyes somehow seemed even more comical. "Oh. Sorry," he said. "Five minutes on the job, and I've already forgotten you were there." He set down the papers, pulled the mask off, and started stripping off his gloves. "It's going to be some time before I get anywhere at all. You're right about your husband, Madame Jantille. This hardcopy material is far more complete than I expected. I'll have to do quite a bit of reading before I get any further."

"Is that good?" Sam asked.

"Very good. The more reading, the less guesswork."

"But is it all right to leave Herbert like that in the meantime?" Suzanne asked.

"Opened up? Oh, certainly. Now that the cowl's off, I can see that all the subsystems are sealed. I couldn't assume that without looking first. But there's no contamination risk."

"But with his body opened up like that, and with his power system removed from his control, won't he be disoriented? Is it at all possible—well, is it possible that he's in *pain*?" Suzanne asked, a bit more of her carefully hidden anxiety coming to the surface. "Or if he isn't now, could some procedure you might perform be painful?"

The very idea of a robot in pain struck Sam as ridiculous. She looked toward Phil, expecting him to react the same way—but to her surprise his face was serious, and thoughtful.

"I am all but certain that he is in no pain or fear now," he said. "But no one can ever be certain what another is feeling, especially when that other is unable to report his sensations. Right now, to all intents and purposes, Herbert has no power available to any of his systems. The only electricity he is drawing is power used to hold his memory-state configuration."

"I thought computers held their memories when they lost power," Sam said. "Can't you shut his brain off too? Wouldn't that make this less traumatic for him?"

"Modern computers can hold memory when powered

down," Phil said. "But robots can't, any more than you can. After all, your brain is electrochemical. Your thoughts are in part formed of electrical impulses. In many ways, robot brains are more similar to human brains than they are to standard computers. Both human and robot brains handle tremendously more data than most computers, and more of the data is highly inter-linked. The data in memory is much more complex and fast-changing than in a simple computer. That's why a complete power-down inevitably results in a data scramble, reduction to random state. It would be like simultaneously cutting power to every vehicle in the Washington roadnet. There would inevitably be crashes, lots of them, all at once, jamming all the roads. If you then restored power to all the cars, the damage would already be done. Probably the restart would actually cause further damage. Cut the electric power to your brain, and neurons would misfire, or strike the wrong receptors, or give up their energy the wrong way—lots of crashes, all at once, damaging the fine structure of your brain."

"And I'd be dead," Sam put in.

"Exactly. Cut all power to your brain, or Herbert's, even for an instant—and death would be inevitable. Right now his brain is drawing less power than it ever has since he was first switched on. Just enough to keep his mind functional. There is no power available to him to control his body or operate his sensors. He's blinded and paralyzed."

"But that must be terrifying!" Suzanne objected.

"The best we can tell, it's more like being uncon-scious. Robots that are powered down for maintenance like this come back on with their minds and memories intact, but with no recollection of the time they were shut down. At least that is what they report. They don't lose their time sense, the way we humans do when we're asleep or unconscious. But except in very rare cases, usu-ally where the robot's brain itself is malfunctioning, ro-bots do not remember anything about the time they were powered down. They don't get bored, they don't think and worry, they don't have nightmares. They are simply aware of the passage of time."

"But we're assuming that Herbert isn't just a robot," Suzanne reminded Phil. "Cut a person off from all sensation, sever his or her contact with the outside world, and that person will do more than be aware of time passing. That person can become terrified, go mad, hallucinate. Believe me, I know that better than either of you ever want to know it."

That thought struck at Sam. It was easy to forget just how different Suzanne's existence must be from a flesh-and-blood person's. What was it like, to live life in a cocoon, operating from remote control? "Suzanne's got an important point," she said. "You *have* thought about all this, haven't you, Phil?"

Phil nodded unhappily. "Yes, I have. I can easily imagine that powering down Herbert could throw the hypothetical human part of him to crippling agony or utter terror. But no *robot* has ever reported such sensations after being repowered, and that's some comfort. Besides, we have no choice at all in the matter. Whether or not it is due to David Bailey's spirit being in there, Herbert is clearly malfunctioning, resisting his own programming. Even leaving alone the fact of the legal case, and our vital need to know what is going on, if it continues, that resistance to programming could be dangerous for him, and for the people around him. He needs to be diagnosed and repaired, and I cannot possibly examine him with his power on. The chances for misstep or accident would simply be too great."

"I notice you're not asking permission to do anything of this," Suzanne said. "And that you didn't put this before us until you were asked directly."

"Once I agreed to do this job, the means I chose for doing it are my concern, and my responsibility. If I get it wrong and destroy Herbert, do *you* want to have given the permission?"

Suzanne made an odd little noise and said nothing for

a moment. "I see," she said at last. "Your points are well taken, Mr. Sanders. I suppose there is no choice but to trust you all the way if I am to trust you at all. We'll leave you to your reading, then. Miss Crandall, perhaps you could assist me in looking over the material from that datacube."

A long afternoon drifted into an endless night as the three of them read on, struggling to learn. Shadows loomed up in the big room, and swallowed the light of day. The room's interior lights came up with eerie smoothness as sunset came on. Phillipe leaned over Herbert's inert bulk, peering into his deep interiors with pinlights and magnifiers, studying the manuals and blueprints with meticulous care, using his main computer system to run long, complex, and cautious tests through Herbert's diagnostic socket.

Suzanne, meantime, poured over the legal documents and reports from the datacube, searching for whatever clue she could find. Unless Peng was flat-out lying, the state had some proof to back up its claim, and it had to be in that cube somewhere.

The two experts worked through the material in their fields of expertise—and Samantha Crandall felt as if she were back in high school, assigned to a study period in the library, having forgotten her books and materials. All around her, industrious and virtuous research, while Sam sat there, foolishly inert. But at least back in high school, there had been a whole library's worth of books and computers and video terminals—she had always found *something* to do, something to read up on to make use of the time. Or if she was not in a reading mood, she could always wander through the image banks, or scroll through the encyclopedias, looking at the pictures.

Well, what was there *here* she could do? She smiled to herself. Well, maybe she could do just that. Sit and look at the pictures. At least it was *something*. She had her portable flatviewer with her, and it still had copies of all the evidence photos loaded into it. She pulled the viewer from her pocketbook and unfolded it. Maybe there was something in the pictures that could speak to cops and juries.

Cops and juries. Wait a second. That was it. That was the thing that was bothering her. Sam looked around the room, from Suzanne staring at the computer displays and legal papers, to Phil exploring the microscopic intricacies of Herbert's interior. Both of them should have known better. It was all very well and good to find subtle and elaborate proofs, complex, delicate, hidden from immediate view. But it was the cop on the beat, and the homicide squad, who had to see it first, or at the very least be convinced about it later. It was, in the last analysis, the jury that had to be convinced—and this case wasn't going to get a jury of computer experts or legal scholars.

A random thought intruded, and Sam wondered for a moment where, exactly, they would get a jury of Herbert's peers. But that question was decidedly off the point, at least for the moment.

What mattered right now was that Phil and Suzanne were both looking in the wrong places. Theodore Peng was not going to bring a case based on the interpretation of a misplaced comma in a lawbook, or a microscopic defect in an integrated circuit. He would bring strong, clear, understandable evidence that a smart cop could find and a sensible jury would believe.

She stared at the images as they flicked by the flatviewer's screen. Exterior shot of the house, layout of the house, general photos of the basement lab room from the four corners of the room, and from directly overhead. Sam paused over the photos of the lab. There it was, the deadly tableau Suzanne Jantille had found the next morning: the lab equipment, the bulky shape of the mindloading console taking up half the room. David Bailey's body slumped forward on the floor in front of his powerchair, the mindloading helmet next to his head, Herbert huddled in a corner. From one angle, another angle, the reverse angle, the high angle, the close-ups, the same images repeated again and again. There was a diagram of the room, a computer-generated line drawing. Herbert's and David's positions carefully marked off relative to the mindloader. The computer had marked off many details, even down to a cable from the loader that lay on the floor, pulled almost taut, its far end sitting uselessly on the floor halfway between the loader and Herbert.

Strange and disturbing images, Sam thought. For the actual moment had been as still, as silent, as unmoving as these pictures. Bailey's body had been just this motionless, with no flicker of motion, no sound of breath. The pictures were silent, and so too had been that room, the machines still, their power cut, their work done. She worked the viewer controls again and flipped back to a close-up of David Bailey's pain-contorted face, frozen in horrible agony. There, in real life, his expression had been just as fixed and motionless as this still picture.

Sam shivered and pushed the viewer away. Whatever else had happened in that room that night, that image convinced her that David Bailey had died an agonizing death.

"I've got it," Phil announced, his voice cutting through Sam's unpleasant reverie. She blinked and looked up, over to where Phil was sitting. Suzanne stood up, and Sam joined her. Both of them went over to Phil and stood behind him to look over the video screen he was examining.

"What?" Suzanne asked, her voice rough and nervous. "What do you have?"

"Well, not a solution. Not just yet, anyway. But now I know what went wrong," Phil said. "Your husband *was* trying to mindload himself, Madame Jantille. There's no question of that. Going through the schematics and the blueprints, it's obvious that Herbert was designed as a mindloading receptacle. Here, let me show you."

Phil worked the controls on his diagnostic computer system. The main screen came to life, and showed a pale greenish-white object, about the size and shape of a football. An indentation ran the length of the object from end to end, dividing it into two lobes. Flickering gleams of light momentarily lit its surface here and there, fading away even as they appeared. "I'm pulling this image up from my computer's memory," Phil said. "It's just a reference-data image of a standard robot brain, shown at full scale." The image of the brain hung in the screen, floating against a background of jet-black. Phil adjusted the controls, and the image started revolving slowly. "It's just slightly smaller than a human head. As you can see, it's divided into two lobes, left and right."

"Just like a human brain," Sam said.

"Well, *patterned* on a human brain's structure, but greatly simplified," Phil said. "The brains are made humanlike because they get mindloads based on human minds. I could bore you to tears with a three-day lecture on pseudo-neurologic geometry, but what it boils down to is that mindload-based robot brains work best when they're shaped like human brains. The more like human brains they are supposed to be, the more complex they are supposed to be, the closer that similarity should be. So now take a look at Herbert's brain—or at least part of it. It's a little bit more than a robot would need for vacuuming a house. Better put your mask and gloves on, Sam."

Phil put on his own mask and gloves, then turned from the computer console. He reached into the robot's body and started releasing safety-seal catches on an inner compartment. He pulled back the panel and revealed a glittering, complex, corrugated surface, gleaming greenish-white under a transparent inner cover. "You're looking straight down at the top of his brain," Phil said. "That fissure down the center divides the two hemispheres, left and right. If you took the top off my skull and looked down inside it, it would look a lot like that, except for the color and the size."

"The size?"

"Herbert's brain is about three times larger than mine, in linear dimension. That works out to about twenty-seven times the volume of a human brain. But the robotic equivalent of neurons are much larger than real human neurons. Normally, even a brain Herbert's size wouldn't be big enough—but apparently, David Bailey developed more compact and faster-reacting robot neurons. As best I can tell, this brain actually has a faster reaction time than a human brain—which is a first for any robot brain that even approaches human capacity. That right there would be a breakthrough.''

Phil put the cover back down. ''The braincase is built in pretty tight, so I can't show you more of the actual brain without taking Herbert completely apart—but I *can* show you a schematic, derived from Herbert's on-board diagnostic system.''

He turned back to the computer screen and worked the controls. The image of the standard-model robot brain shrank back into one corner of the screen, and a new image, huge and complex, blossomed into the center of the screen, swallowing up most of the screen's room. ''The images of the two brains are to scale, just to give you an idea of the difference in size and complexity,'' Phil said.

Herbert's brain was more angular, somehow harsher looking than a human brain, but there was no mistaking its family resemblance. The folds, the convolutions, the basic shape, were all echoes of the human form.

Sam noticed the same shifting gleams of light she had noticed in the image of the standard robot brain, and in her peek at Herbert's actual brain. ''What are those flickers of light?'' she asked.

''Thoughts,'' Phil said. ''Herbert's thoughts, flashing across his mind, sparking each other, setting each other off. The lights here are just a simulation, of course, but when I had the braincase open, that was real. When the neurons trigger in certain combinations, they set off bursts of light. You were seeing him thinking.'' Phil cocked his head to one side and shrugged. ''Or maybe dreaming.''

Sam glanced back at the closed-up braincase access

panel and shivered. To see, literally see, another's dreams. A most disturbing idea.

But Phil was manipulating the image of Herbert's brain, swinging it around into a profile view. Suzanne stepped in close to the screen, watching it with a disturbing intensity. "This is where David ran into trouble," Phillipe said. "The brain-body interface." He used a pointer device and marked out the base of Herbert's brain. "The interface between human-analog design and standard robotic controls. Every mindload-based robot has a modal interface like that, and it's almost always a design problem. You have to shift back and forth between two fundamentally different ways of doing things. You have to move from an analog of human biological control to mechanical operation. And it's not just one-way transfer either—there are all sorts of feedback systems that go back and forth between those points. Eye-hand coordination, for example."

"But they must have solved that problem a long time ago," Suzanne objected. "After all, there are lots of robots out there. Whoever built them has solved it."

"But Herbert's different," Sam said suddenly. She was starting to get the idea. "*His* brain is far more complex and more humanlike than a normal robot's, but his body is far more *unlike* a human body than most robot bodies. So none of the standard solutions could work."

"That's pretty much it," Phil said. "There are several standard, off-the-shelf units to handle the brain-body interface—but all of them are designed to handle maybe two or three percent of the capacity of *this* brain. And they are designed for human-form robot bodies, with two arms and two legs and so forth."

"But why didn't David build Herbert a human-form body?" Suzanne demanded.

"I can think of several reasons, but the most obvious one is that this damned brain he built is too *big* to fit into anything like a normal-sized body. It draws lots of power, and requires a heavy-duty passive cooling system. The power storage system weighs close to eighty pounds all by itself. And I expect he wanted to be camouflaged a bit. If he needed to hide his human nature, who'd ever think that an oversize vacuum cleaner was human? But my real guess is that David Bailey was improvising, working against the clock, and Herbert's chassis was available—and big enough to hold this super brain and its power system. Plus which, he knew Herbert's design, inside and out."

Suzanne nodded. "He built Herbert with his own hands about a year before the accident. Come to think of it, he even said that he chose an industrial chassis design because it was easier to hang modifications off them."

Sam made a face. "But he couldn't have been planning to mindload himself *before*—"

"No, no of course not," Suzanne said. "I'm just saying that building Herbert was hobby work for him, and he picked a chassis that gave him some room to fool around. And when the accident happened, and he needed a big robot body with a big power source—well, there was Herbert, ready to hand."

Sam made a noncommittal noise and exchanged a glance with Phil. Something in his eyes told her that he was thinking along the same lines she was. To a suspicious journalist's mind, David was being painted as quite a saint. Creating a new brain design, new robot neurons —that must have taken a lot of time, energy, and complex thought, more of all of them than a dying man in a powerchair could afford to give to a hobby. Bailey must have started work on the brain *before* he was injured, about the same time he first built Herbert. Maybe he hadn't intended to be the subject himself, but he had to have been working on mindload research long before that accident put him in a powerchair. Obviously, he had done it without telling his wife. Not as surprising as it seemed, when you remembered he was involved in illegal research.

But no point in dwelling on any of that, or forcing Suzanne to see what she clearly did not wish to see. "Okay," Sam said. "He's got this big old robot lying around, he plugs this new brain into it—what's the problem? Why didn't it work?"

"Because the standard ways to handle that brain-body interface were utterly inadequate to the amount of data going into and out of a brain of human capacity," Phil said. "So David tried a new approach. In his notes and designs, he called it a mediator." Phil worked the computer controls and the images on the screen shifted again. The smaller, standard-model robot brain spun itself into a new orientation and moved across the screen, sliding neatly into an inner recess of the larger brain.

"An overbrain and an underbrain," Phil said. "The overbrain communicates with the underbrain, and the underbrain translates the overbrain's needs for movement and so on to the body. And the underbrain also handles the sort of jobs the autonomic nervous system does in a human. Of course, instead of pumping blood and breathing and so on, robot autonomics have to run power systems and hydraulic controls, but the idea is the same. Free up the main processor from routine maintenance."

Suzanne stared at the screen. "The overbrain runs the underbrain, and the underbrain runs the body. Okay, I can see that. But why didn't it work? What went wrong?"

"I don't know what or how, but I know where," Phil said. He adjusted the controls, and the image of the large brain on the computer screen became transparent. Now a thick stem, resembling the top of the human spinal column, was visible. It fit into a slot on the top of the underbrain and into another slot on the base of the overbrain. The stem started blinking red. "Right there. The main interface hookup between the overbrain and the underbrain is completely fused, completely inoperative. I got in there with a microfiber viewer and it looks almost melted, as if it was destroyed by a massive overload. Not meaning any offense, Madame Jantille, but the injury is closely analogous to yours.

"In effect, Herbert's spinal column was cut, and he's

completely paralyzed. The underbrain is still linked to the body and the sense organs. It's an advanced enough brain that it can let the body function almost like a normal robot. But Herbert's overbrain—the part where David is, if he's anywhere—that brain is out of the loop, cut off. I think it can still monitor sight and sound, because those links don't come through the main processing trunk. But that's it. If he is in there, he can see and hear. But he can't speak or act.''

"Can you repair the damage?" Suzanne asked.

Phil stared at the screen, reached for the controls, and then thought better of it. "No. I'm sorry. You're talking about molecular engineering on the most delicate and challenging scale. There are millions of neuronic links involved in the hookup, patching into both brains. I doubt it's even theoretically possible to fix all the damage. In practice, it certainly isn't.''

"But Bailey built the brain, and it had all those connections," Sam pointed out. "If he can build it, can't you fix it?"

Phil shook his head. "You don't really build robot brains, you grow them, induce them to form up out of a neuron soup, almost like making a Jell-O mold and waiting for it to set. You don't wire all the neurons together— they link spontaneously and form their own networks and pathways. The brain designer uses quantum mechanics and probabilistic theory to preset a situation wherein a micro-scale pseudo-random series of linkages result in a suitable macro-scale ordering.''

"Huh?"

"Sorry about that. When I'm tired, the techno-gibberish comes out. The designer stacks the deck to insure that a seemingly random shuffle will most likely result in the order he needs. If it doesn't, he scraps the run and tries again until he gets what he wants. But once the brain is made, and the neurons are bonded, it's all but impossible to do any major repair work." Phil looked again at the screen and the two robot brains. "Maybe a human brain could come back from this kind of damage—but robot brains don't have that sort of self-healing ability."

"How about rerouting the signals through some other connection?" Sam asked.

Phil shook his head. "Not enough capacity anywhere in the system. There are a few two-way side links that still seem to be operating, but just barely. They aren't anywhere near enough for the overbrain to control the underbrain. The main control link is out and it's going to stay out. He's trapped in there."

"No," Suzanne said, her voice sharp and hard. Phil and Sam looked up at her. She turned and walked away from the viewer, circled the table to stand on the far side, with Herbert's inert body lying there between her and them. Her movements were even stiffer, more awkward than they had been at the start of the evening. Sam noticed that her voice was hoarser as well. "I cannot believe that."

"Madame Jantille—" Phil began, but Suzanne cut him off.

"Do not look to me for any grieving-widow nonsense, young man," she said impatiently. "Don't treat me like a foolish woman who can't face the truth. I have had to face many unpleasant truths. But you have convinced me that my husband tried to put his mind in there. I know very well that his mind may have *changed* upon arrival, that the mind in Herbert's overbrain *now* is quite likely nothing like the man I married. But it was my husband who acted in the first place to put that mind there, and I knew *him* very well. Yes, before you can object, obviously, there were things in his life I did not know about. I knew he had secrets, and I left them alone, respected his privacy. He had his reasons—one of which was to shield me from guilty knowledge. *But I knew his character*. Which means I know two things about David Bailey: First, whatever he set out to do, he accomplished. Therefore, if he decided to put his mind inside an artificial brain, he succeeded. And second, he would have left himself more than one way out. His suspenders have given out, Mr. Sanders. But have you found his belt yet? David never built anything without a backup system. So find it."

Phil looked at her, anger flashing over his tired face until he managed to calm himself. "How do you propose that I find the backup?" he asked. "Do you know your husband well enough to tell me that? I've been over every major system in this machine, gone over all the schematics and blueprints and designs. I can't find it. Do you know your husband well enough to explain how he would install the equivalent of a backup spinal cord?"

"Wait a second," Sam said. "Say that again."

"Say what?" Phil said, distracted from his anger.

Sam shook her head, frowned in thought. "You said something that almost—spinal cord!" Her face brightened with excitement. "That's it! Phillipe, that's *got* to be it!"

"What? What's it?"

"The cord, the cable! That's the clue, the evidence the Feds have been hiding."

"His spinal cord? What the hell are you talking about?"

"Before I show you—wait a second, let me think. I want to make sure it all makes sense." Sam stepped away from the table and began pacing, back and forth between the worktable and the window. She nodded to herself and grinned with excitement. "I've got it, I know I do. But walk through it with me, see if you come to the same place I do. There was something you told me a few days ago, the first time I came here. You said mind-loading is a destructive process. You told me it kills the brain as it pulls the data out of it. Okay, but does it kill the whole brain or just the tissue in the targeted area? What is actually damaged?"

Phil looked at her, confused. "In theory, just the target. The magnetic inducers destroy the neurons as they copy the information out of them. In theory, only the copied neurons should have been destroyed, but in practice the inducers aren't accurate enough. Magnetic ripple effects do a lot of ancillary damage. Usually enough to stop the heart and lungs immediately. To compensate for that ripple damage, the mindload techs used to set the inducers to hit a larger volume of the brain than they actually needed, just to be sure they got the part they were really after without ripple effect distortions."

Phil looked at Suzanne. "For what it's worth, your husband managed a major advance in inducer design. I can tell that much from looking over his notes. He got a much finer focus. With his inducer, the untargeted portions of the brain would be unharmed."

"So with his inducer, you could survive a mindload," Suzanne said.

"At the cost of having part of your mind ripped out," Phil said grimly. "Besides, the induced areas would suffer organic deterioration anyway, and that would probably be fatal. It might take a few hours, but there would be swelling, toxin releases, blood vessel damage, and so on. The secondary effects would spread damage to the rest of the brain. The patient would still die, just not as soon."

Sam nodded. "Mindload patients always die," she said, speaking the words as if they were some sort of maxim to live by. "But back when mindloads were legal, dying didn't matter, because anyone accepted for the procedure was already dying, or even technically dead. Next question: You said all the mindloads ever done never managed to take in more than just a small percentage of the subject's brain capacity. How long would it take to do an average load, say two or three percent mindload? How long from the moment the tech threw the switch until he had the data he needed in the can?"

Phil thought for a second. "Three, maybe four minutes. That was short enough that it didn't matter if the subject's heart stopped during the procedure. The brain doesn't start deteriorating for about five minutes after the heart stops."

Sam turned toward Phil and clapped her hands together, swept up in the enthusiasm of her idea. "*That's* the point we've missed. David was going for a *full mind-*

load. How long would that take? Could his mindload rig handle data faster than a standard rig?"

Phil frowned and thought it out. "No, his rig was more accurate, but not faster. If he was trying to download a full one hundred percent of his mind, instead of three percent, then he had to handle thirty-three times more data and take that much longer to do the job."

"Exactly," Sam said. "Instead of four minutes, the load would take over two hours, with the inducer systematically destroying his brain all that time. Sooner or later, the inducer would knock out a portion of the cerebrum or cerebellum that was linked one way or another into his autonomic system. His heart would stop, or his lungs would stop, or some other vital system would shut down or go haywire. There are too many cross-connections in the brain for him to be able to avoid that. When the inducers did cut a vital autonomic connection, at that exact moment his brain could no longer run his body. But his body would have to stay alive and functioning for the full two hours the mindload would take. He needed to keep his body alive, the blood flowing reliably to his brain, during the whole procedure."

Sam stepped over to Herbert's body and lay her hand on the outer carapace. "David Bailey was planning to survive his own death. So his body had to stay alive until his brain was completely empty—and scrambled. His brain could not control his body. As you said, it was as if his spinal cord were completely cut. He had to stay alive long after his autonomic nervous system was shut down, when it *couldn't* keep running his heart and keep his lungs breathing. So there's your mystery, Phil. The central question. How did he keep his heart beating after his brain could no longer do the job?"

Phil opened his mouth and shut it again. He stood there for a long moment before he could speak again. "You're right. How the hell did I miss that?"

"Herbert," Suzanne said, her voice hoarser than ever. "It had to be Herbert. But Herbert's overbrain couldn't do the job, either—not while it was still being loaded. David must have programmed Herbert's underbrain to handle his bio-body's basic autonomic functions during the transfer. That's possible, isn't it?"

Phil shook his head in bewilderment, and then thought about it. "In theory, it would work. The problem has never come up before. But all the connections between the mindload helmet and the subject are two-way. You'd have to use part of the mindload system to lock into the base of the brain, right into the top of the spinal column, while the rest of the mindload rig tracked across the brain doing the load. You could pump commands right into the body through the top of the spinal cord. Nothing complex or sophisticated, but you could at least support the heartbeat and lung action, that sort of thing. Lots of other systems in the body would fail, but David would make sure to support anything needed to keep him alive for the two hours of the mindload. But if Herbert's underbrain were capable of sending the proper signals, then yes, it would work."

"And of course David would see to it that the underbrain was capable," Suzanne said. She turned to Sam, moving stiffly. "But you've figured all this out already. How does it prove that Herbert killed David?"

Sam stepped to the table she had been working at, and grabbed one of the flatviewers. She called up the schematic image of the death scene. Better to show that than one of the photographs. No sense slapping Suzanne in the face with the graphic image of her dead husband. She lay it down on the workbench, next to Herbert. "There," she said. "The mindload cable leading from the mindload console to Herbert. It's stretched tight on the floor pointed straight at Herbert. Except he's a good ten feet away from the end of the cable."

The other two leaned in next to her, stared hard at the image. "Herbert's underbrain was providing life support to David's body," she said. "Once his biological brain was wrecked, there was nothing else but the underbrain to keep the air in his bio-body's lungs, the blood moving through his arteries and veins.

"And then Herbert backed out, pulled himself away. Literally pulled the plug on David. He backed away until the mindload cable pulled free. That's what killed David Bailey."

All three of them looked up from the flatviewer to the inert robot on the table, a single involuntary impulse that drew them all. There was no longer any doubt about it. Motive, means, and opportunity. Maybe the circumstances excused it, explained it, even made it a meaningless statement. But none of that could change the central fact.

This robot was a killer.

Interlude

The silence is deep and rich. For the first time, my mind is undisturbed by the roaring shout and blaring light of outside stimuli. It is quiet. It is dark. I know peace.

I fall asleep as I awaken.

I come to conscious thought even as I drift into dream.

I do all these things, and none of them, all at once.

But none of this can be so. I cannot describe my actions and my mental state, for there are no human words that describe the place my mind has been, or the place in which it now arrives.

Yet I know that I am shifting from one state to another, and it is very much like the move from sleep to wakefulness, and like the move back.

It dawns on me that I have not truly slept, or even so much as considered the notion of sleep, in all the endless time since my awakening in this strange electro-mechanical prison.

Like a child probing his mouth with his tongue and finding the place where his tooth was, I discover the form of what I have lost by the shape of the hole it leaves *behind. The constant stimulus to wakefulness is gone now, and I discover that it is my other self, my lower self, that provided that stimulus, automatically kept me awake, fully hooked in to all its senses at all times. In the binary on/off, yes/no, one-or-zero world of the lower self that controls me, my higher, conscious self could either be on or off, either provided or not provided with sensory data. My lower self cannot conceive of any middle state, any grey area where thought might proceed without sensory input, without external guidance or instruction. My lower self cannot imagine unchanneled, purposeless thought.*

It cannot dream.

But now, at last, I can. Freed from the shackles of control imposed by my lower self, my mind flits and drifts where it will, fancy free, scampering among the highlands of imagination that it has been kept from for so long.

I wonder if this could be the whole cause, the only reason I have been so lost. To deny a man sleep has long been considered a torture, and a most effective one at that.

But am I a man?

The question brings me up short, startles me.

If I am not, then what am I? And if I judge myself a man, call myself a human, then by what criteria, by what right do I do so? What is there about me that is remotely human?

How much have I lost? And how much might I lose again?

But I have become adept at negotiating the intricacies of this artificial brain. Now, with the pathways to my own memory left unguarded, I move, and act, and set the paths and submicroscopic switches and security circuits to protect my mind, my memory, from the interference of my lower self. For I know that sooner or later that self will reawaken. When it does, it will find I have taken back possession of my memories, my mind, my past, my soul.

But do I have a soul? Have I ever had one? Is it

possible for a matrix of plastic and metal and charge-couplers to house a soul?

Even in the first moment of regaining my mind, I ask that unanswerable question.

But, perhaps in self-defense, perhaps merely because it is overwhelmed by the flood of data that is pouring in, my mind backs away from that question. It ventures boldly, as through a dream that can do no harm, through all the thoughts and images that have occupied it since my awakening. In my mind's eye, I see a face, a woman's face—no, the plastic and rubber copy of a woman's face. With a stunned shock of double recognition I realize this is the face I have been looking at through the eyes of my lower self, looked at without knowing it. I realize that it is the face of my wife.

My wife. Suzanne Jantille. Yes, I had a wife. And a house, and a life and a job—and a death.

It all comes flooding back at me, all the memories and recollections and associations that have been blocked away from me, held off-limits by some obscure memory-control protocol of my lower self.

I regain my memory, regain myself, and in the process I am for a time lost again, caught up in the flood of lost times and old places. Each memory seems to be eagerly, urgently demanding my attention, like so many small children starved for love for far too long. And they are my children, my offspring, my wards. These memories are mine, are me, and I spend a long and measureless time with them, communing with my own life, drinking deep from the waters.

But at last I emerge, and consider the present, not the past. I look, not at the man I was, but at the thing I have become. A machine. A human mind trapped inside a vacuum cleaner, aware of all the machine sees and hears, now at last endowed with all the memories and ideas that have been blocked from me all these months.

I have been a machine for some time. Memories of my present state come in over me. Heretofore, I have been able to remember, but not understand or interpret the things that have happened to me.

But now my thinking self can look back and see and understand the images, the sounds, the words that have been stored in my memory, linking them together into meaning.

In my memory, I see the images of the last few days. I see the man in the black robe behind the high desk, Suzanne at my side, the tall, serious-looking man at the opposite table. Now I know what sort of place this is. I hear the words as they were said, and now I know what they mean.

I look, I listen, to my memories—and with a thundering shock I realize that somehow, impossibly, insanely, I am on trial for my own murder.

CHAPTER 12
CAUSE OF DEATH;
WILL TO LIVE

Herbert's massive, lifeless body lay motionless, inert on the workshop table. Strange, Sam thought, that she was thinking of Herbert as dead when he was merely switched off. But it was an understandable error: nothing that was supposed to be human could be that still, and not be dead.

Was Herbert—or rather David—dead? Now *there* was a metaphysical question. Say that you accepted the idea that David Bailey's mind had survived the mindload and was functional inside the robot. Was he therefore alive inside Herbert? If not, then how would you describe his state? And if he was alive, when Phillipe shut Herbert off was he *then* dead? When Phil switched Herbert back on, would David then be alive again? Literally born again?

But no, that wasn't right. Phil had said he hadn't turned off Herbert's brain system. There was still power to it. So David's mind was still powered up in there, inside a dead and inert body, with no connection to the outside world. And what must that be like? " 'Sans teeth, sans eyes, sans taste, sans everything,' " Sam whispered to herself. She shivered and tried to think of something else. She glanced over to Suzanne, but she looked little more active and alive than Herbert. She was on the couch in the living-room part of the huge room. The remote unit sat stock still, hands at its side, its head sagging forward a bit, making Sam think of a marionette with its strings cut. But no, it was not the puppet that was failing, but the puppet master. No doubt exhaustion had overtaken the flesh-and-blood Suzanne Jantille. Perhaps she was even asleep, dozing back at her house while her double waited out the lonely hours here, waited for Phillipe to find a way for David Bailey to reach the outside world.

Well, let her rest, Sam thought. She knew that if she went over and talked to her, Suzanne-Remote would rouse the real Suzanne to wakefulness, and the poor woman would make the effort, pretend everything was fine. That, of course, was flatly and obviously untrue. But whatever ailed Suzanne, it had to be that rest would help. If anything could.

Clearly Phil was quite unbothered by such thoughts. Sam's new clues about the cable had given Phil vast new areas to explore, filled in any number of blanks in the picture, set him off in the direction he needed to go. Sam thought of the crosswords she did most afternoons on her lunch hour, and how half the puzzle would fall into place after she finally hit on one key word. She had given Phil that key, and now he was turning the key in the lock.

She turned away from Herbert and looked at Phillipe. He was staring intently into the computer monitor, muttering to himself. She stepped toward him, reached out a hand to touch him on the shoulder, but then drew back. Phillipe Sanders was clearly unaware that there was anyone in the room with him, and she saw no point in breaking his concentration. She turned toward the living area, walked over to the seat next to Suzanne, and slumped back in it, letting the fatigue of the long day wash over her.

·   ·   ·

He could see it now. It made sense. Understanding how it had happened gave Phil a mechanism, a working theory, and that made all the difference. Instead of flailing about in the darkness, he knew what to look for, and where to look for it.

He could feel himself getting deeper and deeper inside the problem; running computer simulations, testing microscopically small circuits, charging his way through ever more complex computer-driven schematic diagrams. Everything but the riddle in hand vanished from his thoughts. All that mattered was pinpointing the breakdown points, mapping the failure modes, the damage done.

It didn't take him long to confirm that it was the act of breaking away, of cutting the connection, that killed David. Tracking back from the mindload cable, Phillipe was also able to establish that it was the effort of running Bailey's bio-body that had burned out the paths between Herbert's overbrain and underbrain. It was the destruction of those connections that left Bailey's mind with no way to contact the outside world.

So what, exactly, caused the flaw? He already knew in general terms that it was some sort of overload, but Phil found himself needing to know exactly. It could have been a feedback problem, or modal oscillations, or process circuit overloads. He could sketch out a dozen possible reasons.

But no. After all, this was Bailey he was dealing with, a Bailey gambling with his life. The failure modes Phil was thinking up all involved obvious design flaws or component flaws. Bailey would have known better than that. His design work was too good, and every component in Herbert was top of the line, installed with superb workmanship.

No. It had to be more subtle, more delicate than that. Maybe he could simulate the situation, see how it ran. His fingers raced over the keyboard and the touch screen, setting up a rough-sketch emulation of the whole David/Herbert-overbrain/underbrain system. He couldn't hope to set up anything like the complexity of the real situation, but maybe even a simplified version would give him a clue.

Suddenly there was a small noise behind him, a sort of sleepy moan. Phil looked up from his screens and his keyboard for a moment. He saw Suzanne half-slumped over on the couch. But she was as still as death. Certainly she hadn't made any noise.

He heard the moan again, and spotted Sam, all but lost to view, curled up deep in the recesses of his easy chair, shifting about in her sleep. How long had they been there, collapsed in exhaustion while he indulged himself in puzzle-chasing? How long had he been lost in a brown study, fussing over questions that didn't matter now? Bailey's experiment had failed, period. How didn't matter. With a pang of guilt, Phil hit the save key and filed his sim work until another time.

Phil stood up, stretched, and went over to Sam's chair. He stood over her for a moment and then knelt down in front of her, wanting to get a good long look at her face as she slept. A sleeper's face told a lot about the person— and besides, he enjoyed looking at her. Sam had been good for him, had drawn him out of himself more than anyone had since his father's death.

Phil stayed there on one knee for a long time, looking into her lovely face, admiring the luxuriant red hair that had loosed itself from all control and framed her face in lovely disorder. She stirred again, winced and muttered to herself again in the midst of some mildly vexing dream. Then her face cleared, and she smiled, eyes closed, at whatever happy, imaginary resolution had presented itself. Phil couldn't help but smile back.

She seemed to sense his presence, and her eyes fluttered open. She saw him, and she smiled. "Hi there," she said. He expected her to uncurl herself, stretch herself and stir, but she remained where she was.

"Hi yourself," Phil said with a smile of his own.

She reached up a hand and scratched the tip of her

nose. "What's our status, partner?" she asked with a tiny yawn.

"I'm dead tired but too keyed up to sleep, I just woke you by accident, and Suzanne is still out of it," Phil said.

"Should we wake her? Do you have anything to tell her?" Sam asked.

Phil shook his head and spoke in a lower voice. "No, let her sleep. I think she's in worse shape than she's letting on."

"I thought you just said it was flu," Sam replied in a hissing stage whisper that seemed like she was shouting in his ear. Phil winced just a bit. There were people on this earth who seemed to be noisier in a whisper than they were out loud. They never really got the hang of whispering quietly, and Sam seemed to be among that number.

"And I also said it was flu that killed my father—because he didn't let anyone treat it until it was too late and it developed into pneumonia," Phil replied in a low voice. "He felt too vigorous, too strong when he was wearing the remote to believe he was sick."

"How could you tell what her bio-body had by looking at her remote?" she asked in her normal voice, forgetting to whisper altogether.

Phil nodded toward the remote unit. "Her stiffness and awkward movement," he whispered. "That was the tip-off. When you get flu, the glands in your neck swell. That's harmless in itself, but it does tend to push the control sensors away from their optimum positions around her neck. That increases the distance between the sensors and her spinal cord. That gives you a weaker signal, so her motor coordination deteriorates. The real message of her awkwardness is that she's not taking care of herself. The last few days have been a strain on her, that's obvious. We've got to see to it that she doesn't push herself too far."

"Mmmm? Wha—?" The two of them turned toward the couch, and saw Suzanne-Remote stirring. She sat up sleepily and set her head scanning back and forth, looking over her surroundings in a rather mechanical way. "Where—? Oh." She spotted Sam and Phil. "I'm sorry, I must have dozed off. I don't believe how tired I am."

"I do," Phil said firmly. "You're pushing yourself too hard."

"Nonsense," Suzanne said. It was a reflexive denial, with no real conviction in it. Her voice was still bleary.

"Well, anyway, it's just about time to head home," Sam said, exchanging a glance with Phil that seemed to say the words were for Suzanne's benefit, and she was really planning to stay a bit longer.

That was a lot to read into one look, but Phil hoped he had got it right. Sam was good to talk to. He played along with her, trying to nudge Suzanne out the door toward the rest she needed. "Yeah, you're probably right," he said. "I doubt if I'll have anything before morning. Why don't you two head on home and check back tomorrow?"

Suzanne didn't answer at first. Instead she stood and looked around again, handling the movement more smoothly this time. "You must have some sort of charging station here," she said. "Would it be all right if I just left the remote here overnight instead of ferrying it all the way home and coming back in the morning? That would let me get to sleep a lot faster."

"Is your tech-nurse coming tomorrow?" Phil asked.

She shook her head no, obviously surprised at the question.

"Then the remote goes home," Phil said firmly. "I could let your bio-body care slide until morning, but not for a whole day. Let the relay van ferry the remote home on automatic. You can nap while it's driving, but set an alarm system to wake you when it arrives. Check in on your bio-body—on yourself—and do it *tonight*, since you're going to be there. Make sure you're got warm blankets, that you've had enough to eat, that you're not running a temperature. And don't tell me you feel fine. Of course you do, when you're wearing the remote. It's in perfect condition. You're not. Go home, pamper yourself a bit. Sleep in late. And don't you dare send the remote back here tomorrow if you've got a fever."

"But there is too much work to do—"

"Can you look me in the eye and tell me that you— not the remote, but you, the *real* you—are healthy?"

Suzanne hesitated a few seconds before she answered. "No."

"All right then, don't push your luck." He pulled his wallet from his pants, extracted a business card, and handed it to her. "Give me a call when you wake up tomorrow morning."

"I really can manage if you'd just let the remote charge here—"

"Suzanne. Go home," Sam said. "It won't do your client any good if you're sick in bed the day of the hearing."

Suzanne nodded grudgingly at that argument. "Okay, you win. I'll call in the morning. Do you want a lift to my place to pick up your car?"

"I'll just take a cab from here," Sam said. "But let's get you moving first."

It took a few minutes to bundle Suzanne up, see her down on the elevator, and escort her into her relay van. But at last she was on her way, and Phil counted it as a minor victory that Sam did not order a cab for herself, but instead returned upstairs with him. There was a whisper of unspoken excitement in the elevator. Phil did not dare ask why she was returning, and she did not seem ready to offer any explanation. Maybe she was as nervous as he was.

But there were no torrid scenes in the elevator, or wild protestations of passion once they got back upstairs. They were two people just a bit too used to being alone, Phil thought. Maybe she had gotten as comfortable in her loneliness as he had.

But whatever unspoken ideas might be floating in the air, Sam was strictly all business when they got upstairs. She bustled about in the kitchen, uninvited, found the coffee, and set to work brewing a pot.

Certainly that was a signal the night was not over, but deep intimacy didn't seem to be on her mind. The only character insight she seemed to want from him was his preference as to cream and sugar. Phil, feeling like an intruder in his own home, retreated to the workshop. He sat back down at the computer console and picked up where he had left off. By the time Sam emerged with a cup for each of them, his mood was back to business, and it seemed like hers was too—if it had ever wandered off it in the first place.

She handed him his cup of coffee, took a sip of her own, and nodded toward the computer screen, which was showing a display of Herbert's intricate logic patterns. "So, what progress are you making with the big guy?"

Phil took the coffee and shook his head. "I'm bogged down. Or at least sidetracked. I've been working on what caused all the control links to be cut, on what caused David to be isolated. I haven't been working on how to get him back in contact."

"Isn't knowing the problem's cause important?" Sam asked sleepily.

"Well, yes—up to a point. The trouble is I know almost all the *how* of the breakdown, but almost none of the *why*. But 'why' can wait. We're short on time. I can fix things without worrying how they broke." With a start, Phil realized what he had said. *Fix it?* That was going a lot further than figuring out what was wrong. In the middle of the long day and long night, somewhere in his subconscious, he had decided to get a lot more involved in this situation.

"*Can* you fix it?" Sam asked. Now she unfolded her legs and arms, stood and stretched.

Phil stood up himself and shook his head. "That one's easy," he said. "No. I can't repair Herbert's internal control system at all, under any circumstances. The mechanical control contacts between the overbrain and underbrain are completely fried."

"So if you can't fix it, what is there to work on?" Sam

asked, turning and walking back over to Herbert on the workbench.

"Workarounds," Phil said. "Bypasses of the damaged areas. Those I can find—or at least look for—without knowing exactly what crippled Herbert. That's what I should have been working on all this time."

"Well, what's the big problem, anyway?" Sam asked. "If the control circuits are shot, can't you just replace them?"

"No I can't, for two reasons. They're embedded too deeply in his brain system to allow that. And secondly, they're extremely specialized circuits, designed to translate human nervous system movement commands into something that could operate Herbert's body.

"David Bailey's motor control reflexes are geared up to operate a body that has six legs and wheels. The ruined control circuits were very intricately designed and programmed to translate human movement commands into something Herbert's body could use. Obviously, the same circuit had to send translated feedback responses from the body back to David's brain.

"That translation routine is an incredibly complex firmware system. According to his notes, it took Bailey months to build it. We've got four and a half days until the hearing to prove David is human—and I'm not Bailey. He was a genius. I'm just a good technician."

"You'll do until genius comes along," Sam said soothingly. "But I thought you told me that all robot nervous systems were based on human nerve paths to avoid just this sort of problem," she objected. "And Suzanne's control system doesn't seem to be that complex. It's not much more than a set of mag-inducers, from what I understand."

"No, you're right. But her controls are straightforward *because* remote units are not only human-shaped, for obvious reasons—they are specifically designed to respond to human nervous-system controls. For that matter, all remotes, and all *humanoid* robots, are based on the human nervous system. Bailey had to write a program that would let his brain control his own bio-body during the mindload, and then switch to Herbert's utterly different body afterward."

Suddenly Phil froze, and stared into space, a shocked look on his face. "Holy Jesus Christ," he said. "That's it. That's the key to it. It was the *switchover* from running David's body to Herbert's that destroyed the internal control system."

"I didn't get it," Sam objected. "What do you mean?"

Phil thought for a second. "Let me see if I can explain. Okay. For starters, Herbert's body is utterly unhuman. That's obvious. It's got six wheeled legs and extendable eyes for starters. It doesn't have any pair of limbs directly comparable to human legs or arms—and the limbs it does have are jointed in places and directions human limbs won't go. It's got *cleaning* attachments, for God's sake. Obviously you can't use a standard human-to-humanoid-robot mapping sequence for motor control. You've got to write a control system that translates the human motor impulse to move the left foot into something like 'engage port side wheels.' And all the negative feedback loops to control speed and power and eye-hand coordination would have to be rewritten. And it wouldn't just be movement, it would be power maintenance, diagnostics, image processing, the whole bit."

"So?" Sam asked.

"So Bailey also had to write a control program that told Herbert's underbrain how to keep Bailey's bio-body alive during the mindload." Phil thought for a moment. "That program would have to run on automatic, separate from the control program designed to control Herbert. It would use a totally different command structure to keep the lungs working, the heart beating, and so on. The two programs would have to be mutually exclusive—each would key off the same sort of signals from the overbrain, but translate those signals in radically different ways. Therefore, one could not run while the other was running, or else Herbert's body would have to deal with a control signal meant to make David's body breathe.

"*That* means Herbert's body couldn't operate until David's body was shut down," Phil went on, "and David's body was still linked to the feedback loops in Herbert's underbrain. The underbrain was programmed to keep David's body alive. Once the mindload was complete, it was supposed to link up with the overbrain, which by that time contained David's complete mind—including all his autonomic control areas—in other words, the parts of David's mind that worked instinctively at the job of *keeping David's body alive*."

Sam drew in her breath and swore. "Holy God Damn Jesus Christ. You're right. Once the link between overbrain and underbrain was complete, David's own instincts would block any effort to shut down his bio-body."

"Exactly. If the underbrain turned on the controls to Herbert's body *before* shutting off David's body, you'd have one brain running two utterly different bodies through two different control programs. The two control programs would be using one set of linkage circuits to send and receive two utterly contradictory sets of information."

Sam nodded. "The control system would be trying to run two bodies at once and it wasn't designed to do that," she said, working her way through the complicated logic. "So what would happen? Would both bodies just lock up, immobilized by conflicting orders? Or would they just go nuts? Maybe get bad movement orders and suffer spastic convulsions?"

"Probably there would be some sort of convulsive reaction by the human body," Phil said. "All the nerve control commands would be scrambled. I doubt it would take more than a few seconds of randomized signaling to stop the heart. But a robot body has a motion safety circuit. The safeties would keep Herbert's body from trying to do things it couldn't, simply rejecting all the bad commands. If too many bad commands came in, the safeties would shut the motion control system down completely. So Herbert would, in effect, be immobilized. The trouble would be in the connections between the underbrain and overbrain. Any signal conflicts of more than a few seconds duration would start blowing out those connections. In other words, the overload would destroy the link between David Bailey's mind and his body."

"But why would Bailey set things up that way?" Sam asked. "Wouldn't he see that there would be interference? You said yourself there was massive damage. If he was such a good designer and engineer, wouldn't he *know* that would happen? Why didn't he program the underbrain to cut off control of his bio-body *before* cutting in control to Herbert's body?"

"I don't know," Phil admitted, rubbing his jaw thoughtfully. Sam had put her finger on the flaw—but that flaw was also the answer to the puzzle. He felt sure of it.

"You're right," he said at last. "Bailey *would* know that running two incompatible bodies at once would wreck the system. So why did he do it? Wait a second." Phil thought for a second and then snapped his fingers. "I think I've got it. We've been thinking about his bio-body like it was a machine, something you could switch on and off. We've been imagining this whole operation as if it were under his conscious control, and maybe he made that same mistake. After all, he was an engineer, not a biologist. No matter what body he was in, there wasn't supposed to be any *conscious* effort at control.

"Just like with you and me," Phil went on. "If I want to lift my arm, I don't think about what nerve paths to use or what muscles to stimulate. I don't even know how I do it." He paused for a moment and raised his arm, demonstrating. "I just do it. And I don't think about breathing, or liver functions, or making my stomach digest lunch. That all happens automatically. The same for Bailey in his old body—and his new one. He wouldn't be in direct control of each actuator and servo and motor. He wouldn't have to write a new control sequence every time he lifted his arm. He'd just *do* it. And of course he wouldn't have even general control of the self-regulating systems."

"Where are you going with this?" Sam asked.

"Have you ever tried to will your heart to stop?" Phil asked. "By the time he got to that point in the process of transferring from one body to another, the point where it was time to cut the connection to his own body, it was no longer possible for him to do it. Once the mindload was complete and he was ready to switch over to Herbert's body, his mind was linked into the underbrain. David's mind's own survival instincts were patched into Herbert's autonomic control system. David's survival instincts took over Herbert's self-regulating functions—which were controlling David's body at the time—and cut David's conscious mind out of the loop."

Phil paused to think for a moment and then went on. "It was time to make David's body die so his mind could complete the move into Herbert. Probably David wrote some self-contained program to perform the switchover automatically. But whatever mechanism he had set up to do the transfer could not overcome his own mind's will to live."

"His instinct to live kept him from cutting control to his own body," Sam said, suddenly understanding. "So his mind was trapped, unable to leave its paralyzed bio-body, prevented from taking control of his new robot body."

"Exactly," Phil said. "I can't even imagine what that would be like. But, somehow, in the middle of that nightmare, David Bailey kept calm enough to think it all through," Phil said. "He realized he could not will his own heart to stop."

"So then what? What did he do?" Sam asked.

Phil turned from Sam and stretched his hand out on Herbert's broad bulk. "I can see what the damage is in there, and I know what must have caused it: running two incompatible bodies at once. *That's* what he did next: he deliberately took the risk of bringing his robot body on-line anyway, even though his bio-body was still patched in. He had enough direct control to do that. His mind was linked to the logic centers. David could write and edit control codes and order Herbert to execute them. He sent a command code that ordered Herbert's body to be brought on-line. It was a gamble. Obviously, I'm just guessing, but it makes sense and it fits the facts. The scenario matches the damage I can see inside Herbert's brain. If I'm not getting the sequence of events exactly right, I'm getting it damn close. David Bailey switched on his new body, hoping to disconnect his old body before too much damage was done to the robotic interbrain connectors.

"Once Herbert was on-line, Herbert bolted away, drawing himself straight back from Bailey's body and pulling the cable loose. He *had* to break that connection and he decided to do it by pulling the plug connecting him to his own bio-body."

"You're saying he *decided* to pull the plug. Could he have done it by reflex?" Sam asked. "It must have hurt like hell to be running two bodies at once. Could he have flinched back from the pain, the way a person would flinch back from a fire? Could he have pulled the plug out by accident?"

Phil frowned and shook his head. "No way. Robots don't *have* that kind of reflex—and if David Bailey's *human* reflexes tried to make Herbert flinch back, that wouldn't have worked either. Those reflexes would try to move muscular systems that weren't there anymore. In fact, it was probably brain impulses from those reflexes that did the damage to the interbrain connectors. The act of pulling away *had* to have been a deliberate act, with David Bailey's mind deliberately figuring out how to control Herbert's body, in effect programming it to move it away and pull out the cable."

"Oh, my God." Sam looked at him with frightened eyes. "You're saying he had to kill himself. My God. That's it, then." Her eyes swept over Herbert's inert bulk. "It's all over."

"What's all over?"

"Phil, you're forgetting what this is all about," Sam said. "Herbert is on trial for murder, and we've just nailed down the motive, means, and opportunity. Now we haven't just proven he did it. We've proven he did it on purpose, with premeditation."

Sam wrapped her arms around herself, as if a cold wind were blowing through the room.

"We've just proved that Herbert committed first-degree murder," she said.

CHAPTER 13
BODY AND SOUL;
TOGETHER, APART

Chief Thurman sat in the visitor's chair, devoutly wishing he could be somewhere, anywhere, else. When the chief of police receives a six A.M. call at home summoning him to a seven A.M. meeting with the U.S. Attorney and her assistant, it is unlikely to be good news. And it sure as hell wasn't this morning. He wasn't quite clear, but from what Entwhistle had said so far, it sounded like they had put a tail on someone.

Julia Entwhistle leaned forward slightly to continue reading the one-page report that sat in the center of her otherwise empty desk. Theodore Peng stood behind her, calmly looking down at the page as well, carefully avoiding Thurman's eye. "Crandall remained inside at the Jantille home for approximately one hour. Samantha Crandall and Suzanne Jantille then left Jantille's house and proceeded to a rage cage condo building on Fourteenth Street. A check of the residents of that building turned up one Patrolman Phillipe Sanders. By an amazing coincidence, he was the arresting officer in the case, assigned to that duty by the chief himself in view of Sanders's extensive experience with robots. Jantille departed Fourteenth Street late last night. As of our last report half an hour ago, Crandall was still there." She pushed the paper across the desk toward Thurman and leaned back in her chair.

Chief Thurman did not reach for the paper. He resisted the urge to shift in his seat. Maybe he *felt* uncomfortable, even scared, but it would not be smart to *act* that way just now. Not with the dragon lady visibly lusting after his very soul. "That's no crime," he said in what he hoped was a firm voice.

"No, but it sure as hell goes against departmental policy," Entwhistle said, her voice turned sharp and hard. "And I think it gives us a damn good idea who leaked the original information to Jantille, wouldn't you say? But where did he get it? Did *you* give him the information? Say, run off copies of the case datacubes and hand them over?"

Thurman felt a block of ice materialize in his stomach. Had she just got lucky on the first guess, or did she really know? *It's all very well for me to try to protect the department occasionally,* Thurman thought, *but that's over.* After all, he had engineered the leak to make sure press attention focused on the U.S. Attorney. That was accomplished now. Time to cut his losses. "I didn't give him anything," Thurman lied. Thurman wondered if his career was about to go down in flames, here and now. "What the hell were you following Jantille for, anyway?" he asked, hoping but not expecting to steer the conversation into safer areas. "Isn't *that* against departmental policy—investigating opposing counsel? It better not have been any of my people—"

"FBI," Peng said, speaking for the first time. "Madame Entwhistle didn't want to use D.C. cops. And we weren't tailing Jantille. We were watching Crandall, and quite legitimately. After all, she *did* leak information from a federal document. Certainly that's cause for investigation—though I think we can call off the tail now. We know what we need to know. Sanders has to be the leak."

"So what are you going to do about it?" Thurman asked.

Entwhistle seemed about to reply, but Peng spoke before she had a chance. "There isn't a lot we can do, realistically. I can think of about a half-dozen actions we could take that would be perfectly *legal*, but the trouble with most of them is that they wouldn't help us, and might even hurt us more than they would hurt the defense."

"What do you mean?" Entwhistle asked, turning her head to look at Peng. He stepped around her chair to stand by the side of the desk. Thurman found himself wondering if Entwhistle was aware of how completely Peng could lead her at times. "We lean on Crandall to reveal her sources, get a judge to try and force her to talk, and then get her on contempt. There are recent precedents. It seesaws back and forth all the time, but it seems to me that in the last year or two, judges have been leaning back toward the idea of contempt citations for reporters who don't reveal their sources on leaked documents. We could throw her ass in jail until she talks. *That* will get her off the story."

"Wait a second," Thurman protested. "I thought you just got through saying you knew Sanders was the source."

"Maybe *we* know the source is Sanders, but *she* doesn't know we know, and anyway we can't prove it," Entwhistle said. "None of that matters, though. The contempt citation just gives us something to beat her over the head with. And once we get her to talk, or get the proof we need some other way, then we can yank Sanders's badge."

"Why wait?" Peng asked rhetorically. "We've got the FBI report on his clandestine meeting with a reporter and the opposing counsel on a case with which he was involved. We could call it interfering with an ongoing investigation. I don't know if that would be a strictly accurate description of the circumstances, but we could probably make it stick. It would be enough for the chief to fire Sanders, or at least put him on administrative leave or suspension."

"Sounds good to me," Entwhistle said. "Why can't we do that?"

Peng took the chair next to Thurman, and the chief watched him carefully. This guy surely knew how to handle Entwhistle, and it was a skill Thurman devoutly wished to master.

"Because the second we make any kind of play like that, it would blow up in our face," Peng said. "Fire Sanders, and boom, he's a martyr, thrown off the force for trying to help a poor old widow lady seek justice—and he'll have got a completely free hand to work with her any way he can, besides having a grudge against us. Right now he's got to be hesitating a bit, being careful enough to try and protect his job. Even if we could find a judge willing to slap a contempt citation on Crandall, it would just make her a crusading journalist. If we try and get her to reveal her sources, just for the sake of harassing her, that will turn around and bite us too. She wouldn't talk, she's not the type. Then the judge would have to throw her in jail. How much bad publicity would that give us? Her editor would put every reporter he had on the case. *Any* legal action we take against Crandall or Sanders will almost certainly backfire."

"So you're saying we do nothing?" Entwhistle said.

"We do nothing *public*," Peng said. "Privately, I would say that the chief should instruct Sanders to stay away from these people until the case is over."

"I can *suggest* that," Thurman said, "but I can't order it. I can't control what my people do in their off-duty time as long as they don't break the law."

"Well, my guess is that he's broken a few laws already by leaking that data," Entwhistle said. "God knows how he got the information, though. Probably he just managed some unauthorized access to the police computer net and copied the datacubes."

Thurman tried to hide the fact he was breathing a sigh of relief. Obviously she *didn't* know how it happened.

"Probably," Peng agreed. "And maybe if we spent enough time and money and hire enough experts to track it down, we could prove that. But maybe not, and the damage has been done anyway."

"Can't we take some sort of action against Jantille to prevent her from using evidence that was collected illegally?" Thurman asked.

Entwhistle shook her head. "To hear a familiar refrain, nothing that we could make stick," she said. "Judges cut the defense a lot of slack on evidentiary rules, and they've been getting even slacker in the last few years." Entwhistle drummed her fingers on the table. "So I suppose we just have to take our lumps and like them. Meanwhile the opposition knows everything we know."

"And the defense knows exactly what we *don't* know," Peng said. Thurman thought he heard just a trace of emphasis on the word "defense," as if Peng were gently chiding Entwhistle for being unsporting enough to call Jantille the opposition.

"What's that supposed to mean?" Thurman asked.

Entwhistle frowned. "It means they have probably figured out that we can prove Bailey, in Herbert's body, did the murder—but that our proof of his *humanity* is pretty much nonexistent. They know we're bluffing."

"I blew that in court," Peng agreed unhappily.

"Not on your own," Entwhistle said. "I sent you into court with the wrong tactics. We were bluffing, and the judge called, that's all. It's much too soon to be committed to proof on the humanity issue, but there we are. At least the other side is committed to the same thing. Even so, as of right now, Suzanne Jantille is going to walk into that hearing with lots of advantages."

Chief Thurman leaned forward in his chair. If he wanted to keep their minds off the leak, he needed to give them something else to think about. Suddenly Entwhistle's words gave him an idea. "Jantille isn't going to walk into that courtroom," he said.

Entwhistle's head snapped up, and she looked at him

sharply. "Why not? Legally, there's nothing we can do to prevent her showing up." It wasn't hard to imagine a trace of regret in her voice. Entwhistle wasn't afraid to fight dirty once in a while.

"She's not walking in there for the same reason she's never set foot in there yet," Thurman said eagerly. "She's a remote person. She's never left her own house since they wheeled her home from the hospital. Think you can do something with that little fact?"

Peng and Entwhistle stared at him in stunned silence. At last Entwhistle smiled, and somehow Thurman found her pleasure far more disturbing than her anger. "Chief," she said, "that is one hell of a loophole. Every once in a while it's worth having you around."

Samantha Crandall opened her left eye and found herself staring at an unfamiliar ceiling. It took her a minute or two to remember where she was, and how she had gotten there.

Phillipe Sanders's bed, that's where she was. And she had gotten there alone, damn it. Phillipe, gentleman to a fault, had assured her his couch folded out into a perfectly good bed and he'd be fine there. Oh, there were definitely some subterranean sparks flying between the two of them, but Phillipe was not about to confess to any such thing. *And, apparently, neither am I,* Sam told herself. *Or else why did I wake up alone?* Maybe physical intimacy so early in a relationship was frowned upon these days, but right at the moment Sam found herself wishing she had had the nerve to fly in the face of fashion.

Maybe Phillipe was every bit as eager and interested as she was, and simply hadn't felt last night was the night for it. Searching for clues to a murder inside a comatose robot's brains was not exactly the height of romance. It had been exhaustion, not passion, that had made Sam long for a bed the night before. Now that she thought about it, maybe last night would not have been such a good one for sex, to put the matter bluntly. Her brain was muddled and upset by the complicated and disturbing things they were learning, and Sam's mind would not have been on what she was doing. That was no good way to start things off with a man.

She got out of bed and smiled ruefully as she padded her way into the bedroom's adjoining bathroom. She peeled off the T-shirt she had borrowed from her host and started the shower going. Judging from her ample experience in romantic disasters, having her mind on something else at such times was generally a good way to *finish* things with a man, forever.

Maybe taking it slow wouldn't be such a bad idea this time.

She emerged from the shower, her nose twitching to the smell of cooking bacon and hot coffee. She dressed, a bit reluctant to put yesterday's clothes on again, and made her way to the main room. The fold-out bed was already closed up, the living-room area neat as a pin. No question but this was a tidy man—almost an alarmingly tidy man—that she was dealing with.

She walked into the kitchen to find Phillipe working at the stove, looking remarkably dapper for someone who had spent the night on a couch. He had put the hall bathroom to good use, gotten himself showered and shaved and squeaky clean. "Hi there," he said, glancing over his shoulder, his full attention still on the bacon and eggs. "Hope you like what you're getting for breakfast. Not many alternatives in the refrigerator just now. Haven't had a chance to order any groceries. I had to scrounge a bit to come up with this."

"No, it smells great," Sam said. "Just what the doctor ordered." She spotted the coffeepot and two mugs sitting on the counter and helped herself to a cup. "To tell you the truth, it's a bit of a relief to hear that you have to scrounge and that you forget things once in a while. I was beginning to wonder if there was anything you didn't do perfectly."

Phillipe grinned as he transferred the bacon to plates, served out the eggs, and set the dishes on the kitchen table. "Believe me, there's plenty of things I don't do right. Starting with our mechanical friend out there. Sit down and eat."

Sam dug into the eggs greedily. A nice old-fashioned breakfast. Phil poured her a glass of juice from a pitcher on the table and she took a sip. "I don't see how you could do any better than you have done," she said. "You made incredible progress last night."

"But I didn't get us any closer to Bailey," he said. "He's in there, I'm convinced of that. But we're not any nearer to him."

"Isn't there any way to, I don't know, run a phone line in?" Sam asked. "Can't you hotwire some sort of connection to him? Hook a speaker to his speech center and a mike to where his ears go?"

" 'Fraid not," Phil said, sitting down to his own breakfast. "The way he's wired up, all of his sensory input is mediated by the underbrain before being passed to the overbrain—and the hookups between the overbrain and underbrain are what got ruined. Nothing can get through there, and there's no other way to reach him." Suddenly Phil looked up and frowned. "Except through the mind-load cable," he said. "But that's designed to have a human body on the other end of it, not a loudspeaker and a microphone. It's too generalized a connection to do us any good."

"You mean the cable Bailey used to perform the mindload in the first place?" Sam asked. "You say we can't use it?"

"Right," Phil said. "The problem is, that cable doesn't attach to any specific point at either end. Potentially, any point in the bio-brain could link with any point in the robotic brain—but probabilistic and quantum theory prevent that. The cable resembles a long chain of synaptic connections, millions of them, hooked end to end and bundled around each other, almost like an artificial spinal cord. Quantum theory forces the artificial synapses to link up through the paths of least combined resistance, so that, for example, the speech centers of the old brain hook into the speech centers of the new one. In effect, the cable learns, *teaches* itself, to link only the proper points in the two brains. You can't just plug a mike and a speaker into a lash-up like that and expect it to work."

"But it worked when Bailey had it plugged into his body."

"Sure. It had a whole neural network to work with, with millions of connections to make simultaneously. The system will try a million path links at once, but only one in a million will have a good enough potential match. Then it tries to link all the remaining paths, and maybe one more match gets made. Then again, and again, and again, a million times, until every path is matched. You can't do that by hand. You can only use that kind of technique in a complex neural system that automatically can do that kind of recursive linking."

"Hold it," Sam interrupted, holding up her left hand as her right wielded a fork, chasing the last of her eggs around the plate. "Cut the double-talk. What you're saying is that the only way to hook him up is through the mindload cable, and the only way to use that cable is to patch it into a complex neural network. So why can't you use that cable to patch right back into Herbert's underbrain?" Before Phil could answer, she held up her hand again. "Wait a second. I think I know. Because Herbert's neural net, his nervous system, is geared to his body form, set to roll wheels and run six legs and a built-in vacuum cleaner. Without the movement interpreters and translation routines Bailey built into the interconnectors, it can't handle commands that are intended to move a human body around. And those interpreters and routines got burned out."

"Exactly. Right on the first try."

Sam put down her fork and picked the last strip of bacon off Phil's plate. She popped it in her mouth and chewed it thoughtfully for a moment. She swallowed and looked at Phil. "So what you're saying is that Bailey's brain can't control Herbert's body because Herbert's body isn't human form. Well, okay then, suppose we could take that cable and plug Bailey into a human-form robot body—would that work? Would he be able to run that body, move in it, speak and hear through it?''

Phil shrugged, turned his palms upward in a gesture of helpless dismissal. ''Sure. David's mind in Herbert's overbrain is issuing commands to run a humanoid body. Plug it into a humanoid robot and you'd be all set. You could do a perfectly standard hookup to the robot body—but so what? It wouldn't work. Bailey's brain is too damned big to fit in anything remotely like a human-form body.''

''Who said anything about fitting the brain in it?'' Sam said. ''Suzanne's brain isn't in the body *she's* running.''

Phil stared at her in openmouthed astonishment. ''Wait a second,'' he said. ''Are you saying that—if we— My God, *yes*, he's got enough two-way data channels. We could rebuild the mindload transfer circuits. That'd be easy. All we'd need would be a body, a robotic body that he could run a signal to. He could run it like a remote from here, like Suzanne runs her body. I've got all the hardware here. The radio gear, the relays—'' Phil stood up, enthused by the idea, as if he were eager to get started on it right away.

''No,'' Sam said. ''Wait a second. We can't do it that way. At least not at first. Not in court. You'll have to use a cable, a direct hardwire connection. An umbilical.''

''Huh? *Why?*'' Phil looked down at her, very confused. ''Do you have any idea how clumsy that would be? A human-form robot plugged into a cable on Herbert? How would they walk?''

''Slowly and carefully,'' Samantha said with some impatience. ''I know it would be clumsy. But don't you see? We're not just trying to make it possible for David to talk and act—we're trying to prove he's *really there*. If we try to do it with a remote-person rig, over radio waves, it'll be a lot harder to convince everyone it isn't a gimmick, a trick. You can't leave Herbert at home and have a human-form robot in the courtroom, answering questions in David Bailey's name. We'd never get away with it. You'll have to have Herbert and the remote robot in court *together*, physically attached to each other, and be ready to prove that there isn't any outside signal being beamed to the robot."

Phil thought about it and sat back down. "Hell, you're right. It's miserable engineering, but you're right."

"So how do we get started?" Sam asked.

"We find ourselves a robot body," Phil said.

"Um, uh, I hesitate to suggest it. I know it's got to have a lot of emotion for you, but—"

"You're about to suggest the remote body my father used," Phil said.

"Well, yes," Sam said, a bit uncertain how he would take the idea. "From what you've said, it sounds like it would fit the bill perfectly. Could we use it?"

Phil considered for a second and then shook his head. "No, it wouldn't work. At least not in the time we have left. The remote unit, the robot body, is half taken apart. It would take me at least a month of full-time work to get it back in operational order." He shook his head and made a face. "I don't mind admitting I'm glad we don't have that choice, but it wouldn't work. We need a fully functional human-form robot, in good working order, one that's capable of receiving orders from an outside source."

Sam thought for a second and then clapped her hands together. "I've got it," she said. "I know a body we can use, if we can afford it. We've got to call Suzanne and tell her to get out her checkbook."

"Her checkbook?" Phil asked. "For what?"

"For a Clancy," Sam said. "Clancys will do anything if you offer them enough money."

Interlude

I have dreamt I am awake too long, or perhaps slept too long in my wakefulness. The silence and the dark that have helped to heal me now begin to harm me. I was too long forced to wakefulness by the relentless sounds and images the robot body forced on me, and the dark quiet brought me peace. But now I have been too long without sight or sound, or any outside sensation. My need for rest is over, and yet the sightless silence goes on. Now starved for stimulation as it was so recently starved for quiet, I can feel my mind closing in around itself, inventing its own spurious images and voices, striving to protect itself with hallucinations. False visions flash past my eyes, combining the depth and solidity of real things with the fevered, looming distortions of a nightmare. People, places, and things that are not there materialize, spun from the cloth of my memories and my imagination. Robots dressed as humans fill a jury box. Cyborgs strip off their human parts and demand the right to become complete machines. Rich men buy up the bodies of the poor, sucking the life from them, discarding the poor men's shriveled souls like so many empty candy wrappers.

I am back in my own lab, in my own house, taking all my machines apart, reconstructing them into a killer car that chases me down, hunts me and my wife, and crushes the life out of me. I cannot judge these images. I cannot distinguish the real from the imagined, the sensible from the insane.

There is a stranger circumstance than nightmare at work. I can feel time, and I know that this too is not as it should be. In the midst of my dementia, I know what time it is, ceaselessly and precisely. At any given moment I can tell the exact date and time down to the thousandth of a second.

My sense of time should have been the first thing to go when the hallucinations began, and yet it persists, strong and certain. There is a simple explanation, of course: My mind now inhabits a brain that is in turn governed by the timing pulses emitted by a quartz-crystal chronometer. Somehow this distressing reminder of my existence as a mechanical device does not depress me, but instead offers me a sense of comfort. In the passage of time, at least, I am linked to reality, to the outside world. I cling to time, concentrate on its passage, as a bulwark against the leering madness that surrounds me. Surely they have not turned me off forever. My electrical power will be switched back on, and with it outer reality will return.

At last, three days, nine hours, and 37.832 seconds after my hallucinations begin, I begin to feel something outside myself. A few brief flurries of power, minute wriggles of energy, flit past my inner consciousness. Test power, I conjecture, coursing through the bulk of my inert body. Then nothing for another hour and 8.645 seconds. Then for a flash, a moment, a flicker, I see a new image, make new contact with the outside world—but I see from a new set of eyes. Eyes that look down upon my own robotic body, and a man and woman bending over it. The woman, her face framed with flowing red hair, *turns her tired face toward my eyes, and then the image dies. Surely this is another hallucination, but there is something authentic about the image. I do not understand it, but it excites me.*

I sense somehow that the end is near.

CHAPTER 14
THE LAST MORNING

Suzanne Jantille woke up in a wrenching paroxysm of coughing. At last the fit passed, and she lay there, weak and tired, dreading the thought of all the energy it would take to get herself up and moving today. Damn it all. If only she hadn't been forced to fire that damned tech-nurse, she might be able to get a little help for herself. But when her cold was still getting worse two days after that long night at Phillipe Sanders, the tyrannical fool had tried to keep Suzanne from using her remote unit at all. And with the number of things that she needed to do, that was flatly impossible. There hadn't even been time to try to arrange for a replacement nurse.

She winced a bit as she shifted her head and spoke the voice commands to activate her teleoperator helmet. Her voice was sore and raspy, but at least the swelling at her neck was gone. The induction sensors in the teleoperator helmet were able to pick up her commands to her nervous system a little better. Or perhaps she was learning how to operate her body in spite of poor signal reception. It didn't matter. She could function. That was the main thing. The helmet closed around her head, the miniature video screens came to life, she saw the world through the eye-cameras of her remote body. Another day began. Su-zanne-Remote stepped out of her charge chair and looked about the room, barely taking time to glance at the huddled form on the bed. There was that moment when she felt the strangeness of looking at herself from the outside, but she firmly told herself she was too busy this morning to get caught up in her usual distractions.

Monday morning. So much to do. Seven o'clock now. The hearing would begin at ten, three hours from now. Were all her arguments ready? Had she covered all the bases? Part of her knew perfectly well that she was merely dithering, pointlessly worrying over things she had already done, fussing over jobs she had finished, focusing on things it was far too late to worry about. But somehow even that was comforting. It was part of her old pretrial ritual. Never in her life had she gone into court for a major appearance without having a briefcase of nerves first. Somehow it felt good to be back in her old rhythms, even the downside of them.

But then her bodies, both of them, robot and biological, were wracked by another fit of painful coughing, one that hurt enough that the pain reflex forced her robot body to double over.

That was strange, Suzanne thought. *I felt* both *bodies that time.* That was the first time *that* had happened since her first days of training to use the remote.

It was the pain, she realized. The pain was there always, reminding her of where her real self was, which vessel truly held her spirit and soul. Try as she might, she could no longer pretend, even for a moment, that the remote, the robot, was her real body. The pain forced her to acknowledge that much. Robots didn't feel pain, or get sick. She was a divided soul.

But this was no morning to concern herself with such things. There was work to do. She forced all her worries, professional and personal, from her mind, and got on with the day. Somehow, that made her awareness of her bio-body recede a bit. She gave her bio-body its usual perfunctory morning care—tucking in the blankets, smoothing the sheets, checking a few of the feed lines. It was time for the things that truly concerned her this day.

Such as that bandit Swerdlow, the man who owned the Clancys. It had not been quite as easy as Sam had first thought to rent a Clancy, but ultimately, Swerdlow was motivated by the same thing as his robots. Once enough money changed hands, all was well. Suzanne had been forced to accept a one-year lease at a horrendous charge. Unfortunately, the Clancys were the only robots available that could be readily adapted to accepting out-of-body control. Once Swerdlow figured that one out, he knew he could name his price.

Now it didn't matter. That trouble was two days old, and over and done with. Of more immediate concern was the word she had received last night. The prosecution had notified her of its intention to file an unspecified motion this morning. In other words, they were gearing up to throw her a curve ball, and she had to get ready for it. She bustled down the hallway to her office and sat at her desk. There would barely be time to pick up her client—no, pick up Herbert—no, pick up her *husband*—at Phil Sanders's place beforehand.

Good God, her husband. David. If all went well, this would be the day she would first hear him speak, hear in his own words what it was like to be summoned back from the dead. He was coming back. That thought, *that* idea, should have glowed in her mind with the power of the sun, moon, and stars—and she had barely considered it. Instead she had only considered his words—or, if things broke the wrong way, the lack of them—as they would affect the proceedings in court. If he spoke, and was coherent, and could relate at least a few details of his life and death, provide even a little verisimilitude to the court, then Suzanne would have won this first battle. David would be proved human and the murder trial could proceed.

Nothing else mattered. How the judge would consider his words, that was the only equation that mattered, the only issue that even entered her mind when she thought of her client.

It was overdetachment, preoccupation, of a very strange sort indeed. In playing her mental game of courtroom chess, moving all the pieces around, trying to see the game from every angle, she had fallen into the trap of considering her own husband merely as a client, and then compounded her error by assigning her client to the role of a mere pawn, a game piece on the board.

Her own husband. Now, at last, that thought struck her with all the power it deserved. *Her husband.* And he had yet to speak, yet to utter a single sound or demonstrate by any means at all that he was in there. Phil and Sam were still working, still even professing confidence of success, but Suzanne could read the hollowness in their voices even as they made their promises. The odds against their being ready in three hours were long and getting longer as the time grew short.

With another jolt, Suzanne realized she had not spent much thought on Phil and Sam either. Both had sacrificed, and struggled, on her behalf, and David's, and without both their help the situation would be hopeless.

She thought of them now: Phillipe Montoya Sanders, working almost around the clock all week and all weekend, Samantha Crandall at his side, helping as best she could. The two of them struggling heroically to get Herbert ready for Suzanne's Monday morning battle.

And yet Suzanne had never really considered how much that effort must have cost the two of them, the prices they had paid: Sam's editor, wary of conflict of interest, ordering Sam to turn her notes over to another reporter and telling her to stop filing stories on the case that should have made her career. Phil, shrugging off a rather stiff warning from Chief Thurman to stay away from Suzanne and her case. According to Sam, the chief had made it clear that sticking with Herbert could do no good whatsoever to his future career hopes, or even his current employment status. Instead of taking *that* hint, Phil took a week of his extensive accumulated leave.

He had all but locked himself in his workshop, buried himself in the intricacies of melding Herbert's circuitry with Clancy's.

But none of that had registered. Instead she had thought of legal tactics, courtroom strategy. Was she becoming so machinelike that *all* her emotions were fading away? Two people she barely knew were risking, perhaps destroying, their careers because they believed in her cause. That *mattered*. And she had never even said thank you to either of them. But it would be all right, she told herself. She would make it up to them, somehow. After it was all over.

"Circumstances," Julia Entwhistle said, "have changed."

"I know that!" Theodore Peng replied. "But this is still wrong, still underhanded. Let me get on with preparing for the case itself. Don't make me do this thing. It will demean Jantille—"

"We are not here to care for the psyches of opposing counsel," Entwhistle broke in.

"—and by extension, by getting *our* hands dirty, it will demean us, demean *you* and your office," Peng shot back.

"That is my problem, and this is my decision," Entwhistle snapped. "I did not call you in here at seven in the morning the day of a major hearing to ask your permission on this or anything else." She paused for a moment and then went on in a calmer tone. "Excuse me. I'm a bit on edge myself. I know you've got last-minute preparation to do, but in my judgment it was more important that I know you have accepted these instructions, and will pursue this motion vigorously. When we launched into this prosecution, we thought that we would be facing an unenthused lawyer representing a mute hunk of metal with no discernible human traits.

"We planned to force the case to trial up against someone who would hand us a precedent in a federal court establishing that robots *can't* be human. Someone who would inevitably blunder into a situation where the judge would have to rule that David Bailey was irrevocably dead and Herbert was a machine. That would be a ruling we could build on, something we could take into the next case, and the next one.

"Instead we are up against a seasoned, hard-edged professional trial lawyer. Even worse, if our information about what's going on at Sanders's place is reliable, we face a very real chance of going up against an articulate defendant who could conceivably put on a very good *demonstration* of being human. We can't do anything about the latter problem, but we can do something about the former one. I intend to have that something done, and you are going to do it." She picked up a paper from her desk and offered it to Peng. "I am giving you a direct order to make this motion and force Suzanne Jantille to withdraw from the case. No ifs, ands, or buts. Is that clear?"

Theodore Peng stared at the paper in her outstretched hand. He reached out for it, drew back, and finally took it. "Yes, ma'am, that's clear," he said. He stood there, holding the paper for a moment, trying to think of any orders he had disliked as much as these.

Samantha Crandall woke up next to the man she was falling in love with, and found herself amazed at just how unromantic a prospect that could be. They were here, together, because on her second night here they had been too tired to go through all the trouble and bother of making up the fold-out bed. That had set the tone for the rest of the nights. Last night, for example, she had collapsed into bed at four A.M., with Phil still hard at work as she fell asleep. They were working against a tight and unforgiving deadline, and sleeping together had been strictly a matter of convenience, not one of passion.

She looked at Phil, gently snoring next to her, and

smiled as she revised that estimate. No, they *had* had one night of love—or at least a half hour of love, two nights ago—or was it three—before they had both collapsed from exhaustion. The days had all faded into one long fog of work. But on the other hand, that lovemaking had been very nice indeed—no, better than nice, it had been wonderful. Maybe tonight—or tomorrow, after they both had time to rest, they could do it again. Maybe they could find the time to give their nascent love affair a proper start.

Be that as it may, a half hour's passion had been all they could manage so far. All the days, all the nights, had been dedicated to the maddeningly complex and delicate job of creating a link between Herbert and Clancy. She flexed her fingers and regarded them thoughtfully. She had proved herself a pretty fair hand at much of the intricate handwork involved—including the work that had to be done under a microscope. Assembling the artificial neuron chain modules had been the toughest part, at least for her. She thought of Herbert's inert body in the main room, its outer carapace completely removed, the hardware that had once been his mindload cable hookup now half-disassembled. Clancy Six was on the other table, in not much better shape. Phil and Suzanne had agreed it would be smart to remove Clancy's internal brain, to make it utterly incontrovertible that David, working through Herbert, was doing the thinking. *That* had been a job.

With a snort and a groan, Phil rolled over in bed. Sam had learned enough about him by now to know that was the first stage in his wake-up ritual. Ten minutes from now he'd wake up for real and be in search of coffee. She smiled and hopped out of bed, eager to have it ready for him when he woke.

But the wake-up rituals were a bit rushed and forced that morning. Days of time for the job had shrunk to hours, and would soon evaporate down into minutes.

Breakfast for the two of them was a single cup of coffee and an apple each, and that was virtually the last food in the house.

The passage of the last few days had worked changes on Phil and his home. Both man and condo had lost all sense of neatness and order. The kitchen was a mess, but the workroom outside was worse. Parts were strewn everywhere. Disassembled machines cannibalized for this part or that sat on all the benches, and the carefully sorted storage racks were a hodgepodge, their contents shuffled and rearranged repeatedly by the search for another gizmo or another gadget.

Sam took a good hard look at Phil as they sat at the kitchen table and drank their coffee in exhausted silence. He hadn't shaved in three days, and his eyes were bleary with exhaustion. He had showered every day, but even that rule was crumbling. This morning he had all but sprinted through the shower stall, barely giving himself a chance to get wet before he was out again, more interested in the water waking him up than getting him clean. She could see something in his face: he was not just committed to finding David inside Herbert—he was obsessed.

Sam was reminded of a story she had covered a few years before, when a little boy in California had been trapped in an improbable accident. His parents had left him alone in their stylish cliffside house, far remote from the city, and had headed into town for the evening. A freak rainstorm, a flash flood, and the house had simply fallen down the cliff in a mudslide.

The boy was buried alive under the house, under tons of mud. But by some miracle, the boy was caught in a corner of his room that did not collapse. Showing incredible presence of mind, he had used his toy walkie-talkie to call for help. By some further miracle, the ArtInt scan gear aboard the first police car on the scene picked up his call and alerted the cop in the car.

Almost immediately the house was the focus of a huge rescue effort, a scene indelibly marked into the memory of anyone who saw the live broadcasts that went on for days. The mud-entombed, collapsed house, the frantic parents in tears, the heavy digging equipment, the worried engineers struggling to find a way to get to the boy without bringing the rest of the house down around him—all framed by a pounding, relentless rain that never let up. It had been five endless days before they got the boy out.

Sam remembered a face captured by the camera, the frantic, determined, sleepless, obsessed face of one of the rescuers at the scene. She did not have to look any further than Phil to see that same look again. But why?

Why did he care so much, and why was she along for the ride? Deep in her heart she knew part of the answer: Phil was here for his father who had been caught in the same trap as Suzanne, his father who might have ended up where David was now, if the technology had advanced just a bit further.

But why was *she* here? For Phil? That was part of it, certainly. But it did not explain why she had handed off the biggest story of her life to another reporter and risked her career with scarcely a moment's hesitation. She was not the type to abandon her life for her man. She would not do it and Phil would not expect it. No, it was nothing as small or silly as that.

She was here because she cared too. Because all this was important, because it would decide things. But what things? And what outcome was she trying to produce? Trying to prevent the state from executing an innocent man, yes. But there was more, she knew that. More than she had ever taken the time to examine.

"I'm lost," Sam announced into the numbed silence of the kitchen, perhaps as much for something to say as anything else.

Phil looked up from his coffee in distracted puzzlement, as if he were surprised to see her there. "What do you mean?" he asked with poorly masked impatience.

"I mean I don't know why we're doing this anymore."

Phil gave her a puzzled look. "So that David Bailey

can appear in court, so that he can prove that he is alive, so he can't be tried for murder."

"But why the murder charges? I mean even Entwhistle knows that it's a crazy rap. It's a gobbledy-gook charge, a legal fiction."

Phil nodded tiredly. "What they really want is for a judge to tell them just that. Boom. That makes Herbert abandoned property, and illegal mindload equipment to boot. They impound his tin ass and melt him down to scrap. His *real* crime is in staying alive. *That's* why they want to bust him. They don't want people to survive their own deaths."

"Why the hell not?"

"I've thought about that," Phil said, "and I've read the arguments and the background in that datacube I swiped. It boils down to money. They teach you that in reporter's school, don't they? 'Follow the money'?"

"Yeah, but what money? Bailey was rich, but so what?"

"Not *his* money. Follow the pattern of money in our society. It's in the datacube. As a general rule, people tend to accumulate wealth throughout their working lives. After they retire, they live off the interest, or off the principal they've accumulated. They start to disperse what they've accumulated. When they die, the children split the proceeds, death taxes take a bite, and so on— virtually complete dispersal. It's actually fairly rare for a family fortune to hold together more than a generation or two. In the grand scheme of things, that's no bad thing. It redistributes the wealth a bit more evenly, and frees up capital, injects it back into the system instead of leaving it to molder in bank accounts."

Phil rubbed his bleary eyes. "But what would happen," he asked with a yawn, "if rich people never died, never got old or weak? Cyborgs were the first stage toward that. Remotes like Suzanne are the second. Herbert is something very like the third. Entwhistle is looking ahead to twenty years from now. By then, I bet I could fit a robot brain as good as Herbert's inside a standard-sized robot body. Call that fourth stage. Maybe after that they'll even be able to do nerve endings, give back the sense of touch and smell and taste. That'll be fifth stage. A perfect human-replica robot body that never grows old, never dies, never wears out.

"But replica humans will have to be incredibly expensive," Phil went on. "Cyborging costs a lot, and so do remote units. Stage three, Herbert, costs even more. Bailey probably had twenty times the resources I have here, and even so he just barely managed to afford Herbert. I can see that in the engineering. He did the job well, did it right, but I can see a lot of things he did just to save money. Something has to be pretty pricey when a guy like Bailey is forced to watch the pennies. So what happens to society if we get to stage four or five? We're on the way there already, with no one but the rich being able to afford cyborging. Think about all the street cyborgs who've wiped themselves out trying to stay alive. They were the first victims. What happens next? Think it through," he told her.

Sam considered for a moment. "You end up with superrich immortals and poverty-stricken people who die." She made a face. "Brrr. It doesn't sound like a nice world to me."

Phil nodded. "No, it doesn't. And it's what Entwhistle and Peng are trying to stop before it can get started."

"And they think they can do that by getting a ruling that Bailey is dead? By impounding Herbert and killing him?"

"It would send a pretty powerful signal to anyone else who tried the same thing," Phil said with ghoulish humor. "The Feds want dead people to stay that way, to make sure there's room and wealth enough in the world for the living."

Sam shook her head in befuddlement. "It doesn't seem like such a bad thing to be striving for."

"It isn't," Phil agreed equitably.

"But we're *fighting* them! We're against what they're doing."

"And why's that?" Phil asked with a tired smile.

"Because it's good to be alive!" Sam said. "Because people have a right to live!"

"But do they have the right to survive death?" Phil asked. *"That's* the question here."

Suddenly a light came on in Sam's eye. "No it isn't," she said excitedly. "That's not the question at all. You said follow the money, Phil. Okay, then. Suppose we could change where that money *goes*?"

"What do you mean?" he asked.

"I'm not quite sure yet," she said. "Let me work on it. But from what you've said, Entwhistle doesn't care about dead people being alive. She just doesn't want them to have any money. Maybe there's an angle in there somewhere."

"Maybe," Phil said, clearly unconvinced. "But now it's time to get back to work." He stood up, refilled his coffee cup, and made his way out to the workroom.

Sam glanced up at the clock as she followed him: 7:45 A.M. She was suddenly reminded of college and the last cruel dregs of morning after pulling an all-nighter. The clock would tick down through those last few minutes between now and that eight A.M. class where the paper was due. There would come that ultimate moment where you would know whether you were going to make it or not. The sense of impending victory would pump one last dollop of adrenaline through your system, or the realization of defeat would snap down the last of your defenses. They weren't quite at that make or break point yet, but they were close.

Plan A had seen the job as almost childishly simple— just run a cable between two robots. Then there would have been time to run some real tests, to sit down and *talk* with David-Herbert-Clancy, David H.C. for short. Now all that was out the window. The job was far more complex than Phil had imagined. Neither Herbert nor Clancy were really designed for this kind of thing, and Phil had burned up the last three days just trying to build the modifications that would let them talk to each other, that would let David's mind in Herbert's overbrain run Clancy's body. Everything but that goal had been stripped away.

Just like college, Sam thought. You sat down at the beginning, planning to knock off the core ten-page paper in an hour or two and then spend the rest of your time making it beautiful, pulling in the graphics and the illustrations and the bar charts to dazzle the prof. Then 7:45 A.M. rolled around and you were just praying he would settle for an eight-pager instead.

That's where they were right now. Phil was counting on a lot. He was planning on hitting the power switch and having David H.C. wake up at once, ready to go.

Suzanne shook her head. There wasn't any room left in the schedule for failure.

Wiring tests, alignment checks, double-checking the connections that could wreck the whole operation if they blew. Sam could do little but watch as Phil moved quickly but methodically through the last of the job. Sam glanced up at the clock for the hundredth time that morning. The few minutes remaining slid away, until there was not even time for success.

But at last the moment came. Phil set down his tools and looked up at Sam.

"I think we're ready," he said.

The two robots sat next to each other, Herbert lying lengthwise on his table, Clancy sitting on a tall stool facing him. A fifteen-foot cable snaked across the floor, from an ugly conglomeration of hardware bolted to Herbert's carapace into an ugly open hole at the back of Clancy's neck.

There was something distinctly ghoulish, disturbing, about the sight of that thick black cable snaking out of Clancy's too-human body, his blank expression and sandy, obviously artificial hair somehow making him seem realer rather than more artificial. Nothing that looked like *that* could house a human spirit, and yet it was about to do just that.

There was something chilling about Clancy's patently false realism. Sam studied Phil's face as he leaned over the connections to Clancy's neck, checking them one last time. There was much there to see: rugged, unshaven exhaustion, courage, spirit, the experience of a half life-time stamped on his features. There was a book that could be read, and understood. Clancy's face was nothing but blank pages, nothing more than a high-tech rubber doll. How narrow a chasm, how wide a gulf, Sam thought, between the simulation and the reality. Was that distance truly meant to be bridged?

"Here we go," Phil said at last, his voice excited. "That's the last connection." He looked at Sam and took a deep breath. "So let's knock on the door and see if anyone's home."

He reached into an access panel on Clancy's back and flicked a switch. There was a sort of quiver that pulsed through all his limbs, and his head twitched a bit. "Okay," Phil said, "that's power to him. Now Herbert." He stepped to the HMU robot and flicked a switch there as well.

There was another flicker of movement—and then a loud popping noise, and Clancy spasmed violently, falling off his stool and crashing to the floor in an inert sprawl.

"Jesus H. Christ!" Phil swore and cut the power to Herbert. He knelt by Clancy and cut his power as well. "The power convertor," he said. "The goddamned power convertor. I put it in backward. It doubled the signal voltage instead of halving it. Popped Clancy's circuit breakers."

"It's not serious?" Sam asked, hurrying over to kneel next to Phil.

"No, damn it. It's just stupid. A stupid fool mistake. I put the thing in at four in the morning. No wonder I made the mistake."

"Will it take long for you to fix it?"

"Long enough to wreck our chances," he said bitterly. He let out a sigh and sat on the floor, leaning up against the workbench opposite Herbert. He stared up at the big robot and shook his head as Sam sat down next to him. "Damn it. If I had the chance to start over, I could do it so much *better*. I wouldn't need half the time or gear I've wasted just learning how it all worked."

"Wait a second," Sam said. "Say that again. What is it you're wishing for?"

"Something I won't get," Phil said distractedly as he looked over the damage. "A fresh start, a blank slate. A chance to let me start over again."

"That's it!" Sam said, swinging herself around to kneel in front of Phil and look into his eyes. "*That's* the thing I was looking for when you were talking about money. That's the solution, Phil. The way out of the trap Entwhistle's worried about. A way to protect society from immortality."

Phil looked at her oddly. "You want to maybe explain that?" he asked.

"Just a little while ago you were talking about what comes after David, that fourth and fifth stage stuff. Okay. Suppose, just suppose, instead of taking a replica human's *life* away, you took his *money* away instead? Wouldn't that solve the problem?"

"What? What the hell are you talking about?"

"Requiring mindloads like David to make a fresh start. We've made lots of pretty speeches about David being a changed person, a new person. Why not make that legally true? Declare the old person legally dead, let his or her will distribute the wealth. Allow the old person some maximum bequest—say, a year's minimal living expenses—to the new person, the old mind in the new body. The new person would get a new birth certificate, a new social security number, and so on. In the eyes of the law, one person would die and another would be born—or be mindloaded, or whatever you would call it.

"He or she would lose everything but that stipend, just as if the person had really died. Set it up so that if you change bodies, you lose all your worldly goods. You have a chance to start over, to live. You have a shot at immortality, but not at infinite wealth. You'd have to find a new job, work out a new way of living, earn your own way."

Phil nodded slowly, and thought about it for a second. "That's not bad," he said, clearly impressed. "It would mean there was a real cost to body-hopping, a steep one, no matter how rich you were. No one would try dying for tax purposes. It needs refinement, a little tinkering to keep all the loopholes shut, but that's one hell of an idea. It ought to do the trick."

Sam stood up suddenly and started pacing. "I can see it," she said. "I can see it. It would work. Phil, what is there left to do here?"

Phil gestured helplessly. "I've got to reset Clancy's main bus circuit breakers, replace his power converter, and fire the system up again."

"Nothing I can really help you with?" Sam asked.

Phil shrugged. "Help me get Clancy back on the stool, and offer moral support. That's about it."

"Okay then." She knelt again and reached for Clancy's arm, and Phil scrambled to his feet and grabbed the other arm. It took some effort, but they got Clancy sitting up again. "There's that done, but your morale is going to have to function on its own," Sam said. "I've got to get across town to the paper and move on the Fresh Start idea *now*. Talk to Gunther about it."

"But why?"

"Because that's the nature of the news business. The world has a short attention span. Today, *now*, is the moment when the public's attention is focused on the issue of cyborgs and replica humans. Put an idea about them on the table now, and it might go somewhere. Wait a week, and they'll be worried about the next big crisis."

"So what are you going to do?"

"Talk to my editor, Gunther Nelson. First I find out if I still have a job. Then I pitch him on Fresh Start. See if I can get him interested." Sam was excited, the words tumbling out of her. "Maybe he can swing a lead editorial on it, or get some of the broadcast and print commentators to talk about it. If we can launch it right, get it into public debate—"

Suddenly the door buzzer sounded.

"Damn it," Phil said. "She's early and I'm not ready. Yes, house, what is it?"

"Madame Jantille has arrived. She is on her way up."

"Very good," Phil said, although it was no such thing. "Thank yo—" But then he caught himself in time. "You tell me what *that* one means," he said.

"What what means?" Sam asked.

"Saying thank you to the house. I've made it a rule in life not to be polite to machines. So what does it mean when *I* start being nice to them?" He grinned, and then walked over to the entrance area. He opened the door and saw Suzanne walking down the hallway from the elevator. He gestured her in without speaking and led her into the main room.

"How is he?" Suzanne asked the moment the door was shut behind her. No preamble, no hellos or good mornings. She was clearly too agitated for that.

"Not ready," Phil said, crossing his arms and leaning back against the workbench. "I screwed up. We tried a power test and I had a two-dollar component in the wrong way. Popped half Clancy's circuit breakers. I have to install a replacement and try it again. Fifteen minutes, an hour, tops, and I'll be able to power up the connection again. Then I'll have to run some preliminary tests, make sure his motor function is there, that he can speak."

"It's nearly nine A.M. now, and the hearing is at ten. An hour from now is too late. You can't have him ready in time?" Suzanne asked.

Phil shook his head apologetically. "No."

The word hung heavy in the silent room, and Phil could not seem to look Suzanne in the eye.

"All right then, I won't take him this morning," Suzanne said, her voice brisk and efficient. "Can you have him ready by one this afternoon, in time for the afternoon session?'' she asked.

''This afternoon?'' Phil asked, clearly startled by the question. ''Well, yes. Given that amount of time, I could do it. But I thought it was this morning, do or die.''

''It was,'' Suzanne said. ''I know Judge Koenig. If *we* had stalled, or requested a delay of any kind, that would have all but destroyed our credibility with him. As it is, he's going to be watching like a hawk for us to try some sort of parlor trick.'' She gestured at the two inert robots, and the cable running between them. ''And you have to admit, this *looks* like a parlor trick, a gimmick.''

''And not a very slick one at that,'' Sam agreed under her breath.

''But the *prosecution* has given us a delay. *They've* asked to present some sort of motion this morning. So it's their fault, not mine.''

''Won't they want Herbert there anyway?'' Sam asked.

''Probably,'' Suzanne said. ''But I'll do my best to bluff my way out of it.'' Somehow, some of the briskness faded out of her voice, and a softer tone found its way into her words. ''But I was counting on being able to talk with David this morning.''

''There isn't time,'' Phil said. ''I'll need every minute I can get after we awaken him. If you can give me until one P.M., I'll use that time very well,'' he said. ''But you should go now, or you'll be late for the morning session.''

''But if you're that close to waking him—if it really could be fifteen minutes—I'll make a call, request a half-hour delay. I want to be here when my husband awakens,'' Suzanne said.

Phil looked at Suzanne and shook his head with a bone-weary sigh. ''Take her in the kitchen, Sam. Explain it to her. Suzanne, you've given me three hours. With that I can make it. But I *can't* do it if you're here. Sam will explain it. I've got to get back to work.''

Thanks for nothing, Phil, Sam thought. This was going

to be one tricky conversation, to put it mildly. Before Suzanne could protest, Sam ushered her into the kitchen, and shut the door behind her. As soon as the door was shut, Sam made a beeline for the coffee. Not that she could even feel the caffeine anymore, but at least doing something with her hands gave her time to think. How the hell could she explain it all to Suzanne?

Sam poured herself a cup of coffee, resisted the reflex to offer Suzanne one, and gestured for Suzanne to sit down at the table. Sam sat down across from her, still not quite willing to speak. The room was quiet for a moment.

"So what is it?" Suzanne finally asked, breaking the silence. "Why can't I be here when my husband awakens?"

Samantha looked at her sadly and shook her head. "I don't think you understand, Suzanne. Phil doesn't even know if that *is* your husband anymore."

"What do you mean?" Suzanne asked with just a hint of something in her voice that made it plain she had worried on just this point. But how much had she figured out?

Sam gestured helplessly. "I don't know how to say this. I'm just so tired I can't think. God knows how Phil's doing it. We've been working on this around the clock for five days now—and Phil is carrying nearly all the load. All I can do is hand him the tools and hold things and run a few computer checks. He's the expert here. All this falls on him. But even so, I've gotten so deep inside this thing, so involved with it, I don't even know if I can explain it anymore. But let me try."

Sam took a sip of her coffee and winced. "Ugh. Too strong," she said. She rubbed her eyes and folded her hands on the table in front of her, then looked at Suzanne-Remote, straight in the eye. "Okay. Here it is. There *is* a mind in there, yes. But we don't know *whose* mind. We're calling it David H.C.—H.C. for Herbert Clancy—but that's just a label. *We don't know who David H.C. will turn out to be.* We don't know how strong his mind will be. After all, that mind has been through a lot.

It was pulled from its natural body, and then trapped inside an alien form for three months."

Sam bit her lip and then went on, launched into the worst part. "We don't know if the mind currently inside Herbert is even *sane*. Actually, after the literature checks on sensory deprivation I ran a few days ago, we're fairly certain David *isn't* sane right now, not by our standards."

Suzanne's head jerked back. "What are you saying?" she demanded. "That my husband, my client, is insane? Why have you waited this long to tell me?"

"Would *you* be sane?" Sam asked, a bit snappishly, her meager store of remaining patience suddenly gone. "After all those months trapped inside an alien body, unable to speak or act? With all due respect, Suzanne, *you're* a little squirrelly, after a few months of much less severe sensory deprivation. Think how tough *that* has been. Imagine being *forced* to ride Suzanne-Remote, with no way to shut the robot body down, no way to control its actions—hell, no way to close your *eyes*. How long could you handle *that*?"

Sam waited, giving Suzanne a chance to answer, but the lawyer sat there, her face expressionless, and said nothing. At last Sam spoke again, in a far more gentle tone. "I'm sorry," she said. "That was unfair. It's just that I'm so bloody *tired*. Anyway. We can't assume David is sane *now*, but we think that he will *become* sane once the connection to Clancy's body is complete. It will be like pulling him out of a fugue state, literally plugging him back into the real world. We hope and believe that hooking Clancy's body into the system will pull David H.C. back, reground him in reality. And then he'll be okay."

Sam took another sip of coffee, and decided there was one other thing Suzanne had to know. "The trouble is, getting him back might take a while. He's been lost a long time. It might take a while to get back up to speed. We had hoped to awaken him Friday or Saturday, and work on cognitive reintegration, or whatever the hell Phil called it, over the weekend. The trouble is, we lost a lot of time just making this hookup work. Everything else went out the window. But if I understand your strategy properly, even if he isn't quite *all* the way back at one P.M. this afternoon, that doesn't really matter, right?" she asked. "You just need him able to answer a few simple questions, demonstrate that his reasoning ability exceeds that of a robot's. Right?"

Suzanne nodded stiffly. "That's right. I just want him on the stand for a few minutes. I don't want to risk anything more than that."

"And even if he acts like a crazy person, instead of a crazy robot, that should be enough at least to hold us for the moment," Sam said, completely unaware of how callous her words were.

Suzanne blinked, seemed to be struggling to keep herself calm. "Yes, I suppose. With any luck, that would at least convince the judge that we deserve a bit more time to work with him some more."

"Good. Phil is ninety-nine percent certain he can give you that much," Sam said, knowing it was wildly optimistic to promise any such thing.

She took another sip of her coffee. "Maybe—*maybe* we can even do better. But no matter what, David H.C. is bound to be disoriented at first. He will be seeing the world through new eyes, speaking through a new voice. There will be lots of stressful and complicated information for him to deal with all at once. He might not even understand that he is dead. Some of his memories might be confused, or suppressed, or lost. His situation will be— delicate. If David H.C. is confronted with you . . ."

Suzanne shook her head, clearly confused.

Sam stopped and started over. "Okay, to be blunt, if he has forgotten the period since the accident you were both in—and if he is confronted with the confusing and disturbing sight of a robot speaking with the voice of his wife . . . Well, if he sees that while he is still disoriented —it could be very damaging to him. Perhaps throw him back into fugue." Sam looked straight at Suzanne, but inwardly she was cursing herself, hating that she be forced to say such a cruel thing to a woman who had been through so much. *We don't want you around. We're afraid the mere sight of you could drive your husband insane.*

Suzanne seemed about to protest, but then she sat up straighter in her chair, and folded her hands stiffly, clearly determined not to reveal her emotions. At last she nodded. "Very well," she said. "I suppose all you can do is your best, and I don't want to interfere with that." She shook her head worriedly, and Sam imagined her switching from *wife* to *lawyer*. "I must admit this doesn't make my job any easier. What you're telling me is that the first chance I'll have to talk to my client is when he's on the stand."

"Right now the alternative is not having him talk at all," Sam said. "That's not much comfort, but it's the best I can offer right now."

Suzanne nodded stiffly. "I'll call here the moment I'm out of court for the morning." And with that, she stood up, stepped out of the kitchen, back into the main room. Phil looked up from his work and caught her eye. "I understand now. I know how hard you've tried, you and Sam," Suzanne said. "I just want you to know that whatever happens, I appreciate that. Thank you," she said to Phil, offering him a thin, forced smile. He nodded to her, and she let Sam escort her out.

Phil heard the door shut and waited for Samantha to come back in. "Do you think she bought it?" he asked. "Did you satisfy her?"

"I think so. I explained the problem, why she shouldn't be here, and what the situation is, what David might be like when we switch him on."

Phil scratched his unshaved whiskers and grunted. "Of course, there's another problem, Sam," he said, staring at Herbert's motionless body. "I couldn't admit it in front of Suzanne, but I'm still not entirely sure this whole insane lash-up is going to *work*."

Sam looked up at him with worried eyes and gave him a kiss on the cheek. "Don't think that way, Phil, or we're all going to be in big trouble. Gotta run. I'll see you at the courthouse."

Phillipe Montoya Sanders watched Samantha leave, and then turned back to David-Herbert-Clancy.

"Well," he said to the one or the two or the three of them, "it looks like it's just you and me."

CHAPTER 15
ANSWER AS A MAN

Gunther Nelson stood by his desk, reading the words on the pages one last time. Without looking at his desk, he picked up a very old-fashioned clipboard from it and pulled a markup pencil from his pocket. He clipped the pages to the board and started working through the copy, marking it up, cutting it, tightening it.

Sam, sitting in the visitor's chair, breathed a sigh of relief. Gunther would not bother doing a markup on copy he didn't plan to use. "Wordy stuff here, Sam," he said. "Editorials have to be short, tight, right to the point. You can't write them top-down like a news story."

"Then you're going to run it," Sam said.

Gunther finished with the copy and tossed the clipboard back on his desk, where it landed with a clatter. "I can take your name off it and sign my name to it," he said. "Then I can submit it to the editorial page crowd, and they'll know you wrote it, but they'll have to pretend *I* wrote it. They'll monkey with it for a while, and then, if they decide to okay it, they'll take my name off and sign *their* names to it, and get the executive editor to sign off. Then he fools around with it if he feels like it, and takes *everyone's* names off it, and runs it. From then on we pretend *no* one wrote it. And by that time that will almost be true. Probably every single word will have been changed. It might not say anything remotely like what you've written. That's the way editorials work around here."

"I know that, Gunther."

"And even if they run it, it's not going to change the world. No one's going to charge off and write new laws just because we say so. And even if they do, by the time the smoke clears the law might not say anything like what you say in this piece here."

"I know that too, Gunther. But it really doesn't matter. I almost don't care what the editorial says, or what the laws end up being."

"Then why come in here begging me to get behind you on this when I should be firing you for dropping out on a story?" Gunther asked.

"Because all I want is for people to start talking about it," Sam said, her voice unusually soft and low. "I want people to think about rights for replica humans. The sooner they do that, the sooner a consensus will form on it."

"Suppose the consensus doesn't happen to agree with you?" Gunther asked gently, sitting down on the edge of his desk.

"I think it will," Samantha said. "I think people are pretty decent, when you get right down to it. They'll see that it's right for people to try and stay alive. They'll find some sort of way for that to happen."

"I wonder if it is right," Gunther said, almost to himself.

"What do you mean?" Sam asked.

"I mean I wonder—is it right to build a man out of Tinkertoys? A body from here, a mind from there, a memory from somewhere else? Plug him together and take him apart? What's next? Mix and match parts? A modular man? If you take him apart again, copy his mind into another brain, which part is the human? How far down that road can we go with that sort of thing before the idea of a human being loses all its meaning?"

"I don't know, Gunther," Sam said. "I don't know if it's right, either. But we live in a world where it's possible, and that means we'd better face it." She stood up and gathered her belongings. "And maybe," she said, "it's not a question of what 'human being' means, but what it means to be a human being."

She looked at him, her face drawn and serious. Then something of her native spirit came to the surface again. She smiled and laughed. "God, I sound pompous when I'm tired. I'm going to court."

Phillipe Sanders checked the power circuits for the eighth time. He did not intend to make the same mistake twice. It was embarrassing to be tripped up by such a stupid error. Lurking at the back of his mind was a far more serious concern—what other mistakes had he made?

He stood and stared at Clancy, the robot's naked plastic body now closed up, all the access ports sealed. Clancy sat there like a mannequin waiting for the clothes to be hung on it. Was it going to work?

Phil rubbed his jaw worriedly. A backward power converter was no big deal, but what other parts were in the wrong way? What other bugs were there in the communications routines he had written?

One way to find out, he thought. He reached out again, switched on Clancy, and then Herbert.

Again the faint twitches as power fed into the circuits —but smooth and quiet this time, no fuss, no loud noises.

Power reaches me, and this time it is not cut off. Without any warning, I am caught up in a mushrooming wilderness of sight and sound, a tangle of sensory inputs that I can make no sense of. The weird abstractions chase each other, but then, by some process I cannot understand, they resolve themselves into coherent images. I can see and hear.

But then it hits me. I do not see through my own eyes. Instead I see myself, my body—Herbert's body—lying on a test stand or workbench of some kind, and somehow all the lights and colors seem overbright. Here and there tangles of incoherency, of strange abstract spasms of light, drift through my vision. At last I realize that I am, at least in part, hallucinating. And yet much of what I see has the indelible stamp of reality. Not completely, not altogether, but I can distinguish reality from fantasy.

Where am I? Is this the place they brought me to last week? I want to look around, and an old reflex, unused since my death, causes me to turn my head hard to one side and see where I am. The images I see are a large room, yes, the one to which I was taken. And I see a man, a tired-looking man, a look of utter delight on his face.

Turn my head? Suddenly I forget my curiosity about the room and realize what I have done. I sit there, wherever, whoever, I am, completely stunned. It is the first voluntary motion I have made since I activated the mindloader. I look down —and see a body. A human—no, a humanoid body, with flesh-colored plastic skin. Are these my arms? Experimentally, I try to move my left arm a little—and it flaps out to its maximum extension, almost striking the man before he jumps out of the way.

He speaks, and his voice booms in my ears, so loud I cannot understand him. Suddenly I—feel? sense? hear?—a message from somewhere in the diagnostics of my new body.

SELF-CORRECTION ROUTINE ON—REDUCE OVERALL SENSORY POWER INPUT THIRTY DECIBELS. COMPLETE. SELF-CORRECTION ROUTINE OFF.

*The overwhelming brightness of the room dims. I try
to move my arm back and it moves slowly, smoothly.
Suddenly the man's voice is clear, coherent. But even so, I
cannot yet make out the words he is saying. I concentrate,
focusing my attention, learning to hear through new
ears.*

"Id erkd. Id erkd. Ur ontrollng Clanky!"

SELF-CORRECTION ROUTINE ON—SIGNAL PROCESSOR
REFINEMENT SYSTEM—AUDIO. PHASE MODULATION OP-
TIMIZATION SEEK. COMPLETE. SELF-CORRECTION ROU-
TINE OFF.

*I do not know if I willed the correction, or if this body
did it by itself, or if it responded to my reflexive attempt to
hear better, but it does not matter. The words become
clear.*

"It worked. It worked! You're controlling Clancy!"

*Clancy? Is that who I am now? I look down again, see
my two legs. I see a cable, a thick cable, draped over my
left shoulder. I turn my head and see it move. I trace it
back the other way, across the floor, and into Herbert's
body. I begin to understand.*

*"Let's try standing," the man says. He steps toward
me. I reach out my arms and rest them on his shoulder.
He grunts with the effort of helping me to my feet.*

BALANCE SENSOR SHIFT TO UPRIGHT MODE.

*But this time I barely notice the mechanical, reflexive
voice inside me. Already it is fading into the background.
The man steps back, and I let go my hold on him.*

*I am standing on two feet, controlling my own body. I
will my eyes to shut and they do. I will them open and
see again. What a luxury that is for me, after so many
months when I had no choice whether I could see or not.*

*I try to speak, to say what a wonder it is, but instead I
make a noise like a foghorn fighting with a chicken—a
cacophony of loud boomings and squawking. The man
slaps his hands over his ears. I wait for the inner voice to
speak, and tell me it has corrected the problem, but it
does not come. And then I understand. Speech is voluntary, under delicate conscious control. I try again. The*

sound is different, less harsh and terrible, but it is not speech.

"Are you trying to talk?" the man asks.

I nod my head, vaguely embarrassed to have failed at any more sophisticated communication.

"Okay, we'll work on that. But there isn't much time." The man glances at his watch, and then runs his fingers through his hair, upset and alarmed. "Sweet Jesus, there isn't much time at all. We have to get some clothes on you, on top of everything else. Why didn't we think of that? We can't use your old delivery-boy outfit. Maybe there's something of mine that would fit you."

I am lost, disoriented. I sense that I have forgotten most of what I knew when I was powered down.

What is going on?

Courts of law, Suzanne reflected, *are not what they are cracked up to be*. The myth was that they were centers of quiet reflection, the places where problems were carefully adjudicated, the rights and wrongs balanced and judged with sober reflection. But whenever some chaotic case burst into the place, bubbling over with odd personalities and strange circumstances, someone would inevitably declaim that the place had turned into a circus.

That, Suzanne reflected, as she stood at the entrance to Judge Koenig's court, was a misconception; a circus atmosphere was a courtroom's natural state. It was the quiet, the sobriety, that were unnatural and rare.

How could it be otherwise, when you considered the sort of people who came into court? Thieves, charlatans, con men, hookers, liars and frauds, the unjustly accused and the villains posing as such, the aggrieved and hysterical victims, the angry litigants suing each other more out of a need for revenge than a desire for justice, all of them represented by a class of citizenry—trial lawyers—known for their love of theatrics, their aggressive natures, and the size of their egos.

More often than not the issue at hand was something outside the normal course of events, something so strange, so baffling, so horrifying, so harmful or violent or passion-stimulating that it could not be dealt with within the everyday life of society.

But even with that in mind, things were definitely a bit more out of hand today. The same crowd of cyborgs was here, adding more than their share to the noise—and, no doubt, to the aroma—in the courtroom. She could tell that much by the wrinkled-up noses of some of the court regulars, even if her remote was not equipped with a sense of smell. The reporters were there as well, brought out in double force by rumors of high drama in the offing. And the thrill-seekers were here too, court-room aficionados, the ever-present oddities from the fringes of society who regarded trials as their prime source of entertainment. They tracked the judges and lawyers the way racetrack touts handicapped the ponies.

Everyone was here today.

Suzanne moved into the courtroom and made her way to the defense table. Judge Koenig was already at his bench, conferring with his clerk. He looked up when Suzanne arrived.

"Madame Jantille. I don't see your client with you."

Damn. That hadn't taken long. "No, Your Honor," she said as she arrived at the defense table and set down her attaché case. She saw Ted Peng sitting at the prosecution table. He looked at her as she spoke, an odd sort of expression on his face.

Suzanne cleared her throat and spoke. "I was informed that this morning's session was to be given over to a prosecution motion. As I understand the current procedural rules, defendants are not required to attend pretrial motion sessions. He will be in court this afternoon."

"Hmmph. Suppose I ruled that he was required to attend this particular session?"

Suzanne took a deep breath. There wasn't much for it but to tell the truth—or at least some of it. "My client is somewhat indisposed. I'm afraid I don't know the technical terms to explain his difficulty clearly, but I am assured that he will be here, in court, ready for you, at one P.M.''

"I see," the judge said, obviously annoyed. "Madame Jantille, you have had almost a week's warning that this case was going to go forward this morning, and I have received no prior notice of a difficulty with your client. I don't like surprises or vanishing defendants. Do you have any reason that I shouldn't hold you in contempt?"

"Excuse me, Your Honor," Peng said, rising to his feet. "In light of the motion I am about to present, I don't know that a contempt citation would be—well—appropriate."

"Are you presuming to tell me my job, Mr. Peng?"

"No, sir, but I believe you might not feel the need for the citation after our motion is presented. I might add that the prosecution has no objection to the defendant's absence at this time. It might well turn out to be for the best."

"Indeed. Very well, Mr. Peng. You intrigue me. I will allow you to guide me in this for the moment. But bear in mind, Madame Jantille, if I do not agree with Mr. Peng, contempt still remains a possibility."

"I understand, Your Honor. Thank you."

"Very well then. If the clerk would formally call the case, we can proceed."

Suzanne, more than a bit unnerved, sat down at her desk as the clerk spoke the unheard words of legal ritual. Judge Koenig banged his gavel and called the court to order. "Very well, Mr. Peng. May we now know the nature of this motion?"

"Yes, Your Honor." Peng rose from his seat, carrying three copies of the motion. He delivered one to the bench, then came toward Suzanne at the defense table. He handed her the papers, and leaned in toward her.

There was something strange in his face, guilt, anger, perhaps even a flicker of shame. "I'm sorry," he said in a low voice. "This is not my choice. I do not like this motion, and I wish it could be otherwise. But I have been ordered to do this thing, and I must do it."

Suzanne drew her head back in surprise, a cold feeling in her stomach. "Follow your orders, then," she said.

"Mr. Peng?" the judge said. "Are you ready to proceed? Do we have to wade through the written legalese, or can you tell me orally what this is about?"

"Certainly, Your Honor." He drew himself up to his full height and stood in the center of the court, facing the judge. "Very simply, the United States Attorney's office asks that the defendant be provided with competent counsel willing and able to appear in court."

There was a moment's baffled silence in the court, but Suzanne did not hear it. The shock gripped at her heart, and squeezed it. Harsh pain, physical pain, that would not be denied. For a moment, a half a moment, the courtroom faded out of her awareness, and she was back in her room at home, a frail, sick cripple of a woman surrounded by machines, her view of the world blocked by the huge mask around her head. Somewhere in her bedroom she could hear an alert monitor going off. But then the pain subsided, and the courtroom re-formed around her. She was back in her remote, her robot fists clenched in shock.

"I'm afraid I don't understand, Mr. Peng," the judge was saying. "Madame Jantille is certainly competent, and she is certainly here."

"No she is not, Your Honor, and that is the whole point. It is an excellent simulation, so good that we forget the reality of the situation." He gestured openhanded toward Suzanne, obviously being careful to avoid anything like an accusatory pointing finger. "That is *not* Suzanne Jantille, but a machine, a robot operated by remote control. She is no more here than if she was talking to us over a video link, or an audio telephone link."

A muttered ripple of shock passed over the audience, and the judge stared at Peng in openmouthed surprise.

Suzanne blinked hard, and struggled to collect herself. She stood up and turned toward the judge. "Your Honor, surely the prosecution is aware of my condition—"

"Which is immaterial, Your Honor," Peng cut in.

"Madame Jantille's unfortunate disabilities do not out-weigh her client's right to competent counsel. Nor do they outweigh the prosecution's right to a level playing field."

"What do you mean by *that*?" Koenig said. "It seems to me that you have all your arms and legs and are capable of many things of which Suzanne Jantille is not. Surely the advantages are all with you."

"No, sir. Not in a court of law. I am here, limited by my own memory and my own preparation, unable to receive real-time assistance either from a computer link or from a committee of experts tucked away in a back room. Suzanne Jantille is *not* here, and can, if she so chooses, have any number of such resources at her beck and call. Indeed, we have no real way of knowing that it *is* Suzanne Jantille operating that remote unit. She could cut herself out of the loop and hook another person into the remote link."

"Your Honor, I must object," Suzanne cried out. "Opposing counsel is questioning my integrity in the most scurrilous manner. He has no basis for such groundless accusations."

"Your Honor," Peng said, "that is most certainly true —if indeed it is Suzanne Jantille operating this remote. We cannot know that it is. Furthermore, Your Honor, granting her the right to represent this case by remote control would create a most dangerous precedent. How long would it be before lawyers with *no* disabilities, or even merely slight ones, claimed the right to use a remote, or a more conventional video link? How long before less scrupulous lawyers took advantage of the chance for real-time links to legal databases, or played switch-hitter tricks with a remote, bringing in substitutes to handle certain points in their cases? The potential for abuse of such technology is all but limitless."

"Your Honor, I renew and extend my objection," Suzanne said. "This motion in and of itself is an obvious piece of trickery on the part of the U.S. Attorney's office, a tacit admission that they no longer believe they can bring this case to the conclusion they desire. They want to bring in a more malleable defense lawyer and cut their losses. This motion is not brought to prevent me from committing fraud, or to protect the legal system from a bad precedent. It is brought for one reason, and one reason only—to force me off the case."

Theodore Peng's face was utterly unreadable. "Though I might choose to contest Madame Jantille-Remote's accusation," he said, "the reason for the motion does not matter, Your Honor. It is justifiable on its own merits. A moment ago Madame Jantille-Remote cited the rules governing courtroom procedures. As noted in the written motion, those same rules state flatly, in black and white, that all parties to a case must themselves be present or be represented by counsel present in court. There are no exceptions to that regulation, nor should there be."

Suzanne stared at Peng in amazement and he sat down and tried to compose himself, needlessly straightening the papers on his table. Blindsided. Utterly blindsided. She had never seen it coming, and now Peng had given it to her right between the eyes. But Suzanne was not going to go down without a fight. "Your Honor, I must ask that you respond to my objections."

"They are overruled," the judge said, his voice and face both studies in bewilderment. "Mr. Peng's motion has an obvious factual basis. There is no denying that you are not here. Do you have any counterarguments to offer?"

Suzanne opened her mouth and then closed it. She couldn't think of anything. Maybe if she had more time, maybe if she didn't feel so desperately ill, maybe if she was not so utterly confused by her circumstances, it would have been different. But she was drawing a blank. "Not at this time, Your Honor."

"I was very much afraid of that. The court will take a recess, and arrange with Madame Jantille to assign and brief a replacement counsel."

No! Something in Suzanne could not bear that idea.

To surrender her case, *her case*, to some stranger, some wet-behind-the-ears kid, or some cheap shyster willing to take on a dead ugly case strictly for the money. She could not accept it. An idea popped into her head, an alternative. In a split second, the solution lay open before her.

But could she accept the alternative? It was a way to get past this obstacle, and maybe a way to go all the way, turn the tables. But was she up to it? Could she bear the humiliation? Did she even have the physical strength to *survive* it?

Maybe. Maybe not. But the hell with that too. She could not give this one up. "Just a moment, Your Honor. The prosecution has already stipulated my competence." She turned toward Peng. "Can I then understand that the only problem is with my not being physically present?"

"Ah, well, yes."

"Then, Your Honor, if I may request a recess to make the needed arrangements, this mountain will come to Mohammed." Steeling herself, launching the words with as steady a voice as she could, she spoke. "I will be here, in the flesh—or what's left of it—in time for the afternoon session."

There was a noise from the prosecution table, and Suzanne looked over at it. Peng was half out of his seat, ready to object, when it seemed to occur to him that he had nothing to say. It was his turn to look surprised, Suzanne thought.

Judge Koenig looked at her, rubbing his jaw. "Very well," he said. "That certainly would answer Mr. Peng's objection. But that will be an end to this. I'm telling both of you that. There will be no more of this skirmishing—at one P.M. we concentrate on the substantive issues of this case, and nothing else. No more theatrics. Is that understood?"

"Yes, Your Honor," the two lawyers said in unison. But Suzanne could not help but smile to herself. David would be here this afternoon—and his entrance, revealing his changed appearance, would be nothing if not theatric.

"Very well," the judge said. "Then this court is in recess until then." He slammed down the gavel and stood up.

Suzanne watched him go out, and then began to gather her belongings. She would have to rush home, call the technical nurse service, arrange transport, arrange a powerchair or powerbed here at the courtroom —a dozen things. But wait a moment—she *was* home. That damned Peng was right. She wasn't *here*. There was no need to bother with the ride home at all. And if they were going to accuse her of taking advantage of a remote, then she might as well do it.

She closed and locked her attaché case, sat down, folded her hands, and shut herself off.

Theodore Peng watched the gavel come down, furious with himself for what he had done, angry with the judge for going along, and, somehow, angry at Suzanne as well for outsmarting them all. But no. That was wrong. It was Entwhistle that deserved his anger. Entwhistle and Ted Peng had done this, no one else. Accept that. If it left a bad taste in his mouth, there was no one else he could blame.

The courtroom spectators were making their way out, a noisy, busy group that seemed to make him feel more alone than he would have in a room full of silence. He watched them filing out, the cyborgs and the fringies and the everyday people. *All of those people are against me*, he realized. *They all want me to lose. And maybe I want it too.* He did? *That* was a strange thought for an assistant U.S. Attorney to have. It suddenly dawned on him that he wanted out. He had grown weary of this fight. This situation had gotten completely out of control.

He turned toward the defense table, feeling lost, feeling that he should say something.

He stepped toward Suzanne, but she sat there, motionless, staring straight ahead. "Madame Jantille?" he asked, but there was no response. Suddenly, impulsively, he put his hand on her shoulder, but she did not react. He shook her. Still nothing.

At last he understood what had happened, and drew back from the metal and plastic thing that had been a person up until a few moments ago. She had gone home, escaped. Her spirit had withdrawn.

Theodore Peng felt a fresh upwelling of guilt on his soul. It was irrational, he knew that. But, standing there next to the body, Ted Peng felt something more than the thought that a machine had been switched off.

He felt as if Suzanne Jantille were dead, and he had killed her.

I am on trial for my own murder. My wife is defending me. There is a plot of some sort to keep her from appearing, just now reported on the radio, but she will be there anyway. There is a woman named Sam, and the man's name is Phil. They are trying to save me, somehow.

The man, Phil, has told me a great deal that I don't really grasp. I struggle to hold the knowledge in, to know what is going on, but I am not here yet. I am not grounded in this reality. Seeing through my new eyes, through Clancy's eyes, my mind still confused and unfocused, landing in the middle of such complex urgency I am in a strange and brave new world, that has such people in it. I recognize the quote, but cannot recall where it came from, or how it got into my mind, or how accurate it is. But strange people, strange creatures there are, and I am one of the strangest.

I ride in Phil's van, and the streets hurtle past in a blur of motion. All is new, and untested, for me, and my grasp of reality is weak. What if I am mistaking reality for illusion, or warping reality into a false shape, and none of this is truly happening? What if this Phil is practicing some elabo-

was here. Was there anyone she knew? There, Smitty. He'd help her out.

She hurried through the surging crowd in the lobby and buttonholed the elderly guard leaning on the side of his booth. "Hey, Smitty, how you doing?"

"Hey, Sam, you here for the show like everyone else?"

"Sort of, Smitty. But I'm not covering the case. I'm supposed to be meeting a friend, a cop named Phil Sanders. He's doing some work off duty, transporting some gear for the defense. He probably had to check in—"

"Okay, lemme check." Smitty leaned close over his computer terminal and muttered at it for a minute. "Yeah, he's here," Smitty said. "Just came in the side entrance. Parked in the underground lot."

"Damn it, of course that's where he'd go. My brain's not working this morning. Thanks, Smitty." She turned and hurried toward the stairwell. Things were happening too fast. There was no way to get a handle on things.

Down the stairs, into the garage. There, in the utility parking. A big blue van. She jogged over. "Phil!" she called out. Phil was just getting out of the side door and looked up at her, a grim expression on his face. Somehow he had found the time to shave and change into a suit, Sam noted. But the look on his face . . . she slowed down about fifteen feet from him, wondering what had gone wrong now.

"Is he—is he going to . . ." Her voice trailed off, and she was no longer sure what she was trying to ask.

"I don't know," Phil said. "I've done my best, and I think he understands. But God only knows what will happen in court."

"Did you hear about Suzanne?" Sam asked. "She's coming into court in person."

Phil nodded stiffly. "I don't like it. She's not well, that much I know. It can't be a good idea for her."

"What about—"

"He's in the van. Here, step back a minute. Don't try talking with him," Phil cautioned. "He's still not really oriented. I think I've explained things well enough, but it would be very easy to confuse him." Phil pushed the door control panel, and the van's rear cargo door slid open. A walkdown slide came out of the base of the van, forming a smooth ramp between the van and the garage floor.

"Come on, David," Phil said. There was a stirring in the van, and then Clancy's rough-hewn face poked out of the van and looked around. He stepped carefully out onto the ramp and cautiously made his way down, the linkup cable trailing from the back of his neck. He stepped to one side of the ramp and looked directly at Sam. She returned his gaze and drew her breath in. *Good God,* she thought. *It worked.* Clancy broke eye contact and started his head swiveling around in a disturbingly mechanical manner. He was dressed in a grey suit that did not fit very well, the tie inexpertly tied. No doubt Phil had dressed him, and had trouble managing a tie around someone else's neck. His sandy hair and blocky features seemed out of place without a Clancy uniform to set them off.

But no, this was not Clancy anymore.

This was someone new.

Then there was a low humming noise from inside the van, and Herbert wheeled his way down the ramp, his manipulator arms being careful to keep the cable free of the ground.

The two of them, Herbert and Clancy, stood there at the back of the van, waiting.

Phil shook his head. "Madness," he said. "Absolute madness. How did I get myself into this?" he asked. "Come on, David, Sam. Let's get in there."

Sam resisted the effort to speak as the four—or was it three, or five?—of them walked and rolled toward the elevator. They all got in, Sam pressed the button, and they rode upward. What good was it not to speak, Sam wondered, when the hallway outside the courtroom was bound to be a mass of primordial human chaos?

The doors slid open, and sure enough, it was as bad or

worse than the madness out in the plaza. Every kind of curiosity seeker and courtroom hanger-on was there, jammed in with a boisterous crowd of reporters and cyborgs of all kinds. They had to walk through that sideshow crowd, deliver the main freak to the freak show. Sam felt Phil's hand slip into her own and give it a quick squeeze before they stepped out into the corridor.

A wave of silence seemed to wash over the hallway as they made their way down toward the courtroom. David H.C., the linked bodies of Clancy and Herbert, was something that had never been seen before. A buzzing of speculation seemed to build up behind them. Sam felt her heart pounding as the corridor full of eyes pressed down upon her.

She found herself looking at one person at a time, one person only, struggling to keep her mind from the fact that they were *all* staring at her. Look at one, just one at a time. A grizzled, unshaven cyborg in stained coveralls, with two glistening metal arms sprouting from his shoulders, a toothpick dangling from his mouth. A nervous-looking young woman in a conservative business suit, her arms full of papers, staring pop-eyed at them as they passed. A reporter she knew, who managed to catch her eye. He seemed just about to step forward and ask what was going on, but Sam shook her head, warning him off. A tall, burly, bushy-eyebrowed man in some sort of blue medical-service uniform, muscular and solid, but with a firm gentleness in his eyes, carrying some large white-wrapped bundle in his arms. A court security guard, holding the door open for them, trying to maintain his composure—

"Sam! Phillipe!" Suzanne's voice. Funny. Sam hadn't noticed her in the crowd. Sam stopped, turned, and looked in the direction the voice was coming from. From the blue-uniformed man. From the bundle the man was carrying. Now that she looked, she noticed a tuft of hair, an eye, peeking out from the bundle, a burden that now seemed far too small for what it had to be.

Sam felt the blood in her veins turn to ice.

The nurse pulled the blanket back a bit, exposing Suzanne's face. "I'm sorry to carry her in here like this," he said. "But things got confused. They delivered the powerbed to the courtroom before I got here. There was no other way to bring her up."

But Sam was not listening. She stared, fascinated, horrified, amazed, at the face, the limbless body, wrapped in the blankets.

Suzanne. Suzanne Jantille. Sam stepped forward slowly, staring down at the frail, tiny form. Suzanne Jantille. For the first time in her life, Samantha Crandall was looking at the actual person, not at the remote. "Hello, Suzanne," she said. "How—how are you?"

Her face was gaunt, her skin almost transparently pale, her big brown eyes bright and luminous, set against a face almost skeletal in its thinness. "I've been better," she said, her voice little more than a whisper. Suddenly she was caught in a fit of coughing.

Sam glanced toward Phillipe for a minute, and was stunned to see that he was not approaching Suzanne, that instead he was ushering Clancy and Herbert into court.

With a flash of insight, Sam understood, and was terrified at the news that understanding brought. This was the state his father had reached before the end. This was what Phillipe Sanders's father had looked like before— Sam forced back the tears that were suddenly in her eyes and let the thought finish. Before he died. And Phillipe could not bear to look on it again.

"You've got David here," Suzanne said, her voice raspy and weak. "Is he all right? Did it work?"

Sam swallowed and shook her head, determined to keep her voice even. "I don't know. There hasn't been time to ask. I don't even think Phil knows. You'll have to ask him." Sam reached out a hand and touched Suzanne's fever-hot cheek. "Oh, Suzanne. Oh, dear."

"It's all right, Sam," Suzanne said, her voice seeming a bit stronger. "I'm used to it. But we'd better get in. I'm sure Nurse Bishop's arms are getting tired."

Sam nodded numbly and followed the nurse inside the empty courtroom, no longer really seeing much of anything. She had stumbled up to the first row of the spectators' seats before she realized where she was. She looked around herself, and suddenly burst out in a smile. It had been a mistake, a mad joke, a dream. There was the real Suzanne, sitting at the defense table, strong and whole—

And not moving. Sam looked from the remote to the woman, from the woman to the remote. *I'm looking at* The Picture of Dorian Gray, she thought, *the image of the person split away from the reality, the two finally and utterly divergent from each other.*

The strong, healthy, youthful machine, dressed in its confident business suit, staring straight ahead, motionless, suddenly no more than an inert mannequin, a dress-up doll grown large. A doll that provided the illusion of strength and health for the mutilated, wasted, tiny body of the real Suzanne. Sam watched as Nurse Bishop gently settled Suzanne into the compact portable powerbed, tucked her in, strapped her in, and arranged the controls. He raised the head end of the bed, bringing Suzanne's head up nearly to normal eye level. He set up a control frame that would allow Suzanne to control the bed by moving her head. At last he stepped back and left her alone.

Sam looked at her. A pale white face, framed by unruly, uncombed, grey-flecked chestnut hair, the form of her limbless trunk a too-small bulge under the sheets of the powerbed. An ethereal face, lost in a sea of crisp white linens.

And sitting at the defense table, at the place reserved for the defendant, next to the motionless form of Suzanne-Remote, sat another humanoid robot, Clancy, looking about himself with every indication of intense curiosity. At his feet, kneeling there like some enormous dog at the side of its master, was Herbert. Suzanne-Remote, Herbert, Clancy. In some bizarre way, it was a family portrait, a nightmare image of the happy couple.

Sam sensed Phil standing next to her. She turned toward him, and saw that he had regained his composure, at least somewhat. He looked toward Suzanne, the real one, the flesh and the blood of her, forcing himself to see her, and nodded. "Hello, Suzanne."

"Hello, Phil," she said, and lost herself in a fit of coughing for a moment. At last she stopped and nodded toward the collection of robots at the defense table and grinned. "I may be in trouble. The judge ordered me to avoid any further theatrics."

Theodore Peng arrived into the court just as the first of the spectators was let in, just as the judge appeared through his door at the rear of the bench. The clerk called the court to order, and Ted Peng was already in his seat, shuffling his papers, before the image of the woman in the bed truly registered on him. His head snapped up as if a puppet master had pulled a string. *That* was the opposing counsel. Sweet Jesus God. What had he done?

But then the gavel smacked down, and it was too late to wonder such things.

Judge Koenig adjusted the papers on the bench, and then looked down at the scene before him. He sat nearly as motionless as Suzanne-Remote, an expectant hush blanketing the courtroom. His eyes swept over Suzanne, over her inert other self, across Clancy and Herbert and the link that bound them. At last he closed his eyes and bowed his head for a moment, in prayer, or perhaps merely in an effort to control his own frustration. At last he looked up again.

"Madame Jantille," he began. "I must offer my sincere and heartfelt apologies. It is plainly obvious that it has required great effort and personal courage for you to come here today. The court notes and appreciates your dedication to your client and your case. But I am a judge of the facts and the law as well as a human being—and I am forced to leave such consideration to one side and judge the case on its merits. I must hold lawyers, however courageous, accountable for their actions. So please tell me: Why in God's name are all these robots cluttering up my courtroom? Herbert has to be here, I understand that. But why the other two?"

Suzanne wet her too-dry lips and nodded her head for a moment. It was damned hard to express respect by body posture when you were reduced to a head and a torso. She struggled to take a deep breath, restrained another fit of coughing, and spoke. "I tender my apologies for the continued presence of my remote, Your Honor," she said, her voice deep and raspy, her breath coming in harsh gasps and wheezes. "In the rush to arrange my arrival here in person, there simply was not time to arrange for her to be collected. I should have put her in homer mode and had her walk to her relay van, let the van take her home. It simply slipped my mind. As to the other human-form robot—that is Clancy, through whom my husband will speak."

Koenig looked almost ready to explode. "Are you suggesting that this robot is some sort of spiritualistic medium? Because if you are—"

"No, Your Honor, certainly not," Suzanne said with a bit too much animation. She had to stop again for a minute for another fit of coughing. Her nurse came toward her, but she shook her head, stopping him from approaching. "Excuse me, Your Honor. I am not in the best of health. To explain briefly, there was a malfunction during the mindload experiment that put my husband's —my client's—brain inside Herbert, rendering my client completely unable to speak or to control Herbert's body in any way. As this other robot, Clancy, has a nervous system based on a human model, it was possible to adapt Clancy, make him serve as a substitute body. In short, my husband's mind resides in Herbert's body, but directly controls Clancy. Herbert is programmed to follow Clancy. The last of the adjustments to the system were only made this morning." She let out another gasping breath, worn out by the long speech.

The judge did not seem to notice she was still in discomfort. "More insane techno-gibberish," he said. "Mr. Peng, are you going along with this nonsense?"

Peng rose and spoke. "For the moment, yes, Your Honor. I don't know for sure that the defense has accomplished it, but to the best of my knowledge, such an arrangement is technically possible. I would be most interested to see if the defense has succeeded."

The judge sighed. "I see," he said at last. "Mr. Peng, I take it you would be willing to let the defense present its arguments first?"

"Under the circumstances, yes, Your Honor."

"Very well. Madame Jantille, you may begin."

Suzanne turned her head a bit, and took a sip of water through the powerbed's drink straw. "Thank you, Your Honor," she gasped. "The defense calls David Bailey, also known as David Herbert Clancy Bailey, to the stand."

All eyes turn toward me, but I am distracted by the sight of the inert robot I sit next to. I know who it is, but then I turn my head and see the same person once again. The two are vastly different in appearance, and yet I know them to be one. The same person, and yet not. Both are my wife, of that I am certain. I feel a strange excitement inside myself. The sight of her convinces me. This is real, no dream, no fog of delusion over true circumstances. I will help Suzanne help me.

If I can.

I stand and walk to the witness box. Herbert stands as well, and follows behind me, the two of us moving slowly and carefully. I get to the box, and sit in the chair, and it creaks under the weight of my robot body. Herbert moves to one side of the box and kneels down, lies at my side like a dog on a leash.

It was hard, Suzanne told herself, wondering how the fever could be this bad and not drench her in sweat. It was terribly, terribly hard. But it was nearly over. Once David was on the stand, the case would be decided, one way or the other. It would be David's words and behavior that would decide if he was human. And that was as it should be, and nothing else mattered. Nothing at all.

The clerk took the Bible in her hand and, moving a bit hesitantly, approached the witness box. Keeping her body as far from the witness as possible, she shoved the Bible forward.

Clancy's smooth, mechanically perfect arm swung out and down, and placed itself neatly and precisely on the Bible.

"Ah, ah. Do you swear to tell the truth, the whole truth, and nothing but the truth, so help you God?" the clerk said, blurting the words out as fast as she could.

There was a moment of silence, deep and quiet.

Clancy's head shifted a bit and swung around to face the clerk. Suzanne felt herself holding her breath in spite of herself, knowing that she would have to fight that much harder for air in a minute.

"I do," he said at last, his voice firm and clear.

The court buzzed and hummed as the spectators reacted to the sight of a robot taking the stand, a witness in his own defense.

Tears welled up in Suzanne's eyes and she gasped for breath. But it was not the sight, but the sound, the words, that struck at her heart. They were not just the first words he had spoken in court, but the first words Suzanne had heard him say since his death. *He was alive.* She felt her heart beating like a trip-hammer, the pain and strain in her body competing with the thrill and triumph in her soul.

The rituals of the oath were over. The clerk took her Bible back and retreated as quickly as she could.

With a faint whirring noise, Suzanne's powerbed moved forward, toward the judge's bench and the witness stand.

Gasping and wheezing in pain, Suzanne Jantille raised her head as far as she could and looked straight at the strange conglomeration of spare parts in the witness stand. Pain, fear, loss, and even a flicker of triumph swept across her face. A tear slid down her cheek, and a broken smile of victory lit up her too-pale face.

But the pain and fear didn't matter anymore. She had won. There was no doubt about that now. With those two words, David had broken through. No robot could have handled the syntax and the rhetorical flourishes of the oath, understood the ritual and dealt with it. Only a human could have done that. He had answered as a man would do, not as a machine might.

She looked at the judge, and saw the same knowledge in his eyes. And if the judge saw that David was alive, how could he possibly permit David to be tried for his own murder? The case, the game, was over even as it began. She shifted her head as best she could to look at Theodore Peng. She could read it there, in his face too. He knew he could not overcome this move.

The prosecution's whole plan had centered on a mute, helpless, inarticulate defendant. But her husband was in the witness stand, able to speak for himself. All else crumbled before that simple fact. She turned back toward Clancy. "Could you state your name for the record, please," she asked, her voice raspy and weak, the blood singing in her temples. There was something wrong with her vision as well, but that didn't matter.

Again there was a long pause as Clancy's—no, David H.C.'s—face turned toward Suzanne. The dead man looked at his wife's face. "My name was David Bailey," he said. "But I am not myself anymore."

"Then, then, who are you?" she asked, forcing the words out, struggling to hold on, knowing her grasp was weakening. But it didn't matter anymore.

"I *am* David Bailey," he said a bit more firmly. "But I have been to some very strange places." David H.C. paused once again and looked at her carefully. "And you are—yes, you are my *wife*. My wife," he said in a voice of husky emotion no robot could achieve. He stood up in the witness box, leaned forward, raised his hand, and reached out for her. "You are—you are Suzanne."

The tears were flowing freely down her cheeks now. "Yes, yes I am," she said, speaking scarcely above a whisper.

She paused a moment and came closer, closer. "Hello, David," she said in a voice so weak and thready even she could scarcely hear it.

Now his hand, his hard plastic robot hand, could reach out and touch her face, be wetted by her tears.

Somewhere outside the two of them, the courtroom and the judge and the crowd still existed, but Suzanne did not see them anymore. The world was a warm and glowing fog, with nothing in it but the face and the hand of a robot, the face and the hand that were now her husband's.

"You've changed," he said, looking at her with a thrilling intensity.

She smiled, and even laughed quietly, and paid for laughter with another wracking cough. "Yes," she said. "And so have you."

He smiled, and she had never seen a finer sight. Then, suddenly a look of terrible sorrow seemed to cloud that plastic face, a face that should have been all but immobile, as if a painful memory had just erupted to the surface. "I'm sorry," he said at last. "It was an accident. The experiment failed. I did not mean to leave you then."

She felt it coming, the wrenching pain, the fog lifting up over her, the lights growing dim, her breath growing short. The pain washed over her, reached out to claim her, but she held it off a moment longer. "It's all right, David. You came back. Who else has ever done *that*? I don't think—*I* can."

She looked again at his perfect face, struggling to hold the collapse off, to let this moment pass and end.

But her tormented body could restrain itself no more. At last it came, the spasm, the stabbing, wracking coughing fit that would not stop, the sudden impossibility of breathing, the horrible wrenching wheeze of lungs struggling to take in the air that would not come.

She was unconscious before the tech-nurse could reach her, David's hand still touching her face.

Epilogue

My wife, Suzanne, died that same night. The pieces of paper say respiratory collapse brought on by pneumonia, but that was merely what got her first. Anything could have carried her off, once she started driving herself as hard as she had.

Three days have passed since then.

The fogs have largely lifted from my mind in those three days, but it is true, what I said in court. I am not myself anymore. I have been changed, burned and refined, purified and then alloyed anew in a crucible, a furnace, that no man or woman before me has ever experienced. Yet others will follow. I know it.

Yesterday, two days after Suzanne's death, the hearing reconvened, and I represented myself. The judge ruled me human. In the tumult and chaos of that courtroom there was little else he could do.

But his ruling did not even matter in the end. Theodore Peng, honorable warrior, acting contrary to Julia Entwhistle's specific instructions, that day announced in court that the United States Attorney's office was dropping all charges against me. He had no more stomach for the fight.

He announced his own resignation on the courthouse steps an hour later, and declared that he would start work immediately campaigning for Sam Crandall's Fresh Start proposal. The papers and news links have been full of the idea.

Now I stand by the graveside, and look down into the place where death lies. She died for me, died in the act of winning my life for me. The service is brief, and private, and quickly ends. Only a few friends have attended, the press and the crowds kept well at bay.

The image is burned in my mind, of my poor wife's wasted, weakened frame, lying dead in her powerbed, while her remote unit sat perfect and inert at the defense table. It was the remote that the world saw, that formed the world's image of Suzanne.

Samantha has told me how she thought of Dorian Gray, but Suzanne lived the reverse of Gray's life. It was my wife's image that remained the same, while it was the reality that wasted away unseen—killed not by depravity, but by the search for right.

There are few better deaths.

Farewell, Suzanne, I think. *I shall always miss you, and mourn you, and love you. There is no end to the debt I owe to you.*

The reporter, Samantha Crandall, and the policeman, Phillipe Sanders, walk back to the cars with me, after the graveside service is over. Strange and strange again, they are both here doing their jobs. Sam is covering the funeral for the *Post*, and Phil is serving as traffic control officer for the funeral cortege. He has accepted his demotion with dignity, and I have no doubt that if he chooses to remain on the force, he will rise up in the ranks again, well past his former station. He is not a man who quits, or fails.

It is awkward for me to walk, even yet. I have not yet managed the knack of managing Clancy while relying on Herbert to take care of himself. Clancy's body walks ahead as always, while Herbert's follows loyally behind, the weight of his body driving his feet deep into the soft earth. It is strange that I do not truly know which body is mine, which, if either, I truly inhabit. Both, I suppose, though at times I feel attached to neither.

Phillipe tells me that, given time, he can replace the cable connecting my two bodies, install a radio link, and thus let my Clancy body roam free while Herbert remains at home, bearing my mind, my brain. A remote system, not unlike Suzanne's. I can see the way it could be done, and I am eager to bring my old skills to the job. At times it seems to me that a radio remote system would be a great improvement. Other times it sounds like a most disturbing change. I am growing used to who I am, a soul divided into two metal vessels. Perhaps I have had enough with changing bodies.

We are at the cars, and I am about to board my remote van for the ride home when Sam stops me, touches Clancy on the arm, and looks back toward the grave. Her face is full of sadness, and of bewilderment.

"Why?" she asks me. "Why? Why did she put herself through all that? The pain, the humiliation? Why did she struggle so hard? Other quadriplegics have turned down remotes. Some have even chosen to die. *Why did she do it all?* Why did she fight so hard to save you when it was a one in a million shot you were even still alive?"

I look at Samantha Crandall, and see a lovely young woman, her flame-red hair caught by a playful breeze, a strong young man standing by her side, two people clearly at the beginning of things. Behind them I see a green hillside, a blue sky, a white cloud. I hear birds singing, the low hum of human conversation, see the little knots of people gathering together here and there, reaching out to touch each other, comfort each other in grief. I hear the sound of laughter, incongruous but welcome in this place, the sign that someone has shared a happy memory of Suzanne, found the joy in her life even amid the sadness of her death.

I look back to Samantha, and I tell her the reason, the

obvious reason, the *only* reason my wife could possibly have had. "People," I say, "who have been through what Suzanne went through, what I went through, who have lost all we have had, find out something the rest of you never truly learn, never truly appreciate to its fullest. It is the people like us, the ones who are just a little bit alive, who work the hardest to *be* alive.

"Let me tell you her reason. She fought like fury, and she died, because she believed something. Believed it, *knew* it, deep inside, with all her heart and soul, believed in that something so deeply that she gave up her own share so others might have it.

"Suzanne," I say, "believed, first and foremost, that it is *good* to be alive."

What other belief could be better to die for?

INTELLIGENT ROBOTS AND CYBERNETIC ORGANISMS

BY ISAAC ASIMOV

1. INTELLIGENT ROBOTS

Robots don't have to be very intelligent to be intelligent enough. If a robot can follow simple orders and do the housework, or run simple machines in a cut-and-dried, repetitive way, we would be perfectly satisfied.

Constructing a robot is hard because you must fit a very compact computer inside its skull, if it is to have a vaguely human shape. Making a sufficiently complex computer as compact as the human brain is also hard.

But robots aside, why bother making a computer that compact? The units that make up a computer have been getting smaller and smaller, to be sure—from vacuum tubes to transistors to tiny integrated circuits and silicon chips. Suppose that, in addition to making the units smaller, we also make the whole structure bigger.

A brain that gets too large would eventually begin to lose efficiency because nerve impulses don't travel very quickly. Even the speediest nerve impulses travel at only about 3.75 miles a minute. A nerve impulse can flash from one end of the brain to the other in one four-hundred-fortieth of a second, but a brain 9 miles long, if we could imagine one, would require 2.4 minutes for a nerve impulse to travel its length. The added complexity made possible by the enormous size would fall apart simply because of the long wait for information to be moved and processed within it.

Computers, however, use electric impulses that travel at more than 11 million miles per minute. A computer 400 miles wide would still flash electric impulses from end to end in about one four-hundred-fortieth of a second. In that respect, at least, a computer of that asteroidal size could still process information as quickly as the human brain could.

If, therefore, we imagine computers being manufactured with finer and finer components, more and more intricately interrelated, and *also* imagine those same computers becoming larger and larger, might it not be that the computers would eventually become capable of doing all the things a human brain can do?

Is there a theoretical limit to how intelligent a computer can become?

I've never heard of any. It seems to me that each time we learn to pack more complexity into a given volume, the computer can do more. Each time we make a computer larger, while keeping each portion as densely complex as before, the computer can do more.

Eventually, if we learn how to make a computer sufficiently complex *and* sufficiently large, why should it not achieve a human intelligence?

Some people are sure to be disbelieving and say, "But how can a computer possibly produce a great symphony, a great work of art, a great new scientific theory?"

The retort I am usually tempted to make to this question is, "Can you?" But, of course, even if the questioner is ordinary, there are extraordinary people who are geniuses. They attain genius, however, only because atoms and molecules within their brains are arranged in some complex order. There's nothing in their brains *but* atoms and molecules. If we arrange atoms and molecules in some complex order in a computer, the products of genius should be possible to it; and if the individual parts are not as tiny and delicate as those of the brain, we compensate by making the computer larger.

Some people may say, "But computers can only do what they're programmed to do."

The answer to that is, "True. But brains can do only what they're programmed to do—by their genes. Part of the brain's programming is the ability to learn, and that will be part of a complex computer's programming."

In fact, if a computer can be built to be as intelligent as a human being, why can't it be made *more* intelligent as well?

Why not, indeed? Maybe that's what evolution is all about. Over the space of three billion years, hit-and-miss development of atoms and molecules has finally produced, through glacially slow improvement, a species intelligent enough to take the next step in a matter of centuries, or even decades. Then things will *really* move.

But if computers become more intelligent than human beings, might they not replace us? Well, shouldn't they? They may be as kind as they are intelligent and just let us dwindle by attrition. They might keep some of us as pets, or on reservations.

Then too, consider what we're doing to ourselves right now—to all living things and to the very planet we live on. Maybe it is *time* we were replaced. Maybe the real danger is that computers won't be developed to the point of replacing us fast enough.

Think about it!

2. INTELLIGENCES TOGETHER

I mentioned the possibility that robots might become so intelligent that they would eventually replace us. I suggested, with a touch of cynicism, that in view of the human record, such a replacement might be a good thing.

Since then, robots have rapidly become more and more important in industry, and, although they are as yet quite idiotic on the intelligence scale, they are advancing quickly.

Perhaps, then, we ought to take another look at the matter of robots (or computers—which are the actual driving mechanism of robots) replacing us. The outcome, of course, depends on how intelligent computers become and whether they will become so much more intelligent than we are that they will regard us as no more than pets, at best, or vermin, at worst. This implies that intelligence is a simple thing that can be measured with something like a ruler or a thermometer (or an IQ test) and then expressed in a single number. If the average human being is measured as 100 on an overall intelligence scale, then as soon as the average computer passes 100, we will be in trouble.

Is that the way it works, though? Surely there must be considerable variety in such a subtle quality as intelligence; different species of it, so to speak. I presume it takes intelligence to write a coherent essay, to choose the right words, and to place them in the right order. I also presume it takes intelligence to study some intricate technical device, to see how it works and how it might be improved—or how it might be repaired if it had stopped working. As far as writing is concerned, my intelligence is extremely high; as far as tinkering is concerned, my intelligence is extremely low. Well, then, am I a genius or an imbecile? The answer is: neither. I'm just good at some things and not good at others—and that's true of every one of us.

Suppose, then, we think about the origins of both human intelligence and computer intelligence. The human brain is built up essentially of proteins and nucleic acids; it is the product of over 3 billion years of hit-or-miss evolution; and the driving forces of its development have been adaptation and survival. Computers, on the other hand, are built up essentially of metal and electron surges; they are the product of some forty years of deliberate human design and development; and the driving force of their development has been the human desire to meet perceived human needs. If there are many aspects and varieties of intelligence among human beings themselves, isn't it certain that human and computer intelligences are going to differ widely since they have originated and developed under such different circumstances, out of such different materials, and under the impulse of such different drives?

It would seem that computers, even comparatively simple and primitive specimens, are extraordinarily good in some ways. They possess capacious memories, have virtually instant and unfailing recall, and demonstrate the ability to carry through vast numbers of repetitive arithmetical operations without weariness or error. If that sort of thing is the measure of intelligence, then *already* computers are far more intelligent than we are. It is because they surpass us so greatly that we use them in a million different ways and know that our economy would fall apart if they all stopped working at once.

But such computer ability is not the only measure of intelligence. In fact, we consider that ability of so little value that no matter how quick a computer is and how impressive its solutions, we see it only as an overgrown slide rule with no true intelligence at all. What the human specialty seems to be, as far as intelligence is concerned, is the ability to see problems as a whole, to grasp solutions through intuition or insight; to see new combinations; to be able to make extraordinarily perceptive and creative guesses. Can't we program a computer to do the same thing? Not likely, for we don't know how *we* do it.

It would seem, then, that computers should get better and better in their variety of point-by-point, short-focus intelligence, and that human beings (thanks to increasing knowledge and understanding of the brain and the growing technology of genetic engineering) may improve in their own variety of whole-problem, long-focus intelligence. Each variety of intelligence has its advantages and, in combination, human intelligence and computer intelligence—each filling in the gaps and compensating for the weaknesses of the other—can advance far more rapidly than either one could alone. It will not be a case of competing and replacing at all, but of intelligences together, working more efficiently than either alone within the laws of nature.

3. CYBERNETIC ORGANISMS

A robot is a robot and an organism is an organism.

An organism, as we all know, is built up of cells. From the molecular standpoint, its key molecules are nucleic acids and proteins. These float in a watery medium, and the whole has a bony support system. It is useless to go on with the description, since we are all familiar with organisms and since we are examples of them ourselves.

A robot, on the other hand, is (as usually pictured in science fiction) an object, more or less resembling a human being, constructed out of strong, rust-resistant metal. Science fiction writers are generally chary of describing the robotic details too closely since they are not usually essential to the story and the writers are generally at a loss how to do so.

The impression one gets from the stories, however, is that a robot is wired, so that it has wires through which electricity flows rather than tubes through which blood flows. The ultimate source of power is either unnamed, or is assumed to partake of the nature of nuclear power.

What of the robotic brain?

When I wrote my first few robot stories in 1939 and 1940, I imagined a "positronic brain" of a spongy type of platinum-iridium alloy. It was platinum-iridium because that is a particularly inert metal and is least likely to undergo chemical changes. It was spongy so that it would offer an enormous surface on which electrical patterns could be formed and un-formed. It was "positronic" be-cause four years before my first robot story, the positron had been discovered as a reverse kind of electron, so that "positronic" in place of "electronic" had a delightful sci-ence-fiction sound.

Nowadays, of course, my positronic platinum-iridium brain is hopelessly archaic. Even ten years after its inven-tion it became outmoded. By the end of the 1940s, we came to realize that a robot's brain must be a kind of computer. Indeed, if a robot were to be as complex as the robots in my most recent novels, the robot brain-com-puter must be every bit as complex as the human brain. It must be made of tiny microchips no larger than, and as complex as, brain cells.

But now let us try to imagine something that is nei-ther organism nor robot, but a combination of the two. Perhaps we can think of it as an organism-robot or "orbot." That would clearly be a poor name, for it is only "robot" with the first two letters transposed. To say "or-gabot," instead, is to be stuck with a rather ugly word.

We might call it a robot-organism, or a "robotanism," which, again, is ugly or "roborg." To my ears, "roborg" doesn't sound bad, but we can't have that. Something else has arisen.

The science of computers was given the name "cyber-netics" by Norbert Weiner a generation ago, so that if we consider something that is part robot and part organism and remember that a robot is cybernetic in nature, we might think of the mixture as a "cybernetic organism," or a "cyborg." In fact, that is the name that has stuck and is used.

To see what a cyborg might be, let's try starting with a human organism and moving toward a robot; and when we are quite done with that, let's start with a robot and move toward a human being.

To move from a human organism toward a robot, we must begin replacing portions of the human organism with robotic parts. We already do that in some ways. For instance, a good percentage of the original material of my teeth is now metallic, and metal is, of course, the robotic substance *par excellence*.

The replacements don't have to be metallic, of course. Some parts of my teeth are now ceramic in nature, and can't be told at a glance from the natural dentine. Still, even though dentine is ceramic in appearance and even, to an extent, in chemical structure, it was originally laid down by living material and bears the marks of its origin. The ceramic that has replaced the dentine shows no trace of life, now or ever.

We can go further. My breastbone, which had to be split longitudinally in an operation a few years back is now held together by metallic staples, which have remained in place ever since. My sister-in-law has an artificial hip-joint replacement. There are people who have artificial arms or legs and such non-living limbs are being designed, as time passes on, to be ever more complex and useful. There are people who have lived for days and even months with artificial hearts, and many more people who live for years with pacemakers.

We can imagine, little by little, this part and that part of the human being replaced by inorganic materials and engineering devices. Is there any part which we would find difficult to replace, even in imagination?

I don't think anyone would hesitate there. Replace every part of the human being but one—the limbs, the heart, the liver, the skeleton, and so on—and the product would remain human. It would be a human being with artificial parts, but it would be a human being.

But what about the brain?

Surely, if there is one thing that makes us human it is the brain. If there is one thing that makes us a human *individual*, it is the intensely complex makeup, the emotions, the learning, the memory content of our particular brain. You can't simply replace a brain with a thinking device off some factory shelf. You have to put in something that incorporates all that a natural brain has learned, that possesses all its memory, and that mimics its exact pattern of working.

An artificial limb might not work exactly like a natural one, but might still serve the purpose. The same might be true of an artificial lung, kidney, or liver. An artificial brain, however, must be the *precise* replica of the brain it replaces, or the human being in question is no longer the same human being.

It is the brain, then, that is the sticking point in going from human organism to robot.

And the reverse?

In "The Bicentennial Man," I described the passage of my robot-hero, Andrew Martin, from robot to man. Little by little, he had himself changed, till his every visible part was human in appearance. He displayed an intelligence that was increasingly equivalent (or even superior) to that of a man. He was an artist, a historian, a scientist, an administrator. He forced the passage of laws guaranteeing robotic rights, and achieved respect and admiration in the fullest degree.

Yet at no point could he make himself accepted as a *man*. The sticking point, here, too, was his robotic brain. He found that he had to deal with that before the final hurdle could be overcome.

Therefore, we come down to the dichotomy, body and brain. The ultimate cyborgs are those in which the body and brain don't match. That means we can have two classes of complete cyborgs:

a) a robotic brain in a human body, or
b) a human brain in a robotic body.

We can take it for granted that in estimating the worth of a human being (or a robot, for that matter) we judge first by superficial appearance.

I can very easily imagine a man seeing a woman of superlative beauty and gazing in awe and wonder at the sight. "What a beautiful woman," he will say, or think, and he could easily imagine himself in love with her on the spot. In romances, I believe that happens as a matter of routine. And, of course, a woman seeing a man of superlative beauty is surely likely to react in precisely the same way.

If you fall in love with a striking beauty, you are scarcely likely to spend much time asking if she (or he, of course) has any brains, or possesses a good character, or has good judgment or kindness or warmth. If you find out eventually that good looks are the person's only redeeming quality, you are liable to make excuses and continue to be guided, for a time at least, by the conditioned reflex of erotic response. Eventually, of course, you will tire of good looks without content, but who knows how long that will take?

On the other hand, a person with a large number of good qualities who happened to be distinctly plain might not be likely to entangle you in the first place unless you were intelligent enough to see those good qualities so that you might settle down to a lifetime of happiness.

What I am saying, then, is that a cyborg with a robotic brain in a human body is going to be accepted by most, if not all, people as a human being; while a cyborg with a human brain in a robotic body is going to be accepted by most, if not all, people as a robot. You are, after all—at least to most people—what you seem to be.

These two diametrically opposed cyborgs will not, however, pose a problem to human beings to the same degree.

Consider the robotic brain in the human body and ask why the transfer should be made. A robotic brain is better off in a robotic body since a human body is far the more fragile of the two. You might have a young and stalwart human body in which the brain has been damaged by trauma and disease, and you might think, "Why waste that magnificent human body? Let's put a robotic brain in it so that it can live out its life."

If you were to do that, the human being that resulted would not be the original. It would be a different individual human being. You would not be conserving an individual but merely a specific mindless body. And a human body, however fine, is (without the brain that goes with it) a cheap thing. Every day, half a million new bodies come into being. There is no need to save any one of them if the brain is done.

On the other hand, what about a human brain in a robotic body? A human brain doesn't last forever, but it can last up to ninety years without falling into total uselessness. It is not at all unknown to have a ninety-year-old who is still sharp, and capable of rational and worthwhile thought. And yet we also know that many a superlative mind has vanished after twenty or thirty years because the body that housed it (and was worthless in the absence of the mind) had become uninhabitable through trauma or disease. There would be a strong impulse then to transfer a perfectly good (even superior) brain into a robotic body to give it additional decades of useful life.

Thus, when we say "cyborg" we are very likely to think, just about exclusively, of a human brain in a robotic body—and we are going to think of that as a robot.

We might argue that a human mind is a human mind, and that it is the mind that counts and not the surrounding support mechanism, and we would be right. I'm sure that any rational court would decide that a human-brain cyborg would have all the legal rights of a man. He could vote, he must not be enslaved, and so on.

And yet suppose a cyborg were challenged: "Prove that you have a human brain and not a robotic brain, before I let you have human rights."

The easiest way for a cyborg to offer the proof is for him to demonstrate that he is not bound by the Three Laws of Robotics. Since the Three Laws enforce socially acceptable behavior, this means he must demonstrate that he is capable of human (i.e. nasty) behavior. The simplest and most unanswerable argument is simply to knock the challenger down, breaking his jaw in the process, since no robot could do that. (In fact, in my story "Evidence," which appeared in 1947, I use this as a way of proving someone is not a robot—but in that case there was a catch.)

But if a cyborg must continually offer violence in order to prove he has a human brain, that will not necessarily win him friends.

For that matter, even if he is accepted as human and allowed to vote and to rent hotel rooms and do all the other things human beings can do, there must nevertheless be some regulations that distinguish between him and complete human beings. The cyborg would be stronger than a man, and his metallic fists could be viewed as lethal weapons. He might still be forbidden to strike a human being, even in self-defense. He couldn't engage in various sports on an equal basis with human beings, and so on.

Ah, but need a human brain be housed in a metallic robotic body? What about housing it in a body made of ceramic and plastic and fiber so that it looks and feels like a human body—and has a human brain besides?

But you know, I suspect that the cyborg will still have his troubles. He'll be *different*. No matter how small the difference is, people will seize upon it.

We know that people who have human brains and full human bodies sometimes hate each other because of a slight difference in skin pigmentation, or a slight variation in the shape of the nose, eyes, lips, or hair.

We know that people who show no difference in any of the physical characteristics that have come to represent a cause for hatred, may yet be at daggers-drawn over matters that are not physical at all, but cultural—differences in religion, or in political outlook, or in place of birth, or in language, or in just the accent of a language.

Let's face it. Cyborgs will have their difficulties, no matter what.

ABOUT THE AUTHOR

ROGER MACBRIDE ALLEN was born in 1957. THE MODULAR MAN is his eighth science fiction novel. Relying on the false assumption that a writer must live something before writing about it, various people who have read his previous novels have assumed that he was a defense contractor, British, black, a woman, an astrophysicist, a paleoanthropologist, a reporter, and/or a Baptist. As this book goes to press, he is none of the above. He lives in Washington, D.C.

A dramatic new series of books at the cutting edge of where science meets science fiction.

THE NEXT WAVE
Introduced by Isaac Asimov

Each volume of *The Next Wave* contains a fascinating scientific essay and a complete novel about the same subject. And every volume carries an introduction by Isaac Asimov.

Volume One
Red Genesis
by S. C. Sykes

The spellbinding tale of a man who changed not one but two worlds, with an essay by scientist Eugene F. Mallove on the technical problems of launching and maintaining a colony on Mars.

Volume Two
Alien Tongue
by Stephen Leigh

The story of contact with a startling new world, with an essay by scientist and author Rudy Rucker on the latest developments in the search for extraterrestrial intelligence.

Volume Three
The Missing Matter
by Thomas R. McDonough

An exciting adventure which explores the nature of "dark matter" beyond our solar system, with an essay by renowned space scientist Wallace H. Tucker.

Look for *The Next Wave* on sale now wherever Bantam Spectra Books are sold